"ARE YOU SHY WITH ME, JAN?"

There was surprise in Jason's husky voice.

"I think so." Jan's answer was reluctant but honest.

Jason sank back on his heels, his body touched with firelight, perfect in its male beauty. Jan watched him, unable to breathe.

"Don't be afraid, darling. Trust me." Slipping an arm around her, Jason pulled her near him. "We'll have tonight together, then we'll go back to the city in the morning...."

Jan stiffened. "What are you talking about?" she demanded.

Jason's hand traced the curve of her breast. "I'll set you up in a nice flat and you'll never have to worry about money again. Oh, Jan, let me love you now."

Jan shrugged out of his arms and twisted forcefully away from him. She shuddered at what she had almost done. Would she always be so gullible...?

Books by Jessica Logan

SUPERROMANCES

20—JOURNEY INTO LOVE
27—PROMISE TO POSSESS
41—DARK PROMISE OF DELIGHT
99—THE AWAKENING TOUCH

These books may be available at your local bookseller.

For a free catalog listing all titles currently available,
send your name and address to:

Harlequin Reader Service
P.O. Box 52040, Phoenix, AZ 85072-2040
Canadian address: Stratford, Ontario N5A 6W2

THE AWAKENING TOUCH

JESSICA LOGAN

A SUPERROMANCE FROM
WORLDWIDE

TORONTO • NEW YORK • LONDON • PARIS
AMSTERDAM • STOCKHOLM • HAMBURG
ATHENS • MILAN • TOKYO • SYDNEY

Published February 1984

First printing December 1983

ISBN 0-373-70099-7

Printed in Canada

CHAPTER ONE

"JAN, COME HERE A MOMENT, please."

The young woman straightened from her task of tending the injured man stretched out on her bed and went into the huge living room of the big house. She stopped in front of the fireplace, the heat soothing against her legs. It was chilly this afternoon, the nip of winter in the air. Her father stood at the door, a look of uncertainty entirely foreign to his nature twisting his features.

"Ranger headquarters just radioed through. The floatplane is on its way with the doctor. I'll go to the lake and bring him up."

"Please let me go, dad. You look so tired...."

Her father gestured impatiently. "I don't know who's flying the plane and I've no idea which doctor is coming in. You stay here and keep an eye on the boy."

The restlessness Jan Jordan had felt with increasing force the past year reared its insistent head. She found the impulse to defy her parent hard to resist. When on earth was he going to treat her like an adult instead of a child?

Meeting her father's steely blue gaze, the young woman sighed.

"It's five miles to the lake dad, and you know it. You're so tired your legs are wobbling. You aren't at all well and you've no business going all that way and back. Let me—"

"It's out of the question." The way Lewis Jordan repeated the statement left no room for discussion. "You stay here and get the boy's fever down. I think he's headed for a good case of pneumonia if you don't. We'll be back before he needs more of the antibiotic, I reckon. If we're delayed for any reason, give him another injection in three hours." His face was grim as he shrugged into his heavy sheepskin jacket.

"You stay with him, father. You need to rest. I'll go."

"Jan, I'm not prepared to argue with you."

"You carried him for miles. . . ."

"That's enough, honey. You stay here."

"Oh, for heaven's sake!" Jan was fully aware of the real reason her father didn't want her to go. "What on earth could happen to me? Surely the doctor and his pilot must have some claim to civilized behavior. You need to face reality, dad. I can't spend the rest of my life on this mountain never seeing anyone. Other women learn to get along in some manner, learn to cope with strangers!"

Lewis's color drained away, leaving his careworn features bleak, the pain in his eyes searing. His glance swept over the girl before him, taking in the sheen of her honey-brown hair, caught up in a ponytail that hung halfway down her back. The curves of her slender body were barely masked by the thick flannel of the woodsman's shirt she wore. Rust-colored corduroy pants, functional and rough, were belted around her slender waist, the cuffs folded back against the brown leather of her boots. Her feet wide apart on the black bearskin rug covering the floor in front of the huge fireplace, she faced her father in an unconscious posture of challenge. It was a posture that had distressed him with increasing misgiving during the past year. The fact that the girl was unaware of the change in herself only added to his pain.

No matter that Jan was a grown woman. To Lewis she would always be a girl, the precious haunting legacy that was his sole remaining link with the one he had loved beyond reason, beyond pride, beyond honor.

Jan had a special kind of beauty. Her dark brows arched over deep emerald eyes, wide set beside a perfect upturned nose. The sparkle in her eyes attested to her love of life, the sweet curve of her mouth to her generosity of spirit.

A fleeting smile touched his lips. She was so lovely, and her beauty was matched by her intelligence and her independence. She was so like her mother.

Juliana, impetuous, brave....

For twenty years he had been without her, without the central core of his life. Hidden away in this whispering forest he had taken care of her legacy to him, the daughter she had loved so well and had to leave when she was so young.

Had he wronged that daughter, hiding her away, raising her in isolation? Lately the question had bothered him more and more. He was beginning to realize the deprivations that living on this remote mountain had forced on the beautiful and talented young woman now facing him, worried defiance in her clear eyes.

But to tell her why it was necessary to live here, why he had shunned civilization all these years, years of freedom and peace.... The thought of it shook him.

"You stay here and take care of the boy," he growled.

"I'm perfectly capable of meeting that plane," she insisted, doing her best to hide her worry about his physical condition.

"I'm not going to argue with you, Jan. I'll meet the plane and bring the doctor up."

Jan sighed and spread her hands in defeat. There was absolutely no way to talk to her father when his mind was set.

Lewis saw the resigned look on her face. He crossed to her side and folded her into his arms in an unexpected gesture of affection. Jan felt a shudder run through his wiry frame and hugged him close, murmuring sounds of comfort and understanding into his shirtfront.

Tilting her head up with a gentle work-roughened finger, he gazed into her tear-misted eyes. "I'm afraid I've committed a serious wrong, honey, keeping you here with me and never giving you a chance to associate with kids your own age."

"Oh, dad! Don't be silly! I wouldn't change my life for the world."

"Nice of you to say so, but you don't have

enough information to come to any conclusions. Seriously, Jan, I've decided we have to leave here. You need to meet people, get to know something of the way the rest of the civilized world tries to get along. We'll talk about it and work something out. Okay?''

Happiness sparkled in the green of her eyes, lighting the mischievous planes of her piquant features. "Oh yes! Let's do that." He gave her a gentle smile and left, banging the heavy door behind him.

Jan crossed to the window and watched him run down the hand-hewn timber steps fronting the wide veranda, her heart beating with a quickened tempo.

She had never expected to hear him offer to leave this remote mountainside. Lewis Jordan was fanatic in his desire to live away from other men. An engineer gifted with his hands, he'd spent a fortune on the house he'd constructed deep in the mountainous forests of Maine. What was changing him? Her face thoughtful, Jan watched him disappear on the path that led to the lake.

A smile dimpled the corner of her mouth as she caught sight of Bandit, the resident racoon. The furry little thief sat on his hind legs in the shade dappling the clearing. Bandit watched her father plunge into the shadowed path of the trail, then turned his masked face toward the house.

"Forget it you sneaky little character!" Jan laughed. "I'm still here and you can't steal a thing!"

Bandit used every bit of his considerable cunning to devise ways to plunder the hens' nests. He loved eggs, among other things. Lewis spent an infinite amount of time devising ways to circumvent such raids on their food supplies.

Bandit wasn't the only clever predator inhabiting the forest around them, but he was one of the most persistent and challenging. He seemed to regard the cabin and outbuildings as his own hunting grounds. Unafraid he roamed the clearing, confident of his right to be there. Jan watched him with amused tolerance. A partridge rose with a whir of wings as the raccoon moved. A fat squirrel scampered up the straight trunk of an enormous spruce, and a Canada jay, disturbed by the squirrel, flashed across the clearing. Sugar maple blazed in scarlet glory, the wondrous reds interwoven with the vivid yellows of poplar and birch. The somber deep greens of the spruce and pine made a perfect backdrop for the October leaves.

It was all so beautiful, so right . . . and so unsatisfying.

Jan turned from the autumn landscape.

What was wrong with her? Why was she so discontent with the life she'd loved and valued as long as she could remember? If only there were someone she could talk with, discuss her restless feelings. That might solve all her problems.

Teddy, where are you when I need you? The question came swiftly, surprising her. She hadn't thought of Teddy Landry for years.

Skinny redheaded Teddy, who'd had so much trouble with stumbling feet the last year of their acquaintance. The son of a couple who had built a cabin on the lake at the foot of the mountain, he was the only playmate she'd ever had.

Jan had been six when the Landrys had first put in their appearance, and sixteen the last summer they spent on the lake. During the seven years since, the cabin had fallen into disrepair, letting the weather have its way.

Jan had mourned the loss of her friend for ages. She missed Teddy's mother, too. Mrs. Landry had been full of kindness. She had mothered the lonely child, encouraging her visits, seeing her over the rough spots as Jan progressed from a child into a teenager.

Once or twice a week on those long-ago summer days, the children made the trip up or down the mountain to visit each other. Teddy was always a cheerful skinny companion, full of energy and good-will, and Jan had loved him dearly.

They were the same age, but that last year when they were sixteen Teddy had shot up in height, his shoulders broadening, his voice deepening.

In that year their relationship changed in some way.

Jan had begun to long for the sight of him, turning shy when he arrived on the mountain. Their association deepened, becoming something she didn't understand but something she cherished in secret and shared with no one.

Her father had watched them carefully all that summer, not allowing Jan to go down the mountain to the Landry cabin unless he accompanied her.

The Landrys didn't return after that last summer.

Jan had mourned them for years. She had never quite been able to analyze her strange growing awareness of Teddy, not understanding why that last year was so lovely, so different. Now as an adult she realized she had suffered the pangs of first love, the first tentative reaching out to someone she could care for, but she had never summoned up the courage to mention such a thing to her father.

How she longed to meet new people, participate in the give-and-take of friends, become a part of a group! And yet this longing seemed disloyal to her when her father was so protective of his privacy.

A faint stirring in the bedroom alerted her, rousing her from her reverie. She turned from the window and hurried to the sick man. How wonderful it would be if he could speak to her, tell her of his world, his life, his friends.

Lewis wouldn't have left her alone with him had that been the case, and Jan knew it. The broad-shouldered tall young man filling her narrow bed was delirious. He wasn't able to talk to her.

Kneeling beside the bed, she took his hot hand in her cool ones, crooning soft words to him. He opened fever-bright eyes and stared up at her, no comprehension in his gaze.

Concerned, Jan wrung a washcloth out of the ice-cold water in the basin beside the bed and sponged his forehead. His eyes focused suddenly and he reached for her hand.

"W-who are you? Wh-what happened?"

"Sh-shh," she murmured. "You mustn't talk. I'm Jan."

His grip on her hand tightened. "My God," he muttered, grimacing against the pain. "It hurts to breathe. What hit me?"

Prying her hand loose, Jan gave him a rueful smile. "Nothing except the rocks you bounced off on your trip down the mountainside," she told him. "Whatever made you get so close to the edge of that cliff?"

"I w-was taking pictures," he whispered. "Th-the damned ground c-caved in under me."

"Dad thought that was probably what happened." Jan dipped the cloth in the water again, wrung it out and applied it with gentle pressure. "He found your equipment scattered around you. You were in a very remote area. It's just luck that he found you in time."

"What day is it?"

"Thursday. But you shouldn't talk."

"Th-Thursday! G-good night! I was there two days!"

"You must be quiet. You've broken several ribs and you may be coming down with pneumonia. There's a doctor on the way. Dad's gone to guide him up here. They should be here soon."

"I—I'm causing a h-hell of a lot of trouble." Distress showed in his bloodshot gray eyes.

"Not a bit. I'm glad for your company." He grimaced and Jan narrowed her eyes at him. "I have some pain medicine. We're so isolated up here we keep a fairly well-stocked supply of fresh pharmaceuticals in the medicine chest. Dad is adamant about it. Do you want something? I promise not to poison you."

"Th-thanks. It w-would h-help." His whisper became less audible by the moment. "You're an a-angel."

"Hardly. The tablets may be hard to swallow. Do you think you can manage?"

"I—I'll sure try." When he gagged on the hard white pills, Jan ground them to a powder in the spoon, adding a bit of water. Supporting him as much as possible, she raised his head a little and dribbled the mixture down his throat. He choked and she held a glass of cool water to his chapped lips. He gave her a grateful smile as he washed the bitter taste from his mouth. Jan moved him with extreme care as she settled him back among the pillows. His pallor was alarming, as was his clammy skin, but she managed a smile she hoped was reassuring.

"There," she murmured. "Rest if you can. According to my father it won't hurt you as much if you take very shallow breaths. It's awful for you, isn't it?"

"Y-your dad's a s-smart man. I—I'm Tom F—Farrell."

"Sh-shh, Tom Farrell. You mustn't talk. If you'll try to rest, I'll go fix something for you. You must be hungry."

Jan smoothed the covers over him, regarding him soberly. In spite of his size there was something so boyish about him that all her maternal instincts were aroused. He looked, she thought, like an overgrown delightful child who had gotten into mischief and had things go seriously wrong.

Jan grinned at the thought. She had a notion Tom Farrell was old enough to resent any such patronizing idea. Giving the quilts a last pat, she went to start supper.

The stew was bubbling, filling the kitchen with a mouth-watering fragrance. She popped a pan of yellow johnnycake into the oven.

Checking on Tom, she found him asleep and decided to do the chores. Shrugging into her warm jacket, she went out into the frosty evening. She collected the eggs, milked the goat and fed the hogs Lewis was fattening for winter meat. Locking the animals in, she hurried back to the house through the gathering dusk. Her father and the doctor were overdue. Something must have delayed them.

Uneasy, she prepared a tray for her patient. He opened red-rimmed eyes as she carried it in.

"Do you think you can eat a little?" she asked.

He smiled at her, licking dry cracked lips. "L-let me try. I think I'm hungry but I can't tell." His whisper was soft.

"I expect your fever is ruining your appetite," Jan answered, her voice cheerful. "A bite or two can't hurt the cause." She made a place for the tray on her bedside table before she sat down beside him. Carefully she spooned the rich broth into him, adding bits of johnnycake now and then. The young man made a serious effort to eat, the pain of swallowing causing his forehead to bead with perspiration. He hadn't eaten much when he caught her hand and returned the spoon in it to the bowl.

"Th-that's all. It hurts too much."

Jan nodded, understanding. "I'm going to give you another shot of antibiotic and another pain pill. Father and the doctor should have been here an hour ago. I don't know what's keeping them."

She administered the medicine with quiet efficiency, and her patient sagged back against his pillow, his face a dirty gray.

"Thanks...." The whisper trailed away as he slipped into unconsciousness. Jan dropped to her knees beside the bed, running light fingers over his hot dry skin. He was so hurt and looked so helpless. A rush of tenderness washed along her sensitive nerves.

She used the cool cloth on his unresponsive features again, then rocked back on her heels and looked at him with the objective eye of an artist.

As ill as he was, she could see that he was an extremely attractive young man, handsome in a rugged sort of way. His features were in perfect proportion in a square-jawed masculine face. His cleft chin emphasized the forceful shape of his sensitive young mouth and his damp sodden hair curled over his well-shaped head.

He was the most handsome man she had ever seen.

I'd love to draw him, she thought. *He's attractive even when he's sick....*

Embarrassed, Jan smiled, and rising with a quick grace she gathered up the tray of dirty dishes and took it back into the kitchen. Her father and the doctor still hadn't put in an appearance by the time she ate her own meal and cleared away the dishes.

It was totally dark by then.

Jan switched on the powerful floodlights ringing the perimeter of the clearing and heard the big generator at the end of the house come to life. Her father had installed it many years ago, utilizing the

rushing strength of the waterfall just above the cabin
where the little river tumbled over a rocky ledge. It
was a source that never failed, allowing the household to use all the most modern conveniences. Lewis
had brought in the latest in refrigeration. An enormous deep-freeze occupied a space in the laundry
room along with the washer and dryer. The kitchen
was full of labor-saving gadgets, making the task of
preparing meals a pleasure. The house, outbuildings
and clearing were illuminated by the same power
source. Lewis saw no need to deprive himself and his
daughter of the luxuries of life because he lived in the
backwoods.

Jan was accustomed to the comforts of the only
home she had ever known. She enjoyed the way she
and her father lived without question. She had no
idea of the expense of things, no knowledge of how
unusual it was to live in such a remote area and still
have the convenience of modern utilities.

She looked out across the flood-lit clearing. There
was no sign of her father.

Not bothering with her coat, Jan left the house and
crossed the big yard. Pausing at the edge of the
forest, she tilted her head and listened. Evening
sounds filled the night. The river gurgled in the distance. Nothing reached her sensitive ears to indicate
the approach of her father or the doctor he was
escorting.

Frowning, Jan shivered and went back across the
clearing, the chill of the evening air penetrating her
flannel shirt.

She ran up the steps, closed the heavy door and hurried into her father's cosy den. Flipping switches, she activated the powerful two-way shortwave radio installed across one side of the room and called Ken Clark, the area's forest ranger.

"They should be there, Jan." Her uneasiness intensified as Clark's crisp assessment confirmed her own feeling. "The pilot is a man named Jason Farrell. The injured kid's his son. He's bringing in his personal physician, a Dr. John Brogan. He called in three hours ago."

"The plane hasn't run into any trouble?"

"No. They were on the lake when Farrell contacted me. He said they would go ashore and meet Lewis."

"I can't imagine what's keeping them."

"It's a long way up the mountain, honey. Perhaps this Farrell and his doctor aren't as young as they once were. How's the boy?"

"I'm not sure whether he's sleeping or unconscious. He's very feverish."

Ken talked with her about the young man's condition, reassuring her as best he could. "The Doc's on his way. Just keep him as cool as you can. What happened? How did Lewis happen to find him?"

"Dad was out stringing his trapline. He found Tom at the bottom of a gorge by Calamity Gap. He'd fallen a good hundred feet or so, bouncing off boulders and stuff. Dad lugged him out of the ravine and loaded him on a travois. He dragged him in."

"My God! That's miles from your place. I thought Lewis hasn't been feeling too well. That would be a tough job for someone in the pink."

"I tried to go to the lake and meet the plane myself, but you know dad. He refused. I'm worried, Ken."

"Your dad knows that mountain, Jan. He'll be there soon, if I know anything about him. He's a determined man."

"Stubborn is more like it. I'd better go check my patient."

"Call me if you need me, honey. But don't worry about Lewis. He'll be there soon." Jan said goodnight and switched the set off, a smile on her lips.

Ken knew about her father. Lewis was stubborn and immovable once his mind was made up.

When she walked in to check on her patient she found him tossing restlessly, moaning as he moved his head from side to side. He quieted under Jan's soothing hands. She wondered if he'd be more comfortable unclothed, then blushed a fiery red as she thought of undressing him. Her father had removed the sick young man's heavy hiking boots and jacket before pulling the quilts up, but that was all. Those two items of clothing were in a heap in the corner of her neat room. Dismissing the idea of undressing him as impossible, Jan bathed his hot face, crooning to him as she soothed him. He turned his stubbly chin into her hand and settled down with a sigh that went straight to her heart. She sat beside him, not stirring for a while, then giving in to a sudden strong urge she went to collect her drawing materials.

Her fingers flew as she sketched impressions of him onto the pristine whiteness of her sketchbook. Enchanted with him, she scarcely noticed the passage of time until his growing restlessness forced her to close her book and lay it aside.

He was perspiring profusely, his skin cold and damp when she touched him. The heavy shirt he was wearing was soaked through, and he moved restlessly, moaning and jerking his feverish head around on the pillow. It was warm in the room, too warm for Jan's liking, but the young man's teeth were chattering, the sound loud in Jan's ears.

She jumped up, her eyes flying to the Seth Thomas clock ticking quietly on the mantle.

Ten!

Where could her father and the doctor be?

Kneeling before the fire she added logs, then looked up at the sick man. The bed was shaking with the force of his convulsive shivering. Sure that such a chill was not one a human would be able to tolerate long, Jan did the only thing she could think of to aid him. Unlacing her boots and kicking them off, she crawled under the quilts on the other side and slid over against him, slipping her arms around him as she glued her body to his quivering back.

He quieted gradually then, finally becoming still. One of his arms clamped over Jan's and held her firmly in place. Jan lay there, frightened and intrigued. In spite of her worry about her father and the doctor, an odd happiness crept over her, warming her with the thought that she was helping the young man in her arms, and she soon drifted into sleep.

CHAPTER TWO

COLD AIR WHOOSHED AROUND HER, shocking her into consciousness.

Before Jan could open sleep-dazed eyes, she was snatched out of the warm bed by hands that were far from gentle. Her stockinged feet hit the floor as she was marched out of the bedroom. Jerking her head around, she found herself staring into the coldest, grayest eyes she'd ever encountered.

Her accoster towered above her. He was furious. Flaming anger was written in every line of his arresting features.

"Just what the hell were you doing in bed with my son, you little bitch?"

Never in her life had anyone called Jan names, vicious or otherwise. Her rage rose to meet his.

Squirming like an eel, she tried to break his grasp. It was a mistake. Challenged, the stranger smiled grimly. The battle was short and exhausting. Jan wound up completely out of breath and unable to move. She was clinched into his hard-muscled unyielding length and held there, her face pushed into the man's firm chest.

Gasping, she squirmed until she became conscious of the fact that her accoster's breathing had changed.

She wrenched away from close contact with him, her head snapping back as she shook her silky sun-streaked hair from her hot face.

"Let me go!" she hissed at him. "What do you think you're doing?"

His grin wasn't reassuring. His bronzed skin stretched taut against the strong fine bones of his face, making him look positively intimidating. "Just removing you from my son's bed, sweetheart. Sick as he is, he isn't much use to you, is he?"

Jan blushed furiously at the implication. "I was trying to keep him warm."

"Oh, yeah?" It was obvious he didn't believe her, but he dropped his arms and stepped back.

"Jason, I need you!" The imperious summons came from the bedroom. The stranger whirled and vanished.

Two of them!

What was going on? Where was her father? Still feeling dazed, she followed the tall stranger. He was bent over the bed, doing his best to help the second man remove the clothes from Tom's pain-racked body. She knew then for certain who her assailant was.

Jason Farrell, the pilot of the plane. Tom Farrell's father. And the other man must be the Dr. Brogan that Ken Clark had mentioned. But her father was nowhere in sight. What was going on? Snatching up her warm sheepskin moccasins, she thrust her feet into them and went out into the frosty night, dread washing over her.

Something was very wrong!

Lewis was not in the floodlit clearing. Running down the steps, she wrapped her arms around herself and cocked her head to one side. Straining all her senses, she listened to the soft woodland sounds.

A loon called in the darkness. Night creatures stirred. Bandit, his attention caught by her impetuous dash down the stairs into the late-autumn chill, came around the corner of the building and waddled toward her in hopes of a handout.

The night whispered around her, bringing familiar murmurings, familiar rustlings. Jan listened and catalogued each one. None were made by man.

If Lewis was in the vicinity, he wasn't moving. Where on earth could he be? It wasn't like him to send two strangers into his house without accompanying them. His habits were too set, his determination to protect her and keep her isolated too patterned to allow him to even consider doing so. There was only one answer.

He hadn't returned with the two men tending Tom Farrell.

Flying back up the steps, her speed fueled by alarm, she raced through the door, slamming it as she rushed to the bedroom.

"Where is my father? Where did he go after he met your plane?"

"We weren't met, miss." It was the doctor who answered, removing the stethoscope from his ears and looking over his glasses at her. "As a result we lost our way several times. We wouldn't have found you at all if we hadn't finally spotted your lights. Thanks for turning them on."

"But my dad went to meet you. . . ."

"Well, he didn't make it." Jason Farrell's imperious voice cut in with cold impatience. "Get some hot water in here, please. We need it."

Jan's anger rose. Ignoring the crisp command, she appealed to the doctor. "I'm worried about my father. He should have met your plane."

"Your father is the Jordan who found Tom?" Jan nodded, and the doctor went on. "The ranger radioed he was to meet us. It was almost dark when we found the lake and landed. Your father wasn't there. We saw the trail and took it, but it isn't the easiest thing to do to find a way up an unknown trail in the dark."

"Look," Jason interrupted impatiently, "we can discuss your father's failure to keep his word later. We need that water."

The doctor glanced at his friend and spared Jan a smile.

"He's worried," he explained. "We do need a basin of warm water, though. I must clean this young man's scrapes and bruises up a bit."

"My father didn't *fail* to keep his word without a reason. Something's happened to him." Fear trembled on the edge of the words she directed at the man bent over his son. He looked over his shoulder at her, his handsome mouth curved, whether in amusement or disdain she didn't know.

Tossing her head, she turned on her heel and left. Marching into the kitchen, she filled the big electric kettle. Where did a man like that come from, she wondered as she plugged it in.

And when did he think she'd had the time to seduce his son, for heaven's sake? Surely not since
Tom had been in the house. Unbidden, an image of
Jason Farrell formed in Jan's mind. Sketching Tom
had been a pleasure. Sketching his father would be a
challenge. A strange thrill shot through her as she
considered the possibility.

He was so masculine. Tall and broad-shouldered,
he exuded power. His hair was the deep copper of
autumn beech leaves in the rain, she decided. Expertly cut, clinging to the fine proportions of his head,
the dark curls skimmed the collar of his shirt. In spite
of her instant aversion to him, Jan's slender fingers
itched as her artist's mind recalled the decisive set of
his firm chin with its faint cleft, the flash of white
teeth and those startling gray eyes. He was a creature
completely beyond her experience and knowledge.
She reached into one of the cupboards and pulled out
the large stainless-steel basin she used for mixing
bread. When the kettle boiled she filled the bowl, carried it into the sickroom and put it down on the floor
beside the bed.

The men had undressed Tom, scattering the articles of his clothing around the room. He was still
delirious, tossing on the bed, moaning in his pain.

"Would you bring us some towels, miss? And a
facecloth or two?" The doctor didn't look up as he
made his request.

When Jan returned she handed him the towels and
said, "My name is Jan."

"Thank you," the doctor replied. "And I'm
John—John Brogan."

"I'm really concerned about my father's failure to make contact with you. I'll have to go look for him as soon as it is light."

"I understand your anxiety. How can we be of help?"

"There's nothing to be done until morning. I've no idea where he may be. He's too experienced a woodsman to be in serious trouble." *I hope.* She was unable to utter the phrase, to voice her concern. Feeling Jason's eyes on her, she turned to leave the room.

"Could you rustle up some coffee, Jan? We haven't eaten since lunch and we're starved." The doctor's request stopped her in mid-stride.

"Would tea be okay?" she responded to the doctor, doing her best to ignore Jason. "And I've got a pot of stew ready for my dad. I'll heat it if you'd like some."

"Sounds wonderful. I'll just bandage Tom's ribs and get him comfortable, then we'll be with you."

Jan stirred the fire in the giant black iron cookstove and pulled the stew in place to warm. She loved cooking on the ancient stove, the only appliance she had convinced her father not to update. She slid the remaining johnnycake into the warming oven and plugged in the electric kettle before going into her father's den. Flicking on the switches of the powerful shortwave radio in the corner of the room, she checked out the wave bands of her immediate neighbors, none of whom were closer than seventy-five miles. Nothing. No answering calls at all.

It was too early in the morning, of course. Anyone who might know of Lewis's whereabouts was still in bed. There was nothing she could do before daylight. Nothing except worry. Jan shut the set down and went back to the kitchen. She made the tea, then decided the doctor might enjoy a cup as he finished caring for Tom Farrell. Hospitality demanded she put a second mug on the small round tray. Grimacing as she did so, she placed sugar and milk beside the mugs and carried the tray to the bedroom.

Jason was standing at the head of the bed. Looming was more like it, Jan thought. She did her best to ignore the tension. Why was he so hostile? Surely he had been able to figure out by now that she had just been trying to keep Tom warm.

Jan took the tray to the doctor. He thanked her and raised the cup for a quick swallow. Approaching Jason, she refused to allow his hostile attitude to intimidate her. One swift glance at the hard brown planes of his implacable features was enough. She concentrated on watching his lean fingers pick up the mug of tea and scoop sugar into it, then at his murmured thanks she inclined her head and left the room.

She tried to dispel all thoughts of the forbidding man in her bedroom as she set the table. The placemats she chose were the ones she'd crocheted the winter before last. A mass of yellow and orange flowers, they made a pretty background for the thick brown pottery tableware she set on each. She put out a pot of the honey her father had collected from the forest and one of blueberry jam she had made that summer. The johnnycake was hot when she retrieved it from the stove and she placed it carefully on the big pine table. Her father had built the table when they'd first come to the wilderness. It gleamed with a patina of use and good care.

She quickly turned around, intent on getting the stew. To her shock, Jason was behind her, so close she tripped over his feet. The mug he carried flew out of his hand, shattering against the wall, but he caught Jan before she reached the floor. Pressed into the hard expanse of his chest, Jan couldn't move for a moment. In that beat of time, her untutored senses reeled under a whole new set of sensations. She was suddenly conscious of his height, his strength, the firmness of the muscle against her. The scent of him electrified and excited her, triggering a response that frightened her. She tried to escape. Jason laughed then, a full-bodied sound that sent her heart beating wildly as he clamped her against his unyielding frame.

"What were you doing in bed with my son? Been there before, haven't you?"

Jan's head snapped up, green fire sparking in her eyes as she met the cynical gray of his. "I—you—let me go."

"I mean to know. You might as well tell me."

"I'll tell you nothing! Let me go." She strained against his powerful grip, her heart thudding painfully, threatening to deafen her.

"You're the bit of fluff he spent the summer with, aren't you?" He spit the words at her, contempt written all over his lean features. "Quite a hot little number, I presume, to have him neglect his studies and come back for another romp."

Jan stared up at him, speechless.

"What did he promise you? Marriage?"

"Why you—" she choked. "M-my father—"

"Ah, yes. Your father." He cut off her threat with smooth scorn. "Disappeared most conveniently, hasn't he? Part of the operation, I presume. What is his role? The outraged parent who shows up at the proper moment, shotgun in hand?"

"What on earth are you talking about?" she demanded.

His derisive smile deepened the crease in his dark cheek. Twisting in those hard arms, Jan tried to ignore the heat of his body. The panicky feeling that she was about to drown in a sea of emotion gave strength to her effort to free herself.

His laugh matched his smile as he held her easily, glaring at her. "You know what I'm talking about. You can't think I'm unaware of the fact he spent the summer here in this wilderness of yours. Lived with you and those kids from school, didn't he, Jan?"

Again that cold laugh struck her. He was dangerous, she realized, and deadly serious.

"He can't marry you, no matter what he's promised, so you might as well give it up, little girl. The fun is over."

Enraged, Jan refused to respond to his ridiculous accusation. Instead she did her best to break his hold, intent on escape.

His response was predictable. She was jerked off-balance and gathered close, her wrists captured in one strong hand as he dropped his other arm around her slender waist. Jan gasped at the intimate feel of his body. Her head flew back, the streaked honey of her hair swirling around her shoulders. She stared up at him with bitter eyes, doing her best to ignore the sensations his nearness was stirring within her.

Jason glared at her, his angry gray eyes wandering over the delicate perfection of her flushed features. Then his narrowed gaze settled on the winsome curve of her soft lips and stayed there, his expression changing.

Jan's heartbeat slowed to a painful thumping and she stopped breathing, lost in feelings she couldn't understand. Some powerful force flowed from the man holding her captive. It was disturbing, tantalizing, so potent with the unknown that she trembled.

He felt the tremor and laughed. It was a harsh sound, deep in his throat.

Jan felt the rising heat of her blush. "L—let me go, y—you beast." She hated the breathless sob trembling in the words and scorned the quick sting of tears behind her hastily lowered eyelids. How could this man frighten her enough to make her want to cry?

"Let her go, Jase." The doctor came into the kitchen, a hungry look on his tired face. "Tom shows all the signs of having had the very devil of a chill. I'd guess this young lady was in bed with him for the sole purpose of keeping him warm. That right, Jan?" He gave her a friendly smile as though finding a woman in the arms of his friend was nothing out of the ordinary, and sat down. His expression thoughtful, he reached for a piece of warm johnnycake.

Jan squirmed in her captor's unrelenting hold when he showed no inclination to release her.

"You're paranoid, Jase," the doctor sighed. "You think Tom is obsessed with sex. He's not, you know. Don't make a fool of yourself, man. The boy's going to be lucky if he escapes pneumonia. You can thank Jan and her father for saving his life." He took a huge bite of the corn bread he had dribbled honey on and a blissful expression settled on his tired face. "Man, this is good! Apologize to the girl and eat, Jase, eat." He grinned with the assurance of easy friendship. "As a medical man, I want you to know your son wouldn't have had a chance on his own."

Jason stared at the flushed woman in his arms, his features showing little sign of softening, then he released her. Jan sprang away as if shot from a gun, his words scarcely registering. "Never touch me again, y—you—"

The doctor interposed in an attempt to ease the tension. "Nice place you have here. I hadn't realized one could have so many conveniences this far from civilization."

Jan stared at him, not quite able to appreciate the effort he was making on her behalf. What was he talking about?

"I expect your father did most of the work himself to turn this into such a comfortable home." Still unable to answer, Jan stood, fists clenched, doing her best to ignore Jason but so angry she was unable to think at all.

"I must insist you keep your hands to yourself, Mr. Farrell. If you're unable to do so for any reason, please leave at once."

Jason opened his mouth to reply, but his friend managed the first word.

"Good idea. Why don't you go out for some fresh air, Jase, and give Jan a chance to get her breath."

Jason gave the doctor an impatient look, then to Jan's intense surprise he left without a word, scooping up his sheepskin jacket and shrugging into it as he slammed the front door behind himself.

"Well!" She made no attempt to hide her astonishment. The look on her face caused John to smile.

"Don't take Jase too seriously, Jan. That boy of his is always in trouble with the girls. He's a chip off the old block, much as Jase hates to admit it, but as his father he's determined to keep Tom from making the same mistake he did when he was the boy's age. Jase liked the girls, too. It almost ruined his life." The doctor frowned then. "It's a family weakness, I think. May I please have some of that stew? It smells so good I can barely stand it. And some more of your corn bread." He reached for it. "Where do you think your father might be?"

"I don't know. I'm so worried." Now that Jason was gone, her real concern came flooding back. "He should be here. He should have met you at the lake." Jan ladled the thick stew into a large bowl and set it before him. The doctor sniffed the mouth-watering cloud of steam rising from the dish and dug in.

Jan smiled her approval and went to pour tea for both of them.

"Jase has a bad temper when it comes to his son," the doctor remarked between bites. "But he's a reasonable man. This latest little episode of Tom's has really shaken him. He thought the boy was at school in California, you see. To find out he'd injured himself on a mountain three thousand miles from where he's supposed to be has shaken him considerably."

"It has nothing to do with me." Jan carried the teacups to the table, sitting beside the doctor. "I'm very worried about my father. It isn't like him to miss meeting your plane. And even if he did, why hasn't he returned by now? He must know you landed safely."

"Do you think he is lost?"

"He couldn't lose himself. He's lived on this mountain too long and knows it too well."

"Is there any chance he's hurt himself?" the doctor asked. "Has he been ill lately?"

"Anything can happen, I suppose, but I doubt that he's been hurt. I hate to think that he may be lying ill somewhere out there in the cold."

"But it's possible?"

"He had a heart attack several years ago. He doesn't talk about it, but I think his heart's bothering him. He doesn't want me to know."

"Does he have any symptoms you've noticed?"

"He gets very tired, a fact he never admits. His face loses color and he seems in pain. Sometimes he has to lie down, but he hates it. He's such an active man, you see. He's always working on some improvement here, or else he's hunting or fishing. But he didn't even fish much this summer, and he's a great fisherman. We were always at the lake when I was young." She smiled, remembering. That was why she had become so well acquainted with the Landrys. During the summers she had always accompanied her father on his fishing expeditions, except for the last year the Landrys were there. Then Lewis had required her to stay at the cabin.

"How is his appetite?"

"Not always good, I'm afraid. It hasn't been, really, since he had the heart attack when we were in Niagara four years ago."

"What happened?"

"We got out twice a year. In the fall and in the spring, usually. This was in the fall. I was supposed to go to college when it opened that year, but I couldn't after dad's attack. I wouldn't let him stay here alone after what the doctor told me."

"Serious, was it?"

"It was a serious warning. He's had to take nitroglycerin since then. He always carries a supply with him. That's why I'm so worried now."

"I can see why you are upset." Dr. Brogan patted the hand clenched so near him on the placemat. "But if he's had symptoms that long, your father knows how to handle them. Try not to worry. He's probably just been delayed somewhere along the line."

"I can't imagine where...."

"Did you ever get to college?" The doctor was making an obvious effort to distract her. Jan shook her head. "How old are you now?"

The door to the living room slammed causing Jan to jump, her nerves tingling. "Twenty-three," she answered briefly, her eyes on the man stripping off the sheepskin jacket in the other room.

"You've lived here all your life, then?"

"Since I was a toddler. We came after mother died."

"Who saw to your education?"

"My father. He has a degree in engineering and another in business. He's always taught me. I'm fairly well educated."

She watched Jason come into the kitchen and a sensitivity she didn't know she had recorded every movement of his lithe body as he approached. The neat lines of his tailored suit did nothing to disguise the strength of the man. Unbuttoning his vest as he walked, he reached up and jerked at the silk tie around his muscular neck. He grinned at Jan and ran a hand through his tumble of deep russet hair.

"I'm sorry I'm such a bastard. I've been worried out of my mind. Will you accept an apology and allow me to join you?"

Jan's exasperation melted before the glint of laughter in those gray eyes. She felt her spirits lighten. "Why don't you sit down and eat. You look starved. I'd hate it if you fainted."

"Thanks!" He grinned at her, his teeth flashing, his expression changing in a manner that caused her to stare. A glow started deep inside her, and Jan jumped to her feet, startled.

He watched her graceful movement, a strange look on his face. Jan flushed. Why did he have this disturbing ability to affect her as he did? She turned away in an effort to hide her confusion.

When she returned with a bowl of stew, his eyes roved over her and he smiled. Jan felt her color rise once again. What on earth was the matter with her, she wondered with some trepidation. Lewis's unexplained absence had upset her, left her without her usual common sense, she decided as she poured fresh tea and sat down again. That had to be the answer.

"How much education do you think you have, my dear?" The doctor's voice was kind as he tried to relieve the building tension growing between the two.

"Quite a bit, I imagine." Jan sipped her tea, studying Jason surreptitiously. His clean-cut strong features fascinated her. The resemblance between him and his son was marked. In Jason the striking good looks were refined, seasoned. Tom, she realized now, was a handsome boy. Jason was a mature and overpowering man. It was his maturity that was so alarming, she thought.

"I'm sorry. I didn't hear your question," she apologized to the doctor, when she realized he'd been speaking to her.

"I was asking about your studies. What are your major interests?"

"Anthropology and geology, but I love good literature, too, and music. Art is my hobby. I illustrate stories. I speak and read French and Spanish, and since my mother was from Holland, also learned Dutch."

Jason raised his eyebrows and John whistled. "That's quite a respectable list," the doctor commented. "All this on a college level?"

"I think so. Dad has always encouraged me to learn as much as possible. In the winter there isn't much else to do up here. Dad invents things for us. I study."

"I've noticed you live pretty well." Jason tossed the casual statement at her.

John gave her a quiet smile. "I must say I find it a pleasant thought to know one can be so far from the so-called necessities of civilization and still have as many comforts."

"We do live well," Jan agreed. She smiled at the doctor and did her best to ignore Jason. "My father has put his engineering knowledge to good use. We generate our own electricity, thanks to dad's skill and know-how. The cabin is electrically heated, but I prefer the fireplaces. We use them all winter, turning on the electrical heat when the weather gets really cold. We have running water, a deep-freeze and refrigeration. We grow enough food in the summer to last us through the winter. We have books, music and a way to communicate with the outside world if we want to. Our recreation is all around us. We swim, fish and canoe in the summer. In the winter we hunt and trap."

"What is your father's occupation?" Jason asked.

"Occupation?"

"What does he do to supply the money to run this place, buy the equipment needed to make things work?"

"Oh." Jan had never seriously considered the need for money before. Her father just seemed to have it when anything was needed. Because of the isolation in which they lived, the notion of income was one she had not considered. Frowning, she thought about it

now. "Dad doesn't *do* anything, in the way I'm sure
you mean. He traps, and the furs he sells bring in
something, I think. Then he's paid to guide hunters
and fishermen. . . ." Her voice trailed off as she realized the disparity between the money her father
earned and the cost of the supplies and equipment in
the cabin.

Jason gave her an assessing glance. "I see. How do
you get all the stuff you need up here? That mountain trail is a man-killer. You don't backpack it in, do
you?"

"Of course not!" Jan snapped. His probing question had disturbed her. Where did her father get the
money? Did he have a private source of income he
hadn't bothered to discuss with her?

"How do you manage then?" Jason didn't bother
to hide his impatient amusement.

"Things are flown in by helicopter," Jan's explanation was almost brusque. He didn't need to talk
to her as if she were a child. "Dad cleared the area
out front years ago. We've had everything brought
directly to the cabin since I can remember."

"And that's the way it is." The cool voice held an
element of challenge.

"That's the way it is." Jan's agreement was frosty.

"Do you get a chance to see the men who fly stuff
in to you?"

"What are you talking about?" Jan stared at him,
wondering what he was implying.

"Nothing. Sorry. It occurred to me you really
might be as isolated as you seem to want us to believe
you are."

"We have all kinds of people coming through here." Jan didn't hide her annoyance. His statement had suddenly made her defensive. "Hunters and trappers all winter. Canoeists and explorers all summer. I admit most of these are city folk who know little about the woods. But they talk a lot about their homes."

"I'll bet they don't stay long enough for you to get to know much about them." Jason's voice was soft. "Do they?"

"No, of course not. Dad doesn't much care for overnight guests. We never have them, except for old Sim Simmons. He always comes and stays when we go on our trips. He sleeps here, does the chores and takes care of the place. Dad trusts him."

"And I'll bet he leaves as soon as you get back." Again Jason's shrewd guess hit the mark. "I find the whole situation a bit strange."

Jan jumped to her feet.

"What are you implying? Is there anything wrong with a wish to live your life in peace, as my father does? I expect you may be one of those who can't live unless you are surrounded by constant activity. I'll just bet you have masses of people who jump when you say so. You look like the type who'd enjoy it. Thinking of ways to order everybody around certainly fills up an empty mind, doesn't it?" Unable to stop the flow of words, she glared at him. "How dare you judge us when you know nothing about us? Strange, indeed! I find it strange that you know so little of your son's activities that you can think I ever saw him before in my life!" Her hands clenched in an effort to stop from trembling.

Jason watched her, his cool glance inscrutable.

John rose to his feet, and placed a comforting arm around her rigid shoulders. "Why don't you go check on Tom?" he said to his friend.

"Why don't I indeed?"

He went without another word, and Jan shuddered with relief.

CHAPTER THREE

JAN WAS UNACCUSTOMED to having anyone touch her. Embarrassed by the doctor's gentle effort to reassure her, she shrugged away from his arm and reached for the dishes on the table. He let her go.

"What makes that man so insufferable?"

John smiled, his manner easy. "Jason is accustomed to having his own way a good deal of the time." The doctor stacked the dirty bowls together and followed her to the sink. As a rule Jan rinsed her dishes and left them in the dishwasher, but in this instance she needed more activity to calm herself.

Squirting liquid soap into one of the stainless-steel sinks, she turned on the taps. The rush of water against the metal was a perfect accompaniment to the rush of blood charging around in her system.

John continued to clear the table.

"You don't need to help me. I can manage." She was in no mood to be soothed by one of Jason's friends.

"I want to help." He grinned, his tired face taking on an impish cast. "May I say a word in Jason's defense?"

"He doesn't need anyone to defend him!" Jan

sloshed the hot water around and the sink filled with foaming suds.

"Tom did spend several weeks of the summer somewhere in this area, you see. Jason didn't know about it until very recently."

"He didn't approve, I gather."

"He didn't approve. Tom surrounds himself with girls and his father never approves. He's fighting a losing battle, I suspect. It worries the hell out of my friend. The boy has a first-class brain. Young as he is, he only has a year to finish and he'll be through with his university training. He gets good grades, but I do see Jason's point. Tom is a charming kid. He can and often does talk almost anyone into almost anything."

"This includes his ability to talk a girl into being his...companion, whenever he chooses, I presume?"

"Takes after his old man when it comes to that." John didn't bother to elaborate. "Jason is concerned about the boy. Life wasn't easy on Jason. He wants to prevent his son from making the mistakes he did when he was young. It's natural." The doctor smiled at her, deposited the mugs and utensils on the draining board and shifted the conversation with blunt expertise. "I don't want to be overly inquisitive, but I would like to ask a couple of questions, if I may."

"What kind of questions?" Jan shot him a wary look.

"Well...." His grin was reassuring. He flipped a white towel off the rack and picked up a bowl. "It seems to me that you lead a very lonely life up here in spite of how much you may like it. Your father is another matter, I think. I gather he came here just after your mother died?''

''Yes, he did.''

''Uh-huh. Probably loved her so completely he couldn't find any relief from his grief. A man who is deeply in love and loses his loved one will seek solitude. I can understand that kind of desire, that kind of drive to get away from anything that might act as a reminder of happier days. But what about you? Surely you need companions your own age.''

''Do you think so?''

''Any young person does. When a girl of your beauty and intelligence is isolated, it's a crime.''

For the first time that day Jan blushed without being angry. She gave him a quick glance. The doctor was polishing the bowl he was drying, concentrating on the task with commendable attention. Realizing he was making a serious effort to put her at ease, Jan felt her tension lighten.

''You do that very well,'' she told him, laughter in the words. ''I've never seen such a well-polished soup bowl.''

John laughed and gave her a broad wink.

''I haven't always been just a handsome doctor, you know. Back in my gritty and uncomfortable past, I once washed dishes for a living. Takes a lot of money to get a poor boy through college.''

''You were poor?''

''Yep. Poor and struggling. Until I met Jase. He loaned me the money to finish my degree in Sybaritic comfort. Can't tell you what it meant to me.''

"Oh. That was nice of him." Somehow Jan couldn't conceive of Jason as a benefactor. "What did he demand for security? A pound of flesh, perhaps? Or your instant obedience to his every wish."

"Now who's judging?" Jan flushed. "As a matter of fact, he didn't want the money back even when I could finally afford to repay him."

"You're right of course." Jan found herself apologizing. "It's just that he makes me so angry. I've never met anyone like him before."

"I can see that. This is why I wondered about you. Must you stay up here all the time? Couldn't you go out, meet people, get some experience that would allow you to deal with a person of Jason's caliber?" He laughed then, a gentle self-derisive sound Jan found attractive. "I wouldn't want to mislead you. There are very few of Jase's caliber out there, and learning to deal with him is something of an experience. But you need to learn what others are like, learn to hold your own."

"I do know what you mean." Jan had longed to leave, to go to college. It had been a wonderful dream—a dream that had shattered when her father had his heart attack. "I will one day. As soon as I know dad isn't in danger. I'm afraid to leave him alone."

"Because of the attack he had?"

"He refuses to admit there is anything wrong with him," Jan answered. Remembering the effort it took to keep her father from working himself to exhaustion, she shook her head in resignation.

"Stubborn, is he?" John gave her a swift glance as he stacked the crockery.

"Muleheaded is the term, I think. There's so much to do around here. And he's always inventing something that demands a lot of his energy before it works. He won't listen. He just grits his teeth and slugs away."

"How far is it to the spot where he found Tom?"

"Miles."

"Miles! Did your father carry him in? Tom's a hefty youngster."

"No. Dad jerry-built a travois and tied him onto it. Tom was unconscious and feverish. He couldn't be left. Dad was afraid he'd found him too late as it was, so he brought him in."

"He was almost right about that. Tom's condition is serious. He couldn't have taken much more exposure and cold."

"Dad understood the necessity of quick action. I'm sure it didn't occur to him to leave Tom and come for help."

"The hours he saved made a great difference in Tom's chances for survival," the doctor confirmed. "Your father sounds like quite a man to me. Hasn't it ever occurred to him that you may need to go away from here, to be around people?"

"He's so independent himself, I really don't think it has until quite recently. He said something about it today. I was surprised when he mentioned it."

The doctor's face was thoughtful. "Were you enrolled in a college when he had his attack?"

"No, but I had filled out all the application forms.

We were going to see about it when we returned from that trip to Niagara Falls. I didn't send them."

"Didn't he object? Couldn't he see the sacrifice you were making when you decided not to go?"

"I know my father. When I realized he mustn't be left alone on this mountain, I just approached the subject in the right way and he never questioned my motive."

"And that was?"

"I told him I couldn't bear the thought of leaving here and going out on my own. I said I much preferred staying with him, staying where it was quiet and peaceful."

"And he bought it?"

"Well, he hates crowds, hates to be constantly surrounded by others. He seems to have such a powerful need for solitude that he didn't find it at all odd that I should want to stay."

"But surely you don't expect to spend the rest of your life tucked away here," John said gently. "Don't you have any wish for a career, a life of your own?"

"Oh, yes. I write children's books, which I illustrate. I plan to try to sell them one of these days."

"It's a tough market. Are they any good?"

"I hope so. I seem to have a flair for drawing and there are a thousand stories out there in the woods."

"I'd like to see them a bit later, if I may."

"Certainly." Jan gave him a shy smile. "No one has seen what I've done except dad. I'm not too sure his opinion is unbiased, but he thinks they're good."

"Let me get some rest, then allow me the privilege

of seeing them, would you? And now, if you don't mind, I'll borrow a blanket and bed down somewhere." He stretched his muscles and gave her an apologetic grin. "I'm dead tired and I expect Jason is, too."

"You can sleep in dad's bed." A frown creased her forehead. "It doesn't look as though he's coming back tonight."

"Perhaps he stopped off to see someone and...."

"We are the only ones living on the mountain," Jan interrupted. "He had nowhere else to go."

"That is odd. If he wasn't feeling well, is there anywhere he could find shelter?"

"There are always places, of course. Windfalls, caves, things like that. But—"

"Show John where he's to sleep. He's dead on his feet." Jason interrupted abruptly. Jan whirled around. She hadn't heard his approach. He gave her a cold smile. "You can finish your little chat tomorrow, after we find your father."

"We? You aren't going with me...."

"I'm going with you. You'd better get some rest, as well. It isn't long until daylight."

"There's no need. I can find him myself."

"What if he's ill or had an accident? You'll need help. I'm going. Will you please show John where he's to get some sleep?"

"If something's happened to him, he may need the doctor—"

Again Jason interrupted. "Tom needs John's attention. I'll go with you. I'm capable of rendering comprehensive first aid."

"If your father's in trouble, Jase is the best person to have with you. He's terrific in an emergency. You could do with forty winks yourself, Jason," the doctor interjected hastily.

"Go ahead. I'm not sleepy."

John gave his friend a sharp look, then shrugged and followed Jan into her father's room. Sitting on the bed he kicked off his shoes.

"I'll just stretch out on top of this if you have an extra blanket. Is that your mother?" He yawned, his tired gaze on the photo beside the bed. "She was beautiful," he smiled when Jan nodded. "Do you know you look like her?"

"Dad says so, but I think he's prejudiced. I can't believe I resemble her all that much."

"Take my word for it—you do."

Jan gave him an uncertain smile and left, disturbed that he had mentioned her likeness to her mother. Lewis had remarked on the same thing several times in recent months, his face sad when he did so. She knew that as she grew older her striking similarity to her mother worried and upset her father. He didn't discuss the source of his distress with her, but she knew him too well not to be aware of it. Her resemblance to the mother she couldn't remember was a source of unhappiness to Lewis and she had no clue as to the reason why.

She thought about it as she went into her room to check on Tom, unwilling to go back into the living room, where Jason waited. She didn't want him to go with her when she went to look for her father. His presence was much too disturbing to her.

She dawdled as long as she could in the sick man's room, her worry about her father gnawing at her, causing her to move around restlessly. She folded the young man's discarded clothing, picked up her sketch pad and put it away, straightened up the room and generally stalled as long as she could. She hoped Jason had followed his friend's example and gone to bed. It was a vain hope.

He was waiting for her, his long frame propped against the facing stone of the fireplace. He straightened as she came through the door and stopped.

"Come on in," he ordered, his command impatient. "I want to find out more about you. I need to if I'm to help."

"I don't need your help," she told him. "I'll be okay."

She knew she sounded breathless. Deciding to take the offense, she came to stand beside him. For the second time during this interminable night she was grateful for the warmth of the fire on her legs. However, the soft heat did little to nullify the chill emanating from the stern man facing her.

Jan had always considered herself to be tall. Jason topped her five feet six by a good eight inches. Her head barely cleared his shoulder. She stood there meeting his enigmatic gaze, doing her best to stare him down.

He considered her, his eyes partly hidden behind lashes that were thick and curved. Jan concentrated on them, her artist's eye noting their length.

Jason frowned. "That was quite a bill of goods you were trying to sell my friend just now." His voice was a deep murmur.

"I beg your pardon?"

"Just an unselfish, innocent young thing, aren't you? I don't know what your game with Tom is, lady, but let's get the whole business finished and wrapped up."

Jan's expression registered her utter amazement. "I don't know anything about your son," she retorted angrily, "but even if I did, he looks like an adult to me, and surely you have no right to interfere with his life. You certainly have no right to make accusations about me. And now if you'll excuse me I have more important things to attend to."

She left him standing by the fireplace and stamped her feet into her boots. Pulling on her sheepskin jacket, she went to the door, digging her woolen gloves out of her pocket. She knew those smoky gray eyes followed every movement she made.

It was too early to do chores, not yet light in fact. But if she got them done now, she could leave at dawn to find her father.

Anything was welcome if it removed her from the suffocating presence of her unwanted guest.

CHAPTER FOUR

By FIRST LIGHT Jan had finished the task of caring for the animals. The basket of fresh-laid eggs over her arm and the bucket of goat's milk in her gloved fist, she shut the door behind her and looked up into the morning sky as a sound caught her attention.

High above the clearing a flock of Canada geese honked and fluttered, then wheeled in behind the leader and fell into their V formation. They crossed the pale wash of visible sky, pointed due south.

Winter was coming.

Jan shook herself and headed for the cabin. Now that it was light she had to find out what had happened to Lewis.

Jason was no longer in the living room when she went in. Perhaps he'd succumbed to his fatigue and gone to bed.

She carried her burdens into the kitchen and put them away with quick efficiency then plugged the electric kettle in. If only she could get away without waking anyone.

The house stayed quiet. Grateful to be free of Jason's disturbing presence, she went into her bedroom. Tom was breathing in short noisy gasps, the covers pushed partially off his large frame. She covered him and touched his forehead with light fingers. He still had a fever, but it had come down considerably.

A noise attracted her attention and she glanced at the door. Jason was there, watching her with hooded eyes. He ran his hand over the stubble on his chin, the sound rasping in the stillness.

"Are you making tea?"

"Yes," she answered shortly, brushing by him. He followed her to the kitchen.

"Are you ready to look for your father?"

"I am." She poured the boiling water over the tea leaves in the pot and unplugged the kettle.

"I'm going with you." It was a flat statement, leaving no room for argument.

Jan tried anyway. "Oh no, you're not. I'll look for dad by myself. He's my responsibility. Tom is yours."

"John says your father's symptoms make him a prime candidate for a heart attack. Since his attempt to help my son may have weakened him, I'm going. You may need my help."

"Please yourself." Jan couldn't admit his offer was welcome, even to herself, but the look of strain that had shadowed her father's face haunted her. Heart attack...dear God!

She gulped the rest of her hot tea and put her cup into the sink.

A grim look on his face, Jason followed suit.

"It was close to freezing last night," Jan told him. "We really must leave at once—if you insist on coming. Hypothermia is a grim reality in the kind of chill we had last night."

"It is. I've been so concerned with Tom's condition I forgot about that danger. I'm sorry."

A swift look told Jan he was indeed contrite, and this gave her the oddest feeling.

She turned away and prepared a thermos of hot tea. While she rummaged in a cupboard for the bottle of whiskey her father kept, Jason went into the other room for his jacket.

She had filled a flask with whiskey by the time he returned. Taking the thermos and the flask from her, he shoved them into his jacket pocket. "Let's go then. John will see to Tom." Pushing the door open, he followed her into the crisp air, taking command without hesitation. Jan stifled the impulse to rebel and led the way down the forest trail.

The morning was fresh, full of awakening life. The glimpse of bleached-blue sky through the bright foliage told of the coming winter. A sugar maple flamed red against the dark green of spruce and fir. They wound down through a tiny meadow, its stand of birch molten gold in the early sun.

Jan loved these first hours of a day. Usually a morning walk filled her with exquisite pleasure as she savored the beauty surrounding her, but this one was wasted. Her attention was centered on her father.

Jason followed as she stamped down the trail. Lengthening his stride he reached out, his long fingers wrapping around her arm. Jan whirled, facing him, her head high.

"Keep your hands off me, Mr. Farrell!"

"Jason," he commanded as he dropped her arm. "Look, I apologize. I mean it. I know I shouldn't have jumped to conclusions yesterday. But Tom's usually so predictable—and you're so damned lovely. I was sure you were the reason he ditched school. A natural mistake.''

"I assure you I never saw your son before dad dragged him into the yard yesterday morning." Jan's words were as crisp as the frosted leaves underfoot. "And you don't need to try to flatter me, Mr. Farrell. Now may we continue to look for my father?"

"Jason," he reminded her shortly, his eyes intent on her indignant face. "And why don't we call a truce?"

"You have tried your best to irritate me since the moment you saw me," Jan began, "and I see no reason to try to be friendly with you beyond the dictates of good manners."

"Don't like me much, do you?"

She stared up at him, her brief laugh grim. "I don't like you at all, Mr. Farrell. You are overbearing, arrogant and disgusting, and I feel sorry for your son. Now shall we go?"

"What about our truce?"

Jan sighed. What was the point of arguing with him? "If you insist," she replied, then moved away from him in a sudden rush to put some distance between them.

Jason's voice sounded behind her. "I saw your mother's picture in your father's room. You look very like her."

"My father has told me I resemble her a little."

"She was beautiful." It was a flat statement.

"Yes. The picture is all we have of her. I don't remember her, of course. I was so young when she died. My father never really got over her death.''

"Is that why you live on this mountain, so far away from others?"

"I think so. He's never been able to face the world since he lost her."

"Where was he born, Jan? Here?"

"Sh-shh!" A small sound touched her ears and she stopped, listening. Jason halted behind her, his eyes never leaving the curve of the cheek he was able to see as she held herself rigid, her head to one side. She identified the sound and shook her head, continuing down the dim trail. "I don't know his birthplace. His father was English, he told me once. I think he was born in London, but he has never wanted to talk about it much. He attended university there, I know. I've seen his diploma. But he has never told me anything of the past. I don't even know where I was born. I don't know where my mother died."

She changed the subject with determination, suddenly wary of the lazy probing questions coming over her shoulder. "Why was Tom here on the mountain?"

"He was supposed to be at his university in Palo Alto three weeks ago. I've no idea why he isn't out on the West Coast, but I plan to find out as soon as he is out of danger."

Jan heard the grim overtones, but she caught a glimpse of their destination at that moment.

"Look! There's the lake." She stopped and raised her arm to point.

The path was steep here, and her companion could

not avoid a collision. He crashed into her. Jan slipped and staggered, clutching at the nearest support. For the second time in less than twenty-four hours, Jason saved her from falling to his feet.

Jan caught her breath as his arms encircled her. She turned her face upward. The morning sun filtered through the trees, touching flame in the dark auburn head bent over her. The surprise in the gray eyes changed, becoming deeply intent and dark with a meaning she didn't understand.

He smiled then, a tender expression lighting his face.

Jan stared up at him without the least inclination to break the spell, her lips parted in wonder. She felt the tremor pass through his muscular frame and trembled in return. Jason groaned softly, lowering his head. His mouth, cool with the morning chill, touched hers.

Fire shot through her and she clung to him, the blood singing in her veins, the sweetness of her first kiss intoxicating, exquisite.

Birdsong quivered on the air, filling her world with music. The scent of pine, the familiar musty odor of the leaves crushed underfoot mingled with the fragrant after-shave of the man holding her. All her senses were heightened, alerting her to wonders she'd never dreamed existed. She accepted his kiss with a fierce longing that seemed to trigger Jason's sensual nature. Tightening his arms, he kissed her with a deepening passion.

It was then Jan heard the sound.

A muffled moan, it carried through the clear

morning air, at odds with the trilling songs of the woodland denizens.

She broke away and stood poised, electrified by the faint cry. Jason reached out for her, then was instantly alert himself. Tension closed around them as they waited, willing the sound to come again.

When it did, Jason touched her arm.

"This way, Jan."

She followed him without a word, her anxiety for her father dispelling all thought of their passionate kiss. Weak with apprehension, she ran behind Jason, leaping over deadfall, stumbling over the rough ground but keeping up with his longer strides.

He led the way fifty yards through the undergrowth, then came to a halt at the edge of a steep little ravine cut into the floor of the forest by a creek long since gone. Jan pushed around him and stared down into the V-shaped bottom of the ravine. It was filled with brush and autumn leaves. Nothing stirred.

Then the sound came again and Jan was over the edge in a flash. Burrowing into the dead leaves, she unmasked a fallen tree trunk that spanned the ravine close to its bottom. Jason dropped down beside her and together they uncovered the man who was sheltered underneath the protection of the trunk and the leaves.

Lewis's face was ashen and his breathing restricted. He was unconscious. His left leg was twisted beneath him, oddly askew. He moaned, twisting with pain, but didn't open his eyes.

Frightened, Jan turned in silent appeal toward the man kneeling beside her. He reached for her, pulling her head into the rough comfort of his shoulder in an instinctive answer to her unspoken appeal. His other hand smoothed the satin sheen of her hair.

"Don't fall apart, Janet," he counseled, his deep voice gruff. "Stay here with him. Don't touch him. I'll be right back. I've got a stretcher on the plane. Brought it for Tom. We have to get him out of here and to a hospital—fast." He held her a moment, then let her go and headed downhill.

Released abruptly from his compassionate embrace, Jan suffered an acute feeling of loss she didn't understand. Impatient at her own weakness, she knelt over her father, working with care as she brushed off the blanket of leaves covering him.

Cautiously she unzipped his heavy jacket a few inches and felt in his shirt pocket, breathing a sigh of relief as she found his bottle of medicine. Pulling the zipper back up, she opened the bottle and shook out a tiny pill, thrusting it under his unresisting tongue.

Hurry, Jason. Hurry, she cried in silent frustration.

Thank God there was a doctor at the cabin!

The relief this thought gave her didn't last long. The cabin was almost five miles away. Even with the stretcher Jason was bringing, Jan knew she wasn't strong enough to struggle that far with her end of the burden.

Whatever would they do? Jason couldn't do it alone. One of them would have to go up to the cabin and bring the doctor back. But that would take so long!

Her father moved restlessly and cried out, still unconscious. Jan shot up out of the ravine.

Oh, why didn't he hurry?

She saw him then, running uphill, the rolled stretcher in his hands.

"Hurry, Jason! Please hurry!" she screamed at him.

He ran through the underbrush and scrambled down the slope behind her. He was panting from the uphill run but worked with quick efficiency, straightening Lewis's leg, easing him onto the stretcher, then producing a thin temporary splint for the injury.

"We won't be able to carry him back up to the cabin," he said, his voice grim.

"I'll get Dr. Brogan." Jan was on her feet as she spoke.

"Help me with this." He handed her a roll of bandage. "And stay right here, young lady. I need your help if we're to save your father."

"How? Do you think we will be able to carry him to the doctor?"

"No, I don't. Even if you were strong enough to carry your end of the stretcher that far, it would take hours. This man needs attention as quickly as possible."

"That's why I should be going to get...."

"You couldn't be back inside of three hours," he cut in with brusque impatience. He finished wrapping the bandage on the splint holding Lewis's broken leg. "We'll take him down to the lake and load him into the plane. We can have him in one of the world's finest hospitals in just over an hour. He's going to need good care, Jan. Being out here all night hasn't been the best thing in the world for him."

"All right. But let's hurry."

"Let's go, then." Jason tucked the blanket he'd remembered to bring around the man on the stretcher. "You take that end of the stretcher. Now lift gently."

It seemed to take forever to reach the plane. Loading Lewis into the floating plane was an experience Jan never wanted to repeat. Once they were airborne she sat beside him, holding his hand. He moaned occasionally but didn't regain consciousness. Jan spoke to him softly, paying no attention to Jason's crisp voice as he snapped orders into the microphone of his headset.

"For God's sake, man!" His exasperation did penetrate this time. "This man saved my son's life. I want the best for him and I want it now!" He paused to listen to a voice she couldn't hear. "Well, make sure he's at the hospital and get a room ready!" His command rang in the cabin and Jan was suddenly less anxious. Jason was in charge. He would see to it that her father received the best care. Assurance came, and with it a tiny flame of gratitude. There was a comforting security in trusting this man. She hadn't known it existed.

They flew into Boston, into one of the busiest airports in the world, Jason landing on the sheet of water they had flown over.

As they touched down Jan heard the wail of a siren and glimpsed the flashing red lights of an ambulance. She heard Jason mutter with evident satisfaction as he turned the plane toward shore. By the time he taxied into position and cut the motor, the ambulance was standing by, the doors open, a large cradle of a stretcher ready.

The plane's door opened and men swarmed in, instruments and oxygen at hand. Jason came to take Jan out of the plane.

"They'll take good care of him," he murmured, bending his head close to her ear. "Let's get out of the way."

Jan allowed him to help her from the plane. She flinched as a throng of television news-cameras loomed before her.

Someone thrust a long slender microphone into her face. "Are you the girl Mr. Farrell found on the mountain?"

Jan was caught off guard. She shrank back and felt Jason's arm go around her. "I—"

"Miss Jordan's father found my son," Jason interrupted her. "After he rescued Tom, he broke his leg going for help. I've brought him in so he can receive proper medical attention."

"Where was Tom this time, Jase?"

Jason shot the man a glance of cold dislike. "Up in the wilderness, Johnson. On a school project."

"Yeah. Research in the form and development of gorgeous girls, maybe? Can't say I blame him, if Miss Jordan was his project."

Jason stepped in front of Jan, the anger in his face enough to blister the newsman.

"This young lady's father has just saved my son's life." His words were so quiet Jan almost missed them. "Keep a civil tongue in your head or you'll answer to me personally."

The obstreperous reporter backpedaled. "Sorry, Jase. Where's Tom?"

"Still back at the Jordan cabin."

"By himself?" someone else asked.

"Of course not. He's with a doctor. He can't be moved yet, so the doctor will stay there with him until he has recovered enough to be flown out." He turned and took Jan's arm. "If you don't mind, we need to move on. The ambulance is ready to go and we should be at the hospital when it arrives. If you'll excuse us, gentlemen."

"Which hospital, Mr. Farrell?"

"Was Miss Jordan there in the wilderness when you arrived?"

"She looks. . . ."

"How'd you get so lucky, Jase?"

"Sorry," Jason replied brusquely. "We've nothing more to say at the moment. I'll keep you posted." A pressure on her arm was propelling Jan through the crowd of assembled reporters. Helpless and confused, she surrendered to Jason's strength and allowed him to direct her toward a limousine parked beside the waiting ambulance.

"Aw, Jase," someone in the back of the group wailed. "Give us a break. She's beautiful and she's news."

"Back off," Jason's response came from deep in his throat. "This isn't the time to tangle with me."

They reached the limousine and a smartly uniformed chauffeur opened the rear door.

"It's never time," Jan heard. She watched as a beautifully manicured hand extended itself from the interior of the big car and guided her in. "Admit it, my love. You know you can't stand reporters!"

Jan found herself in the middle of a luxurious back seat. It offered impeccable comfort. Jason Farrell sank down beside her with a weary sigh. Paying no attention to the person beside her, Jan twisted around to watch the attendants rush the big stretcher across the black tarmac to the waiting vehicle. One man ran beside it, supporting a bottle of something swinging from a shiny metal hook attached to the stretcher.

"Why can't I stay with my father?" she demanded sharply.

Jason shook his head. "Paramedics are very competent in an emergency. They know what they're doing. You'd only be in the way if you rode with them."

Jan gave him a strained glance and sat back on the seat. She knew he was right.

"Are we going to the hospital?"

"We'll follow them," he answered. "Thanks, Lucille." He spoke to the woman who occupied the other corner of the long seat. "I appreciate the use of your car. I didn't expect you to come along."

"Oh, Jason, you know I wouldn't be left out of one of your adventures for anything in the world. What have you been up to now and where did you find this beautiful child?"

"Lucille, this is Jan Jordan. Her father saved Tom's life. He injured himself in the process. Jan—"

he turned, a cool look on his face "—this is my very good friend, Lucille St. John."

Jan glanced at the woman beside her. She had never seen or imagined such an exquisite creature. The perfect oval of her face was set off by dark almond-shaped eyes. Long silky lashes curled up and out, shading those black depths with languorous seductiveness. Velvety brows arched in perfect harmony, accenting the black widow's peak of her thick and magnificently styled hair. A proud and classic nose was faultless above the flawless full lips. She was clad in a form-fitting pantsuit of scarlet suede, with gold at her throat and ears.

Jan stared at her, stunned. A complacent light in her eyes, Lucille St. John reached over and patted Jan's gloved hand.

"Welcome to our town, Miss Jan Jordan. You are miss, I presume?" Her words were sincere, her voice lovely and welcoming.

Jan nodded, feeling overwhelmed by the woman's presence.

"Who the hell alerted those news hounds?" Jason's angry voice shattered the calm.

"Oh, Jason. Don't be so naive!" Lucille admonished him. "You know very well the Farrells are front page. The least hint of something new and the press turns out in full force. There's no way for you to keep anything as exciting as this a secret!"

"Damn kid! He needs iron-handed discipline."

Lucille's laughter tinkled lightly. "Don't be droll, Jason. You were unable to spank the boy when he was small enough for you to get away with it. You can't begin at this age."

"Are you implying I couldn't do it now?" Jason sounded every bit as menacing as Jan thought him to be.

"Even if you could, you wouldn't, Jason, my love. You're such a pussycat. What are you trying to do? Frighten this poor girl you've hauled out of the north woods?"

Jason folded his arms across his sheepskin jacket and stared out at the gathering dark.

Jan sat back, her eyes glued to the flashing lights on the top of the ambulance speeding ahead of them. Why had her father been unconscious so long? Pain? Perhaps, but her fear told her no. A broken leg didn't cause unconsciousness as a rule. Had the combination of pain and exposure been too much for Lewis's tired heart? The thought was devastating.

Oh, Dad, she prayed. *Be well. Be strong.* A sob caught in her throat.

Lucille heard the sound and turned to her, her eyes glowing in the flash of lights illuminating the interior of the car as they sped down a busy street. "Poor dear. Don't cry. I know the situation is quite nerve-racking, but you must not worry, Jan. May I call you Jan?" A soft hand touched hers.

Jan looked into those lambent eyes and her nerves prickled a warning. She had little experience with people, but she had survived in the deep woods in conditions few would have welcomed. That survival had depended many times on her ability to sense danger before she knew what it was. Something triggered her warning system now.

"If you wish," she replied. She couldn't keep the coolness out of her voice even as she realized she was probably extrasensitive because of her father's condition.

"My dear child, you needn't distrust me." Lucille's lovely mouth curved in a smile. "Just ask that handsome man sitting beside you. He trusts me completely, don't you, Jason, darling? And we're so concerned with your father. Such a wonderful thing he did, bringing our Tom in when the poor boy might have died."

My dear child! Jan was not used to being patronized but she was too confused to take offense.

"Jan is not a child." Jason threw in the dry remark, his eyes on the racing ambulance. "May we drop you somewhere, Lucille?"

"I really must get back to the plant." Lucille reached across Jan to lay a tapered hand on Jason's wrist. "You know that planeload of buyers is here from the Middle East, Jason. They've been in the showrooms all day. I was hoping you would be able to attend the dinner this evening."

"You'll have to handle it. I have to take care of Jan and her father. Then I have to fly the supplies John needs back to the lake."

"They will be annoyed." Her sweet voice was crisp with censure. "They have been asking for you."

"You can manage, Lucille. Just turn up the charm and carry on." Jason sounded weary, Jan thought, and very impatient.

"Oh, Jason, darling. Whatever am I going to do with you? You know how these men are about dealing with the head of any company in which they have an interest. You may be insulting them."

"Don't be ridiculous. They won't expect me to be there. Not with my son ill and needing me. Explain and carry on."

"You're stubborn when you decide to be, Jason. Will I see you before you leave to fly back up north?"

"Sorry." Jason rubbed his hand across his chin. "I've had one hell of a twenty-four hours. I've got to see to Lewis Jordan and get Jan settled somewhere. Then I'll have to pick up any supplies John may need. He's going to be isolated on that mountain a while. I don't think Tom can be moved for some time. I'll have to get back tomorrow and I don't want to carry supplies up that trail in the dark, so I'll leave early. I'll call when I get back." The big car drew up to the portico of the hospital as he made his apologies. Jason pushed the door open and jackknifed out before the chauffeur left his seat. He held his hand out for Jan. "We'll take cabs. Don't wait for us," he instructed Lucille.

"You can bring her to me, Jason. I have that extra room, as you know. I'd be happy to look after her for you."

Jan wondered how such a kind offer could make her feel so unhappy and out of sorts. She shook herself, her irritation mostly with her own ridiculous reactions to a charming woman. What on earth was wrong with her?

"I don't think so," Jason interposed smoothly before Jan was able to think of a civilized way to say no. "Jan will want to be close to her father. I'll find some place nearby for her."

Grateful for that small reprieve, Jan managed to smile at Lucille. "Thank you for your kind offer. Perhaps we'll meet again." She moved away from the car, unable to understand her reaction to the beautiful woman.

Jason shut the car door and swung his long frame beside her. "Don't mind Lucille," he commanded, his deep voice quiet. "She's my vice-president in this area and a bit too inclined to organize things along the lines she thinks appropriate for the president of the shop." He sounded amused and tolerant.

"Shop? President?"

"Actually it's an electronics firm. I head it. Her father was head of the eastern division and my good friend for several years. Lucille was his personal secretary while he was alive. She had enough experience and the qualifications to take over when he died unexpectedly. She's a good administrator and she runs a tight ship. She's also one hell of a saleswoman. I called her on the way in, told her what I wanted and she laid it on."

"Oh. Please thank her for me." Dismissing the woman without a further thought, Jan gave in to her anxiety. "How will we find dad? Do you know where they have taken him?"

"Through here." Jason led her into the hospital.

Leading her down a quiet hall, he stopped at an imposing desk. The nurse in charge gave him the directions.

"This way, Jan." Jason took her arm in his and led her into the elevator. Jan stripped off her gloves and unbuttoned her sheepskin jacket. When the elevator stopped she followed Jason down another quiet hallway. They found Lewis in a high bed surrounded by banks of instruments that ticked, muttered and clicked. Two white-jacketed men and three nurses were working over him. One of the men glanced up, his sharp eyes inquiring.

Jan glanced at her companion in an instinctive appeal for help.

"This is his daughter," Jason informed him. "I'm Jason Farrell. I flew him in."

"Yes, I see. Wait outside. We'll let you know as soon as we get him stabilized."

Jason led her from the room. Jan, white faced, allowed him to do so without a murmur of protest. Her father looked so—so awful!

Jason took one look at her and headed her back toward the elevator. "We can't do a thing here, and I've just remembered we haven't eaten."

Jan was too stricken to protest.

He took her on a short cab ride and escorted her into the breakfast room of an old elegant hotel, ignoring the fact they were hardly dressed for such a place. In a fog of misery Jan didn't notice the raised eyebrows her rough clothes and Jason's unshaven chin triggered among the other patrons.

Although she was too upset to be hungry, Jan downed the food Jason ordered her to eat and drank her coffee like an obedient child. She was too numb to resist.

If anything happened to her father, what did the future hold for her? She shrugged the thought away with a characteristic lack of fear and concentrated all her energy on the fierce belief that her father would live.

Jason watched her and said nothing. When they were finished he led her to a phone in the plush lobby and called the hospital.

"Jan—" he turned to the young woman beside him "—they aren't able to tell us anything yet. There has been little change in his condition, but he is no worse. There are reporters all over the place. Will you stay here, please? I'll get a room for you and you can get some rest."

Jan was sure sleep was impossible, even though she was very tired. Exhausted, in fact. How long had it been since she'd really slept? Her last attempt had been effectively shattered by the man watching her now.

"Why are reporters showing such an interest in my father?" she asked.

Jason shrugged, his expression rueful.

"Heaven only knows why, but anything I do seems to generate a lot of press activity. This time the bizarre situation is one they can't ignore. Natural, I guess." A wry grin lit his face and gave it a boyish cast that arrested her attention. "My only son falls off a cliff and is rescued by a woodsman who carries him out of a forest. To add spice to the whole thing, the rescuer himself has to be rescued, by me and the man's lovely daughter. Makes the best story they've had since the time I saved Tom from an Italian gang in Rome. They had kidnapped him and were holding him for ransom. He was ten and thought it was great fun. That boy's always in trouble."

Jan stared at him. "You've got to be joking. And I'm not lovely."

"No," he assured her. "It happened. And don't tell me what you are."

Jan looked at him, then down at her clothes. She'd slept in them, done the chores in them, struggled in and out of the ravine in them. She glanced back up into his impassive face. "I'd like to get out of these clothes. I'm a mess. I'll check in and clean up, but I won't be able to rest until dad is okay."

Suddenly Jason became very impatient. "Jan, I've got two or three hours' work to do. You've got to rest. I'm going to check you in and you must sleep a few hours. I'll keep track of your father. I'll send someone to the hospital to keep an eye on his progress. You'll be phoned the minute we know anything."

Jan was utterly weary. Common sense told her Jason was right. Again she felt the warmth of her trust in him.

"All right, if it isn't too much trouble to keep someone there. It is kind of you. Thank you."

"I'm the one who is grateful in this case. Let's find you a bed, shall we?"

"You've been in touch with Dr. Brogan?" she asked as they walked through the hotel lobby.

"I talked to him as we flew in. He knows what happened to your father and where we are. He'll take care of Tom. The boy is doing as well as can be expected, but I do have to get back up there."

"If you're flying back to the lake you'll need some rest, too."

"Worried about me, Janet Jordan?" A smile touched his lean mouth.

She was really too tired to reply. Lack of sleep and the shock of finding her father had combined to drain her reserves of energy.

Jason arranged for a room and led her into the ornate elevator. After glancing at her strained face, he kept a firm hand on her arm.

The room was a new experience to Jan, one she was almost too tired to appreciate. Finely appointed, full of good antiques polished and gleaming with care, color-coordinated from the rug on the floor to the luxurious and lovely spread on the bed, it was a standard of luxury she hadn't experienced when traveling with her father. Lewis always kept a low profile, staying at more modest places.

Jason stood aside as the bellman checked lights and heat. When they were alone, Jan turned to him.

"I haven't any money with me," she told him. "I won't be able to pay you for all you've done until dad and I get back to the cabin."

"The question of money doesn't arise, Jan. I'll never be able to compensate you and your father for saving Tom's life. Surely I owe you the comfort of a decent place to live for a week or so. Let's wait until your father is well before we discuss such things, shall we?" He reached for her arm. Jan quelled an impulse to resist and let him lead her to a chair. "Sit down, please."

"Why?" She sat, more in the effort to break contact with him than anything else.

It was then she remembered the kiss they had

shared high on the mountain slope. Her throat tightened and her heart began to beat with a pained thudding that shook her slender frame. Glancing up she met Jason's smoky gray eyes. Frightened by the intensity she saw in them, she blushed, her lashes sweeping down to hide her sudden awareness of him.

She heard him sigh, then he hunkered down beside her, balancing on his heels. Long hands reached for her booted foot.

"What are you doing?" Jan looked at him, her clear green eyes dulled with confusion.

"Taking off these boots of yours," he answered, his tone teasing. "It might be hard to explain if you mess up the sheets with these great clodhoppers." He bowed his dark head over her slender leg, his fingers tangling in the laces.

Jan stared at the wealth of dark auburn curls, feelings she had no idea existed welling up inside her. Unable to say a word, she was caught in a sudden devastating wave of intimacy.

It was a sensation she couldn't handle with confidence. As much as she wished to deny it, she knew the man at her feet attracted her, affecting her in ways she had only dreamed about. Unprepared to deal with the potent force of his personality, she felt threatened by a danger she couldn't assess. After pulling off the first boot, his fingers rested a moment on her stockinged feet. His light touch on her flesh sent an unbearable thrill shooting through her responsive system.

He stood with an easy flexing of muscle, her second boot in his hand, his gaze inscrutable. "Is something wrong, Jan?'' The question held a quality that sent a wild sweetness surging through her.

"No. Certainly not.'' She fought to steady her breathing.

His gray eyes gleamed under those long lashes, a smile causing the attractive creases that emphasized his lean good looks to appear. Jan rose to her feet, mesmerized by the glow in those lazy gray eyes, her hand touching her slender neck where her heartbeat pounded erratically. Unable to bear his scrutiny any longer, her own lashes fluttered down.

Jason chuckled deep in his throat. "Get some rest, Jan. I'll be in touch.''

The fleeting pressure of his knuckles brushed her soft cheek, then he was gone. Jan stood staring at the closed door for a long time, painfully aware of his masculinity, his sound, the warmth of him as he knelt before her, the feel of his hands on her feet.

New sensations swept through her, filled the world around her. It was exhilarating, wonderful. The pulsating of her heart grew, her whole body throbbing with a loveliness she was afraid to identify.

Was this a part of the world she had missed on the mountain? Was this wonderful frightening feeling part of the restlessness she'd felt so long and fought with such little success? She had no way of knowing for sure, but she knew now that she would have to come to terms with herself once her father was well.

The phone rang then, shattering her distracted thoughts.

Startled back to reality, she snatched it. Who could be calling her?

It was Jason. He told her he was still in the hotel lobby.

"I've just checked the hospital again. Your father is sleeping now. His condition has stabilized. They have moved him from the intensive care unit. He has improved."

Jan swallowed, unable to speak as relief and gratitude flooded through her.

"Jan! Did you hear me?"

"S-sorry," she stammered. "Yes, I heard you. Thank you very much, Mr. Farrell." She used the title in a frantic effort to gain some distance from him.

His laughter whipped across the wires. "I can see we're going to have to have a serious talk about friendliness, Jan. I'll call you later." He hung up.

Jan gripped the phone with fingers that trembled. What a wonderful caring person! Tears stung her eyes, threatening to overflow. He sounded so concerned.... She dropped the receiver.

"That's enough, Jan Jordan," she told herself sharply. "You've never met anyone like Jason before and you've let him get to you. He's only being kind and it's going to your head. You've seen Lucille. You've heard her call him darling."

Suddenly she felt depressed. She took a long hot shower, washed out her clothes, hung them on the towel rack to dry and fell into bed and into a dreamless exhausted sleep.

CHAPTER FIVE

AN INSISTENT CLAMORING awakened her.

Jan struggled to sit up. The noise continued as her mind flew around in wild disorder, trying to orientate herself.

The phone!

Jan reached for it and the noise stopped. She almost dropped the receiver as she juggled it, trying to find the proper end to speak into.

"I take it you were asleep?" Jason Farrell's deep voice was amused. "Sorry. The hospital will let you see your father in a couple of hours—after a much-needed nap he's taking. Want to see him?"

"Don't be ridiculous, Mr. Farrell. Of course I want to see him."

His sigh was melodramatic. "You can cut the 'Mr. Farrell' routine, Jan." His chuckle took the sting from his reprimand. "Have a couple of packages arrived for you yet?"

"Packages? No. Why should I get packages?"

"Just a little something to make your time out of the wilderness more enjoyable. A change of clothing, to be exact."

"You must not buy things for me. I won't accept anything."

"Refusing, when you don't even know what it is? Come on, Jan. Be sensible. We rushed away from your home with no idea of the gravity of your father's situation. You have no money with you and you'll be here several days, probably. You need a change of clothing."

The idea of having Jason Farrell buy clothes for her upset her. Her dainty chin set in a stubborn cast, she pulled the receiver from her ear and stared at it, her wrath rising.

"You can repay me just as soon as you get back to your woods."

There was an indifferent bored edge to his voice Jan didn't like. "There's no way you're going to be able to avoid the newshounds. The story of Tom's rescue is all over. You might be more comfortable in more conventional clothing, that's all. At least try the things I've sent up, Jan."

She brought the receiver back to her ear. "They won't fit. You don't know my size. I'll be much happier in my own things, thank you."

"They'll fit, Jan." His assurance offended her. How many times had he bought clothes for a woman, she wondered. She didn't like the answer that came to her. "Just get dressed when your outfit arrives."

"What time is it?"

"Twelve o'clock."

"Twelve o'clock. Do you mean twelve noon? It can't be!"

"It is. You were exhausted."

"I've never slept so long in my life...how awful!"

Guilt tightened Jan's voice. "Dad must think I've abandoned him. How could I have been so—so thoughtless! Are you sure that he's all right? I should have been there with him!"

"I had someone at the hospital constantly. He is stable and he rested well. The last thing he needed was to have you pacing around and stewing over him, Jan. Believe me. You had to have some rest. Lewis has had the best care possible. He isn't out of the woods, of course, but he is doing well under the circumstances. And he wants to see you. Says it's important. So get ready. You can eat there at the hotel or after you get to the hospital."

"I'll wait. Have you heard from Dr. Brogan?"

"Yes. Tom is getting better thanks to the help he received from you, John says. I'm to take a few things up to him. I'll go this afternoon, weather permitting."

"I'm glad. Thank you so much for phoning to tell me about dad. I'm so relieved. Can I walk to the hospital from here?"

"It's too complicated for a stranger. Just get dressed and wait. Unfortunately I'm tied up here for another hour. Lucille has volunteered to pick you up. She'll be there shortly. See you at the hospital." With that he hung up, leaving unvoiced Jan's protest that she didn't want Lucille to pick her up.

She banged the phone down as a knock sounded at the door. Scrambling out of bed, she went to the door and demanded to know who was there.

It was the bellboy. She opened the door a crack and peeped out. His arms were loaded with a stack of gaily tied boxes. "Packages for you, Miss Jordan," he hesitated. "Mr. Farrell sent them up." Deciding he looked impertinent, Jan hesitated a moment. How did one deal with such a situation? She knew she didn't want him in the room. At the same time, she wanted to see the things Jason had sent.

"Leave them there, please. I'll bring them in."

"But—"

"Leave them."

When she was sure he was gone, Jan went to the bathroom and retrieved a large bath towel. Clad in a terry cloth sarong, she peeked into the hallway. Deserted. She pushed the pile of packages stacked at the door into the room.

What on earth had Jason done?

The pile of boxes was intriguing. The brief tussle with her conscience didn't last long. Her curiosity demanded to be satisfied. She hadn't had many surprises in her young life.

Opening the packages, she was thrilled.

She found a beautifully tailored suit in a gold green tweed and a cashmere turtleneck in chocolate brown. An emerald green silk scarf picked up a fleck in the tweed, matching her eyes with amazing accuracy. There was silk lingerie and cream-colored stockings. One box contained a gleaming leather bag the color of mountain honey. Another held an exquisite golden clasp designed to control the long hair she wore pulled back in a ponytail. Three inches across at its widest part, it was shaped like a shell, a filigree of gold that fit the nape of her neck in a perfect curve.

Jan shook her head and reached for the last two boxes. One contained a toothbrush and other necessities, all tucked away in a striped-silk purse especially made for them.

There were shoes in the last box.

Jan had never seen anything so pretty. A series of scanty straps the exact shade of the handbag were gathered together on a slender spike of a heel she was sure no human could possibly walk on. They were delightful.

"Jason Farrell, you've lost your mind!" She rocked back on her bare heels and stared at the lovely loot.

In the mountain vastness Jan called home, she had given little thought or attention to clothes. Without the companionship of girls her own age, her fashion sense hadn't developed to any marked degree. Her father always insisted upon buying her at least one fashionable outfit on their rare trips down from the mountain. These items hung in her closet, neglected at home where more practical garb was needed. As a result her wardrobe was rather ordinary. Good things randomly selected, but lacking in the flair and perfection of this expensive coordinated selection.

For a moment, kneeling there, her slender body gleaming in the soft filtered light of the late-autumn day, Jan was sorely tempted.

Then she sighed and thrust temptation away. Working with quick efficiency, she folded the lovely items back in the rustling tissue wrappings and returned them to their boxes. The only article she didn't repack was the silken purse containing the toothbrush and the toiletries.

Taking a quick shower, she towelled dry and used the hairbrush included in the kit.

Climbing into her own pants and bra, she grimaced as she thought of the soft and lovely underthings she had packed away.

Forget it! she warned herself. *If I read him right, Jason is very much at home buying gorgeous things for women. I wonder what he considers adequate compensation when he goes to that much trouble? More than I'm prepared to pay, I bet!*

With that in mind she dressed, buttoning her flannel shirt and zipping into the corduroy jeans. She pulled on her thin woolen socks and looked for her boots.

One was missing.

She looked behind the chair she'd sat on so many hours earlier when Jason had removed those boots. Nothing. Pushing the chair aside, she looked under it. The boot wasn't there.

Exasperated, she examined every inch of the room. It just wasn't there. Nor was it in the large closet. Jan plopped down in the chair and thought about it.

Had Jason taken it?

Of course! That had to be the answer. Crossing to the bed, she retrieved the shoe box. Opening it, she regarded the leather confections. The dainty sandals looked as if they might fit.

What an outrageous man he was! He must have walked out with her boot, his mind already made up about supplying her with this expensive change of clothing! How had she failed to notice?

Remembering the effect he had on her, she knew the answer to that. Anything less than an earthquake would not have been noticed by her. Color wavered in her cheeks as she thought of his impact on her.

Could one win a prize for being gullible? If so, she just might be a prime candidate. A man of Jason's caliber had no interest in a woman with her lack of sophistication. Trying to see herself through his eyes, she knew what the contrast must be if Lucille was an example of the kind of woman with whom he associated regularly. She must realize he was grateful to her father. Any attention he spared her was grounded in that gratitude.

The phone rang, interrupting her thoughts.

"I've been sent to collect you," Lucille's well-modulated voice informed her. "Jason is knee-deep in problems. I'm in the lobby. May I come up?"

"Please do."

A few minutes later Jan answered the knock at her door. Clad in a full-length black mink that was striking with her sleek black hair and dark eyes, Lucille looked beautiful. Jan thought of the lovely clothes in the boxes with regret.

"You aren't ready to go to the hospital!" Lucille took in Jan's work clothes with amused disapproval. "Aren't you planning to wear the outfit Jason sent for you?" She glanced at the boxes on the bed.

"Certainly not!" Lucille's comment had sounded more amused than critical, but Jan felt herself flushing. "Jason has taken my boot, I think. Did he give it to you by any chance?"

"Oh dear!" Lucille's amusement grew. "He means well, Jan. It's just that he's generous to a fault when it comes to expressing gratitude. I'm sure the idea you might reject the things he sent never entered his mind."

"Did he take my boot?"

"I expect so. He probably took it in order to determine your shoe size. Nothing in this world is more uncomfortable than shoes that don't fit."

"There was no need. I'm not going to wear anything except my own clothes."

"This is no time to be proud, Jan." Lucille gave her a worried little smile. "Don't you see he is trying to protect you? Haven't you seen the news clips on television?"

"No, I haven't. Are you referring to those men who tried to stop us at the airport?"

"Oh, my dear, you should see them. You photograph so beautifully. And you look so confused, so frightened. With Jason protecting you with that fierce expression on his face, those shots turned into a reporter's dream. I expect you have been a big news item this last sixteen hours or so."

Jan stared at her, stunned. "I can't believe I'm news."

"Under the circumstances you're the hottest news to come to the East Coast since the last royal wedding. Which is why you must not leave this room still looking like a miniature edition of Paul Bunyan, my dear. The news media will have a heyday if you do. One can see the headlines—'Beautiful Hermit Rescues Jason Farrell's Son'—for example. They'll make a comic figure of you. Jason is trying to protect you, dear child.''

Lucille was truly concerned. Considering her earnest frown, Jan felt her resolve weaken. ''It doesn't seem right to accept clothes from a—a strange man....''

''Jason is paying for your hotel room, I presume?''

''Yes, but only until I can see my father and get the money to repay him.''

''Well, then.'' Lucille smiled and came up with a practical answer. ''You can ask your father for enough to take care of the clothing at the same time.''

''You really believe it's important for me to wear the clothes?''

''Yes, I do. And Jason is a proud man. It would humiliate him if you didn't dress in the things he's sent to you. He has impeccable taste as a rule. Surely he hasn't sent you an outfit that is unbecoming?''

''Everything is so beautiful. It's hard for me to believe a man like Jason could assemble such a pleasing assortment of lovely things. Or any other man, for that matter.'' Her father couldn't have done it. ''Did you help him?''

''Jason is well qualified,'' Lucille laughed. ''He's been choosing lovely things for lovely ladies for years. I didn't help him. He didn't ask me. Are you going to be reasonable? We need to hurry. Your father is waiting for you.''

"If you're sure...." Suddenly Jan felt young, in need of guidance.

Lucille's smile was warm and comforting. "I'm positive. For all his roaring around, Jason is a man you can trust implicitly, Jan. He's the soul of honor in spite of the gossip about him. And he's the best friend I've ever had."

"Okay!" Jan gave in. "I'll hurry, if you don't mind waiting until I can get changed."

"Would I insult you if I asked to do something with that wonderful hair of yours?"

"My hair?" Turning, Jan stared at herself in the clear mirror on the wall. Pulled back, her hair was held firmly in place by the rubber band she used to keep it captive. It tumbled down between her shoulders in a warm honey-brown fall. "What's wrong with it?"

"Nothing, I expect. But if you'll sit down and lend me your brush, I'd love to try something. It won't take long."

Brushing the long tresses, Lucille piled them on top of Jan's small head, capturing them in a crown of burnished beauty. "If I just had a comb or a clip," she agonized, pulling small tendrils down to frame the bemused and piquant features of her subject. "You're absolutely gorgeous, you know."

"If people don't stop telling me that, I'm going to start believing it and then we'll all be in trouble." Jan's laugh was rueful. "Will the clasp Jason sent me be of any help?" In spite of herself, a little shiver of happiness ran through her. Retrieving the gold clasp from its box, she gave it to the other woman.

"Just the ticket!" Lucille cried and inserted it firmly. "There! Now go and change and we'll go to your father."

Jan gathered up the boxes and headed for the bathroom. The phone rang as she reached the door.

Jason!

The thought stopped her in her tracks.

"Shall I answer for you?"

"Yes, please." She didn't move while Lucille picked up the receiver.

"Hello?" The soft word questioned the caller. "I beg your pardon. Would you repeat that, please? I see. Just a moment." Putting her hand over the mouthpiece, she turned dark eyes on the younger woman. "Do you have a cousin named Peter, Jan?"

"No. I have no relatives. Except my father, of course."

"This man says he is Peter Goud and that he is your cousin. I expect he's a reporter trying for a story."

"Tell him he's mistaken. I have no cousins." Jan went into the bathroom and pushed the door shut. She could hear Lucille's tart rebuke, then the sound of the receiver being replaced in its cradle.

"That should take care of the opportunist. Some reporters will try anything to ensure an exclusive. Cousin indeed! Cute!"

"One must give him an *A* for effort and ingenuity, at the very least." Jan smoothed on the silken stockings Jason had provided and slipped into the lined fitted skirt of golden tweed. The cashmere sweater was a whisper of luxury, topped with the cloudy green of the scarf. Strapping on the dainty sandals Jan stood and stared, incredulous, at her reflection in the big mirrors of the bathroom.

Dizzy at the transformation, she left the boxes where they were and walked into the other room.

Lucille laughed, her eyes sparkling with genuine appreciation.

"My dear, you are stunning. Jason has done himself proud this time!"

"The clothes are nice," Jan agreed. "You seem to know Jason so well. Have you worked for him very long?" Jan rustled among the things remaining on the bed and found the leather handbag.

"Years," Lucille replied. "I inherited the job when my father died, but I've known him much longer. We grew up together. Our fathers were friends, that sort of thing. My husband died shortly before my father. It was almost too much to bear. I loved them both very much. I retreated into a corner to lick my wounds. I expect I was headed for a breakdown when Jason hunted me down. He wasn't the least bit tolerant of my self-pity, as he called it. He gave me a lecture and put me to work. I'd worked for father, so I knew something about the job. I've been at it since then."

"You don't mind his sarcasm?" Jan found she was beginning to like the other woman.

"Jason can be sarcastic, but in my case he was only being concerned. I've known him all my life. It's been nice for me. As I was an only child, Jason has always substituted as my big brother."

Jan felt an odd sense of relief. She wasn't sure why, but she knew she was seeing Lucille in a completely different light.

There was a knock at the door then.

"Would you mind answering it for me?" Glancing up from the task of arranging her new handbag, she smiled at Lucille.

"If it's a reporter I'll get rid of him." Lucille's sweet voice sounded determined, Jan noted. "Some of them are so insistent."

Quite willing to let Lucille handle the intruder, Jan went on with her task without bothering to look up.

"Yes?" Lucille's tone was crisp. "What may I do for you?"

Silence was the only answer. Jan zipped the center section of her new handbag closed and picked it up, sending a curious glance over her shoulder.

A tall blond man stood there, the blue of his eyes gleaming with a strange fire. His mouth dropped open as he stared. A sense of danger rippled down Jan's spine as she turned to face him.

"It's true...!" The words were hoarse, spoken with a faint accent. "My God! After all these years...!"

Lucille gave Jan a puzzled look. Jan, equally bewildered, shrugged and shook her head. The action seemed to galvanize the stranger.

"Excuse me..." he leaped past Lucille and burst into the room, the tan suede jacket he carried falling to the floor. Ignoring it, he reached for Jan.

Her instincts fully aroused, she dodged behind the

chair, unwilling to let him touch her. "Who are you?"

Pulling up short, he smiled in an obvious attempt to reassure her.

"I'm your cousin. Your mother was Juliana van Eck! My aunt!"

"Juliana Jordan," Jan corrected him. "My mother was Juliana Jordan."

"Jordan!" The name sounded hoarse as he said it. "Lewis Jordan." Again Jan heard the ghost of a foreign accent.

"Is your name van Eck?" Perhaps he was a long-lost relative. At least he seemed to know who her parents were.

The look he gave her was closed, secretive. "No, I'm not van Eck. I'm Goud. Peter Goud. Surely your mother talked about me. about her family?"

"My mother died when I was very young. I scarcely remember her. My father has never talked about our family."

The man smiled then, relief breaking over his handsome face, happiness sparkling in the blue of his eyes. "You are my cousin. Please believe me. It was a miracle when I saw you on television last night. I thought my eyes, my mind was playing tricks on me. I thought you were Juliana. Then they said your name, said Lewis was injured, and I knew you must be Juliana's daughter. You are so like her. She was your age when I last saw her, I think. How old are you, little cousin?"

"I turned twenty-three last month."

The man narrowed his eyes, a swift look of triumph flashing across his features then vanishing instantly.

"Yes, that's about right. I was ten or eleven when I last saw your mother. I'm thirty-four now."

"As interesting as this is, I think we'd better get to the hospital, Jan. Your father will be awake and asking for you. I must get back to the office."

"Of course, Lucille." Giving the man before her a wary look, Jan left the safety of the chair she'd put between them.

"You're going to the hospital to see Lewis? Mind if I come along?" Peter smiled at Lucille, his manner deferential, pleading. "I can't wait to see my—uncle. It's been so long. You understand?"

Hearing the slight hesitation in the request, Jan gave the man a sharp look. His smile was charming and he looked so anxious, so eager that she dismissed her misgivings.

"Are you sure you're not a reporter, Mr. Goud?" Lucille interjected. "Jason wouldn't be very understanding even if you do claim you are related to Jan should this—happy event—result in a news exclusive."

"I assure you I am not. I am an insurance investigator for an international consortium." Reaching into the back pocket of his superbly fitting trousers, he flipped out a wallet and opened it. A badge glittered from its fastening beside an official-looking photo. Lucille glanced at it and nodded.

"I see. Where were you when you saw the telecast of Jan?"

"In California on my current investigation. I

caught the first plane to Boston." His smile was beguiling. "I couldn't wait to find out if the gods had finally favored me, you see. Lewis and Juliana made excellent work of disappearing. I still can't believe my luck. To have found Jan, to have her be so beautiful...."

"We'd better go." For some reason his praise stirred a warning in Jan. Why had her father never mentioned this man, never discussed the van Ecks with her? Lewis was entirely self-sufficient, of course, and fiercely independent. Had he quarreled with these relatives? Was he related to them, too, or was it only her mother? As soon as she knew her father was on the road to recovery, she would find out. Picking up the key to the room, Jan turned to Lucille.

"Will it be all right if Mr. Goud accompanies us?" she asked.

"Certainly. We can talk more while we're in the car."

"I'm not sure dad will be able to see you...."

"I won't go in if he isn't," Peter assured her hastily. "Please allow me to make up for lost time, lovely cousin. I have so many questions to ask, so many things to find out." Again that secret look of satisfaction crossed his handsome face, vanishing before Jan was able to interpret it.

"I think it will be all right, Jan." Lucille smiled at Peter as he stood back and bowed them through the door. "After all, it isn't every day one has the chance to meet such a good-looking relative. Where is your home, Mr. Goud? In California?"

"Oh, no. I live in Amsterdam. My work takes me around the world." So that explained his accent. Was her father from Holland, too? "I was very fortunate to happen to be in the States at this particular time. Otherwise I would have missed the broadcast that located Jan for me. I shall be forever grateful to the fates that I was here." He escorted them into the elevator. "Call me Peter, if you please. And may I know who you are?" He smiled down at Lucille as he pushed the button for the lobby.

"I'm Lucille St. John. How did you happen to lose sight of Jan and her parents?" The doors opened and he followed the two women out.

"It's a long story." Peter shrugged into his leather jacket as he strode across the hotel lobby with them. The chauffeur had the limousine waiting for them. He opened the car door, then closed it before climbing behind the wheel.

Peter, seated in the middle, turned to smile at Lucille. "I really don't want to go into it now. It wouldn't be fair to Lewis. It is rather obvious Jan has never heard the story, so I expect she should hear her father's side of it from him first." The tone of his comment conveyed an understanding that forgave and tolerated his uncle's failure to inform his cousin of her relatives.

"I don't think dad is in any shape to deal with old problems at the moment." Jan didn't want her father disturbed or upset. "He isn't well enough to be bothered."

"I wouldn't dream of it," Peter assured her, hearing the concern in her voice. "I'll just peek in. I can't tell you how much it means to me to actually see him after all these years! You will allow me that pleasure, won't you, little cousin?"

Jan frowned. His endearing address was annoying. "Only if he is well enough. You knew my mother well?"

"We were a close-knit family. I was a frequent visitor in her home. As a ten-year-old I was smitten with her. She was so beautiful, so kind to me. I will never forget her."

At least that sounded sincere, Jan thought, surprised at her continued suspicion of the man. "Her home? Surely you mean my father's house, as well?"

"I—yes—of course. I keep forgetting you have no knowledge of the situation, the—er—disagreement that drove Juliana...and Lewis into exile." Fear touched Jan again. What was there about this man? Why did she feel threatened?

"It's so romantic, finding a new relative," Lucille commented. "Are you a big family? How many cousins and aunts and uncles does Jan have?"

"Quite a few." Peter laughed. "She has English relatives as well, you know. Were you aware of that, Jan?"

"No, I wasn't," she answered shortly. "It's all very interesting, but I'm sure you'll understand I have other things on my mind. I'm glad you came, glad to find out I do have a family, but right now I'm only truly concerned about my father. As soon as he is well we can discuss this further. I'm sure you must know how I feel."

"Yes, I do." He reached across and his hand enfolded her clenched fist, his fingers warm. "We won't talk about it until later. Okay?"

"Thank you." Jan withdrew her hand, wondering at her relief as the chauffeur swung the big car into the entrance driveway of the hospital. "Oh, here we are." Opening the door as soon as the car stopped, she got out.

"I'm going to leave you here, my dear," Lucille told her. "I must get back to business. Will you be all right?"

"I'm sure I will. Mr. Goud can go with me while I check on dad's condition. Then, if the doctor thinks it won't bother him, I'll take him in to see my father. Thank you for your kindness. I do appreciate it."

"I'm sure he's doing well, Jan. Jason will be here shortly, I think. He wants to see you before he flies back to your mountain. Good luck and keep in touch." Reaching up, she touched the soft curve of Jan's cheek. Jan smiled, deciding she really did like ElPac's vice-president. "Goodbye, Peter." Turning to him, Lucille extended her hand. "I'm happy we met and had the chance to talk. Perhaps I'll see you again soon."

"Thank you, kind lady." Peter straightened and followed Jan across to the entrance and down the long passageway to the big hospital desk. The same young woman who had been there the previous day greeted them.

"I didn't recognize you for a moment, Miss Jordan," she exclaimed. "My, how nice you look."

Embarrassed, Jan thanked her. There were several people waiting in the lobby. If any of them were reporters, none of them knew who she was. One could hardly blame them, she thought, looking down at her new clothes.

As they rode up in the elevator, Peter stood beside Jan, silent. She had the feeling he was watching her but she didn't look up. Her uneasiness about him had returned and she wished he hadn't come. As she stepped out of the opened doors, the knowledge that she looked poised and well-groomed gave her a sense of assurance. She walked quickly toward the nurses' station.

"Mr. Jordan is doing very well, considering," the duty nurse said. "The doctor was with him a few minutes ago. I'll check on him if you'll wait in the visitors' lounge, please. If the doctor is finished I'll come and take you to your father."

"Thank you." Jan went along with her, Peter close behind. The nurse showed them into a comfortable lounge. It was empty.

"Wait here, please. I'll return as soon as I can." She paused on the way out. "He is only allowed to have family as visitors, I'm afraid."

"He's my uncle," Peter informed her.

"That's okay, then. I'll be right back."

Jan turned to the window and stared out over the city skyline, hardly seeing the wind-whipped trees and swirling leaves foretelling the approach of winter.

"It's very strange that dad has never mentioned you," she said. "I wonder why?"

"I've said it was a long story your father ought to tell you," Peter replied.

Jan turned to face him, feeling on the defensive. "Was he in trouble? Was that why he and my mother left Holland?"

"It's your father's story, Jan. There is much bitterness, much unhappiness connected with it. I know one side of it. His may be completely different. We'll wait, ja?" He sounded coaxing, reasonable, as if he truly was concerned with giving her father a chance to explain the mystery in his own terms. "Just trust me," he told her.

Why then did she feel this growing dislike for him? Why did he seem to be gloating? Or was she imagining things?

She cursed her lack of experience with people. How did she know which instincts to trust? Throwing caution to the winds she strode over and stood before the watching man. Lifting her proud head with its crown of glorious, honey-brown hair, she stared up at him, her green eyes probing. He looked down at her, his own eyes quiet but giving nothing away.

"I don't know whether I can trust you or not," Jan told him bluntly. "I haven't dealt with enough people to know that. But I'm afraid for some reason. Should I be afraid of you?"

"Ah, little cousin! How candid you are!"

Jan saw something flicker in the blue of those eyes and a shiver ran through her. She suddenly felt like a very small mouse at the mercy of a very large cat.

"You haven't answered me. Should I be afraid?"

He slipped an arm around her waist. "Do you have any idea of your charm?" he asked, his voice deepening.

"She is charming, isn't she?" The words filled the room with raw tension. Tearing herself from Peter's easy embrace, Jan whirled around to meet the icy gray eyes of the man behind her. Jason scowled at her and stalked into the room, his contempt evident in the set of his lean body. "Who is this fortunate man? Aren't you going to introduce us, Jan?"

"I—you—this is Peter Goud. He—he is my cousin. From Holland...." Jan stumbled over the words, overcome by the sight of him.

"Cousin!" His laugh scorched her. "I might buy that, too. Except that less than forty-eight hours ago you were telling me you and your father were the only members of your family. And now you come up with a cousin!"

"How dare you!" Jan's cheeks suddenly became inflamed. Why was Jason so angry? Confused, she lashed out at him. "You have no right to speak to me so—so hatefully!"

"I *am* her cousin," Peter interposed.

"Let me handle this, Peter," Jan shot a fierce look at him.

"Ja!" Peter gave a tight grin and walked to the door. "You get on with it. I'll wait outside while you settle it."

Jan faced her accuser, hands clenched, green fire in her eyes. "Who do you think you are, Jason Farrell? What right have you to speak to me in the tone of voice you just used? You have no right to criticize me.''

"Don't come on to me about rights, Jan. My first impression was correct, wasn't it?" He turned away and went to stare out the window. "From the looks of this Goud guy, you know a good chance when you see one. Who is he? Some man you picked up at the hotel?''

Speechless, Jan stared at his lean and unyielding back. When she didn't answer, Jason spun around, clearing the distance between them with a couple of long strides. His hands gripped her arms.

"Looking for a man, are you? Well, try me! With proper encouragement I might buy your deal...."

Where was the tender caring man from the night before? Confused and hurt, Jan tried to free herself.

"I don't know what you are talking about," she retorted, struggling against his restraining grip.

"Stand still," he commanded. "This is a hospital. Have the good sense to keep your voice down.''

"I'll shout if I want to," she shot back. "Let me go this instant. I hate it when you touch me!''

"I'll touch you!''

The next instant Jan lost her balance and fell against him. Her head came up as she glared at him, angry words on her lips.

She didn't have a chance.

Holding her squirming body with an unrelenting strength, he lowered his head. His mouth, hot and demanding, descended, and his marauding tongue touched hers. Sweetness shot through her with a paralyzing force and her knees weakened. Clinging to him, she was lost in a surge of sensuality she was unable to handle. In seconds her latent sexuality sprang to life. Sight, sound and touch coalesced as she melted, becoming one with the man holding her.

At last he lifted his proud head and stared down at her dreaming distracted face, his own breath rasping in his throat. Jan clung to him, eyes closed, her heart thundering in her ears, unable to move. She felt the response in his heart. It joined the pounding of her own, shaking her, engulfing her. He ran enraptured eyes over her, the flame still alive in their gray depths.

Jan buried her head in his shoulder as she tried to regain the intimate closeness they had shared. The throbbing of her body, the electric response of her nerves, the warm and enchanting flush that heated her were a magic she didn't want to give up.

Jason looked bewildered himself for a moment, and then his eyes hardened and his face settled into a cynical cast.

"You do that very well. No wonder Tom is bewitched. If I didn't know better I might even be gullible enough to fall for it myself."

Numbed, Jan staggered then caught herself as he released her. Jason's laughter grated on her ears as he reached out to steady her.

"Beautifully done! Your father included acting in his tuition, did he? He's coached you well, I must say. Shall we get on with it? I still have to fly up to that lake before dark."

Jan stared at him, her hand going to her mouth. He laughed again, a sour sound. Unable to understand the implication of his grim statement or the expression of intense dislike on his hard face, she choked off a sob of despair and pulled herself erect, brushing off his restraining hand.

"Leave me alone...." The command was barely a whisper. Resisting the impulse to rub at the tears welling up in her eyes, she rushed to the door.

Jason was there first.

"Yes. I know. You hate me." He handed her the gold clasp that had fallen from her hair and opened the door without attempting to conceal his cold amusement. "I'm not my son, Jan. Don't lie to me anymore."

"I've no idea what you mean." Jan forced some degree of control back into her own voice. "I have no wish to continue the conversation. Where has Peter gone?"

He was nowhere in sight, but the nurse was coming toward them.

"There you are," she bustled up to them, a warm smile taking in Jason's lean features with evident appreciation. "Mr. Jordan is asking for you. Come with me, please."

Confused and unhappy to the point of tears, Jan hurried along with the nurse, doing her best to ignore the man striding beside her.

"He's doing very well," the nurse murmured, "so we've moved him from the intensive-care unit." She turned the corner, stopping so abruptly Jan bumped into her. "Oh, my goodness!"

Chaos filled the passage. Uniformed figures

rushed around, pushing equipment into and out of the second room down the passage.

"Dad...!" Jan wrenched away from Jason's reaching grasp and rushed through the doorway. White-clad men and women worked frantically, clustered around her father's bed.

"Heart...crash cart...infarction...." Staccato words whose significance escaped Jan reached her ears.

Impelled by the fear that seized her, Jan dodged through the confusion and rushed to the bedside. Only then did she notice Peter Goud flattened against the wall.

Lewis opened his eyes.

He stared up at her for a moment, such bitter pain in his face that his daughter cried out in response to it. His eyes shifted then and fastened on the tall blond man who had moved to stand beside Jason. Sweeping the attendants aside with a mighty surge of strength, Lewis sat up, reaching for his child. Hate leaped into his fading eyes along with something else—fear. His sick gaze bore into Peter Goud.

"Stay away from Jan," he shouted. "Stay away, I say!" He crushed her against his chest with a strength that was unbelievable. Jan cried out as his body convulsed. He turned to look at her.

"Oh, God," he cried. "The pain...."

He gazed down at her for an instant, tenderness written on his gray drawn features, before he fell back into the pillows.

Jan sobbed and buried her face in the hospital

gown, unaware of the decisive shake of the doctor's head as he answered Jason's questioning glance.

Jason watched her as long as he could bear it, his expression soft with concern. Then he extricated her from the tangle of equipment the hospital staff had used in their attempt to keep Lewis alive. Leading her from the room, he murmured words of comfort against her silky hair as he soothed her.

CHAPTER SIX

THE DEEP TURQUOISE of the lake burst into view as the floatplane topped the shoulder of foothills. Flaming crimson, orangy browns and a whole palette of yellows were reflected in the crystal water, echoing the rioting blaze of the shoreline. Shedding leaves the color of sunlight, silver birches stood white and lovely against the wondrous autumn foliage.

Winter wasn't far away.

"I can see why you're fond of it here."

Jan turned from savoring the familiar scene. Jason kept his attention on the task of bringing the plane down and Jan had a chance to examine the strong profile of the man who had taken charge of her life these last three days.

He had been so gentle with her. Then, unpredictable, he had changed in the past twenty-four hours. His attitude had become cold and withdrawn. He was so morose. Jan was confused, unable to understand what had happened.

Had she managed to offend him in some way? Wrapped in her grief, she doubted she had said or done anything to make him angry. Whatever its source, his mood was making him very quiet.

"I thought I saw Peter, that man who said he was

my cousin, as we were taxiing away from the airport.''

"Why didn't you tell me?" Jason demanded. "Don't you know I'm trying to contact him?"

"I didn't. Why should you want him?" Shuddering, Jan remembered the tortured words her father had shouted at the man. Lewis's strained angry expression was one she'd never forget. It haunted her.

"I thought it might be useful to find out why his appearance upset your father the way it did," Jason answered, easing the plane over the rippled water. "I'd like to know more about what went on between them."

"I never want to see him again. He caused my father's heart attack. I'm afraid I can't forgive that."

"Your father had a very shaky heart, Jan."

"I know, but there was something almost furtive about the man. I don't think he was father's friend even if we're related as he claimed."

"I doubt that he was." Jason concentrated on guiding the plane across the lake to the dock. "You seemed to think he was okay before your father died, however." He shot an oblique glance at her.

"I don't understand."

"I saw you in his arms in the waiting room. How long had you known him then? A few hours at the most."

"I was not in his arms." Jan's flush was dull, her voice weary. "I was speaking to him about dad when you came into the room. Talk about jumping to conclusions! Whatever your opinion, let me assure you I want nothing to do with the man.''

"What if he is your cousin? Aren't you interested in finding out if you have other relatives?''

"No, I'm not. I haven't the least idea why my parents left Holland but their reasons were probably good ones. As far as I know, the relatives have never tried to get in touch with us before. If they were the cause of my father's need to isolate himself as he did, then I don't wish to know them.'' The stubborn set of her chin reinforced her words.

"You may be making a mistake.'' Jason eased the plane into the dock, cutting the motor. "Can you tie up for me?''

"Certainly.'' Unfastening her safety belt, Jan scrambled over the backpacks containing additional supplies for John Brogan. Jason had been unwilling to leave her alone to deal with Lewis's death. With all this going on he had not neglected his son, and the day Lewis died he had sent a planeload of things John needed to the cabin. Since then he'd been in radio contact with the doctor, calling him each day to monitor Tom's progress.

Opening the plane's hatch, Jan jumped onto a rocking float, tossed the tie rope over a timber and pulled the light plane in. Scrambling up the ladder, she took a deep breath of crisp autumn air. Wind ruffled through her hair. It was good to be home.

Oh, Dad. What will I do without you? The endless question had been ringing in her mind since Lewis's death. A sob caught in her throat.

The man loading the backpacks onto the dock heard her in spite of the chuckling sound the water made sloshing over the floats of the plane. A grim look thinned his mouth and his gray eyes were bleak.

Jan shrugged into one of the packs and started up the trail without a backward glance.

John welcomed them with undisguised relief.

"It's a good thing I misspent my youthful years down on the farm," he scolded as he assisted Jan with the cumbersome backpack. "Milking a goat, for Pete's sake! Never milked a goat before in my life, young lady."

"I'm so sorry!" Jan was horrified at her own lack of concern over the animals. Generally care of them was one of her first priorities. How could she have forgotten them? "I didn't think. Did you manage?"

"Certainly." John's smile was gentle. "Under the circumstances, you couldn't be expected to do anything but think of your father. I'm so sorry, my dear. It's been very hard on you, hasn't it?"

"Yes, it has. Mr. Farrell has done so much for me. I couldn't have coped without his help, I'm afraid. He's been very kind."

Looking over at Jason stripping off his own burden, the doctor nodded. "Jase is a good man to have around when a person needs help," he said quietly.

"How is Tom?" Jason shed his sheepskin jacket, his eyes on the doctor.

"He's coming along nicely. His fever is down and he's beginning to recover his appetite. Another three or four days and he'll be well enough to move, maybe.''

"I can't see dragging him down that trail in such a short time." Jason's frown drew his straight brows together. "No way. He'll have to stay here a couple of weeks, I think. Then perhaps he can leave under his own steam."

Two weeks!

Jan knew she couldn't bear to have Jason around that long.

"We have an air-charter service that will fly him out by helicopter," she said hastily. Jason, starting for the room his son was in, turned to look at her, a question in his eyes.

"Where would he land? I thought the lake was the nearest spot."

"Dad cleared a landing pad several years ago. I told you that before. We use the lake when we are flying out, but we always bring our supplies and equipment in by helicopter. There is no other way to bring in things such as dishwashers and generators. You must be able to see that!" Jan knew she was babbling but she couldn't stop the flow of words. "Dad used Mike's Air Charter all the time."

"Did he?" Jason's brow shot up into his distracting tangle of dark russet hair. "Wasn't that kind of expensive?"

"We aren't discussing expense." Jan's reply was frosty. What business did he have questioning her about her father's finances? Her face stormy, she turned her back on him. "It was only a thought.

Your son might be more comfortable in a hospital where he has the proper facilities, that's all.''

Jason turned and left the room. Jan shrugged. Taking off her jacket, she put it away then went into the kitchen to start a meal. She quickly assembled a chicken casserole and slipped it into the oven. Fixing a cup of tea, she sat at the table, a forlorn heartsore figure, loneliness and grief welling up. She was close to tears when the powerful radio called her to her father's den.

"Jan, honey," the ranger's voice was warm with concern for her. Through the years he had often risked Lewis's wrath as he bullied him into letting Jan visit the ranger station. Jan loved the time she spent there. She adored Sarah, Ken's motherly and childless wife. At the sound of Ken's voice, the tears she had been holding back came flowing down her cheeks.

"Can I be of any help, love?" The ranger's voice was gruff with feeling.

"Oh, no, Ken, thank you very much. It—it's all been taken care o-of." She choked on a sob and stopped talking.

"Why don't you come over here? You could talk to Sarah, get yourself squared away. You'll need to make plans. We could help."

"M-make plans?"

"You must, Jan. You can't winter up there all alone. We've been worried to death about you these last several years."

"What do you mean, Ken? Why were you worried?" She was in control once again.

"Well, dammit, Lewis hadn't been in the best of health and you know it. What would have happened to you if he'd had an attack in the middle of a blizzard? He was foolish to take such risks, but he was as hardheaded as a mule and you know it. Come stay with us for a bit, Jan."

"Thanks, Ken. You're good to me and I love you and Sarah. But I can't come right now. There are the animals to care f-for and...and...."

"Sim is on his way. He passed through here yesterday. I told him about Lewis. He'll stay all winter if you'll let him help. But you come to us. He can handle that end but you can't stay there with him, you know. It isn't as if he were family."

Old Sim had been a fixture during the past few years. A trapper with his own lines on the mountain, he earned a living as a guide for hunters during the fall and spring. During the summer he escorted groups of campers and hikers back into the far reaches of the wilderness.

Lewis had hired him on a regular basis to do the chores and care for the cabin during the short trips he took with Jan. Sim always turned up at this time of year. It was after hunting season and before the snowfall justified the winter trapping that was his main source of income. A burly rough-hewn man, Sim was well past his middle years. Taciturn almost to the point of being morose, he nevertheless seemed to enjoy his stay at the Jordans' mountain retreat. Lewis had respected him for the skilled woodsman he was, and valued him for his blunt honesty.

However, her father would not have chosen him or

any other man as a live-in companion for his daughter during the long winter months just around the corner, Jan knew.

Should she go live with Ken and his wife, leaving Sim here to tend the cabin and the animals? He could probably handle Lewis's trapline as well as his own.

It might be the right thing to do, but Jan wasn't ready to commit herself to a decision.

"I'm glad Sim is coming," she told the ranger. "I don't know what I want to do this winter. It's too soon. I'll let you know. Please don't worry about me, Ken. I'll be all right."

"I'm sure you will, honey. It's only that these first few weeks are so hard in any case. I'm afraid it might be more difficult for you because you have no one out there to turn to, as most people have when losing a loved one. How is the young man doing—the one your father found. He's still with you, I take it?"

"Yes, he is. The doctor his father flew in is here with him. He's recovering but he's still very sick."

"How's the doctor? Is he okay?"

Jan laughed in spite of herself at the droll-sounding question. "Oh, Ken! You're as bad as my father. Dr. Brogan is a charming respectable man and I'm sure he's never taken advantage of a lone female in his life. Tom's father is here too, you know." *Jason, who might take advantage of any female.* The thought shamed her even as it formed in her mind. Convicting a man because she disliked him left a lot to be said for her sense of fairness, she knew.

"Just you be careful, young lady. I'm not sure your experience with charming respectable men is anything to brag about."

"How can you say that when I have you for a model? Give Sarah my love and thanks a lot."

"All right, honey. Just be careful. And do consider turning the place over to Sim. We'd enjoy having you with us for the winter. And maybe by the spring you'll have had time to come to some sort of decision about what you want to do with the rest of your life. One thing's for sure. You can't stay there on that mountain all by yourself."

"I'll think about it. You're a dear, Ken. Thanks for your concern. Goodbye." Her smile was soft with affection.

"Goodbye, honey. Keep in touch. Let me hear from you soon." When he signed off, Jan flipped her own switches down and turned to face Jason. He stood framed in the doorway, a mysterious expression on his dark face.

"Eavesdropping, Mr. Farrell?" Nettled at the strange, almost frosty look in his eyes, she marched toward the door, head high, expecting him to step aside and let her pass.

He didn't move.

Within three feet of his hard-muscled frame, Jan came to an abrupt halt, a wary expression settling on her face.

"Excuse me, please."

He straightened, a tight grin giving him a danger-ous look.

"Who is 'dear' Ken, Jan? And Sim? Are these

woods full of men who can't wait to take care of such a little innocent?''

"For heaven's sake! Don't you ever mind your own business? What possible interest can it be to you if a couple of people care about me enough to want to help me?'' She knew he hadn't heard enough of the conversation between herself and the ranger to know exactly what had been said or why, but she was too fed up with him to try to explain. Why on earth did he assume he had the right to interfere with her life? She drew herself up and met his demanding stare.

"Let me pass, if you please.'' She stood there, slim and defiant, confused by the strange look in his eyes.

Just who did he think he was?

Even as the question formed, Jason moved. Reaching for her, he caught her arms above the elbows, his hands hard.

"Okay, Jan,'' he muttered. Her heart jumped as his arms slipped around her. She was aware of the heat of his body even before she touched it.

"Don't tell me anything, if that's the way you want it.'' His words had a bite. "But let me tell you one thing. I'm not leaving you here to spend the winter with your playmates of the wilderness.''

Rigid in the circle of his arms, the hot whisper of his breath doing strange things to her body, Jan did her best to remain cool. Her color flamed under his interested gaze, then vanished leaving her skin with the delicate clarity of alabaster.

"At the risk of becoming monotonous, Mr. Farrell, I must ask you to take your hands off me. I'm very tired of repeating—''

His odd laugh cut her off. With an effortless surge of pure male strength he quelled her abortive attempt to struggle as she realized her imminent danger.

His head came down, his seeking mouth muffling her gasp of frightened protest.

He kissed her with a consummate skill, his passionate demand destroying her resistance as he deepened the contact, and she felt the hard thrust of his arousal against her sensitive body.

The thrill of raging response fired through her, causing her heart to race in a crazy out-of-control manner. The pulse in her throat threatened to shut off her breath. A deep need shuddered through her slender form, causing her to melt into his hard strength, her hands caressing his broad back as they sought to explore the flexing muscles beneath them.

Jason raised his head an instant, took in her heightened expression, then lowered his lips to hers once again.

The infinitesimal pause was his undoing. Jan's electric response had frightened her out of her wits, and the instant Jason pulled away she came to her senses.

Sobbing, she pushed him away and fled, dodging past his reaching hands.

He let her go, a somewhat bemused and incredulous look in his eyes.

Fleeing in blind haste knowing only that she had to escape, Jan stumbled blindly into the living room.

John, coming in from the sickroom, gave her a

glance full of curiosity. Jan tried to ignore him as she dashed to the coat hooks by the door.

"What time did Jason say the copter was coming to pick us up?" he asked as she snatched her jacket from its peg.

"It's coming for you," she informed him. "I'm not going. You'll have to ask Jason what time it's due." She slammed the door behind her, not seeing John's puzzled expression.

All arranged, was it? Jason must have radioed the air-charter service while she was preparing the casserole. Well, just let him try to take her away from here! Jan's retreat left something to be desired as far as dignity was concerned, but it was fast. She flew up the path, past the outbuildings, and was into the dense forest in seconds.

Jason was still searching for her when the big helicopter he'd ordered to transport the four of them back to Boston arrived.

He stood in a small clearing, his plea still echoing on the clear air. Sunlight struck a pathway through the foliage, illuminating him with spotlight clarity. Jan, high on a rocky ledge, watched him. He looked so strong, his head thrown back, his legs in a determined stance as he called to her. Blood drummed in her ears and her heart raced. How fascinating he was....

But instinct told her that danger lay in any further contact with such a powerful individual. He had aroused a surge of powerful feelings in her, and she was frightened.

She didn't understand him, didn't understand his

ability to awaken desire within her, and her response to him intimidated her.

She needed time...time to be alone...time to become accustomed to Lewis's absence and her new independence. She had to learn how to get along without the support of her father.

She stayed out of sight and the shadows grew longer, forcing Jason to give up and go back to the cabin.

Jan watched as Tom was bundled aboard the big machine, stretcher and all. The doctor, dressed in his outer gear, stood beside the aircraft arguing with his friend for a long time. His vigorous gestures, the shouted bits of sentences drifting upwind were clear indications of his strongly worded protest.

Jason stood with his arms folded across his jacket, apparently unmoved by his friend's vehement words. Coming to the edge of the trees, Jan saw the sun glint off his auburn head as he shook it. At last he clapped the doctor on the shoulder and gave the pilot a thumbs-up signal. The helicopter motor throbbed, the huge blades began their lazy rotation.

The doctor shook his head and picked up his bag before climbing up into an empty seat. The helicopter rose straight up, hovering above the cabin a moment, then headed in the direction of the lake, the sound lingering long after it disappeared.

It was some time before peace and quiet was restored to the darkening timberland. The chirping of woodland birds settling down for the night took over then. Jan shifted her position so she could watch the man who had gone to sit on the front steps of her house.

He was still there when darkness fell.

CHAPTER SEVEN

DID HE REALLY BELIEVE she was foolish enough to go back into the house with the other two gone? Jan trembled, halted her imagination and sought the strengthening refuge of anger. It didn't come.

He fascinated her, and it was this fascination she was unable to shrug away.

Jan was able to recognize her own lack of experience with men and her vulnerability because of it. Her isolation had left her without the knowledge of men most young women took for granted.

The thought caused her to smile. Would any woman be safe from a man with Jason's personality? The last few days had convinced her he was a man who demanded, expected and got his own way in this world. She was sure this included any woman he desired.

He was intelligent, talented, full of charm. He had drive and determination plus a boundless energy that swept obstacles away. He was handsome, and the sheer power of his physical presence made him hard to resist.

Jan had read enough to have a rudimentary knowledge of the bounds of her own sexuality. During the last few years she had been plagued with sensations she was unable to account for, vague longings and feelings of emptiness.

Externalizing the energy, she had sketched and painted, creating children's stories about the creatures in the forest where she lived. They were stacked on the chest beside the worktable in her room, wonderful vignettes woven into charming stories. She created pen-and-ink drawings that were alive. Sometimes she worked the illustrations in watercolors.

Lewis had recognized his daughter's talent and had encouraged her, seeing that any material she might need was available. It was he who delved into the latest publications on techniques and mediums, buying the books and making sure she had access to them as she explored her natural ability.

Her feelings, her longings, her lonely moments were all sublimated as she channeled energy into the pictures that flowed through her fingers. Whenever she was disturbed she picked up a pencil or a brush.

Now as Jason stood in the doorway of her house silhouetted against the light he had flipped on, Jan felt the itch in her fingers. How she longed to sketch his lithe strong body, paint the rugged handsome lines of his features.

But nothing could induce her to go into the house as long as he was there. She was scared of him.

Not of him as a person. It was her own reaction to him that scared her. She had spent the long afternoon tracking him through the forest as he looked for her, following him, spying on him, listening to his frustrated rage as he asked her to give him a chance to apologize and repair the damage caused by his actions. Those hours had convinced her of one thing. He was a caring person, more sensitive than she had first thought. It was her own untutored reaction to his masculinity that filled her with panic and apprehension.

She was proud, independent, sure of her ability to channel her own impulses. To have her confidence in her self-control shattered in seconds was devastating.

The thought of facing Jason without John and Tom as buffers terrified her. She would rather spend the night outside.

She slipped through the dark and into the shed where Lewis stored the equipment for his traplines.

She took her down-filled sleeping gear from the shelf and checked her backpack to make sure it contained matches and a small hatchet. Using a lighted match she found the small but powerful torch she would need to help her find a place to sleep. The backpack also contained a pot for cooking and tea to make a hot drink. Keeping an eye on the house, she gathered up the equipment and went into the animal shed. Exploring in the dark, she found six eggs laid that day. While she was wondering about the advisability of milking the goat, the lights came on in the compound.

Jan dashed to the door and opened it a crack. Jason was coming down the path from the house, the milk bucket in one hand. So he had enough knowledge to realize the little goat had to be milked twice a day, did he? That was surprising, given his city background.

Jan knew she couldn't leave the building without being spotted in the flood of light illuminating the area. But she also knew Jason didn't have a chance to find her if she reached the edge of the clearing before he caught up with her. Settling the backpack firmly, she took a deep breath and dashed into the light, her heartbeat outstripping the flash of her long legs.

Jason cried out as soon as he spotted her. She heard the clang of the milk bucket as he dropped it and gave chase.

It was close. Jan could hear the sound of his racing feet drawing near, the hard rasp of his breath as he gave up shouting and put his energy into closing the gap before it was too late and he lost her in the darkness of the forest cover.

He didn't make it.

Jan leaped into the dense shadows of the trees. Her heart thundered as Jason dashed past. Standing as still as a post in the darkness of a towering spruce, she forced her breathing to slow as she listened to the man crashing into the forest. By the time he understood his mistake and stopped thrashing around to listen for her, Jan had herself under rigid control. Breathing quietly, she forced herself to absolute silence, waiting without moving until he knew he couldn't hope to find her. Muttering forceful imprecations, Jason strode back toward the well-lit clearing. None of the light penetrated the absolute dark of Jan's hiding place. Stepping from behind her tree she followed him, her booted feet silent as she moved. Standing well back in the black shadows, she watched him snatch up the empty bucket, his action expressing his aggravation. He stormed on into the animal shed and Jan turned away, her eyes dancing with satisfaction. At least she didn't have to worry about milking the goat!

It was easy to see that Jason suffered frustration badly. Jan resolved to keep far away from him in the future. It was a resolution she shouldn't find difficult to keep. They hardly moved in the same circles.

With a sure knowledge of the terrain, she moved silently to the little river bubbling its merry way over the nearby falls. The falling water provided the power source to turn the generator that supplied electricity to the homestead.

Climbing the crude stairs her father had cut into the granite near the place where the water fell, Jan switched on her torch, sure the beam of light couldn't be seen from the clearing. Following the noisy watercourse she walked upstream to the cave she was looking for. The entrance was low in the sheer rock face, forcing her to crawl in on hands and knees. The torch picked out the well-defined path to the interior. Once inside, Jan stood up and planted the flashlight firmly against a wall. Using one of the branches she had pulled in after herself, she swept the cobwebs off the dry stone of the irregular walls. The same broom served to sweep the sandy floor.

Smiling to herself she recalled when she and Teddy had discovered the place. They'd been young at the time, eight or nine, probably. It had served as a pirate's cave all that summer. They had pledged eternal friendship a la Tom Sawyer and Huckleberry Finn.

Then her father discovered the secret hideaway. They hadn't been allowed to use it after that.

At the time she hadn't understood her father's angry reaction.

Now she realized that he had tried to protect her from any knowledge of life. He hadn't wanted her to know about people or how to interact with them. He had started to circumvent her awareness very early in her life. It suited the way he wanted to live. Jan could see that.

But he'd been wrong. His need for privacy had not helped her. It had arrested her natural development.

For now she had to leave this sanctuary he had created. She had to find her place among the crowds he so despised. Ill-prepared, with only her strong sense of independence to rely on, she knew she must face the world beyond the mountain.

Would she be able to cope or would she be a social misfit? Only time would tell, of course.

Jason's effect on her was a clear indication of the fact she must leave here. She needed to be with others to test her intelligence and her instincts against her peers. This need was a real hunger she could no longer deny. Jason had torn at her veil of innocence, shredding it and wrecking her belief in her ability to handle any situation that presented itself.

Now it was time to push onward, to marshal her forces and to learn, to see and accept the world as it was, not as she imagined it to be.

I will learn, too! she muttered, remembering her disastrous encounters with Jason. Shards of light glittered off the hatchet blade as she swung it energetically, chopping the limbs at her feet into firewood. No man would ever throw her off-balance again. She'd show Jason!

Jason. She never wanted to see Jason again.

The thought made her strangely unhappy. Annoyed at her weakness, she piled the dry wood and started a small fire, the smoke escaping through a natural vent in the cave ceiling. She did her best not to think of Jason.

Instead her attention turned to the mysterious Peter Goud. Had she seen him at the airport? She tried to recall her impression of the tall blond she had glimpsed as Jason taxied away from shore. The floatplane had taken to the air before she could be certain.

Peter had disappeared from the hospital, vanishing before Jason had calmed her enough to leave her and look for him. He hadn't put in an appearance at the brief memorial service for Lewis. Remembering her father's strong reaction to him, Jan felt dislike stir within her. It was impossible to determine the source of Lewis's agitation, but she knew that the sight of the man from Holland had touched off emotions responsible for his death.

Lewis's heart hadn't been able to withstand the shock of seeing the stranger from his past. Sight of the man had aroused such strong feelings that his weakened heart had given out. Knowledge of her own part in bringing Peter Goud to the hospital was bitter.

What had happened so long ago? Why hadn't her father shared his troubles with her? Had he been hiding from Goud and his past all these years, only to have his nemesis led to him by his own daughter?

If that was so, what ironic games Fate played! The thought took away any pangs of hunger she might have had, and she put the eggs aside to eat in the morning.

Tending the fire, she banked it so it would last through the night, then unlaced her boots and rolled her jacket into a respectable substitute for a pillow. She crept into her sleeping bag and zipped it up. In spite of her troubled thoughts, Jan fell asleep moments after her head touched her makeshift pillow.

She dreamed that a blond giant was chasing her through the forest, vanishing and reappearing in the trees behind her as she tried desperately to attract Jason's attention. Jason was striding down the path before her, his burnished auburn head glinting in the sunlight. She couldn't reach him no matter how fast she ran. He vanished around a bend in the trail just as the frightful monster leaped to seize her.

Waking with perspiration cold on her flesh, Jan rolled to her feet, clutching at her sleeping bag. The fire glowed at her through the gray of the wood ash. Even it looked hostile. She shivered, then shook herself out of the nightmare. Rebuilding the fire, she settled back down into uneasy sleep. She didn't dream again.

Awakening at first light, she washed her face and hands in the cold brisk waters of the river. There was nothing like ice water to eliminate any lingering cobwebs of fear! Grinning to herself, she ran her fingers through the silk of her hair.

Dawn held the promise of frosty sunlight. The brilliant red of sumac punctuated the patchwork of birch and maple. Evergreens raised lofty shards to the washed blue of the morning sky. Jan breathed deeply, despair and doubt sloughing from her as she welcomed the day. Feeling better, she gave in to her natural optimism. Her father would have hated the thought of a prolonged period of mourning, in the same way that he would have decried her cowardice where Jason was concerned. He may have deprived her of the company of others but he had raised her to be supremely confident.

There was only one thing to do. She would confront Jason head on.

Marching down beside the busy stream she refused to allow her imagination to construct pictures of the impending scene. When she came to the edge of the clearing, she saw that the lights were still on. She wondered why he hadn't turned them off before going to sleep. She ignored the cackling of the hens wanting to be let out and fed, the grunting pigs rooting around, searching for food, and the plaintive bleat of the little milk goat. She'd take care of the chores after she dealt with Jason. First things first. Otherwise, her resolve might weaken.

She stamped across the porch and slammed the heavy door back against the wall and marched into the middle of the room.

Her noisy entrance produced no startled sounds of a man rudely awakened. The house was silent. In the fireplace a well-tended fire glowed, properly banked beneath its covering of gray ash.

Gray as his eyes. The thought set off Jan's alarm system. Face grim, she closed the door and went to the bedroom Tom had occupied. The bed had been stripped and left to air, the blankets folded neatly across the bottom end of the mattress. There was no sign of the dirty linen. The other bedroom was the same.

Where on earth had he gotten to?

Her pulse picking up, Jan hurried to the kitchen. It, too, was perfectly neat. There was a white sheet of paper torn from one of her sketchbooks, propped against the teapot on the table. Black letters slashed across its smooth surface.

In spite of herself, her hand trembled as she picked it up to read the distinctive sprawl of writing:

Jan,
    Since you aren't going to allow me to apologize, this note will have to do. I am sorry. You can't know how much. I'm leaving now since it's obvious you won't come back while I'm in the house. Don't stay in the woods all night. I can't bear the thought.

                                                        J

Staring at the decisive, boldly written initial he used as a signature, Jan felt fear rise and grip her. He'd gone down the treacherous mountain trail and back to the floatplane in the dark!

Even to those who knew it, the trail was dangerous at night. Her father's accident proved this. Lewis had known the track better than anyone alive and had still fallen victim to it. How could a city person, with no more experience in the wilderness than Jason had, expect to make it safely?

Flying through her chores she snatched up an apple and rushed after the man she told herself she disliked so much.

When she reached the lake the floatplane was gone, the surface of the water a serene reflecting pool. Jan sat down on the dock and wrapped her arms around her legs.

How could she be so anxious about a person as self-assured as Jason? She was still sitting there, watching the fall breeze skip leaves over the ruffled surface of the lake, when Sim Simmons came by on his way up the mountainside.

His craggy face drawn up in the strain of his effort, he tried to tell her of his feelings as he expressed his sorrow at losing one of the few friends he had.

Jan gave him an impulsive hug. This startled him immensely and put a shy smile on his mouth, which lasted all the way back up the mountain.

CHAPTER EIGHT

"WILL YOU BE ABLE to stay the winter if I leave, Sim?" Jan asked him at the supper table that night.

Sim chewed on his mouthful of food and looked at her with careful eyes.

"You planning that?" he asked after he washed down the bite with a healthy slurp of hot coffee.

Jan blinked. "Yes. Yes I am." Her mind was made up in an instant, a characteristic her father had deplored. All her life he had warned her about her tendency to be impulsive. According to him it was an inherited trait, one of Juliana's most endearing qualities, but in Jan he saw it as a flaw. Jan didn't know why her snap judgments, her intuitions, worried him so. He had admonished her constantly, trying to get her to make reasoned, logical conclusions the way he did. He hadn't been very successful, she thought with a grim smile. It was probably the rash side of her nature that found Jason's dangerous personality so fascinating!

"You gonna go over and set with Sarah Clark a spell? She's kinda 'specting you, I take it."

Jan wasn't surprised Sim knew of the Clarks' offer to her. Neighbors might be seventy-five miles apart, but they were a close-knit group with few secrets from one another. This had been one problem her father had battled with all his life!

"Not this time. I think I'll fly out to California." Jan's mind was settled on her destination, but she wondered about money. That would need checking into. And she must radio Sarah, let her know.

"Gonna stay long?"

"I think I will. Perhaps I'll look around, find a job. Then I could probably stay all winter. How about staying here? You could run your traplines along with dad's."

"Share the profits?" His shrewd brown eyes took in her reaction, gauged it, then he smiled.

Jan smiled back. "Sure, Sim. You use dad's traps and locations and live here. Your living will cost you nothing. In return, I want fifty percent of your take."

"Just on your dad's lines. Not on mine."

"Okay, you old fox. Just on dad's lines."

His grin lit up his grizzled face. "Shake on it. You allus was my favorite young one, you know."

"I had no idea, Sim." She gave him her slender hand and he wrung it, his expression sincere.

"Yep. Allus was. I'll leave at first light. Go collect my traps and be back afore the week's out. That all right?"

"Fine. I'll use the time to get my things together and get ready to go. After you get back, I'll call Mike's Air Charter and book a plane out."

"Yeah. Reckon I better hurry so's you can get out before the lake starts to ice. You won't want to wait till it freezes solid enough to support the weight of a ski-plane, I shouldn't think."

"Good idea. It's settled, then."

"Sure enough, Jannie girl. I better hit the sack. I'll be up and off early. Sooner I get back the sooner you can be on your way."

She watched him wander off toward her father's bedroom, where he always slept when he minded the cabin. The old man was pleased with the arrangement. He was getting far enough along in age to appreciate a solid roof over his head during the cold winter months. Feeling good about her bargain, Jan cleared away the supper things and went to contact Sarah Clark.

The ranger's wife answered the call.

"Hello, honey. How are you feeling?"

"I'm going to be okay, Sarah. I'm calling to thank you for your kind offer, but I'm not going to take it, I'm sorry to say."

"Oh, Jan! I'm so disappointed. It would be wonderful to have you here with me this winter. I was looking forward to it."

"You're so sweet. You know I'd love to, Sarah, but I truly must get on with the business of learning to make a living. I can't do that tucked away here in the Allagash. I've got to go out and try."

"There's a young man here who says he's related to you. Are you planning to go with him?"

"A young man...! Who is it, Peter Goud?" Jan knew it had to be.

"Yes, that's his name, dear. I wasn't aware that you had folks, although it's only natural, I reckon. He came yesterday, looking for you. Ken was out and we couldn't reach you when we called."

"Ken isn't bringing him over, is he?" The ranger flew his own twin-engine plane. Specially built for the region, it was capable of landing on either land or water. Ken used it to keep abreast with happenings in the area. Jan found the idea that he might be flying the man responsible for her father's death into their lake abhorrent.

"Of course not, dear. Ken wouldn't do such a thing without your permission. He's planning to get in touch with you about it as soon as he gets back in the morning. He had to fly to Bangor today and won't be back tonight. Isn't young Goud telling the truth? Isn't he your cousin?"

"He may be, but he went into dad's room at the hospital while I w-was busy e-elsewhere." Memory of the nature of her occupation in those few minutes when she should have been with her father caused her to suffer from a rush of guilt. "I—I don't know what he said or did, but I th-think whatever it was, it caused dad to react so violently he had the attack that killed him. I—I don't want to see him, Sarah. Please tell Ken not to bring him over."

"Anything you say, dear. Are you sure that's what you want? He went to a great deal of trouble to get here."

"He doesn't know about the lake?"

"I don't know for sure. Ken talked to him about it last night, but he will have no idea of where it is, of course."

"Please, *please* talk to Ken, Sarah. I don't want to see the man. I—I think dad hated him." She muffled a sob as she recalled the fiercely protective anger in her father's face as he spat his last words at Peter Goud.

"Don't worry, love. Ken will handle it. Where are you planning to go and when will you leave?"

Sarah sounded scandalized when Jan told her she was going to California, but she couldn't dissuade her. "Call me before you go, Jan. And do keep in touch. I'll be worried with you so far away."

"I know," Jan was sorry for the anxiety she was causing the motherly woman but her mind was made up. "I'll write often. I'll expect replies, too."

They chatted awhile, Sarah lamenting the decision but resigned to it when she understood Jan wasn't going to change her mind.

"I expect you know best, dear. Young things need to try their wings. Just don't get yours bent or broken, you hear?"

"I won't," Jan laughed. "If anything gets close enough to bend them, I'll come rushing back to the wilderness."

"See that you do, miss. When will you leave?"

"As soon as Sim gets settled in. He's leaving in the morning to collect his traps. It will be a few days yet."

Jan finished her talk with Sarah in a thoughtful mood. The fact that Goud had gone to the extent of tracking her as far as the ranger station was unsettling. Why should he have gone to so much trouble? Had she seen him the day she and Jason left the city to return to the mountain? Why should he continue to look for her? She was glad he was with the Clarks. Ken could be counted on to send him away with no information about her whereabouts now that he knew she didn't want to see the man.

She couldn't sleep that night. Thoughts of Jason kept intruding, even though she told herself it was futile, she would never see him again.

Finally she gave up, and wrapping her warm robe around her and slipping on her woolly slippers, she went to the kitchen and brewed a pot of tea.

She was sitting there, staring at the cooling liquid, when Sim arose just before daylight. Coming into the cosy kitchen he gave her a curious look.

"Been up long, girl? I could get my own breakfast, you know. No need fer you to get it fer me." He banged a big skillet onto the stove and went to rummage for bacon and eggs. "Want a bite?"

"No, you go ahead." Jan took her cup to the sink and dumped it. "I just wanted a cup of tea."

"Mustn't've tasted like much." Sim cocked a knowing eye at the brown liquid running down the drain.

"I'm going back to bed, Sim. You carry on. I'll see you when you get back."

"Yeah," he agreed. "Try to get some sleep, Jannie girl."

For an old codger, Sim didn't miss much, Jan decided as she crawled back into her warm bed. She did fall asleep, and when she finally awoke he was gone.

Pushing her troubled thoughts behind her, Jan set out to put her house in order for the winter. Her father had money stashed away in his room and in the den. Jan found almost a thousand dollars, but there was no sign of a bankbook or securities. She knew he had a bank in New York, and there was some man he visited regularly. She thought the man was a lawyer of some kind, but her father had never mentioned his name or discussed the reasons he consulted him. For the first time she was faced with the fact that she knew nothing at all about his business affairs. What *had* been the source of the income with which he maintained his home? She had no idea.

Jan knew she must find employment immediately if she left the mountain. A thousand dollars wasn't much. How long would it support her while she looked for something she could do? How did a person even start looking for a job in a strange place?

Frowning, she turned the problem over in her mind as she worked. Her stories. Were they good enough to sell? Would they interest children?

She went to sleep that night wondering whether she might be able to support herself by her art.

The next day she took her stories into the big living room and curled up in the corner of the comfortable divan in front of the huge stone fireplace.

She spent most of the day going over the illustrated manuscripts, trying to project herself back into childhood, trying to read them with the mind of an eight-year-old. In the end she had to give up as she wasn't sure of her objectivity. The stories seemed interesting to her, full of adventure and humor, written in a manner a child would enjoy.

But she wasn't sure. In the end she left the manuscripts on the long low table, stacked neatly in their individual folders.

Two days later Sim still hadn't returned. Jan de-

cided to run her father's trapline and draw a map for
Sim so he would know the location of each trap. She
left early that morning. When she returned it was
dark, and she did the chores before going to the house.

Jason had been there during the day. She found
the note he had left on the kitchen table when she
went to prepare her meal. In his bold firm hand it
read:

I came for you. I had to leave. Be back in two
weeks. Be ready to go with me, Janet. I won't
take no for an answer. Lucille has agreed to let
you stay with her until you find a place of your
own.

You can make up your own mind about your
future, but I refuse to allow you to remain alone
on this godforsaken mountain all winter. Your
father saved Tom's life. I owe him. I'll take care
of you, strictly business. You can repay me as
soon as you are able. You have my word on it.
See you in two weeks.

Again, it was signed with the impressive *J*.

His initial represented him perfectly, Jan decided.
Arrogant, demanding recognition no other man
would presume to exact.

Thank goodness she would be in California by the
time he returned! At least she'd be spared the con-
frontation with him. A long shudder shook her and
she knew she was lying to herself. No matter how
stressful a meeting with Jason would be, she longed
to see him.

The thought was enough to send her to bed with a restless feeling that precluded any attempt at sleep. Daytime hours weren't so disturbing. Knowing everything had to be shipshape, she filled her time with hard work. She had to prepare for the proper care of the animals during the winter. Sim could be relied on to care for them, but he needed things organized.

She was busy enough to keep thoughts of Jason at bay.

Nights were another story. Jason moved out of her subconscious then, taking over her sleep. She awoke each morning flushed and out of sorts.

"All you need is to fall in love with someone your own age," she told herself. "Maybe if you had some real experience to stack him up against, Jason wouldn't strike you as so marvelous."

But given the chance, would she welcome another man's kiss?

Oddly enough the thought had no appeal to her. Perhaps it was because she had no idea whether one man's kiss could be compared to another's.

"I'll just have to find out, won't I?" she mused.

By the time Sim returned, things were shaping up rather well. He helped her service the generator, then they checked all the lines and switches as her father had taught her.

The next day they carried in the firewood Lewis had cut and stacked in a clearing not far from the house. The cabin was electrically heated, but it had been their custom to use the fireplaces all winter. Nothing could match the comfort of a roaring fire on a snowy day!

The day before she was to leave, Jan helped Sim with the final task of putting up the storm windows. It was Friday, and she wanted to be gone before the first of the week. Jason would come sometime then, if she took his note seriously.

She had no inclination to deal with it in any other way. When he arrived, she planned to be far away.

They were almost finished with the storm sash when Sim glanced over his shoulder, narrowing his eyes.

"Company." The laconic remark hung in the air as Jan whirled to face the edge of the clearing.

Jason!

Jan froze, her heart in her throat.

The man emerging from the trees saw her abrupt motion as she turned her head. He waved enthusiastically, breaking into a galloping run, his unzipped jacket flaring out as he charged across the wide clearing.

The sun glinting off his dark bronzed head, Tom Farrell covered the distance to the cabin with astounding speed, considering how sick he'd been when she'd seen him last.

Jan's heart settled back into a more comfortable rhythm and her breathing began once more.

"I had to come back and thank you for all you did." Tom skidded to a halt at her side and threw his arms around her.

Sim caught the storm window she was holding and balanced it, a wry grin on his weathered face. Jan, tall as she was, found her nose buried in a flannel shirtfront covering a chest that rivaled Jason's for breadth. Young as Tom was, no one would have questioned his relationship to Jason. All the ingredients were there. He was going to be a carbon copy.

He hugged her and whirled around in a dizzying dance. Jan emerged from his strong embrace, her cheeks rosy and her eyes sparkling as she laughed at his exuberance.

"Put me down. You'll find yourself back in the hospital if you keep this up."

Sim watched their antics, his face twisted in astonishment. Tom released her reluctantly as the old trapper's critical grunt informed him he was trespassing. Sim squinted, registering his disapproval.

"Yer're the young sprout Lew dragged in out of the cold, I reckon." He measured Tom with a frosty eye. "Don't seem to be too much wrong with you, youngster."

"Nope, I've always healed fast," Tom agreed, his voice so like Jason's that Jan flinched. "Let me help you there, sir."

He grabbed a storm sash, his easy smile charming. Feeling an instant empathy with him, Jan performed the introductions to Sim and they got back to work.

"You walked up from the lake, I take it."

"Sure thing." Tom's smile included the old trapper. "I had a hard time finding the charter company that knew where it was. I just had to come up and thank you, Jan."

"It's a nice thought, but you shouldn't have made such a trip," Jan scolded, feeling immediately at ease with her former patient. "You've been very ill and it's a five-mile hike up here."

"I had to come." He grinned at her. "How else would I know if I'd dreamed you or not. Besides, I brought you something."

"That wasn't necessary," Jan protested.

"Sure it was." Balancing the sash he was holding for Sim, he reached into the pocket of his jacket and dug out a gold-foil-wrapped box. "Here you are. Something to remember me by."

Jan took the proffered gift, thanking him but unsure of the proper response. If Tom noticed her uncertainty, he ignored it. "I have to be back in class in California Monday morning if I don't want to get kicked out of college. I thought it would be a good idea to stop by and see you on the way." He turned back to the task at hand as if stopping by a cabin in the remote wilderness were a common practice done by everyone.

Jan wondered about the cost of the stopover. The young man smiling down at her carelessly didn't seem a bit bothered by it.

"Why don't you open the box?" he asked, teasing her.

Sim gave her an odd look as he removed the screen covering the window they were working on. Acting as if he'd done it all his life, Tom fitted the sash he held into the opening with a deft movement. Sim grunted his approval, then tramped onto the next window.

Jan slipped a nail under one of the golden seals, folding the expensive wrapping back with care.

The box contained a beautiful crystal bubble full of an enchanting scent. Her exclamation of surprise pleased the young man. "Thought you might like it. I asked Doc for some ideas. He suggested it."

"Dr. Brogan? How is he?" Jan had almost forgotten about the doctor.

"Fine. Actually, I weaseled the name of that charter company out of him. Dad hired his floatplane from them. Doc wasn't sure I should take time to come up. I really do have to be in school Monday or dad will have my head." The prospect of his father's displeasure didn't seem to affect him much.

"Your father isn't going to approve of this trip if you're really supposed to be in California," she told him.

"It'll be okay," he assured her. "I managed to get Doc's promise that he wouldn't say a word to my old man as long as I am back at school in time to beat the deadline."

In spite of herself Jan smiled at Tom's description of his father. Old man! Served Jason right.

"I figured you wouldn't mind putting me up overnight." He gave her an ingenuous grin and followed Sim to the next window. "I'll leave in time to get to the lake. Tomorrow's Saturday. I've got a ticket for an afternoon flight out. I'll have all day Sunday to get my act together."

"Guess he could bunk with the goat," Sim said in a tongue-in-cheek tone of voice. Jan caught the expression on the older man's face and nodded in solemn agreement.

"I don't give a hoot where I bunk," Tom assured them. "I figured it might not be convenient, but I had to come back up here and see if my angel of mercy was as gorgeous as I thought she was or if I was hallucinating.'' He was serious now, his face intent as those gray eyes roved over Jan's slender form. ''I wasn't delirious. You're even more beautiful than I dreamed possible.''

Jan's color rose, tinting her cheeks.

''I...well, I'll just go and make sure we have enough to feed you.'' She beat a hasty retreat, dashing up the steps and onto the porch.

''You are, you know,'' Tom shot after her. ''I'll stay and give Sim a hand, but hurry. I could eat a bear!'' His laughter followed her into the house.

After she had the meal on, she went into her room and surveyed the packing she'd started the night before.

She hadn't much left to do. Her choice had been limited and her suitcase was light. There were very few of her clothes that would be appropriate for life in a city. Most were suited to the rough environment on the edge of the Allagash. They wouldn't do elsewhere. Some of her limited supply of money must go for a better wardrobe if she was to be successful in her search for a job.

She had a fair idea of the importance of appearance when one sought employment. In her case it would be even more important as she had no formal training. She was going to have to find some position where the employer was willing to take her on and train her in the techniques of the job.

And that kind of employment might be hard to come by.

Her painting materials and her sketchbooks made

a tidy bundle. The only other thing she was taking was the box in which she was going to carry her manuscripts. They were still in a stack on the table before the fireplace in the living room. Tom would have to bunk on the big couch the table fronted.

I'll pack them up tonight after we eat, she told herself. It was then that another thought struck her. She'd planned to radio for a floatplane to take her out the next day, knowing it would make a sizable hole in her cash to do so. Maybe Tom would let her go back to Boston with him. She could share the expense.

Tom was not only agreeable, he was enthusiastic.

"I'd do a lot more than that for you, Jan," he told her as they finished supper. "You and your father saved my life. I'll never be able to repay you, but I'd sure like to try. Anything you want, you just ask. If I can't get it for you I'll enlist my dad's help. He can do anything."

Sim grinned at them and left to do the chores. Surprised by Tom's outburst, Jan stared at him, horrified at the thought of his asking Jason to aid her in any way. She rose from the table, her hands full of dirty dishes. Tom was on his feet in an instant, stacking up the remaining clutter. Jan stood quietly a moment, her thoughts sorting themselves out.

"Tom, I want you to promise me something."

The young man looked up from his task and smiled at her. "Anything, Jan. Anything at all!"

"You didn't tell your father you were coming here, did you?"

"Hell, no. He's in Europe for a couple of weeks.

Doc Brogan is the only one who knows where I am and he said he won't mention it as long as I get back in time.''

"I don't want you to tell your father, ever. I'm going to California, too, but I don't want him to know that, in case you run into me there.''

"You're joking! Where are you going to be? Do you have friends there? Can I see you sometimes?''

Laughing at the flood of questions, Jan carried the dishes to the sink and turned on the tap. "I'm not joking,'' she assured Tom as he followed her with his hands full. "Put them there.'' He did and went back for another load. "I don't know where I'm going yet, and no, I don't know a soul out there. All my friends are here on the mountain, but I feel I need a complete change of scene, and California has always appealed to me. And I expect you'll be much too busy with your schoolwork and your girl friends to bother with me.''

"That'll be the day,'' Tom muttered. "Where do you plan to go? Los Angeles? Frisco? San Diego?''

"I've no idea. I thought I would go someplace and get a job while I try to sell my stories.''

"Just like that!'' The scorn in his voice told her what he thought of the idea. "Do you have any money? Have you ever lived in a city? Do you know what you're letting yourself in for?''

"Nope. I'm quite accustomed to taking care of myself,'' Jan told him with a careless amusement. He sounded exactly like her father, she thought.

"Yeah. I bet.'' His drawl was caustic. "What are these stories you're talking about?''

"I'll show you when we finish here."

They worked together in companionable harmony, laughter flowing in the big room as they teased each other, becoming acquainted.

Tom looked so like Jason, but how different he was. . . . Jan felt an odd sense of longing.

By the time they finished in the kitchen, Sim returned from doing the outside chores. Jan and Tom walked into the front room as he was entering the house.

"Guess I'll hit the hay," he announced, proceeding to leave them as he went into the bedroom for his usual early night.

Tom sat on the couch beside Jan and picked up one folder after the other, leafing through each with absorbed attention.

"These are absolutely fantastic, Jan!" His face glowing, he turned to her and repeated the praise once more. His comments as he turned over the pages filled Jan with a sense of accomplishment. Lewis was the only one who had seen her work previously. He too had praised it, but Jan tended to discount his judgment as a bit prejudiced. Tom's spontaneous appreciation gave her a wonderful sense of achievement she hadn't experienced before.

"You really think they're good?"

"Well, it's been awhile since I've read children's stories," Tom chuckled. "I wasn't privileged to have anything of this quality to read when I was young. As an adult I find them fascinating. I think they're wonderful, Jan."

"Do you think they will sell? Please give me your

honest opinion, Tom. I want to get off the mountain this winter. I need to give myself a chance to find out about the world out there. I figure if I'm away from here I'll get over my father's death a lot faster. But I do need to be able to support myself. I have very little money.''

Tom gave her a thoughtful look. ''I don't know very much about the writing game, but dad has a friend who makes a lot of money at it. I could ask him about it.''

''I wouldn't want to be a bother. . . .''

''Aw, c'mon, Jan. As if you could! You haven't really decided where you want to locate yet, have you?''

Shaking her head, Jan began to pack her manuscripts into the box in neat order.

''Tell you what then. Why don't you come to the coast with me? I live at home during school and drive the twenty-five miles each way every day. You'll love the place. It's been in the family for years. My grandfather fell in love with the peninsula when he was just a kid. He bought the house when it was miles out in the country, all by itself. You should see the people now! Granddad would have a fit . . . but we do have the sweetest housekeeper in the world. She took care of dad all his life and now she takes care of me. Her name's Tilly. Tilly Jense. Her husband works for us, too. Jense oversees the orchards and the grounds. Keeps everything shipshape.''

''Thanks a lot, Tom, but I couldn't.'' Jan picked up another folder and put it away carefully, her skin prickling.

"Aw, Jan, don't be silly. It'd be super for you. The house isn't too far from San Francisco. You could get a job there. It's a great place to work. And this guy I was telling you about—dad's friend, the writer—lives in Frisco."

"I've told you I don't want to bother him!" Jan didn't try to keep the sharp edge out of her voice. "Nor can I go to California with you."

Tom was silent for several moments, watching her as she packed her box.

"What is it, Jan?" he asked, his voice quiet. "Tell me the truth. Why won't you let me help you? Are you afraid of me?"

"Hardly," she laughed. She liked Tom. There was a warm sincerity about the young man that she trusted. "I—well, you see, it's your father, actually. I have an awful time trying to get along with him. The last time I saw him, we—we had a terrible..." words failed her for a moment. What would she call their final encounter? "Row," she finished.

"Dad stays in New York. We'll never see him." Tom grinned at her flushed face. "What did you fight about?" He cocked an eyebrow at her, looking exactly like his father. "Don't tell me if you don't want to," he added kindly.

"Jason doesn't like me," Jan hedged. It was the best she could do.

"You must be joking!" Tom exclaimed. "I know my father better than that. Jase has always admired intelligent good-looking women. And he's too sharp not to have noticed you're both of those things. So what gives? Come clean."

"Believe me, Tom. I won't go to the coast with you and chance running into him." A thrill of danger danced down her spine.

Jason's house, Jason's son. . . .

Surely she wasn't reckless enough to think she could live in Jason's house without him being aware of it? She felt her senses stir as she thought of the challenge.

"Dad never comes to the West Coast anymore, Jan." Tom sounded honest as he told her this. "He prefers New York for some obscure reason. It's the women who live there, I think. And his business is centered there, but that's only because he wants it that way. He has enough clout to have his headquarters anywhere. You can come with me if it's only the thought of meeting dad that is standing in the way. I promise you he hasn't been in the house for years. When he does come to California he stays in San Francisco when he's in the north. Or sometimes, Sacramento. He doesn't come to the house. Even if he did he'd let Tilly know before he came. Otherwise she'd have his head. Please believe me, Jan. It's such a good solution to your problems and there's no way Jason will ever know."

"Why do you call your father Jason?" Jan found this off putting. Tom wasn't insolent when he spoke of his father, but she felt a faint challenge in his attitude, his words.

"He is Jason, and I sometimes find it hard to think of him as my father." Tom looked rather sheepish as he made the admission. "He's so sure of himself, if you know what I mean. It bothers me sometimes.

Especially when he plays the heavy with me and tells me what to do.''

"Usually right, is he?" Jan guessed shrewdly.

"He is! That's what makes it so hard to take. But he might approve of my idea this time."

Jan raised an eyebrow, her skepticism plain.

"C'mon, Jan. Dad would be the first to admit we owe you something. This is the perfect way to pay our debt to your family. It'll cost practically nothing, not that price matters. Tilly will love having you. You will have shelter that isn't going to break you financially. You can pay me back as soon as your books sell, if you insist. Don't be stubborn. Listen to reason."

Jan gave in to temptation. "I'll pay you back as soon as I get a job."

Tom caught the drift of her words immediately. His reaction startled her. He leaped up, pulled her into his arms and danced her around the room in a wild imitation of a polka. Jan, laughing in response to his spirited mood, allowed him to whirl her around. They were both out of breath when he stopped. He plopped her back down on the couch and handed her the rest of the manuscripts, one at a time, to pack.

"This is great, Jan. You're never going to regret it."

"I should hope not. It does seem the practical thing to do. Perhaps your father's writer acquaintance can tell me who to see, how to get started. Remember, though, I won't go near him if he is liable to get in touch with Jason."

"It's not likely." Tom opened the last folder and turned the pages thoughtfully. "This book of yours about the ranger and his work is outstanding, Jan. If I'd seen it when I was eight or so I'd probably be studying forestry now. Who is the ranger?"

"His name is Ken Clark. He heads the district here. I love him and his wife, Sarah. They wanted me to stay with them this winter, but I feel I must get away for a while. I'm so lucky to have Sim. He'll stay all winter."

Tom was turning the pages, his face thoughtful.

"You made a sketch of me, didn't you, Jan?"

"Yes, I did." She glanced up from her packing, surprised at the question. "The first night you were here I did a pencil drawing of you while I waited for my father to come back from the lake with the doctor. He never did, of course. Why do you ask?"

"I was pleased with the likeness. It's very flattering."

"Where have you seen the sketch? I guess it must be around the cabin somewhere. I don't know where it is."

"Didn't you give it to dad?"

"Your father? Certainly not!"

"Well, he has it. Framed and on the dresser of his bedroom in that apartment of his in Manhattan."

"Manhattan?" Jason had taken it! Something stirred deep within her.

"Sure. Didn't you know that's where he lives? I went down there when they let me out of the hospital in Boston. He wasn't home, but I always stay there if I'm in New York. It's convenient and the guy he has for a servant is just great. John Brogan practices on Fifth Avenue, you know.''

"No, I didn't. I thought he was from Boston. I hadn't realized Jason brought him out from New York.'' Jan was taken aback by the information that Jason and John Brogan both lived in New York. "Where does Lucille St. John live?''

"Ah, the lovely Lucille. Our handy little widow lives in Connecticut, and I hope to heaven she stays there.''

Amused by his expression, Jan laughed in spite of herself.

"Problems?''

"Not really. I don't like Lucille. She and dad are too cozy to suit me. She runs one of ElPac's plants. She's good at it, I guess, but she hides a lot of bossiness under that glamorous exterior. I don't like it.'' His brows drew together. "He'll never marry her, you know.''

"Why not?'' Jan couldn't have stopped the question if she'd wanted to.

"Dad's never going to get over the thing my mother did to him. He hates women, really, but every one he meets is fascinated by him. It's his macho looks, I suppose. They all want him, young and old. He manages to run around with some pretty classy dames, but he won't marry any of them. He's a regular misogynist. Hates marriage, and I can't blame him. The only trouble is he wants me to hate it, too. He's always on at me about it. That's why I generally stay on the West Coast. He can't tell me what to do all the time if he's here and I'm there. I *like* women!''

Jan took another look at her guest. There was a decided petulant small-boy look on his clean-cut features. She had no inclination to delve further into his personal affairs as she remembered John Brogan's comment on the number of times Jason had retrieved Tom from difficult situations. What was there between Jason and his son? It was, she decided, none of her business.

"How old are you, Tom?"

"Old enough...." He let the implication drift between them. Jan gave him a cool look, and Tom had the grace to blush. "I'm a senior at Stanford this year," he told her.

How old did a senior have to be, Jan wondered. Twenty-two, probably, if he entered at eighteen. Something in Tom's answer didn't ring true. Jan suspected he wasn't that old, even if he wanted her to think so. She didn't have much experience in guessing the ages of people, but Tom seemed young to her in spite of his height and breadth.

He grinned at her. For some reason she couldn't find it in her nature to be truly upset with him.

"I suspect you use that charm of yours to get what you want in this world, Tom Farrell," she admonished with some severity. "It won't work on me, you know. I'll go to the West Coast with you, but I'm not going to commit myself to anything further until I look things over. Then I'll make up my mind. Okay?"

"Good grief! I've been waiting for the most beautiful woman in the world all my misspent life, and when I meet her, what happens?" He struck his broad forehead in a classic gesture of grief. "I'll tell you what happens! She turns out to have a mind of her own and a practical one at that. Mama mia! What have I done to deserve this?"

Jan laughed at his tragic expression. "You needn't flirt with me, Tom. It isn't part of the bargain. We need our sleep if we're going to cross the continent tomorrow. Here are your blankets." Raising the lid of the oak chest sitting against the wall, she showed him a store of fluffy Hudson's Bay's best. "I'll get a pillow and sheets for you."

Taking them from the hall linen closet, she gave them to him and told him to sleep well.

As she went to her own room she remembered her mother's picture. The door to her father's room was open, Sim's gentle snore telling her he was fast asleep. Slipping through it, she tiptoed over and picked up the only photo in existence of the woman Lewis had loved so fiercely. Carrying it into her room, she wrapped it in a sweater and put it in with her things.

She couldn't go off across the United States and leave it behind.

CHAPTER NINE

UNMOVED BY TOM'S IMPATIENCE the next day, Jan radioed her goodbyes to the Clarks. She left Tom's address and phone number with them. With no mail service and no telephone, the information was useless to Sim. He stood on the porch and watched them go.

Her young companion was in a rare mood. Laughing and teasing, he kept her entertained all the way down the mountainside. The floatplane he had hired came in on time and they were in Boston in the early afternoon. With a two-hour wait until their flight to California, Tom took her to a plush hotel near the airport.

"You look nervous," he told her as they sat along the counter. The seats were well-padded armchairs rather than the usual lunch-counter stools. The restaurant was crowded with men and women lingering over drinks.

Jan watched them with a feeling of pleasure. The men and women looked friendly to her. The room was full of their laughter and voices, a kaleidoscope of movement and color she rarely had had time to enjoy when she traveled with her father.

Her manuscripts were in a box at her feet. Tom

hadn't wanted to check them through with the rest of the luggage when he'd gone to buy her ticket.

He hadn't allowed her to pay for it. Jan, helpless in the face of his insistence, had finally agreed to his plan. She was to let him pay for all her expenses until such time as she sold her books or was able to find employment paying enough to support her needs.

"Are you?" Tom gave her one of the two menus the hostess had handed him.

"Am I what?" Jan looked at him in some surprise.

"Nervous. You look jumpy, unsettled."

"Perhaps. I've never flown cross-country. I know people do it all the time, but three thousand miles seems like a lot of flying to me."

"Just put yourself in my hands, fair lady, and all will be well." Tom leered at her, the effort pulling his face into a comic pattern.

"You are incorrigible."

They ordered, then Jan went to the ladies' lounge, leaving her things on the floor. While she was gone Tom struck up a conversation with the man beside him, but when she returned he directed all his attention on her once again.

"Let's start work on my account with you while we're waiting," Jan suggested. "I don't want to lose track of anything and I'm already on my way toward owing you the national debt."

"Heard about such things even up on your mountain, have you?" Tom produced the small accounts book he had purchased for her from his jacket pocket. "Here you are, hardhead. Get on with it."

Jan scowled in mock anger and scribbled in the

record book, noting everything he had spent already, including half the floatplane cost.

Tom leaned back in his chair, staring at her profile as she worked. "Where are you from, Jan?" he asked suddenly.

"You know where I'm from. You've just been there." She closed the little book and leaned back, giving him a soft smile. "I live on a mountain on the edge of the Allagash in the state of Maine."

"That's not what I meant, Jan. Where were you born? You have such a clear skin. It really is peaches and cream, you know. I've heard a lot about your kind of complexion, but yours is the first I've ever seen, and I'm a connoisseur of such things."

"I'll bet you are." The tart edge to her voice was caused by the thought that he was truly a chip off the old block. Jason Farrell gave every indication of having lots of experience where women were concerned.

"No fooling, Jan. I mean it. You don't even wear makeup and you look better than any woman I've ever seen before. Your hair is such a wonderful rich color. It looks like silk. And those eyes of yours! Wow! They're so clear and green and lovely. They can look right through a guy. Like now."

His grin was only a bit uncertain. This young man had a fair idea of his own charm. He'd probably started perfecting it while he was still in his crib, Jan thought to herself. He was able to use it with some of his father's flair. "You look exotic," he continued. "You're different from anyone I've ever met before, and I've met a few."

"I have no idea where I was born, if that's what you mean."

"Don't you have a birth certificate?"

"I don't think so. Not that I know of, anyway."

"Who was this Goud guy John Brogan was talking about? Isn't he a relative of yours? John told me he said he was."

"He claims he is," Jan said abruptly. She had dismissed him from her thoughts since he'd made his fruitless contact with Ken Clark. She had probably seen the last of him. She certainly hoped so. Thought of the man made her uneasy and restless. "He said he was one of my cousins, that he was related to me through my mother."

"Do you think he was?"

"Yes. There is no reason not to. He seemed to know things only my father or another member of my family would be likely to know. I didn't like him much."

"Has he been in touch?"

"He disappeared from the hospital. Jason couldn't find him after dad died. He came to the ranger station, though. I don't know why. I asked Sarah and Ken not to let him know where the cabin was. He told me he was from Holland."

"Holland! Did he say you were from Holland, too?"

"He did, if I remember correctly. I'm confused about it. If my father was English, why did he speak Dutch so well?"

"Did Goud know you planned to go to California?" Tom asked.

"No," Jan grimaced, then smiled at the waitress depositing the steaming plate of stuffed sole in front of her. "It's none of his business. Thank you, miss."

The young woman gave her a vague smile in return, her attention centered on the handsome man at Jan's side. Tom winked at the waitress and she blushed with pleasure. "Enjoy your meal," she instructed them.

Jan laughed at the smug look on her companion's face.

"I can't help it, Jan," he grinned at her. "Have to fight them off all the time."

It wasn't until they stood to leave that she discovered the wallet she had left in her jacket pocket was gone. She had taken off her heavy sheepskin jacket and thrown it across the box of manuscripts beside her. The wallet wasn't there. It wasn't anywhere. She ran back into the lounge, although she couldn't remember taking it in there with her.

White-faced, she went back to Tom. He took one look at her stricken expression and folded her into his arms.

"Don't, Jan. It's not the end of the world. I won't let anything happen to you."

"But I feel as if I should never have come down off my mountain, Tom. That was all the money I have in the world and now it's gone."

"Sh-shh," he soothed her. "You have a fortune in these manuscripts of yours. Leave it up to your old Uncle Tom. You'll see."

Jan wanted to believe him. She pulled away from his warm embrace.

"What if you're wrong, Tom? How will I ever earn enough to repay you?"

"Dunno," he told her with a cheerful disregard of consequence. "But where there's a will there's a way, as the saying goes." He picked up her things and started toward the door, his determination to have his own way written clearly in the firm set of his mouth. "You'll think of something."

"I could get in touch with Peter Goud. He was very anxious to take me to Amsterdam with him. And if he is a relative. . . ." Jan winced at the idea as she followed her escort.

Tom shouldered his way through the huge glass doors of the hotel lobby, holding them for her with an exaggerated look of patience. "I gather you don't even like this Goud guy. Why the hell would you want to go charging off halfway around the globe with someone you don't even like? Or am I in the same category? Don't you like me, Jan?" He handed the box to the driver of the cab, who put it in the trunk. Turning, Tom frowned at her, a concerned expression on his handsome face.

"Don't be ridiculous, Tom. You know very well I have the best feeling in the world toward you. You're like a—a younger brother to me, I think. I'm becoming very fond of you."

"Ouch! Younger brother!" His scowl deepened and the gray of his eyes darkened. "I'm not younger and I don't like the role of brother one bit."

"Well, you are. At least I think that's how one would feel if one was so fortunate as to have someone like you for a brother. Don't you see what I mean? If Peter is truly who he says, I probably have family in Holland. Maybe they wouldn't mind taking care of a penniless relative.''

Tom's laugh dealt a deathblow to her idea. ''I think you'd best listen to your own instincts, Jan. You don't have enough experience to deal with people any other way. If Goud makes you uncertain, check him out before you commit yourself to any of his schemes. We can talk about it once we get to the coast. And we better hightail it or we're going to miss that flight.''

Jan allowed him to bustle her into the waiting taxi. She was sure he was right when he said she must trust her instincts, and those instincts told her quite clearly she was safe with Tom Farrell, for all his attempts to convince her he was a full-fledged lady-killer.

In any case, it was easy to trust Tom. Jan knew he was sincere in his desire to help her. She believed him when he said he felt he could never repay the debt of gratitude he owed her because her father had saved his life. And Lewis had done just that.

Full of plans for her, Tom talked nonstop as they cruised high over the changing terrain. Jan kept her eyes glued to the small window most of the time, drinking in the plains below, breathless as they crossed the Rockies and cruised high over the basin country dividing them from the Sierra Nevadas. The coast itself spread out under the jet, a sparkling jewel in the bright sunlight. They touched down lightly at San Francisco's International Airport and Tom rented a car to drive down the peninsula to Palo Alto.

Jan came out of the terminal building and moved

through the marvelous air with a distinct feeling of unreality. The feeling grew as she sat back in the bucket seat of the rented car and watched the scenery with increasing fascination. Despite the dark, she saw the palms and eucalypti rising against the pearled luminescence of the sky. Flowered shrubs flashed by, guarding the center dividing strip of the multilaned roadway running south. Scents such as she had never experienced filled her nostrils, intriguing her.

"Enjoying yourself?" Tom caught a glimpse of her rapt expression in the dim light thrown up by the car's dash.

"I'm not really sure. Are you certain I haven't died and gone to heaven? It was so cold in Boston. . . and worse at home. How long has this kind of weather been going on? Why haven't I heard of it before?"

"The secret we've tried to keep is being spread all over the world, I'm afraid. Even my dad says the rest of the world has its uses, but good old California is the only place fit to live in on a long-term basis."

"Does that mean he'll be coming back?" Jan's response was instant.

"You really don't like dad, do you?" There was a kind of wonder in his voice, a disbelief. "Why not, Jan?"

Honest all her life, Jan found it hard to handle the questions about Jason. There was no way she knew how to explain to Tom the powerful effect he had on her, how threatened she felt by him.

"He's so bossy," she replied evasively. "He's always telling me what to do. He acts as if I were a child."

Tom bought her explanation. "Yeah. I know what you mean."

"Tell me more about Tilly and her husband," Jan said, changing the subject.

Tom was still talking about Jense and the housekeeper when he pulled up under the portico of an enormous white house set amid beautifully kept emerald lawns. They had driven through tall gates and followed a curving gravel drive between hedges of flowering shrubs as tall as trees.

Jan jumped out of the car, savoring the soft air, the exotic fragrances.

"It smells so wonderful, Tom."

His arm around her waist, he led her up the steps. "Just wait till you meet Tilly. I forgot to phone. She'll scalp me."

He didn't seem very concerned, though, as he ran up the steps onto the wide veranda, taking Jan along in an impetuous rush she couldn't resist. He pushed the doorbell and she heard chimes ring somewhere in the house. Impatient, Tom grinned at her and beat out a rhythm on the polished panel of the heavy door.

I'm crazy, Jan thought wildly. *What am I doing here? What if Tom was mistaken and Jason is home?* It was too late, of course....

The little woman who opened the massive door was snatched up and whirled around, her skirt flying. "Put me down, you silly boy! This minute...." Her protest was lost along with her breath as Tom hugged her with enthusiasm. He steadied her on her feet then, and her hands flew to the wisps of gray hair he had loosened from captivity around her rosy face. Tilly was so short Jan was able to look down from her own five feet six height onto the top of the housekeeper's head. As she straightened the hair she wore in an old-fashioned bun, the round little woman did her best to glare at her tormentor with her soft brown eyes. Tom smiled at her and put out a hand, ruffling the order she was trying to impart to her wayward locks.

"Stop that, Tom! What do you mean coming home without warning me? How are you feeling, lad? You're looking fit."

"I'm fine," Tom assured her. "They let me out of the hospital this week and here I am."

"I see that. And who have you with you?"

"This is Jan Jordan... Tilly Jense... Jan." Tom dropped a casual arm around Jan's waist. "Her father saved my life and Jan took care of me until dad and Dr. Brogan could fly in to where I was. Jan's going to stay here for a while. Wait till you see the stories she's written, Tilly! They're fabulous. I'm going to help her sell them."

Tilly gave Jan a cautious smile and offered a small hand.

"Thank you for helping this rattlebrained young sprout, Miss Jordan. I was dead set against that photography trip in the first place. Then to think he didn't have sense enough to take a guide with him or let anyone know where he was! We were all worried to death...."

"Later, Tilly," Tom interrupted. "We're starved. The stuff they dole out on airplanes as food isn't enough to keep a canary alive. Where's Jense?"

"He's out at one of those meetings he goes to. Come with me, Miss Jordan. You bring in her things, Tom."

"Sure." Leaving the door open to the warm air, he ran back down the steps.

"This way, please," Tilly gestured toward the graceful stairway curving up to the second floor. "I am very happy to make your acquaintance, miss. Will you be staying long?"

"Please call me Jan. I'm really not sure how long I'll be here. I must find a job and see if I can sell my stories. Tom seems to think I may be able to. He says he knows someone...." Jan followed the little woman upstairs.

"Tom is just like his father." Tilly's smile was gentle as she headed down the carpeted passageway running the length of the upper floor. "Jason always knows everyone and Tom inherited the same flair. They are so alike, those two. It is uncanny at times." Coming to a door at the end of the long hallway, the housekeeper opened it and went in. "I'll put you in here. The bath is just through that door and you'll be able to see over the back garden all the way to the mountains. When you look out from this room it seems as if we are still in the country instead of in the middle of a growing city." She sighed, then smiled. "Never mind. It's just that we were so isolated when I first came here as a young woman. Things have changed so. Progress, I think it's called."

"I've lived in a very remote area all my life," Jan told her, laughter sparkling in the green of her eyes.

"I'm looking forward to a bit of crowding, people around me."

"I can understand. Will you be all right here?"

Jan looked around at the charming bedroom full of lovely graceful antique furniture, the windows covered with fluffy curtains of a sprigged yellow print matching the ruffled bedspread. The carpet on the floor was richly patterned. Warmly tinted in earth colors, the trailing design woven into it was golden brown with hints of a clear green. A velvety chaise longue was mated with a small mahogany table, its piecrust edge fluted in a most attractive manner. Tilly had touched a switch as they entered the room. The lamp on the table shed warm light on an exquisite figurine in subtle shades of blues and grays.

"It really looks wonderful."

"I think you'll find it comfortable." Tilly crossed the lovely carpet and opened the door on the other side of the room. "Here's the bath." She turned on that light and a cheerful bathroom tiled in yellow and white came to life. "Does Jason know you are here?"

"No he doesn't." Instant panic gripped Jan. "Tom told me he never comes here. Was he wrong?"

"Tommy was telling the truth," Tilly's voice held an edge of unhappiness. "He's stayed away since just before his father died. I haven't seen him for almost a year. He's always so busy."

Jan could hear the regret in the housekeeper's words, but her own relief was immense.

Tilly regarded her a moment, reading the expression on her mobile features. "Would you like to wash up? Then come down to the kitchen. I'll fix the two of you something to eat. That Tommy is always starved. I hear him coming up with the luggage. He'll show you the way to the kitchen. I'll lay the table there this time so I'll have a chance to talk with you and that young scamp."

Jan agreed, smiling at the affection in the older woman's voice. "Thank you, Tilly. And thank you for letting me stay."

On her way out, Tilly turned back to give her a surprised look. "It's Tommy's home, Jan. I have nothing to say about guests, as a rule. He can have anyone he wants here. I wouldn't get far trying to interfere with that young man's wishes. I'm only grateful that he's such a straightforward youngster.... Your meal will be ready in a few minutes."

After washing her hands in the ample bathroom, Jan went back and ran the comb she had in a jacket pocket through the dark honey of her hair. A brisk knock announced Tom's arrival at the open door. He brought in her suitcase and the box containing her manuscripts and put them both on the chest at the foot of the big four-poster.

"Is the room okay, Jan?" He looked up at the ruffled canopy stretched across the top of the bed. "It's pretty fancy."

"I'll feel as if I'm some sort of a fairy princess," she laughed. "Don't worry, Tom. I'll take off my jeans before I get into bed," she teased.

Tom looked offended. "That's not what I meant and you know it. Your cabin on the mountain is so comfortable. Everything there is practical and you use it.''

"All the time,'' Jan agreed.

"Yeah, that's the difference. My grandfather and his father collected most of this junk. Looks nice, maybe, but that's about the limit. I like your place better, almost.''

Jan smiled, mischief in her green eyes. "I'll have to do my best to put up with this. I really don't think it will be a problem.''

"I want you to be happy here, Jan," he said, his face serious. "This is your home as long as you want to stay. Let's go eat. Tilly is dying of curiosity and I'm starved. Besides, I think I heard Jense pull in a minute ago. Might as well go down and get the third degree over with.''

"The third degree" turned out to be a rousing session of exchanged information. Jan was completely at ease with the housekeeper and her husband. They made her very welcome.

Both Tilly and Jense spoke of Jason as if he were no older than his son. They laughed about incidents of his childhood, bragged about him as an adult. Jan was fascinated. These two older people loved the man. Their affection showed in the fond way they recounted some of his more outrageous indiscretions.

Tom came in for his share of attention. Under Tilly and Jense's gentle questioning, Jan found herself sharing with them some of the more amusing events of her own cloistered life.

Tilly whisked the dishes off the table, refusing to allow Jan to budge. "Tomorrow you help. Today you sit," she ordered. Pouring fragrant coffee from a porcelain coffee server, she filled man-sized mugs for them and placed a plate of delicate sugar cookies before them.

"Jense and Tommy like to drink their coffee from cups that hold something," she remarked, sitting down herself. "Have one of the cookies, Jan. They're from the old country. I use my mother's recipe."

Jan took one of the feather-light delicacies and popped it into her mouth. It promptly melted, leaving the most delicious taste.

"Oh. Fantastic. What are they called?"

"Fattigman. It translates to mean poor man, even if a poor man may not be able to afford to make them." Tilly's face crinkled with delight as she watched Tom and Jan eat. "Egg yolks, cream and butter. Goodness! So expensive!"

A short while later Tom led Jan from the room. "Like 'em?" he asked, tilting his head back to the kitchen where the older couple still sat.

"Love 'em," Jan answered, following him across the broad hallway.

There was a phone on the carved chest beside the living-room door. It rang.

"Hello?" Tom answered. "Farrell residence. Certainly. For you, Jan." He handed the instrument to her.

"For me?" Jan felt an instant panic. Who on earth would be calling, asking for her? Her immediate thought was Jason. Tom read her concern and shook his head. "It's your ranger friend."

Weak with relief, Jan took the receiver. "Hello? Ken?"

"Jan, honey, Peter Goud showed up at your place. I'm sorry to have to tell you he roughed up old Sim."

"No! Why would he do a thing like that?"

"Seems he wanted to find you and Sim refused to say where you were. He was trying to get the information out of him when that other fellow. . . you know. . . the kid's father, arrived. The kid Lewis found."

"Jason?"

"Yeah. Jason Farrell." Jan felt stunned. Jason must have returned early from Europe. Thank goodness she had decided to leave with Tom. "I reckon he isn't as old as I thought he was," Ken said. "I've talked to Sim. Farrell got rid of Goud, according to the old man."

"Is Sim all right?" Jan voiced her concern for the old trapper. Ken assured her that he was fine. "That awful man! How did he find out where I live?"

"He hired Mike to fly him in. Seems he came in sometime after young Farrell. He paid rather handsomely to charter a plane, fed Mike some cock-and-bull story about being your only living relative. You know how accommodating Mike is when his air charter can pick up a buck. He flew him in. Goud sent him back to base. Said he'd radio for him when he was ready to come out. Farrell seemed to think the guy had been following young Tom. It's the only way he'd know which charter company to use. Mike pointed out the trail to him."

"How would he have known who Tom was or where to find him, for that matter?"

"It was in the papers and on television when Jason Farrell airlifted his son out and put him in the hospital. He could have picked up the trail easily enough. He knew you lived up here somewhere, you know. When he came to the ranger station and ran into a dead end, he found another way to reach you, that's all. Farrell radioed me from the cabin and explained briefly. Sim is mad as a wet hen. Goud better stay away. Sim won't be caught napping next time."

"When did this happen, Ken?"

"About mid-afternoon. Farrell wanted to know where you were, Jan. I didn't tell him. He didn't like it much. Are you hiding from him? How can you do that if you are at his home out there on the coast?"

How indeed?

"I'm not really hiding, Ken," she tried to allay his fears. "I want to find my feet, that's all. Tom was kind enough to offer to let me stay here until I get myself sorted out. My arrangement is with him, not with his father."

"I don't understand, honey, but I guess you know what you're doing. Farrell gives me the impression he is really concerned with your welfare. Are you sure you're doing the right thing?"

"No, but I'm committed."

"I haven't met him in person, so I may not be a good judge, but this Jason Farrell sounds all right to me. Just be careful, Jan. And if you need anything or get in trouble, you know our number. Keep in touch, hear?"

"I will. I'm so sorry about Sim. I had no idea anything like this might happen...."

"It's not your fault, honey. Sim can take care of himself. This Goud surprised him, that's all. Keep well and let us hear from you."

"I will. Thanks, Ken. 'Bye."

Hanging up, she met Tom's interested glance. "Jason has been to my cabin. He—"

The phone shrilled again and Tom gave her a rueful grin. "Want to bet it's my old man? Just don't say a word." He fixed a stern eye on her. Heart racing, Jan was still. Tom let the phone ring a couple more times before picking it up.

"Hello. Farrell residence. Oh, hi, Jason.... Yeah, I got home this afternoon...."

The instrument vibrated with the deep sound of the male voice calling from across the continent. Jan felt her blood rush.

"Yeah... yeah, I know you thought I was going to come straight home, but I still had a week...."

Interrupted again, he looked at Jan. She was watching him with a stricken expression. Tom winked at her, the picture of naughty innocence.

"My courses are in great shape, dad. I've nothing but independent studies this semester. I arranged it that way so I could go on this photography trip... I told you...." He grinned. "Sure dad... I know, but I wanted to thank this Jan Jordan for all she and her father had done for me, so I flew in... no, she left instructions with the man at her cabin not to tell anyone where she had gone... sure it's aggravating, but she can probably take care of herself... I'm sorry. Sure. I have finals in two weeks. I'm going to be too busy to get into trouble. I'll keep my grades up, don't worry."

Tom was beginning to sound exasperated. Jan felt as though her knees might actually give out. She realized her friend had avoided giving his father any information without resorting to actual falsehood. How had he managed to do it? She knew she couldn't have flirted with the truth in such a skillful manner.

"I don't know whether to be horrified or grateful to you, Tom. How did you get to be so devious?" she asked as he replaced the phone.

Tom waved a careless hand at her. "I never tell my dad a lie. It's just that sometimes he doesn't ask the right questions. I always answer the ones he does."

"He'll have a right to be furious if he finds out."

"He won't find out. He knows you asked Sim not to give anyone a clue as to where you were. The only thing he doesn't know is that I was there when you said it."

"What if he calls and Tilly or her husband answers the phone? They won't know he has no idea I'm here in his house."

"Just go on up to bed and stop worrying. I'll talk to Jense and Tilly. I'll show you around in the morning, okay?"

In spite of the luxury of the big bed, Jan had a most unsatisfactory night, tossing and turning. Jason's dark face wavered in and out of dreams she didn't remember, filling her with a deep longing.

The next morning Tilly gave her a thoughtful look as she arrived in the kitchen.

"Tom tells me you don't want Jason to know you're here," the housekeeper ventured. "Is this so?"

"Yes, it is," Jan answered, taking the mug of steaming coffee Tilly handed her. So Tom had talked to Tilly about the situation. "I'm so worried about being here. It—it seems unscrupulous, somehow."

"You didn't get much sleep last night from the looks of you. You mustn't get yourself so upset about it. Tom is right when he says Jason would do the same for you if he had the chance."

Jan didn't elaborate on the real reason she didn't want Jason to know of her whereabouts. Instead she gave Tilly a wan smile. "Do you think he would?"

"I'm sure of it. Tommy says someone stole your wallet."

"I'm afraid so. It had all my money in it."

"Well, then! What else could he have done? He had to bring you here."

"I shouldn't have left my wallet there in my jacket. It was so stupid. It didn't occur to me that anyone in that room would have taken it. They all looked so prosperous! I still can't believe it happened."

"It's probably for the best. You'd be on your way this morning if you had the money, wouldn't you?"

"Yes, I would. I could find a room somewhere." *And be gone if Jason should show up.*

"It's better for you to be here. A young girl like you hasn't any business living in some old smelly room. No, Tommy did right bringing you home. Jason would agree about that, I'm sure. You haven't had enough experience to be out on your own."

"I guess losing my wallet proves that," Jan agreed ruefully. "I shouldn't be let out without a keeper, I think."

"You mustn't worry about it. You can't be expected to realize how bad folks can be, what with your sheltered life and all. But you'll learn. You look smart enough to me."

"I hope you prove to be right," Jan laughed, feeling better. Would she ever learn to control her longing for sight of the arrogant man who lived in her thoughts whether she was awake or asleep? That, she decided, was a must. There was no reason, no excuse for her continued fascination with Tom's father.

"Is it that you don't like Jason, Jan? Is that why you don't want him to know you are here?"

"That's not the case." Sipping her coffee, Jan stared out over the smooth green lawns of the estate. "He makes me so—uncomfortable. He's so—overpowering—I think is the word. I don't think he likes me much."

"Upsets you, does he? Thinks you can't take care of yourself?"

"That's right, I'm afraid." Jan's firm jaw set and she flushed.

Tilly considered this a moment as she buttered hot toast for the younger woman's breakfast.

"I can see how he might affect you." She put the toast in front of Jan and went to a cupboard for a jar of jam. "You haven't had much experience with men, have you? I doubt very much that Jason could dislike you. I think you've mistaken the way he tries to help as an invasion of your privacy, perhaps."

"I suppose you may be right, but I'd rather take care of myself without his help. I had to get away from my home but I didn't want to be involved with Jason.''

"I see. Well, Jense and I will do our best not to let him know you are here until you tell us it's all right. Is he looking for you?''

"Heavens, no. Why should he do anything like that?''

Tilly gave her a look full of speculation. "I just wondered. Do you want eggs this morning?''

Jan refused, not very hungry, and they talked of other things until Tom put in his appearance.

Her uneasiness left her as she responded to the teasing attitude of her young guide. He took her to the rooftop of the sprawling Victorian mansion and showed her the gently rolling land belonging to it.

The house was surrounded by fifteen acres of grounds, he told her. Jense tended the fruit trees and the big vegetable garden and oversaw the men who did the actual labor and kept the expansive lawns in top condition. There was an enormous swimming pool behind the house, shaded by a stand of lovely and exotic trees she'd never seen before. Tom told her the names, but she knew she would have to get closer to them, inspect them, before she could hope to identify the lovely things.

"I want to show you our shopping mall," he told her as they ran down the stairs. "Put your boots on and we'll run over now."

"What's wrong, Tom? Don't you like my rugged look?" Jan laughed at him, looking down at her jeans and checkered shirt.

"You look fine, but you'll have to get some differ-

ent gear, I'm afraid. The house is always full of guys.''
He let the implication that he'd like her to impress his
friends unsaid. ''Besides, you'll want to wear something to wow that agent when we see him.''

Jan thought of the outfit Jason had bought her.
She had taken it off and packed it away after her
father's funeral. She hadn't worn it since but she had
it with her. What would Tom say if he knew about it?

''I really want you to get something special,'' he
rushed on. ''When the guys come, I want them to be
livid with envy.''

''Will you tell them I'm living in your house?'' She
made a quick guess at the direction his mind was
moving.

''Sure. That's half the fun.'' He wasn't quite able
to meet her eyes.

''Are you going to let them think I'm—sleeping
with you?'' she pinned him with a stern look, her disapproval easy to read.

''Er, no, of course not!'' Tom blushed. His embarrassment was plain as he pushed a hurried hand
through his tousled mop. ''I know you wouldn't
want that.''

''You're right. I wouldn't and I don't.''

''Jan, you're a guest in my house. I'll never do
anything to make you uncomfortable. Don't give it
another thought.'' He had the look of a small boy
caught with a fistful of cookies and an empty jar. Jan
felt a rush of affection for Jason's son. He was so
transparent.

She put on her boots and allowed him to drive her
the mile to the shopping mall.

"The shops in here aren't too bad," he told her as they drove through the complex. "Of course the place to do real shopping is San Francisco. Everyone knows that. Once I get rid of my finals, we'll go there."

The mall looked fabulous to Jan. And expensive. She was beginning to realize that Tom wasn't too concerned about the money he spent.

"Get something nice. I want you to look super."

There was a ring of command in the words that brought Jason to mind. Jan tried to protest, but she didn't have a chance.

"I'll leave you some money in the morning in case you feel like coming back and doing some shopping. You can keep track of it, put it in that blasted book of yours." His rush of words cut off her objections. "I have to be out of the house early, I'm afraid. You needn't wait for me."

"I'm not going to need all that much. I don't want my debt to you to pile up so that I'll never be able to repay it."

"You need to look like a knockout when we find an agent for you," he protested. "It doesn't hurt, you know."

"I'll sell my work because it has merit, Tom, or I won't sell it at all. It doesn't matter whether I'm dressed in jeans or the latest fashion."

"That's what you think," he told her sternly. "It never hurts to impress the guys you want to deal with. You can be impressive in a spectacular sort of way. Listen to me and trust me, Jan. I know what I'm talking about."

There wasn't a trace of flippancy in his voice or on the smooth planes of his face. She patted his arm, grateful for such support.

"Thanks, Tom. You're good for a person's ego. It was well worth my time helping to save you, I see," she said lightly. "Where else would I get such a loyal promoter?"

They drove home in the best of spirits.

Jan overslept the next morning and came running downstairs long after Tom had left the house.

"There you are." Tilly greeted her with sparkling eyes and a cheery smile. "Tired, weren't you? I thought it would catch up with you. Just sit yourself down in the breakfast room and I'll have something ready in a jiff."

"Let me help," Jan protested. "I'm good at it."

"Go along with you." Tilly shooed her out with a firm hand. "The rest of the house is yours, young lady, but the kitchen is mine. The morning paper is on the table. Catch up on the news."

The breakfast room, just off the kitchen, was a cheerful place furnished with rattan and plants in a tasteful manner that fit perfectly into the Victorian setting. Tilly poured coffee into a china mug. "Tom asked me to give you this."

Jan took the thick envelope from the smiling housekeeper and ran a nail under the seal as Tilly left the room. Tom had written a note and wrapped it around a thin sheaf of hundred-dollar bills. The writing showed signs of becoming as distinct as his father's.

Go get yourself something nice. Take a taxi to the big mall. Tilly will call one. Jense isn't home today or he'd take you. Or, if you'd rather, wait for me. I should be home about three and the stores will be open late, I think. Have fun!

He had scrawled "with love, Tom" across the bottom.

Jan sipped the delicious coffee and stared at the sheaf of bills with some consternation. There were ten of them. How did one deal with a young man who had a thousand dollars lying around the house as loose change?

She tucked the money away in her jeans and read the newspaper she found on the table until Tilly bustled in with a tray.

"How about some freshly squeezed orange juice, lovey, along with ham and eggs this morning?"

The tantalizing aroma of the food filled the room. Jan pushed the paper aside and thanked Tilly.

The housekeeper smiled. "Enjoy your breakfast, honey. If you need anything, holler. I'm making a batch of bread for Tommy. The boy loves it."

"Speaking of Tom, how old is he?" Jan broke off a piece of warm toast, popping it into her mouth.

"Won't tell you, eh?" Tilly chuckled. "He's always trying to pass himself off as older than he is. Full of the old Nick, just like his father. But he's a love and everyone is fond of him—including Jason. Tom is eighteen."

"Eighteen! But Jason...."

"Jason was seventeen when his son was born,"

Tilly told her in a gentle voice. "He ran away with an older woman when he was just sixteen. He came back the next year with Tommy."

Stunned, Jan stared at the housekeeper.

"Is that why—?"

"Why he keeps such a close watch on Tommy? I expect so. He's such a bright boy. Jason wants him to have the best. He wants the lad to get a good education, give himself a chance, not make the same mistake he did." Tilly smiled and bustled from the room.

So Jason had run away to be married when he was sixteen. That explained why he showed so much concern about his son's affairs.

What had happened to his wife? Tom's one reference to the woman who was his mother had been filled with quiet scorn, she remembered. He'd seemed to approve of his father's action in separating him from his mother while he was still an infant.

Why?

Restless, she finished her breakfast and cleared away the dishes. She decided it might be more interesting to wait until Tom came home and then let him take her on her first shopping spree. For the rest of the morning she helped Tilly. The housekeeper flew around the old mansion, cleaning, polishing and shining. Jan enjoyed the work and Tilly's unbroken flow of chatter.

"Tom looks so much like Jason, but he's much easier," the plump little woman confided. "Tom has all sorts of friends. The house is full of them more often than not. But he doesn't have Jason's horrid reputation, thank the Lord. It was very bad when Jason was Tommy's age. He was very handsome, you see, and so full of life. Girls just wouldn't leave him alone. I'm afraid he took advantage of the situation. Not that he ever neglected Tom, mind you. The child came first. I think maybe Tom is such an outstanding young man because Jason gave him so much love. He'd had very little from his own father, you see. He tried hard to be different with Tom. He was much better.''

Jan finally stemmed the tide of information Tilly seemed intent on sharing. They talked of Tom and his friends, his interests, the problems his wealth and his looks brought to him. Tilly delighted in illustrating the clever ways he used the charm and intelligence he had inherited from his father to solve those problems.

She adored Tom—and his father. Anything praiseworthy about him was due to Jason being his father, she was quick to point out. As was anything regrettable. But as Tilly told it, the two men were perfectly wonderful.

Jan had other ideas. She was sure Jason kept the continent between himself and his son for purely selfish reasons—to prevent his son from finding out about the women in his life, perhaps? The thought made her angry as well as strangely restless.

"I'm going to overhaul my manuscripts," she told Tilly after lunch, unable to listen to another word about the Farrell men.

Climbing the stairs, she returned to the lovely old room. It was peaceful and quiet, at the back of the house away from everyone, but she couldn't work. Tilly called her down to the phone three hours later. She hadn't accomplished a thing.

"Hi," she replied to Tom's cheerful greeting. "Thanks for the loan. It's far too much, you know."

"I doubt it. Have you priced a good dress lately? Go. Spend. Have a ball," he said laughing at her. "I won't be home until about eight, I'm afraid. I have some studying to do that must be done here in the library, then my frat is having a policy meeting and I've got to go to it."

"I've read some very strange things about frats," Jan teased.

"My dear young lady, fraternities are much maligned. Most are dedicated to good works and other things. The one I belong to is mostly dedicated to other things, I'm afraid, but I'm an officer and I have to be there or suffer. Will you be okay?"

"Yes, of course. Perhaps I'll go shopping in that enormous mall we drove through yesterday."

"Great. Buy something luscious and seduce me. There's a good girl."

"Don't try to be outrageous, Tom. I've got more important things to do than waste time seducing a minor."

"Tilly! She's betrayed me. Why did she have to tell you my age?" Tom sounded aggrieved but not at all astonished. "I suppose this puts us right back to that brother thing you were talking about?"

"I expect it does." Jan was unable to help laughing at his mournful tone. "I told you you made the best brother in the world."

"Yeah, I know. But do me a favor, will you? When I bring guys around, act like you really go for me. Please, Jan. I've been telling some of them about the smashing girl I found in the mountains. They can't wait to meet you. And I can't wait to show you off," he added, the charm she knew he possessed working full-time.

"We'll see," Jan replied not willing to commit herself to anything. "I take it you won't be home for dinner, then?"

"Nope. Let Tilly know, will you? She hates it when she cooks for me and I don't get there. Makes her cross."

"I will. Bye." Jan hung up and went to find Tilly. By the time she'd imparted the news that Tom wouldn't be home, her own mind was made up to go shopping. It would probably be a lot of fun.

She ran upstairs and changed into her one white shirt. Of a soft cotton, it was nothing spectacular, but it did look dressier than the flannel ones she was accustomed to wearing this time of the year. She brushed her hair until it shone like dark molten gold, then tied the heavy silken fall at the nape of her neck with a shoelace. Putting on the one hand-knit sweater she had with her, she went downstairs with five of the hundred dollar bills in her jean's pocket, sorry she had no footwear except the soft leather boots she had on.

One of the first things she would do, she decided as she went to the kitchen to tell Tilly where she was going, was to buy herself a decent pair of sensible shoes and a handbag and wallet.

Tilly was horrified that Jan wanted to walk.

"That mall is at least a mile away, dear. Maybe farther. If you'll wait a half hour Jense will be here. He'll take you. Or you can call a cab."

"A mile isn't far, Tilly," Jan protested, thinking of the miles she'd walked every day back on the mountain in Maine. "And it's all practically flat. It's no walk at all."

Tilly came to the door and watched her all the way to the gates at the end of the curving drive. She was still shaking her head when Jan turned to wave good-bye to her.

CHAPTER TEN

JAN ENJOYED THE WALK to the shopping mall. She took one wrong turn, but a quick word with a woman passing by set her straight. Wandering from store to store at a leisurely pace, she inspected the offerings in the windows for the sort of thing she was sure would suit her.

The mall was full of shoppers, cars moving smoothly in and out of parking spaces. Drivers were really quite considerate of each other, she decided, wondering if she had the ability to control an automobile herself.

I'll have to ask Tom, she decided as she came upon a lovely looking shop with windows displaying some fantastic fashions. Deciding she had procrastinated long enough, she went in. The assistant who greeted her took an instant liking to the long-legged young woman with hair the color of burnt gold. If she found anything incongruous about the slim-figured customer clad in rough jeans and a man's white shirt, she did not let it show.

Within a short time Jan found herself dressed in the most becoming suit she had ever dreamed of. A butter-soft ultrasuede, it was the color of crushed raspberries, with an enchanting silk blouse and a short jacket. The skirt fit closely to her hips then flared gently around her legs. Feeling pleased with the stunning suit, Jan went all the way and indulged in a smart shirtwaister with a charming mandarin collar. The dress was of a silky material, the background a geometric print that matched the color of the suit. It was easy for the saleswoman to persuade Jan she must have a handbag and a silk scarf to match her purchases.

And then there were her boots.

She turned in front of the mirror. "What on earth would you advise?" she asked the attractive young woman helping her.

"Go next door and buy some sandals," was the quick reply. "And then take yourself over to the Hair Place and see Michael. You have beautiful hair. He can style it and you'll look like a million dollars. Shall I give him a call and see if he can take you?"

"Why not? How much will the shoes be, do you think? I didn't dream I would spend so much money and I only have about a hundred and a half left."

"That should more than cover it. Don't you have credit cards?"

"Afraid not. What are they?" Jan laughed at the woman's astonished expression. "I've spent my whole life on a mountain in Maine. We had no need for such things."

"Oh, you're the one who rescued Tom Farrell. Your father broke his leg and Jason Farrell was there!" The young woman smiled at her in recognition. "Lucky you! Isn't he fabulous? Did you fall in love with him? I saw him once and that's what happened to me. Flat out, no contest. He's so handsome!"

Jan experienced a twinge of pain at the mention of Jason's name. In love with Jason! That would really be living dangerously.

"Mr. Farrell is a very interesting man," she ventured, caution signals going off in her head.

"You're something of a celebrity, you know," the saleswoman told her. "I remember your picture now. You and Jason were bringing your father in for treatment, I believe. The papers picked up a picture of you and him. It was an absolutely stunning photo of the both of you. Did you know?"

"No, I didn't. Are papers allowed to do that?"

"Sure, if it's news, and you'd better believe anything Jason and his son do is just that. Jason travels in the jet set a lot. Some of the women he has his picture taken with are stunning. I wondered why all three of the papers ran the same picture. They usually try to outdo each other with their shots."

Jan remembered Jason's crisp dismissal of the reporters at the airport as they watched the medics' swift transfer of her father from the plane to the waiting ambulance.

"Mr. Farrell was responsible, I expect. He was rather short with them."

"Your father died, didn't he? I heard that on the news, too. I'm so sorry. He was a real hero, wasn't he, saving Tom the way he did."

"I think perhaps he was. I was very proud of him."

"Let me make that call to Michael, then I'll take

you around to the shoe shop and show you where
The Hair Place is.''

The thought of her father saddened Jan, and she
waited quietly while the woman made the phone call.
When she came back she was all smiles. Michael, she
said, had just received a cancellation from one of his
regular customers and could take her in half an hour,
which would give her plenty of time to shop for appropriate footwear.

Jan came out of the beauty shop into the early
dusk, her hair reshaped into a sleek fall which fluffed
around her face attractively. Michael had shown her
how to care for it, singing praises to the silken quality
of her hair as he cut and shaped it.

Jan knew she had never looked better in her life.

It never occurred to her, as she trekked blithely out
of the confusing shopping complex, that she was
striking, breathtaking, in the lovely suit and high-
heeled sandals. She swung along, her graceful stride
catching the attention of more than one man as she
walked by, her packages swinging. It was great to be
alive, and the day was wonderful. She was happier
than she had been since Lewis died.

The streetlights came on as Jan walked. It was then
she realized she wasn't quite sure of her direction.
The street was vaguely familiar, but she supposed
that could be because of the tour Tom had given her
the day before.

Stopping, she looked around to get her bearings
and knew she was lost. Just ahead of her was a fast-
food establishment. A car and a pickup truck were
parked outside. As she walked toward them she re-

membered she didn't know the name of the street Tom lived on. Nor did she know the name of the town, for that matter, although she assumed she must still be in Palo Alto.

The two men leaning against the door panel of the pickup watched her approach. Jan returned their friendly smiles.

"I'm lost," she told them. "I wonder if either of you know the place I'm looking for?"

"Don't know, ma'am, but we'd sure like to help you." The taller of the two pushed himself upright and stared at her with interest. Close to six feet, he was well built and moderately attractive, dressed in a dark blue T-shirt and jeans tucked into cowboy boots. "I'm Bob Jones and this is my buddy, John Smith. Where do you need to go?"

"I'm staying at the Farrell house," Jan felt a surge of relief at the stranger's willingness to help. "Do you know it by any chance?"

"Old man Farrell's place? Shore do, little lady." He opened the door of the pickup and reached for her packages. "I live on past the Farrell place. Hop in and I'll take you home."

Jan moved, sidestepping the long arm. "That's kind of you, but I can get there if you'll be so kind as to point me in the right direction. . . ."

"Wouldn't think of letting you walk, miss. Tom and I went to school together. He'll have my head if I let you walk, a guest of his. It's getting dark, don'cha know. Pretty things like you shouldn't be walking alone in the dark. Isn't that right, Johnny?"

"That's true," the man named John agreed. "Better let Bob run you home, ma'am. Tom sure won't like it, you being so far from the house and it getting so late and all."

"You both know Tom?" Jan, accustomed to the easy hospitality of the few neighbors she knew in the Allagash, didn't think twice about trusting these two. After all, they were acquainted with Tom, were schoolmates of his. It didn't occur to her to question their words. "Well, if you're positive I won't be taking you out of your way."

"Not a chance, pretty lady. Hop in and I'll run you over to old Tom's."

"Thanks." Jan climbed into the truck and held her packages on her lap. "It's very kind of you," she added as the man called Bob swung himself lithely through the door. He slammed it and reached for the ignition key.

Bob dropped his arm along the back of the bench seat as he turned to stare out the back window. He backed the truck out. Jan heard the other car start up. Then the man beside her straightened the pickup and started down the street toward the mall.

"You look older than Tom," Jan remarked casually, her attention caught by the headlights reflected in the long side-view mirror. "Were you in the same classes in school?"

"Hardly." He hadn't removed his arm from the back of the seat. "Tom's younger'n me. Three or four years, I reckon. I was held back, so's to speak. And he speeded up. We weren't never in the same classes."

"I see." His hand crept to her shoulder and Jan picked it up, ducking under his arm and sliding over into the corner of the seat.

"Don't like me touching you, huh, baby? Why not? Doesn't Tommy touch you?"

"I'm sorry." Jan was beginning to realize she had made a mistake. Whenever was she going to learn? "Please stop the truck and let me out. I recognize this part of the shopping mall. I can find my way from here."

"I wouldn't think of it, little lady."

Suddenly Jan knew she was in trouble. Her father had always warned her about New York, never allowing her to be alone on the streets there. He'd always seemed much too concerned. She had never been accosted in any way. The need for caution had escaped her there, and it hadn't occurred to her that she might find herself in a dangerous situation in this area, but her senses were alerted now.

"Stop this vehicle at once! I want to get out."

"Darn! An' here old Johnny an' I thought we'd show you a real good time—"

"The car following us is your friend's, I take it?" Jan interrupted him, her voice icy.

"Noticed, did you? Sharp as well as pretty, eh? Well, we just thought we'd go by my place, see? Have a party, you know? Drink a little beer, have a bit of fun."

He leered at her in the soft light reflected into the truck's cab.

Jan squelched her feeling of panic, realizing this was no time to lose her presence of mind. Bob, if that really was his name, wheeled the small truck out of the shopping complex and made a right turn. They were on the wide street Tom Farrell's house was situated on. Jan recognized the shrubs growing down the center divider. The Farrell house was about a half mile ahead, she thought.

Turning her head, she took in the complacent expression on the driver's features and felt her tension mount. With only herself to blame for her predicament, Jan knew she would have to handle the situation on her own. Adrenaline shot through her system as she stared at the man's profile, her thoughts clear.

"Stop at once and let me out."

A raucous laugh greeted her command.

Jan allowed her packages to slip to the floor and folded her hands together, clenching them into a tight double fist. "I want out of this truck and I want out now."

"Not a chance, lady. We've always sort of envied ol' Tom, see? How can you ask us to give up a chance to share a bit of his goodies? He has so many. Now you look to be a little of the best. It ain't right we should pass up such a fine chance to share ol' Tom's wealth, seems to me. Just sit tight. We don't aim to hurt you. Just want you to get to know you can have a good time on our side of the tracks, too. Tom ain't the only man you can enjoy, you know."

The Farrell gates were just ahead. Jan wasted no time.

"Look here!" she yelled.

Startled, the man swiveled his head and Jan

chopped at his nose with her clenched fists. He howled, his hands flying to his face, and Jan clipped him again, behind his ear this time.

The pickup veered wildly and flew across the road, plowing into the hedge of shrubs. The man wrenched the wheel, blood flowing from his nose. The truck swerved on its spinning tires and did an about-face, coming to a halt before the flashing red and blue lights of the police car that had roared up behind it. Jan was on the ground, her carrier bags and purse gripped in her hands, before the incredulous officer reached the truck. The wild ride had shaken her.

"What the hell is going on here?" the officer demanded.

"I'm not really sure." Jan forced a calmness she didn't feel into the words. "The man who was driving needs help, I think." Bracing herself, she waited for the man she had injured to accuse her.

He just moaned and clutched his face.

"Get out of there, buddy, and let's have a look at you."

Her accoster climbed out of the cab with considerable reluctance.

"Oh, it's you is it, Hever. Thought I warned you about staying out of trouble?"

Jan gave the driver a quick look, realizing she'd been right. His name wasn't Jones. He'd never gone to school or anywhere else with Tom, either, she was willing to bet. A child would have known enough not to accept a ride from a man like that, she thought.

"I ain't doing nothing, Gary. I just was helping

this little lady home. She was lost...." His voice was muffled in the dirty rag he was holding to his nose. He stared at Jan in mute appeal.

"That so, miss?" It was plain to see that the officer didn't believe a word Hever said.

Jan took a quick glance at the road. The street was empty, the car that had been following them had gone.

"He did say he knew where the Farrell house was when I asked about it," she said, her tone neutral. "He said he'd take me there. I was lost."

"It's just over the way," the officer tilted his head toward the gates. "You sure that's all there was to it, miss?"

The memory of television cameras crowding around her, reporters shouting questions, rose in her mind and she made an immediate decision. "Yes," she stated firmly. "This unfortunate man was a victim of a sudden nosebleed just as we were approaching the gates. I can't imagine what happened, but he cried out and then lost control apparently...." She let the explanation trail off.

"I see. Are you hurt?"

"No, I'm not. If you don't need me, officer, I'll go up to the house. It was a harrowing experience. I need to get over my fright."

"You're staying with the Farrells?"

Jan told him she was and gave him her name. Her would-be assailant seemed glad enough to let her go without a word, she noted with a grim amusement.

Never, never, never do a foolish thing like that again, she warned herself as she walked up the curving gravel drive.

Prudently, she decided not to mention anything to Tom Farrell.

Tilly was horrified to find blood spots spattered on the left sleeve of the ultrasuede jacket. She took it to the kitchen at once, dabbing it clean with cold water and demanding an explanation of how such a thing could happen.

"Nosebleed," Jan told her.

Fortunately Tilly assumed it was Jan's nosebleed and asked no more questions, cleaning the garment with a swift efficiency.

The two of them were eating a delicious snack of chocolate cake and drinking tea when Tom came home. He had three of his classmates with him, and they were staying for the night.

Laughter echoed through the old house as Jan and Tilly held their own against the crowd of young men, but when Jan finally went to bed she found it difficult to sleep.

The next morning she went to breakfast to find Tom and his visitors gone. Restless, she spent a profitable day revising and checking her manuscripts, getting them in tip-top shape.

That afternoon she sat out on the grounds behind the spreading old mansion and sketched, taking time to talk to Jense about the care that went into keeping the place in first-class condition.

Tom came home full of good news. He had contacted his father's friend, the author, who had given Tom his own agent's name. Andy George, the agent, wanted to see her manuscripts the following afternoon at four.

"Everything's working out great, you'll see! Andy is going to like your stuff and if he does, he'll sell it. I told you things were on target!" He grabbed her and hugged her.

Caught up in his enthusiasm, she forgot to ask Tom whether he had told his father's friend not to mention her name to Jason if they happened to be in touch.

"You're going to make lots of money, Jan," Tom assured her. "I know it."

"Tell me more about Mr. George," Jan asked.

"Andy wants to see a few samples of your work. He'll look them over, let you know if he likes them. He mentioned a publisher who's beating the bushes trying to find some decent children's stories that are different. Yours are different and they're good. You've got it made, babe. Just stick by me and I'll have you in the front line yet."

The next afternoon they took six of Jan's finished manuscripts to Andy George. He looked them over and his evaluation made Jan feel optimistic about her future as an author. She signed the contract he offered her and left his tidy office feeling better than she had for some time.

It was hard to get to sleep that night, but at least it wasn't disturbing thoughts of Jason that kept her awake.

JAN FELL into the relaxing rhythm of the Farrell household. Toward the end of her first week she began swimming before breakfast. The air was crisp, but hardly more so than most summer days back home. The water in the Olympic-size pool was heated, though, and was considerably warmer than the lake in which she had learned to swim.

She watched the news on television as she ate breakfast, sometimes watching a game show or a drama in the evenings if Tom didn't return until late.

Tom was engrossed in his studies, she realized as the week went on. He wasn't content with a surface understanding of the subjects that interested him. He dug in and explored each one with dedication.

His photography was a fine example of this character trait, she thought. He had a darkroom and did his own developing and enlarging. Shots he had taken were displayed around the house. They showed a sensitivity and depth of perspective well beyond his years. He was an artist with a camera.

On the weekend he decided to teach her to drive. They covered miles of the flat Salinas Valley, California's salad bowl, both days returning to the house in the late afternoon.

Sunday night, Jeff Allen, one of Tom's older friends, brought a pamphlet of driving rules to her. Issued by the state's motor-vehicle department, it contained all the laws of the road she needed to know to obtain a license to drive. Jan promised to study it.

When he returned the next evening she fended off his attempts to stump her about some of the more obscure rules. Jan knew them all. The night before, she had taken the pamphlet to bed with her, studying it, using it to hold thoughts of Jason at bay.

Jeff finally gave up, shutting the booklet with a satisfied smile. "You can take your test next week. I don't think they'll stump you at all. But I'll bring some sample test sheets over so you'll know what you're up against."

"Thanks, Jeff. Aren't you all out of school next week for Thanksgiving?"

"Yeah. We have the week off. Don't know what we're gonna do yet."

There had been some talk of going to a ski lodge in the High Sierras. Jan was interested. She'd skied, of course. Skis and snowshoes were often the only means of transportation during winter in the Allagash region. Skiing on slopes designed for the sole purpose of having fun was different, however. She hadn't done that and she found the idea intriguing.

"If Jeff's father gets back in time we'll borrow his plane and Jeff will fly us into Reno. We can either fly to Tahoe from there, or if the weather is bad we'll rent a car and drive. Susie James has a lodge up there."

"Who is Susie James?" Jan asked.

"A girl I know." Tom flushed a little as he looked at her, his lashes lowered.

Jan met that glance and felt her heart lurch. How he resembled his father. Immediately she pushed the thought away and gave him a questioning smile.

"She's a girl I met last summer. She invited us up this winter."

"Oh. I thought you spent the summer in Maine."

"I did. That's where we met her, wasn't it, Jeff?"

So both Susie and Jeff had shared his vacation. In Maine? Remembering Jason's concern about his son's summer activities, Jan looked at Tom with new interest.

A secretive expression crept into his dark gray eyes and he grinned at her, his disarming smile a challenge. Jan refused to take it. After all, his behavior was his father's affair, not hers.

Her sleep was disturbed again that night, Jason's gray eyes staring at her, accusing her. When she awoke she was restless, her mind racing. Unable to relax, she dressed and reached for her sketching materials.

Immobile for long minutes, a lovely creature frozen in the soft light of the lamp, she stared at the block of paper before her. Then the charcoal she held began to move as if of its own volition. Once started, her fingers flew.

A long time later she finished and dropped the charcoal on the thick rug underfoot. She stared at the portrait in her hands.

It was Jason.

His strong face laughed up at her, wonderful, warm, compelling.

Shocked, she studied the drawing. Where had it originated? When had this impression of him entered her consciousness? The man she had drawn was loving, a compassionate creature with humor and sadness in the virile lines of his handsome face. He was gentle, passionate, sensual. How could she have drawn him this way?

She put the pad of paper aside, unable to believe the story the portrait was telling her. Until the sky lightened and she could go downstairs without arousing anyone's curiosity, she stood and stared out over the dark grounds.

Jason wasn't like that. She knew it. He was a businessman, cold, calculating, even ruthless, she suspected.

Loving? Compassionate? He couldn't be. No man who was would have abandoned a small son to his housekeeper for months of the year. Her subconscious longing was responsible for the loving, wonderful image she had created.

There was no question that Jason was concerned about his son's activities now. Jan was fond of Tom, but his conversation that evening had shaken her. What if he did have some of the tendencies his father was worried about? She didn't want to believe Jason might be right, but Tom's brief discussion of Susie James, the sidelong, almost sly glance at Jeff had worried her.

The best thing for her to do was to finish work on her new story, then get on with her own life, a life far away from the disturbing Farrell men.

CHAPTER ELEVEN

JAN STARED at the jangling phone. She had been in the living room with Tom. He was intent on his books and she was sketching. Needing a harder pencil to finish the drawing, she had run upstairs to fetch one. As she crossed the gracious entry on her way back, the phone pealed.

Reluctant to answer it, she transferred her glance from the phone to the living-room door. Tom's books and notebooks were scattered over the polished coffee table, his work spilling onto the rug between the table and the welcome fire crackling away in the huge stone fireplace. Tom wasn't in the room.

The phone rang again and Tom's voice drifted down the hallway. "Answer it, will you, Jan? It's probably Jeff. He wants to take you for your driving test Friday. He's through with his finals in the morning. I'm not."

"Okay." Jan reached for the receiver. "Hi, Jeff. I'm ready and willing—"

"I beg your pardon?"

Jan's fingers stiffened and she almost dropped the phone as Jason's puzzled question registered, rendering her speechless. "I didn't understand...hello? Who is this please? I want the Farrell residence."

"I—y-you have it."

"Who are you? I'm Tom's father. Jan, is that you?"

Wild-eyed, Jan snatched the receiver away from her ear, reacting as if she'd been stung.

Tom approached from the library, a reference book in his hand. He took the phone she thrust at him.

"What's wrong? You look like you've just seen a ghost."

Jan shook her head and fled into the living room, not trusting herself to say a word. She huddled in the corner of the comfortable sofa, trembling, her blood thundering in her ears.

"Just a girl from school," she heard Tom say. "Yeah...she's one of Jeff's friends. He had to go get a book he forgot. Yeah...he'll be back to pick her up.... I don't have time for that. I'm studying for finals, you know...yeah, yeah, sure.... Dad, you're out of your ever-loving mind. I already told you I went back to that cabin to thank the Jordan girl for all the effort to save my life.... Yeah, well, who can say where she has gone. I'm sorry Jeff's girl friend sounds like Jan. She sure doesn't look like her.... No, sorry. I can't come east for Thanksgiving. I've already made plans to go to Tahoe. Yeah, skiing. How about Christmas? Okay...hang in there. Bye."

He came storming back into the room. His eyes hot with anger, he flopped down on the sofa, arms folded. Jan sat in her corner, her fingers tightly laced, vibrating with her heartbeat.

"I'll have to leave here, Tom. Will you lend me some money?"

"Leave? Why do you want to leave? Don't be dumb!" He was angry and incredulous.

"Jason knows I'm here. I can't stay now."

"That's ridiculous! He doesn't know anything of the kind! You heard me. I told him you were just one of the girls who are always hanging around...."

"You don't really think he believed you, do you?"

"Yes I do, damn it! I never lie to him. I haven't since I was about six and he knows it. That's what makes it so bad. He hates a liar so much...because of my mother, I think. She was a constitutional liar, unable to tell the difference between the truth and a falsehood, according to my grandfather. I made up my mind a long time ago not to be like her. But I guess I am like my mother, hard as I try not to be."

He looked miserable, but Jan wasn't able to comfort him. All she could think of was that Jason knew she was here. She felt it in her bones.

"You aren't a liar, Tom. I—I'm awfully sorry I've caused trouble between you and your father. I n-never should have come here with you. It—it's my fault." Tears stinging her eyes, she jumped up.

Tom leaped to his feet in response and wrapped his arms around her.

"Don't cry, Jan. I'm not blaming you. You haven't done a thing. It's just that I get so mad at Jason sometimes. He loves me but he's like a mother hen—wants to protect me from myself all the time. He's never sure about me because he thinks I'm a chip off the old block and it scares the very devil out of him. He thinks I'm going to be as stupid as he was and run away with the first woman who bats an eye at me. Little does he know!''

His voice had such smug complacency in it that it caught Jan's attention, in spite of her own upset. Was he bragging in that hidden way of his? He met her glance with artless openness and she wasn't sure of anything.

"You're wrong, you know. Jason recognized my voice. I'm sure he did. He knows I'm here, Tom. I'll have to find somewhere else to stay. I don't want him to find me here, living in your house." *Living with you!* That is how Jason would see it. "He accused me once of spending the summer with you in the Allagash, you know.''

"What!'' Tom stared at her in utter disbelief. "You must be joking!''

"'Fraid not. That's why I don't like him.''

"I see!'' Tom nodded and let her go, his expression clearing. "So that's what's wrong between the two of you.''

"That's it.'' Jan knelt beside the couch and began gathering up her materials and her manuscript. "Now you can see why I can't risk having him find me here, can't you? Will you lend me some money until I receive an advance? I must go.''

"Maybe not. At least not until after Thanksgiving. Dad's busy in the East. He won't be out. That's why he called me.... Tell you what. Friday's the last day of school. Then we're going to fly to Reno and go to Tahoe for the week. You stick around and go with Jeff to get your driver's license Friday, then we'll all go skiing. When we get back, Jeff and I will find you an apartment. Please think about it, Jan. Don't say no." Tom knelt beside her and took her things away, putting them on the coffee table so he could catch her hands in his. "Please, Jan?"

"I don't want your father to find me here. You can see why, can't you?"

"Yes, but he won't, Jan. Even if he were thinking of coming—and I give you my word he isn't—he wouldn't now. I told him I'm not going to be here. Say you'll do this for me, Jan."

"I—I'm not sure I should...."

"Aw, c'mon, Jan. You won't regret it, and dad will never know. I promise you." He raised the fingers he held captive and kissed them.

He looked so young, so vulnerable. And so like Jason. Jan pulled away, uneasy in his embrace. Calmer now, she sat on her heels and looked at Jason's son.

"Why is your father so afraid you'll be like him, Tom? You aren't at all as far as I can see. Except you do look and sound like him, of course. That's natural, I guess."

He shot her a troubled glance and went to his scattered books, kneeling to pick them up. "Dad's a—a rogue, I guess you could say. He's afraid I'll follow in his footsteps as he did in his father's."

"How is that?" She was unable to stop the question. There was danger in becoming better acquainted with the background of the man who fascinated her so, but she wasn't able to resist the temptation to probe. "Why do you refer to him as a rogue?"

"I don't know," Tom replied. "Maybe that's not fair. I heard granddad described like that once by one of the women he'd just dumped. I was about ten at the time and it stuck in my mind. I've always thought dad had exactly the same attitude toward the other sex as my grandfather. He's had reason enough."

"And he thinks you are wild?"

"He doesn't want me to end up like him or his father. Granddad was a chaser. It killed my grandmother, so the story goes." He stacked his books and notebooks in a neat pile. "Dad is doing his darnedest to keep me from following them both, you see. He was only little, four or five at the most, when his mother died. Grandpa never married again, but he paid a lot of attention to his women and very little to his son, according to my great-aunts. They are all gone now. While they were alive they filled me in, book and verse, on the antics of dad and his father. When dad was sixteen he ducked school and ran away with my mother. She was ten years older than he...and not possessed of an exemplary reputation, according to grandpa and my great-aunts. Created quite a scandal, Jason did."

Pity stirred in Jan. For the first time she began to see the reason behind Jason's obsessive efforts to keep his son free of the kind of entanglements that had shaped his life and turned him into a misogynist.

"Was your mother a—a bad woman, Tom?"

"I'll never know." He ran his hands down the stack of textbooks. "I was only two weeks old when dad came back home with me. He refuses to talk to me about her in any way. My birth certificate says I was born in Los Angeles. My mother's name is on it but I have no idea where she was from. I look exactly like my father, of course, as he looked like his. Since I have a brain or two, I have to assume she had reasonable intelligence, although I suppose I could have inherited it all from dad. He's probably the smartest man I've ever met.''

He stood with the lithe grace so like his father's and gave her a crooked smile. ''Want to have some cocoa before we go to bed?''

Recognizing his need to lighten the mood, Jan put her own feelings on temporary hold and went out to the kitchen with him. As he rummaged around in the refrigerator looking for the milk, she put a couple of pottery mugs on the table and looked for the cookies Tilly kept on hand.

''Was your mother in the habit of lying to your father, or do you know?'' Jan watched Tom's face as she asked the question.

Stirring the chocolate powder into the milk he had measured out, Tom looked moody. ''Sure she was, according to my relatives. She lied about her age, lied about loving him, lied about wanting me. He was awfully young. He needed to belong to someone as much as he needed someone to love, I think. It was probably because he was so young that she hurt him so much. His father disinherited him, of course. When she found out he wasn't rich anymore, it didn't take her long to let him know the only reason she'd bothered to marry him. I guess dad stuck with her like glue until she had me. He was scared she'd have an abortion if he didn't prevent it. She didn't want me. Thank God he did.''

"What did they do for money?" In spite of her desire to remain detached, Jan had a clear picture of the young boy who had wanted love so desperately he had pursued the first person offering him anything approaching it.

"Dad had a considerable inheritance from his mother, which came to him when she died. His father managed it, of course, but Jason was able to get his hands on a fair piece of change when he decided to elope. I've a notion my mother would never have considered going with him if she hadn't known about the money.''

He gave her an odd little glance. "Something one of my great-aunts let slip when I was a kid gave me the idea my mother really wanted to marry granddad. He had big bucks but he wasn't interested, so she took Jason and ran, according to what Greataunt Amanda said. I never had the chance to find out for sure. Both granddad and my aunt were gone by the time I was old enough to question them without getting punished." Putting the empty pan into the sink, he filled it with warm water. "Anyway—" he grinned and sat down "—dad, his money and the woman all disappeared. When the money was gone, he reappeared—with me.''

Jan stirred her cocoa, her eyes on the swirling liquid. She warned herself it wasn't safe to feel sorry for Jason Farrell.

"Tilly took care of me, and dad went back to

school. Granddad never let Jase forget what a sap he'd been. Dad stuck it out till I was thirteen. He'd already made a bundle by then. He got out... went east.''

"And left you here? How could he? Weren't you unhappy?''

"He didn't want to interrupt my schooling. I missed him. Of course I did. But he didn't neglect me. I spent all my spare time with him. He's the guy who taught me to fish. I learned to snorkle and skin-dive from him. We're always sailing and surfing together. He's teaching me to fly. I'm not ready to apply for a license yet. I will be when Jase is through with me. He always insists on checking me out himself and he's tough, but I don't mind. He's a great teacher and he's fair. Dad taught me to ski and we still go somewhere together a couple of weeks every year. He's a good father, Jan.''

"Why did he decide to go east? Did he quarrel with his father?''

"They always quarreled. It wasn't all Jase's fault. Granddad was a tough one. He died when I was fifteen. I couldn't change schools then because I was ready to go to university at the end of that year. I was pretty young. Dad thought I should stay here where my friends were.... Dad and I are close. Closer than a lot of guys and their fathers.''

"Why did you lie to him tonight, then?''

"I don't want him grabbing the first flight west. I know how you feel about him. I won't have him bothering you.''

"He has a right—''

"Not in this case," he interrupted her protest. "You saved my life and you need a little care yourself now. Dad might agree with that, but he wouldn't like it if he knew you were living in the house with me." He looked at her wryly. "He hoots at the idea of a platonic friendship, you know."

"Well, I like being your friend, Tom."

"I'd like to be more, Jan. You think of me like a brother or something. I want you to love me."

"Oh, Tom!" Jan protested. "I do love you. You know I do. You're the dearest sweetest creature!"

"Yeah. I know. And I know when I'm licked." He stood, catching her shoulders in gentle hands as she rose with him. "Let's clean up our mess and stay out of trouble with Tilly, shall we?"

The next two days Jan felt as if she were walking on eggs. Her work didn't go well. Unable to concentrate, she flinched every time the phone rang. Jason was coming. She was sure of it.

Tom laughed at her fears and advised her to concentrate on learning the driving code. By the time Jeff came to take her in for her driving test she was a bundle of nerves, but she went through the motions like a well-programmed robot and passed the test with ease. The written test was no problem, either. She emerged from the building, temporary license in hand. The permanent one, complete with her picture, would be mailed to her.

In spite of her fears, Jason wasn't at the house when she and Jeff returned. Could it be that her instincts were failing her?

Convincing herself that this was so, she went out

that night with Tom and his friends to celebrate their week of freedom ahead.

They went to a popular jazz club where the clientele was mostly university students. During one of the musicians' breaks Jeff turned to address Tom.

"My old man isn't going to get back with the plane until late tomorrow," he said. "We won't be able to head for Reno until Sunday. The plane will have to be serviced before we go. When did you tell Susie to expect us at Tahoe?"

"Not till she saw us."

"That's all right, then."

"Which reminds me—" Tom turned to Jan "—you've got to have some skiing gear. Let's go to San Francisco tomorrow. You can get something there."

"It'll cost the earth."

"Not as much as it would in Tahoe. Don't worry about money. I'll add it to your tab."

"You're going to own my soul, Tom Farrell."

"I know." That endearing leer of his appeared. "Part of my master plan, my dear girl."

The thought of spending the day away from the house was a welcome one. Anything to relieve the strain of expecting Jason to pop out of the woodwork any second! "Okay. At the risk of permanently mortgaging my future, I would like to go."

The next morning Jan dressed in the ultrasuede suit. The cashmere sweater Jason had given her was perfect with it. Unable to resist the temptation, she'd put on the scarf he'd given her, tying the emerald silk under the roll of the soft collar. She touched her lips with lipstick and brushed her shining hair, feathering it around her face before she went downstairs.

Tom gallantly bowed her into her chair in the kitchen.

"I have a slight expansion in our plans," he announced with sunny good humor. "That is, if you don't mind."

"What is it?"

"I had a call last night from our old neighbors. They want me to meet their daughter at the airport and take her to her hotel. It's on the way. Is that all right? I told them I would."

"Certainly. Old neighbors?"

"They lived next door for years. Nancy and I grew up together. At least, we were bosom buddies until her parents moved east." He grinned, a faraway look in his eyes. "We were about ten, then. I was sorry to lose her. We studied anatomy together."

"You what?"

"Anatomy. At least, introductory anatomy. I've defined the concepts and extended my knowledge since then, of course."

"Whatever are you talking about, Tom?" Jan asked.

He laughed, mischief dancing on his face. "Look way over in the corner there. See that bunch of trees?" He pointed with his cereal spoon. Jan nodded. "You can't see it from here, but there's a perfect tree house up in there. That's where Nancy and I played doctor and nurse. I was always the doctor. Sometimes I could talk Nancy into being a patient instead of a nurse."

Jan laughed in spite of herself. "Introductory anatomy! I *see*. No wonder they took her to the East Coast. Doctor indeed!"

"It wasn't as bad as it sounds, Jan. Didn't you ever play similar games with friends when you were young?"

"I had a friend for a few years," Jan told him. "He came with his folks to that old cabin you saw on the lake. But the most we ever got up to was playing Tom Sawyer."

Tom clicked his tongue at her and tried to assume a doleful countenance. "A waste of time, in my opinion."

"If such a thought even entered Teddy's mind, he kept it a careful secret." Jan laughed. "Have you seen Nancy since those days?"

"Oh, sure. I always go to see the Stones' when I'm in New York. Nancy grew up to be a real beauty. You'll see! She goes to Harvard. She's going to Honolulu for Thanksgiving, but she'll be in San Francisco for a couple of days. Maybe she'll join us and we can do something together after we pick her up."

Nancy Stone proved to be the prettiest redhead one could imagine. She was petite, barely reaching Jan's shoulder. Her lovely face had a sprinkle of golden freckles, and her flaming hair exhibited a natural curl that defied any efforts to confine it. She charged into the lounge, filling the area with electricity.

"Tommy!" Throwing her arms around his neck, she met his kiss with an enthusiasm that caused smiles to appear on the faces of people standing nearby. "You're such a dear to meet me. I have two whole days! Let's not waste a minute!"

Jan didn't hear a word as she stared at the man who came into the lounge a few steps behind his son's bubbling friend.

Jason had indeed come home.

CHAPTER TWELVE

"DAD!" TOM GAVE THE YOUNG WOMAN in his arms a final squeeze then put her down and reached for his father's hand.

Jason smiled and Jan was lost.

A surging singing happiness such as she'd never known overwhelmed her, and at the same time she felt scared out of her wits. *I hate him,* she tried to assure herself. *I must!* She knew she was lying to herself as she struggled to ignore the true message her heart was giving her. There was no way the emotion she felt for the commanding individual watching her with such cool amusement had a chance of being identified as hatred. No way at all!

Fighting the tidal flow of emotion threatening to wipe out her remaining good sense, she faced him, her chin lifted.

"You've cut your hair." There was an edge of censure to his words. He reached for her, and before she could react he brushed her mouth with an easy kiss.

Jan felt as if she had touched fire. Jerking away, she felt her face flame.

"This is Nancy, Jan," Tom interposed. "Jan is the angel I found when I fell off a mountain, Nancy. Jan Jordan, Nancy Stone."

Jan put out a hand she was sure must have been trembling and mumbled her pleasure at having a chance to meet Tom's childhood friend. If Nancy noticed Jan's agitation, she was diplomatic enough to ignore it.

"I'm so happy you and Tom were able to meet me." Her cheery disposition was plain in the laughing tone of her voice. "I hear we're going to take a tourist's view of San Francisco today, with one of the handsomest escorts in the world!" She thrust her arm through Jason's. "Two, if we can entice Jason to join us! Help me persuade him, Jan. Let's go collect my luggage and get down to work." Irrepressible, she linked her other arm through Jan's, and Jan found herself hurrying along on the way to the luggage carousel.

What am I to do? Jan despaired. Jason strode along on the other side of Nancy, her arm linked through his. He didn't appear to be in the least put out at being commandeered by the spritely imp between them.

Jan looked straight ahead with rigid determination, trying to still her wild heart. Grinning, Tom loped along beside her, perfectly happy with the situation.

"Will you come with us, Jason? We'll have a blast."

Jan felt like shaking her erstwhile benefactor. Couldn't he see how impossible the whole thing was?

Apparently he couldn't. Jason slanted a look at the stiff profile Jan was presenting.

"Sounds like a winner," he drawled.

Jan could hear the amusement in that deep voice of his. He was teasing her. It was in the laughter under his smooth words. She tossed her head, ignoring him.

"Give me your baggage claim checks, Nancy. Tom will help me collect your bags. No need for you two ladies to get in that crowd."

"Thank you, Jason. There are two of them. I tied pink pom-poms on the handles. You can't miss them." She handed over the slips of cardboard and Tom followed his father through the barrier. Jan watched them, fascinated, unable to help herself.

They stood face to face, talking earnestly, eyes locked. Suddenly Jason reached out a long arm and draped it across his son's back. Tom laughed and punched his father's shoulder. When at last they picked up Nancy's two suitcases, they were still deep in a discussion about something. Two pairs of smoky gray eyes fixed on Jan as they came back to the young women. She knew very well she had figured in the conversation.

The idea destroyed the little equanimity she had left. To her embarrassment she stumbled when she got out of the car at the restaurant the men wanted to try for luncheon. Unaccustomed to high heels, she would have fallen if Jason hadn't steadied her. Still annoyed with herself when they were seated, she extended her hand for her glass of water, longing for a drink. She knocked it over, then proceeded to dump the lacy basket of hot rolls onto the floor in an attempt to right the glass.

Scarlet, she bent to pick up the bread and crashed

into Jason's descending head. Leaping to her feet, she bumped into the chair. Jason caught her, keeping her from embarrassing herself further, and laughed with fiendish delight. Jan didn't know what to do, and ended up giggling like a schoolgirl.

When the diplomatic maître d' whisked them away to a dry table screened by a discreet fan of lacy palms, Jan's green eyes were brilliant with the effort to get control of herself. Jason looked her over, smiled his sympathetic understanding, then proceeded to interrupt Tom and Nancy's nonstop dialogue by asking his son some penetrating questions about his studies.

Tom's witty answers had them all laughing again. Jan relaxed and drew in a deep breath of air, appreciating the respite Jason had provided by diverting attention from her. Smiling, she touched the roll of the cashmere sweater and adjusted the knot of the emerald scarf. When she put her hand on the table between them, Jason covered it with his. Startled, Jan stared straight at him. The smiling look she received was so full of intimacy she felt her color rise again.

She gasped. Was he flirting with her? She rejected the idea with hurried scorn. Nevertheless, a warm glow started somewhere in the far reaches of her being. It burned with a steady heat, which strengthened throughout the rest of the afternoon.

They drove to Fisherman's Wharf after a delightful lunch and spent an hour there and another in Ghirardelli Square. Afterward Jan rode beside Jason in the front seat as he drove Tom's sports car up and down the steep streets. He kept up a constant stream of tour-guide patter as they went.

Jan hung on for dear life as the powerful car shot up what must have been the steepest street in the world. Jason laughed, his gray eyes glowing as he took in her flushed enjoyment. In the cramped confines of the back seat, Nancy squealed with horrified delight and clung to Tom, burying her face in his broad shoulder. He offered no objection as he settled her small frame into his large one.

Jan caught a glimpse of satisfaction on his features in the rearview mirror as she shifted in her own seat, responding to the pull of gravity. Then she spent the next few minutes gazing into the blue sky of this late November day. The heavy sports car crested suddenly and Jan lost her breath entirely as they shot over the top and dipped down the other side.

"Oh! How can people live on streets like this? If anything is dropped it must roll for miles downhill!"

"If you think this is unique," said Tom, "just wait! Take her down Lombard Street, Jason."

Jason shot an amused glance back at his handsome son. "You think she can take it?"

"Hey, Jan's a mountaineer from Maine, remember?"

"Okay. Let's go."

He turned a corner and they went down a series of switchbacks edged on each side with interesting houses.

"Look at this one," Jason challenged her, a hand on her arm.

Shocked by his touch, Jan sat still, staring down a

long series of wide steps that were layered into a steep
hill. There were houses on either side of them, as
well.

"Surely no one can drive down there!"

"You're right." Jason scanned her profile, amusement in his expression. "But it is used as a street at
times. By drunks and the likes."

They drove to a lovely park high above the bay.
Tom and Nancy murmured in the back seat, their
words soft, inaudible. Jan maintained a dignified
silence in front, holding herself in tense readiness,
unsure of the cause of her tension except that it was
the direct effect of sitting so close to Jason.

What on earth was she doing here? More to the
point, what was he doing here?

The air between them grew so charged Jan was
sure she heard it crackle. When he stopped the car,
she scrambled out. She had to break the spell whose
magic threatened her.

Raising her face to the glow of the sun, she shook
her head. Cool fingers of wind blew through the silk
of her hair. Breathing deeply she stood transfixed by
a singing happiness she couldn't suppress. Never
mind why Jason was here with her. The knowledge
that he was, and that he seemed to be determined to
please her, filled her with a joy she was scarcely able
to contain.

Standing there she let her senses absorb her sur-
roundings. Fog lay like a blanket across the distant
hills. As she watched, it rose, a silent soft curtain of
gray, lifting coyly at the edges to drop and lift again.
Finally, through that gray veil, the ghost outline of a

bridge became discernible, the hills and mountains beyond were sensed rather than seen. She was suddenly conscious of the birdsong filling the air, the smell of the sea, the scent of the earth. . . .

And the powerful thrust of the man who came to stand so close, his warmth reaching out to enfold her. Miraculously, as he stopped, the curtain tore, the sun striking through its hanging tatters. The Golden Gate Bridge lay at their feet, spanning the great arm of the bay as it opened to the sea.

"How lovely. . .!" she exclaimed.

Dazed by the force of her feeling, she tilted her head and turned to look at Jason. His own eyes were as soft and smoky as gray velvet. The smile he gave her enticed, intrigued, as his teeth flashed white in the darkness of his face.

They spent the rest of the afternoon driving around the bay, stopping at Cliff House to watch the seals cavort on the wet slippery rocks. And all afternoon Jan was enthralled by Jason, bewitched, hardly aware of the other two people with them.

When at last the sunset flared in scarlet and golden fire behind the fogbank far offshore, Jan felt it was a part of her and she was one with its blazing display.

They made their way to the hotel were Jason said he had reservations for dinner.

To Jan, it seemed impossible that anything could top the wonders she had already experienced that day. She was wrong.

They dined in a room high above the lights of the city. Awed by the place, the view, the day, Jan's

sense of euphoria grew. She gave herself over to en-
chantment.

Jason kept her glass filled with a wine that tasted
like the gods had made it, and overpowered her with
his attention. They danced after dinner, and sometime during the evening Tom and Nancy disappeared.

Jason didn't seem in the least concerned about
their departure as he led Jan to the car, his arm
secure around her waist, her head nestled in his
shoulder. The fog had blanketed the city. It was rolling over the peninsula as Jason guided his son's sleek
automobile down the highway. When he turned into
the curving driveway of his stately home, the thick
mist followed behind.

He parked under the portico of the dark house,
then shut his door and went around to draw Jan out
of the warm nest of the car's bucket seat and into his
arms.

Holding her, he dropped one arm and drew her
slender hips into the strength of his body. Unwilling
to break the magic, Jan leaned against him, her
hands spread across his chest, her face pressed into
it.

Jason laughed then. The sound excited Jan and
she breathed deeply, drawing in the exotic fragrance
of the man, the scent of his body. She raised her
head, and for the second time that day, he kissed
her.

The rush of sweetness Jan felt left her without the
use of her muscles. Collapsing against him, she put
her arms around his neck and drank in the wonder of

his mouth touching hers. His tongue feathered her soft lips and she answered its demand, seeking his deepening kiss.

Jason moved suddenly, sweeping her into his arms as he bounded up the steps. He kicked the door closed behind him and crossed the dark hall without hesitation. The grandfather clock struck ten as he carried her into the living room, closing the door behind them.

Jason let her knees slide from the cradle of his arms as he came to the warm glow of the fireplace. He drew her to him, his mouth seeking the melting sweetness of hers once more. Jan moaned, a low wondering sound. Wrapping her arms around his lean waist, she shifted against him, seeking mindlessly the unknown magic she yearned for.

Unable to control her movements or her reactions, she followed the dictates of her sensitized body, stirred by primitive instincts long neglected. Her flesh suddenly glowed with desire, and she became a living flame in his arms.

Sliding his hand down the arch of her back, Jason cupped the sweet curve of her hips, pulling her firmly into the thrusting strength of his arousal.

Jan gasped, trembling with the force of the fire consuming her, and he laughed against her lips.

"Ah, we're going to be good together, wood-nymph. . . you'll see."

He touched her ear with the tip of his tongue then traced its outline with consummate delicacy.

"What do you mean?" Jan whispered.

"I mean I want to make love to you." His tongue

moved down the column of her slender neck, probing, seeking.

His hands slipped under her sweater and jacket
and were on the tender flesh of her narrow waist, exploring her silken skin, touching, loving.

A tremor rippled through her. Attuned to it, Jason
laughed again. The sound was seductive, thrilling.
The jacket fell from her shoulders and he eased the
sweater over her head, his fingers impatient.

Firelight touched the beauty of her. Jason's groan
was a cry of need, and Jan felt him tremble as he
pulled her to him, sinking to his knees, firelight
touching the hard planes of his face as he buried it in
the softness of her breast. His lips touched the
wonder of her, the communication of his desire ex-
plicit, and Jan felt the heady sweetness of her
womanhood.

Instinctively she twisted to her knees, holding the
demanding lips away, fingers laced in the silk of his
hair. Jason allowed her to escape, his eyes gleaming
in the firelight.

Intuitive, innocent, driven by the exquisite hunger
his touch awakened, Jan rose to her feet with a flow
of grace that deepened the desire in him, turning his
eyes to dark velvet. His smile a gentle curve, he
watched her undress, the magic of the fire gilding her
silken flesh.

"Jan...." The sound tore from him, husky, passionate. She moved but he caught her, burying his
face in her slim waist, his arms locked around the
curve of her buttocks. She collapsed against him, her
longing a fever out of control.

His sigh, deep, seductive, touched her, thrilling, enticing. The small moan that answered him triggered an unexpected response. His hands and body were trembling as he scooped her up and deposited her on the long couch, then tore at his clothing, discarding it in seconds.

He towered above her. "Ah, Jan, sweet Jan." The sigh tore through him, the words husky in a way that enflamed her. "I want you. I must have you."

With her hands she explored him, touching, caressing. A smile formed on her lips as he trembled beneath her fingers. The wonder she was feeling, the power she had over this man who wanted her was heady, delicious.

He roused himself then, and with insistent lips teased her sensitized skin, her slender thighs, her smooth stomach, the sweet roundness of her breasts. Moaning, Jan reached for his head, her fingers tangling in his thick hair. Jason took her hands, kissing the palms, increasing the fire of her longing.

He pulled away then, his face tender as he stared down at her, his knowing eyes acknowledging the flame that burned in her.

In that moment, shyness hit Jan. She withdrew her hands from his, and covered the sweet thrust of her breasts.

"Are you shy with me, Jan?" There was surprise in his husky words.

"I think so." Her answer was reluctant but honest.

"Why should you be?" He sank back on his heels, virile, his physique touched with firelight, perfect in its male beauty. Jan watched him through her thick lashes, unable to breathe.

He was smiling, the creases in his cheeks deep.

"Don't be afraid, little woods sprite." His voice deepened as he sought to reassure her. "I adore you. No one will ever be able to make you unhappy without answering to me. You'll never be alone again, Jan." Gentle hands brushed back her hair and his kiss enchanted her. "Trust me, darling. I know you're alone in the world but you won't be any longer. I'm going to take care of you from now on."

Slipping an arm under her, he pulled her near him. Jan arched against the taut flesh molding his muscular frame. Jason smiled down at her.

"We'll have tonight together, then we'll go back to New York in the morning."

"New York? Why?" Jan leaned back into the couch. What was he talking about?

"I spoke to Tom while we were collecting Nancy's luggage. He told me your situation. I want you, Jan. And I want you to belong to me. We'll go to New York." He reached out a long-fingered hand and touched her throbbing breast. Then his hand moved down, smoothing the curve of her waist, tracing the swell of her hip.

"I'll set you up in a nice flat anywhere you like. And I'll see that you never have to worry about money again. Oh, Jan, let me love you now. I must, I must!"

He sought her mouth, his kiss blazing with passion. Jan stiffened, a warning she didn't understand sounding within her.

"What are you talking about?" Struggling, she tore away from him.

"Come on, Jan! This is no time to talk. I said I'd set you up. Clothes, car, anything. For as long as you want. Come here!" He made no effort to hide his impatience.

"I—are you saying I'll be your mistress?"

His laugh was harsh. "Where did you resurrect *that* Victorian term from? This is the twentieth century, my love."

"You want me to go with you. You're willing to make love to me just so I'll agree to live with you."

She flinched from the truth even as she recognized it. Jason saw her as a threat to Tom. He was willing to use any means to protect his son from her. What had she almost done! How could anyone be so gullible?

Shrugging out of his arms, she twisted away from him, off the couch and reached for her clothing with fumbling hands.

"What are you doing?" Jason's question was impatient, and his arms extended to grasp her.

Jan dodged him and scooped up her shoes. Tears streaked down her cheeks, glistening in the flickering firelight. Without thinking of the consequences, she turned and ran, leaving an astonished Jason staring after her in disbelief.

"Jan!" he commanded as she jerked the door open. "Come back here! I want to talk to you."

As she tore down the dark hall she heard him behind her. Naked, she sped through the unlighted kitchen, then slipped through the back door and out onto the long veranda. She could hear Jason's footsteps pounding up the stairs. She had lost him. Without a sound she moved down the steps and ran into the fog-enshrouded grounds. Shivering with cold and anger, she stopped to dress, her fingers stiff.

An aching unhappiness filtered through her. How could Jason be so cruel? How could he?

CHAPTER THIRTEEN

JAN STUMBLED ALONG ON LEGS that were suddenly unreliable. She couldn't stop crying. What a mess she had made of her life.

It was impossible to consider going back to the house. Even if Jason returned to New York and never appeared again, he had ruined her innocent ease with Tom.

How could he have even suggested that he set her up, to be used at his convenience!

By the time Jan reached the gates, her tears had ceased and anger had taken over. She marched through them, her thoughts bitter. She didn't notice the car parked at the curb, hidden in the heavy fog. Nor did she see the man who moved away from the shelter of the gate pillar.

"Jan!" The shout barely penetrated her consciousness. "Jan! Jan Jordan! Wait! I want to talk to you!"

The sound of her full name brought her to a halt.

She turned and stared at the man through the thick mist. Dazed she didn't recognize him.

"It's me, Jan. Your cousin, Peter." The tall blond man bent and gave her a searching look. "You do remember me, don't you?"

Jan realized immediately that she still didn't like this man. "What do you want?"

"Want? Is that any way to greet me, now that I have found you, little cousin?" He peered at her, a smirk on his bland face. "I've been searching all over for you. Why didn't you get in touch with me so we could make the arrangements."

"Arrangements? What arrangements?"

"Why, the arrangements to restore you to your relatives. We must go to Holland. I told you."

"I'm not going to the Netherlands with you. I didn't say I would. Not ever."

"Be kind to me, little cousin. You need to go to your homeland. There's a fortune waiting for us if we are intelligent and work it right."

"I don't understand." Jan watched him with wary eyes, the same feeling of danger she had experienced once before telling her to be careful of this man.

"Come back to my hotel room with me and I'll explain the whole thing to you."

Jan sidestepped his reaching hand instinctively. He moved his shoulders in an impatient shrug.

"Let's not be coy, Jan. You're coming with me, like it or not. We're going to Holland together. Once I collect what's coming to me, you can do as you please. Now come along."

"What are you talking about?" Jan backed away.

"Trust me, little cousin. Come with me and we'll both be rich, I promise you." His voice was soothing, persuasive. "It will be so easy."

"I want nothing to do with you," she told him.

There was something about the man that set her teeth on edge. ''I don't know what you have in mind, but it has nothing to do with me. My father was English...."

His laugh cut her off. "You don't know anything about it. Just come with me, Jan."

He reached for her and Jan reacted instinctively, turning to flee into the thick fog. She kicked off her slender high-heeled pumps and took off like a deer.

She ran for ages, a stitch in her side almost doubling her over. As she tore around a corner she crashed head-on with a uniformed police officer. They both went down in a tangled heap. The policeman stood up first. He dragged Jan to her feet, his own chest heaving as he tried to recover the breath she'd knocked out of him.

"What's going on here, young lady?" he demanded.

Jan was unable to answer. Switching on his powerful torch, the policeman flicked it over her strained features.

"Catch our thief, Gary?" Another officer appeared in the glare of the flashlight a moment before his partner turned it off.

"I'm not sure. Where did you come from, miss?"

"I—er—I was trying to escape," Jan panted. She stood between the two policemen, trying to get her breath. She didn't know what to say.

"Want to tell us about it?" The officer named Gary asked the question in a neutral tone.

"I—I...." Her lungs weren't responding as she tried to recover both her breath and her wits. Jan staggered, and a firm hand closed on her arm. "Th-thanks. Could I sit down a minute?"

The officer opened the door of the squad car and Jan tumbled in, grateful for the seat.

"Where are your shoes, miss?" Gary's question was sharp and official sounding. Jan shook her head, unable to answer as her chest heaved with the effort of recovering from the fast sprint she'd just completed.

The two looked at each other when she didn't answer.

"Better take her in, Gary. Looks like she's one of them. I'll ask for a backup and carry on here."

"Okay."

The car door closed with a decisive click, and the light went out. It wasn't until the officer called Gary opened the front door on the driver's side that the interior was lighted up again. Then Jan noticed the heavy mesh screen denying her access to the front seat. Realizing it existed to protect policemen from the dangerous suspects they dealt with, Jan felt a rising hysteria.

She had really made a mess of things this time, she told herself. What was she to do now?

Call Jason at the old Victorian house on the hill and ask him to come vouch for her? Impossible.

The policeman drove her to the station and escorted her into a brightly lit room. He told her someone would be in to talk to her in a few minutes, then left.

A short time later another officer strolled into the little room. Jan raised her weary head from the scarred tabletop where she had been resting it and stared across at him as he seated himself. Another man came in and leaned against the wall behind her. He gave her a cool smile when she twisted around to glance at him.

"I'm Officer Johns," the man seated opposite informed her, his voice neutral. "What is your name, young lady?" He didn't bother to introduce the man leaning against the wall.

"Jan Jordan," she replied. There was no way she could be linked to Jason if she gave her own name, she hoped. Would she be able to cooperate with these men and get herself out of this mess without involving Jason? Visions of television cameras and reporters formed in her mind. She had to try to avoid any publicity.

"Do you have any identification, Miss Jordan?"

"No, I'm sorry, I don't."

"Isn't that a bit unusual?"

"I'm not sure. Is it?"

"Even in a police station, we seldom see a beautiful young woman without shoes or any kind of identification," the officer told her in a stern tone. "What happened, Miss Jordan? Why were you running barefoot through that fog? Where do you live?"

"I—I would rather not tell you," she answered hesitantly. "I can assure you I haven't done anything wrong...." *Except to fall in love without using my head,* she thought.

"Did you get confused in the fog and run into Officer Mason when you thought you were running in the opposite direction?"

"I had no idea there was a policeman within a hundred miles. I wasn't trying to avoid him."

"Who were you running from then? As a rule we don't find young women running through the streets at this time of night. You had been crying, hadn't you?"

"Yes, I had!" Jan's answer was crisp. "It isn't really any of your business, you know. I've done nothing at all to interest the police. Please let me go and I won't waste any more of your time."

"Without shoes?" Officer Johns looked at her skeptically. "Without knowing you have a safe place to go to? It's obvious you haven't any money. We have a duty to protect you, you know. Are you going to tell me what happened?"

"Nothing happened." Weariness was beginning to erode Jan's ability to think. "I've done nothing. I just want to go about my own business, please."

Johns stood and jerked his head at the other man. The two of them left the room and Jan put her tired head on the arms she rested on the table. She was asleep in seconds.

A firm hand on her shoulder shook her awake.

"Want to talk to me now, lady?" It was Officer Johns who stood beside her.

Jan raised sleep-dazed eyes. "I—no, I don't."

He gave her a look of pained patience. "I don't know what you are hiding, miss, but I can assure you that it is better for you if you tell me who you are and why you were in that particular neighborhood, running through the streets so late at night."

"What time is it?" Rubbing her tired, dry eyes, Jan turned to gaze at him.

"Almost midnight. Time for decent girls to be home in bed. Tell me about yourself and I'll have an officer run you home, where you should be."

"I can't." The thought of going back to the Farrell house and facing Jason was almost as horrifying as the thought of the hue and cry of the news media if they found out.

"I'm going to have to book you if you don't co-operate." He did seem reluctant, Jan observed. "You look like a decent sort. I'd hate to have to do such a thing to you."

"What do you mean when you say 'book me'?"

"Don't make fun of me, little lady."

Jan gave him a blank look and he came to the re-luctant conclusion she had no knowledge of police procedure.

"You were found in a very sensitive area, you see," he explained. "It has been staked out. There've been several robberies around there. We were there because of a tip we received tonight. Personally, I don't think you are involved in the burglaries, but if you won't tell me why you were running in the dark and won't give me any way to determine your in-nocence, I have to fingerprint you. And I have to de-tain you for prowling and failing to identify yourself. Want to talk?"

"No. I—I can't."

"What are you afraid of? Why don't you want us to know who you are?"

Jan shook her head.

And so Jan Jordan was booked, fingerprinted, photographed and turned over to a matron, who led her into an empty room and ordered her to strip. Embarrassed beyond belief, Jan did as she was told without a word. When she was allowed to dress, the short woman in the severe black uniform led her down a long echoing corridor.

"Phone's over there in that cell," she was told. "You can make a local call before I lock you up."

Jan stopped. Tom might be home by now, but what if Jason answered the phone? With her luck, he would do just that.

"I need to think first," she told the impassive matron. "May I still make it later if I decide to?"

"Perhaps. Come along."

Jan found herself in the holding tank of the area. It was occupied by three rather tough-looking women who were unjustly accused of prostitution, according to one of them, and an old woman in tattered clothes who had been arrested for panhandling.

Jan spent the next few hours sitting on a bed, wide awake. At last the matron came and opened the barred doors to order her out. Exhausted, Jan followed the matron back down the hallway in the direction she had come from before.

"In here." A door was opened and Jan found herself in a large open area in the entrance of the police station.

Tom Farrell, bewilderment on his handsome face, caught her up in a fierce hug. "Jan, honey! What on earth are you doing here? What happened? Dad is out running around like crazy, looking for you! How did you wind up in the slammer?"

For the second time that night Jan broke into tears. Unable to speak, she clung to him, sobbing. Officer Johns leaned toward them over a long counter.

"I've a few unkind words to say to you, Miss Jordan," he told her, his admonition severe and blunt. He proceeded to point out book and verse to her concerning her irresponsible behavior. "With your attitude, I've every reason in the world to send you to court, young lady. But I won't this time. You can count yourself lucky Farrell is willing to vouch for you. I'm not going to press charges. Go on home and make sure nothing like this ever happens to you again, do you hear?"

"Yes," Jan replied, "and thank you."

Tom took her hand and hurried her out of the place. "How did you find out where I was?" she asked as he helped her into his sleek sports car. "I—I didn't dare call you."

"Why not? Dad's out of his mind with worry. And I've spent a few bad moments myself. What made you run out the way you did? Tell me, Jan!"

He twisted in his bucket seat and gave her a grim look.

Jan looked down at her hands.

"What's going on? What's between you two, Jan?" Tom asked in exasperation.

"D-don't be silly," she replied impatiently. "There's nothing between your father and me! He despises me."

"Tell me what happened tonight."

Tell him! How could she?

"We had one of our disagreements, that's all."

"Some disagreement! You left the house without even taking your handbag or your keys. Jan, didn't you realize how dangerous that was? How did you get mixed up with the police?"

Jan told him then about being accosted by Peter Goud and losing her way in the blanketing fog, which still swirled around the car as they sat talking.

"Running into that officer was probably the best thing I did all night," she concluded.

"Probably," he agreed, catching the hands she was still twisting in her lap. "Lucky for you he was the same one who had seen you in front of the house once before. He said something about seeing you when some guy wrecked his pickup because of a nosebleed. I couldn't make sense of it at all, but he remembered where he'd seen you before when the station reported to him that you weren't about to talk. He came up to the house to find out what he could about you."

"And Jason was there?" She felt a sudden relief.

"As a matter of fact, he'd just left. He came back to the house a couple of times to check if you'd called yet. I stuck by the phone. I thought you'd surely call. After all, I'm the only one you really know."

"I was afraid your father would answer. That's why I didn't phone you when they said I could."

"Oh, Jan. I can't bear to think of you in a cell with criminals."

"It wasn't so bad. The others were really quite

decent. They had a good laugh because I had no shoes.''

"What happened to your shoes?" Tom let go of her and reached for the ignition switch.

"I left them when I started to run." Jan gripped his arm, and he turned to look at her. "Where are you taking me? I can't go back to your house!"

"Why not? What *is* going on between you and Jase? Level with me, Jan."

"I—he—you must believe me. There's no way I can ever talk to your father again."

"It can't be that bad."

"Oh, Tom! Please! Just believe me, won't you?" Jan pleaded. "I won't go back to your house. Even if he isn't there now, he will be back and you know it. I doubt there is anything either of us could do that would keep him away."

"You really don't want to see him?" Tom didn't argue the point any further. He knew there was no way to keep Jason from returning to the house.

"I really don't. I won't, in fact."

"Hmm. You're dead tired and I'm not in much better shape. Tell you what. There's a fairly nice motel over by the university. It's one that caters to parents who come up here to see their kids. It has a good coffee shop. Why don't I take you over, find you a room and let you get some sleep? I'll go home and hit the sack, then tomorrow, after we've both rested a bit, we can decide what to do."

The thought of a welcoming bed sounded heavenly.

"You won't let your father know anything about this?"

"C'mon, Jan. I'll have to tell him you're safe and sound. He'll go crazy if I don't. But I won't say where you are. Okay?"

"Okay." Why did life have to be so complicated, so frightening, she wondered. And why had she been so stupid as to fall in love with Jason?

Tom took her to the motel and installed her in a comfortable room, promising to be back for her. Jan tumbled into bed and fell asleep instantly, exhausted by the emotional trauma of the day.

When Tom called later that morning she felt much more rested. He asked if she'd like him to bring some of her things with him. Grateful for his thoughtfulness, she gave him a list of articles she needed, including a replacement for her lost shoes.

She was dressed and ready when he came. She put on her shoes and took the handbag he'd brought.

"Hurry and get your hair combed," he told her. "I'll even wait till you put on some lipstick. Then let's go eat. Have I got a plan for you!"

Jan laughed at him. "I don't think I want a thing to do with plans of yours, Tom Farrell. Your last was a humdinger."

"Got a little messy, didn't it? But you're gonna love this one. Nancy and Jeff are waiting in the coffee shop."

"Nancy!" Jan followed him through the door.

"Yeah." He looked slightly abashed. "I talked her out of Honolulu. It's all right. We called her parents last night. They're all for it. She's going to Reno skiing with us."

"Us? I can't go with you, Tom! I'm going to get in

touch with the Clarks and ask them to loan me the money to fly home. I can't stay here."

"Fly home!" Tom stopped in front of the coffee-shop door and swung around to grab her shoulders in his strong hands. "You're joking! You can't go home. What about your writing? How will Andy George get in touch with you? And you don't need to borrow money from anyone. I'll give you all you need."

He looked so fierce that Jan reached up and patted his cheek.

"I know you would give me the money, Tom. I won't take it. If Mr. George wants me bad enough, I'll leave my address with you. Our mail is delivered to the ranger station. I must go home. I love being with you, but I can't stay."

Her longing to go back had surfaced while she slept. She needed the north woods, needed the peace, the solitude, the serenity she had left there. In the final analysis, she had neither the tools nor the experience to live with people like Jason. The answer to the question she had asked as she left her isolated cabin had been answered.

Jan Jordan was not able to cope with the outside world. She was going home. It sounded so simple, and yet it was a heart-sickening defeat.

"I wish I could stay, Tom," she said softly, sorry her decision had been such a blow to him.

"But I can't do without you, Jan. It's been wonderful having you around the house when I come home. I can't tell you how much it means to me, just to sit studying while you work on your stories. You help me so much. I'm not nearly as wild...."

"Were you wild?" She laughed. "I never noticed. I'm sorry, Tom. I must go. In fact, you can put the phone call through to the ranger station for me before we eat, if you will. Then it will be all settled and you can get on with your life."

"I can't believe this. Jason is the cause of it, isn't he? Why didn't he stay where he belongs and leave us alone?" His voice was bitter, his face set in somber lines.

"Let's go make that phone call." Jan tugged at his arm and led him past the restaurant into the lobby of the motel. Muttering his wrath, Tom dialed the phone number, giving the operator his credit-card number.

"I'll owe you for this, as well." Was there no end to the debt she was piling up with Jason's willing son? *This is the last,* she vowed silently. *From now on I'm on my own, sink or swim.*

"It's ringing." Tom handed her the black instrument, his frown expressing his feelings.

"Thanks." Jan took the phone from him, listening to the ring clear across the continent.

"Hello. Red Mackay here. May I help you?"

"Hello, Mr. Mackay." Jan knew the ranger. He was often in the region. "This is Jan Jordan. May I speak to Ken or Sarah, please."

"Sorry, Jan. Ken took Sarah to Hawaii for two weeks. They aren't due back here until the middle of next week."

Jan's spirits dropped with a thud. "Oh, dear. I did need them."

"Something I can do?"

"Thank you, Mr. Mackay, but I'm afraid not. It's rather personal, you see." She didn't know him well enough to ask him for money to buy a transcontinental plane ticket. She told him she would call back later. Hanging up, she shot a despairing glance at Tom. He was standing there, one husky shoulder against the edge of the kiosk, a pleased grin on his handsome face.

"You were listening," she accused him, shaking her head in disapproval.

"Yep." He grinned, his good humor restored. "Now that you haven't an excuse you can come to Reno and Tahoe with us, Jan Jordan."

"No, I can't...."

"You can and you will." He fastened a hand firmly around her elbow and steered her into the coffee shop.

"Here's our missing member, gang!"

Jan slid into the smooth curve of the booth, Tom right behind her. The other two gave her an enthusiastic greeting.

"It's going to be great fun," Nancy said enthusiastically after they'd ordered. "Tom says we'll stay in Reno a couple of days, then go to Susie's at Tahoe for the rest of the week. Aren't you excited, Jan?"

"Intrigued," Jan smiled. "What is Reno like?"

"You'll love it, Jan. We can see a show, play the slots, shoot craps, just have fun gambling."

"I'm not exactly sure about your terms. Slots? Shoot craps?"

"Haven't you ever gambled, Jan?" Tom asked.

"Certainly. I play a mean hand of poker, among other things, but I don't know anything about slots, whatever they are, or craps, either."

"Your education's been neglected," Jeff told her. "We'll take care of that as soon as breakfast's over. My dad hasn't unloaded his gear yet, but the plane is ready to go. It's been fueled and serviced. He'll unload when we get back."

He buttered the stack of pancakes the waitress put before him, then poured syrup over the golden brown heap. "C'mon, slowpokes! Eat up! Let's get moving."

Tom turned to Jan, who had hardly touched her food. "What's the matter, Jan? Don't your scrambled eggs taste good?"

"So many things have happened. I can't get a grip on myself. I shouldn't go off with you like this."

"Why not? It'll do you good, take your mind off things."

Did he mean Jason? Jan avoided the piercing glance he turned on her. "I wish I could have talked to Ken and Sarah. I'm sorry I missed them."

"Old friends are fine. But new ones are okay, too. Aren't we, guys?"

Jan smiled. "But I shouldn't be going. I have no money...."

"Forget about that, Jan." Tom's scowl was fierce. "I'm not going to listen to another word about the little bit of money you owe me. What you really owe me is a chance to show you a good time."

Until Sarah and Ken were back she couldn't return home, and there was no question of her staying at the Farrell home. Jan had no choice. She was going to Reno.

CHAPTER FOURTEEN

IT WAS COLD when Jeff brought the Cessna around to the apron at Reno's windy airport. They climbed out and ran through the frosty air, their teeth chattering by the time they reached the lounge.

Tom quickly hired a taxi and soon the four of them were booked into the opulent high-rise hotel. Eager to start gambling, Tom led the way down the thickly carpeted steps that curved across the front of the lobby and headed straight to a cashier's booth. He spilled the silver change he received into two large paper cups and handed one to Jeff.

Moving over to two enormous machines standing side by side, they began to play. Jan watched, fascinated, as the two of them fed the machine and pulled down handles at least four feet long.

"Let me try, Jeff," Nancy begged. He laughed and stepped aside.

"No, thanks." Jan declined Tom's invitation to try his machine. "I'll watch for a while." Thirty minutes later his cup had only a single coin rattling around in it.

"Your turn." He handed it to Jan. "I'm gong to wash my hands." He gave the last coin to her, holding out his black hands. "Who says money isn't filthy?"

Humoring him, Jan dropped the coin in and gave the handle a sharp pull. Disks flew. Jan turned her head and saw Jeff walk off in the same direction as Tom.

Suddenly a bell went off behind her and pandemonium broke loose. Jan clutched at Nancy as the machine clanged into action. Lights flashed, sirens screeched and the garish machine spewed out money. Nancy, her arms around Jan, squealed and jumped up and down. Tom and Jeff sprinted back across the floor to see what was happening.

When it was all over Jan found she'd won five thousand dollars.

"I knew it!" Tom grabbed her and whirled her around. "I knew we'd be lucky with you along."

Jan refused to take the money, and a heated argument ensued, Nancy and Jeff siding with Tom.

"Don't you see, Jan," Nancy pleaded with her. "You have a string of luck going. You have to use it or it'll go. Take the money. Use it to make more."

"It was Tom's dollar."

"Jeff's, too," Tom informed her. "We pooled our cash for the gambling kitty. Half of everything's Jeff's."

"Okay. You and Jeff share it."

"How about this?" Jeff interrupted reasonably. "We'll put the original hundred back in the kitty, then split the rest four ways."

He looked so eager Jan didn't have the heart to turn him down. They were such an uncomplicated, happy lot, full of fun and life. She had spent her own slice-of-life caring for her father. Why on earth shouldn't she have some fun now and relax with them? Unable to think of a good reason not to, she gave in and surrendered to the gaiety of their mood.

It was the beginning of a wild and unbelievable time. Nancy was correct in her assessment of Jan's lucky streak. Everything Jan played paid off. The other three watched her in awe, cheering her on, plying her with instructions. They went from one casino to another, the cold nipping at them as they dodged in and out of taxis, the chill wind blasting them into each new place.

By early evening their winnings had doubled. It was pitch dark outside and getting colder.

"Are we still going to Tahoe?" Jan asked as they trooped into yet another pleasure palace. The entrance was a spacious arcade lined with glass-fronted shops exhibiting all sorts of expensive items. One of the display windows full of attractive ski clothing had caught her eye.

"Sure. We'll probably go up first thing in the morning. Too much of this can't do a body much good." Tom laughed.

"I haven't a thing to wear," she told her companions. "How about taking a break and doing something sensible, like letting me spend some of this ill-gotten gain."

Tom struck his forehead in a gesture of tragedy. "Here she is, lady luck in her pocket, and she wants to go shopping."

Tom and Jeff stayed outside wandering around the corridor and looking in the plate-glass display windows while Jan and Nancy went into the ski shop.

Buying an outfit didn't take Jan long. In no time at all she had tried on a striking one-piece designer ski suit. In turquoise and white, it fit like a dream. Feeling extravagant, she added the companion après-ski outfit, slim-fitting pants and bulky knit sweater. She also chose a cap, gloves, goggles and boots, all in the same lovely blue and white. The salesclerk packed them all in a matching knapsack along with the thermal underwear Nancy insisted was a must.

Tom and Jeff met them in the wide shopping passageway, mischief crinkling their good-looking faces. Tom took charge of her purchases, rushing them up a long and extremely elaborate escalator to the main gambling floor.

After checking in the knapsack, he escorted his friends toward a crowd of hopefuls clustered around a dice table. "C'mon, Jan. I want you to try your hand at this. I have the weirdest hunch your luck is going to hold!"

"I can't, Tom." She resisted his firm grasp. "I haven't the least idea what this is all about."

"You don't have to know a thing. Just throw the dice. I'll see to everything else."

He shouldered his way between two men. They glanced up, saw Jan and made room.

"Thanks, fellows. My fiancée wants to learn how to play craps." He winked at them, ignoring Jan's outraged sound of dissent.

Jan leaned against Tom's shoulder, watching as the man beside her shook the dice in both hands then sent them spinning the length of the taut green surface of the dice table. The red cubes bounced and came to rest, the croupier chanting a litany she had no way of understanding.

The player beside her threw the cubes three more times, then the man in charge swept the dice in front of her.

"I don't..." she started to protest.

"Come on, little lady. Change our luck...warm 'em up...throw those galloping dominoes..." Comments flew as the men at the table offered encouragement.

"Shake 'em and throw 'em hard enough so they bounce off the end of the table," Tom instructed her, placing a neat stack of chips in the rack fronting him.

Jan glanced at the croupier. He had hair almost the color of Jason's and he was watching her with steady brown eyes. Although he didn't much resemble the ghost haunting the back reaches of her mind, the dark auburn sheen of his hair stirred her to action. Galvanized, Jan shook the dice in two hands, then threw them with a quick snap of her wrist. Recoiling off the backboard, they came to rest, twin dots showing on each. Four was her point.

"Get four again," Tom told her.

The stickman swept the dice back to her and she threw a three and a one. Jeff and Tom whooped.

"Do it again!" Tom laughed, as the quick sweep of the stick left a pile of chips in front of him.

Jan threw a five and a one this time.

"Make your point, little lady!" said the croupier. "Do it again...!"

"What's my point, Tom?" she asked.

"Six. Any old six will do. Yee-ha!" He yelled as she did it. "Lady luck has us spotted!"

The excitement of the crowd had its effect. Realizing the requirement was to throw a number, then get the same number again, Jan concentrated on the dice, thinking of the different combinations needed to make each point. She'd done this six times before she paid much attention to the racked chips in front of Tom and Jeff. The men who had made room for her also had columns of chips. Everyone was talking and laughing, urging her on.

All at once, she had a clear idea of her position.

Pointing to Tom's neat stacks she asked the inscrutable man in control what would happen if she failed to make a point.

"You lose, lady, he loses, too."

"How much are those chips worth, Tom?"

"In the neighbourhood of twelve thousand, if I haven't lost count."

"Twelve thousand dollars?" Jan was horrified.

"Yep! Throw them again, Jan."

"You're betting it all?"

"Sure thing! I can recognize a hot streak when it hits me in the head! Throw them, Jan." His request was seconded by the crowd around the table.

Jan gave Tom a long look. "How do I stop?" she asked the stickman.

"Just pass the dice along."

Jan promptly handed the red cubes to the man beside her and backed away from the table.

"Aw, Jan! You can't do this to me."

"Place your bets, ladies and gentlemen...place your bets," the croupier called.

"Smart move, lady." The man she'd handed the dice to passed them on and began filling his pockets with his chips. Tom hesitated, then followed suit. Jeff and Nancy had already picked up their winnings.

Tom and Jeff each came away from the cashier's booth with more than twelve thousand dollars. They promptly divided the spoils with the two young women.

Nancy danced around, bubbling with excitement. "Six straight passes! I still can't believe it! How did you do it, Jan?"

"I've no idea," Jan laughed. "By the time I knew no one really expected me to do it, I'd already done it. Then I noticed all those chips in front of Tom. It scared me to death when I realized he was betting all of them. How did you get so many?"

"Just let 'em ride," he grinned at her. "Every time you made your point the bet doubled."

"It's just as well I didn't know what you were doing. The stickman knew I couldn't go on forever, didn't he?"

"He was counting on it, young lady." The gambler who had been the first to pick up his chips stopped beside them. "May I buy you all a drink?"

"Oh, thank you, but no," Jan replied before the others were able to accept. "This is my first time here and I've been promised a midnight show."

"Well then, let me treat the four of you to the best one in town." He pulled out his wallet and extracted four slim tickets from it. "These are for the late show at my place. Starts in about an hour. Go on over and enjoy yourselves."

"Thanks, buddy." Tom accepted them. The man raised a couple of fingers and strolled away.

"What do you say? Shall we go?"

"I'd like to." Jan was conscious of a lack of energy. "I really don't think I'm up to any more gambling."

"Aw, Jan! I want you to try one more thing." Tom retrieved her purchases from the smiling woman behind the counter before he led her out into the wide courtyard. Jeff and Nancy followed close behind. "Brrr. It's getting colder, isn't it?" They hurried into the taxi and Jeff gave the driver instructions.

A silence fell as a taxi swished through the cold night. The blazing lights of the gambling halls sparkled and danced in the clear crisp air. To the west, the Sierra Nevada towered over the town, dense black against the lighter sky. A full moon shone, a pale lantern in the night.

The mountains called to Jan. How wonderful it would be to be deep in their silent strength. How wonderful to draw on their serenity and stillness, to find her own peace of mind again. *I will go home,* she vowed as the taxi sped down the garish street. *I will leave all this and go back where I belong.*

The taxi drew up to an elaborate entrance where thousands of lights created a miniature galaxy. Jan and Nancy found their teeth were chattering in spite of the quick dash into the warm lobby.

"It's almost an hour until show time. What say we try keno?"

"I'd rather not." Jan began to protest.

"Say you will, Jan," Nancy pleaded. "After all, we're here to have fun and we've won pots already. Let's give it one more try."

"Only once and only a dollar each," Tom put in. "I'm dying to try an experiment."

They all looked so eager Jan didn't have the heart to refuse. "Okay, let's go play keno. But I'm going to hold you to the dollar maximum."

"If I'm right, that's all it's gonna take." Tom dropped a long arm around her waist and hugged her. "C'mon!" He herded them into the keno area and ordered Bloody Marys from the cocktail waitress before they settled themselves in the comfortable lounge chairs.

"I've got a plan," he intoned solemnly as the scantily clad waitress vanished on the way to fill the order. "Everyone give me a dollar."

Laughing, they each handed him one. Picking up a long grease pencil, he poised it above a packet of unused keno tickets, his motion dramatic. "Stand up, Jan, and turn your back to the counter."

Jan did as he asked.

"Now give me six numbers. Any six that pop into your beautiful head. They must be less than one hundred."

Humoring him, Jan rattled off six numbers at random.

Marking two tickets, Tom gave one to Jeff, along with two of the dollars. The two young men went to the tellers ensconced behind the impressive desk and came back with officially marked papers. The waitress was there with the drinks by then. Tom threw a five-dollar bill on her tray. Her smile was dazzling as she left.

"Good friends, good fun!" Glasses clinked in salute.

Jan sipped her drink, liking the spicy taste. She stirred it with a length of crisp celery.

"This could grow on a person. What is it?"

Jeff told her and they fell into a lively discussion of the composition of mixed drinks. Conversation ceased when the announcer closed the game, sending a myriad of little caged balls into a frenzy of spinning action. Occasionally he plucked one out, calling the number it contained. A board behind him filled with the random numbers as he called them. Jan sensed a growing tension in the two young men seated by her.

Suddenly, Tom leaped from his seat, shouting. He and Jeff rushed up to the play windows.

"What happened?" Jan turned to Nancy. "I reckon the noise means we've won!"

"I think we've just won twenty-six thousand dollars. Each!" Nancy laughed. "Look at the odds. Six numbers, twenty-six thousand. For one buck."

Two incoherent young men hustled Jan and Nancy straight to the casino's office.

"You two get your share of this loot converted to cashier's checks," Jeff demanded. "Then go to the ladies' room or something. Tom and I will be right back. Don't go away and for Pete's sake don't gamble anymore. We're all going to owe the IRS our souls as it is.''

"But...!"

"No buts! See you." Tom vanished through the door on the heels of his friend.

"What was that all about?" Jan asked.

"Don't know, but let's get rid of this cash." Nancy took hers to the man watching them from behind the desk.

Jan had a sense of relief as she converted all the money except for two thousand dollars into a crisp check. A quick bit of mental arithmetic convinced her that was enough to take her skiing and to buy her ticket home. She could bank the check and send Tom the money she owed him after she reached the East Coast. It would be nice to have her own checking account. If her stories sold as well as Andy George seemed to think they would, she was well on her way to financial independence. If only she were able to find a way to counteract the corrosive effect of having fallen in love with Jason, she'd have a decent chance to work out some sort of a life for herself.

Tom and Jeff were nowhere in sight when they left the office. After waiting a while they made their way back to the lobby. Tom and Jeff were coming in from the outside, grinning like happy children. Each had an outsized garment box clutched under one arm.

In unison they presented the astonished women with gorgeous full-length minks. One for each of them.

"I can't possibly accept such an expensive gift," Jan protested, horrified.

"You went back to those shops where Jan bought her ski stuff, didn't you?" Nancy hugged the fur Jeff had given her to her small frame. "I've never seen anything so beautiful."

"You two have lost your minds," Jan exclaimed, trying to shrug away as Tom draped the supple fur over her shoulders. "You can't buy an expensive mink for me, Tom Farrell!"

"I've already done it." He caught her slender shoulders and turned her toward him. "And a better dollar was never spent. You look great."

"Tom, you and Jeff must take these back at once."

"We won't, you know. They hardly made a dint in the loot you won for us tonight. It's our way of saying thanks for a wonderful evening. Want to hurt our feelings?"

Nancy capitulated without further ado, throwing her arms around Jeff's neck and giving him a kiss.

"Show time!" Tom grinned and headed toward the theater.

Jan followed, fuming. "You're going to be just like your father, Tom Farrell," she warned him.

"What do you mean, Jan?" Nancy asked, curious.

"He's well on his way to thinking he has to have his own way all the time just like Jas...." Too late, Jan realized where her unwary tongue was leading her. She blushed under the interested gaze of her three companions and was relieved when they reached the wide doors leading to the large dinner theater. The maître d' took one look at their tickets and became very attentive. He seated them in a curved and padded booth, front and center, and two bottles of champagne in ice-filled coolers appeared as if by magic.

"Enjoy the show," he told them after filling their goblets.

And enjoy it they did. The nightclub act was full of glitter and panache, and Jan found that she was almost happy. Throwing her reservations to the winds, she relaxed. She wasn't in the mood to quarrel with Tom tonight, but she'd have a serious talk with him the following day. The price of the coat would be added to the amount she already owed him.

Exhausted, she was pleased when the consensus of opinion sent them to find the taxi ranks after the performance.

"We'll have to get an early start," Jeff reminded them. "We won't be able to fly. I've checked the latest report and there'll be heavy snow by midmorning tomorrow. I won't risk flying in, so we'll have to drive. It means going up in a snowstorm, but the skiing will be great when the storm stops."

"You're sure we can't get going early enough to miss it if we fly?" Tom asked. "Driving up may be a drag."

"Until weather prediction becomes an art of the absolute, I insist on giving the weather birds room for error." Jeff looked serious. "They say midmorning. That means anytime between sunrise and noon, as far as I'm concerned. I don't want to take the chance of flying in."

"Hey. You're the pilot. Anyway, hitting the sack sounds good to me. I'm ready. It's almost two."

In spite of the hour, a restless crowd milled in and out of the lobby doors. "How do they do it?" Jan wondered as they went toward the entrance.

"The old adrenaline gets flowing. Every time they win a little it gives them a spurt of energy, spurs them on to greater things," Tom told her. Grabbing her fur-clad arm, he pulled her up the steps toward the entrance, weaving expertly through the crowd.

Suddenly Jan froze. The glass doors before her slid open, and a grim-faced Jason strode through.

CHAPTER FIFTEEN

JASON'S EYES DIDN'T LEAVE Jan's face, shadows of intense pain flickering in the gray depths.

"I've looked for you for hours," he said simply. "You are needed in San Francisco, Jan. A Mr. Clark phoned. He's frantic. His wife is ill."

"Sarah!" Jan whispered the name of the only mother she could remember. "What happened?"

"I'm not sure what happened, but she isn't expected to live, apparently. Her husband is trying desperately to reach you."

"It was good of you to come," Jan said quietly.

"Let's go back to your hotel and get your things. We need to hurry. Clark doesn't expect her to last very long." He took Jan's arm and guided her through the doorway, snapping his fingers at the cab rank.

"Why didn't you call us, dad?" Tom asked in a reproving voice. He followed his father into the cab, and Nancy and Jeff climbed into the front seat.

"The Silver Palace, and hurry," Jason instructed the driver before turning to his son in exasperation. "How in the devil was I supposed to contact you? I had no idea where you were until I just happened to get in touch with Jeff's father. Even he wasn't sure whether you were in Reno or Tahoe. I checked your flight plan out and tried to locate you by phone. Nobody had you registered, so I caught a flight over. I've been here since six, combing the casinos for you. I finally found your hotel. If we catch the next flight out, we may be in time.''

"I'm sorry." Tom's voice conveyed his regret.

"I can't believe Sarah is so ill," Jan said. "Mr. Mackay told me they were in Hawaii.''

"According to her husband, they were returning early. They wanted to stop in San Francisco for a couple of days and see you. His wife became ill enroute. By the time they reached the city, Mrs. Clark was delirious. He took her to the hospital, then tried to reach you.''

"But what is wrong with her?''

"Nobody knows. The doctors suspect she may have been bitten by something poisonous or something she has an allergy to. The trouble is they can't find any evidence of an insect bite. They are working frantically to discover the cause. She keeps murmuring your name. That's why he wants you to come. He thinks you may help.''

"I'm very grateful to you for taking the trouble to come here and find me. It's wonderful of you.''

"The man is out of his mind with worry. He needed help," Jason answered. "There was no other way to reach you.''

''Sorry," Tom sounded uncomfortable. "I should have let you know where we were staying.''

"You should have," his father agreed. "But the important thing is to get Jan to the coast. Her friends need her.''

Jan remembered then why Tom had not advertised their plans, and she was glad Nancy chose that moment to turn around and give her hand a squeeze.

"Everything will be okay, Jan. You'll see. Mr. Farrell will take care of you."

"Yeah. Don't worry, Jan. Just let dad handle it for you."

Inexplicably she found she was willing to do just that. Where was her much-vaunted independence? Somewhere deep in her consciousness there was a sweet relief that the dark man beside her in the crowded car was in charge.

Jason called the airport from the hotel room, hanging up the phone with an impatient gesture.

"I'm afraid we're too late. There isn't a flight out of here until morning."

"Oh, no! What shall I do? Can I rent a car and drive?"

"Not by yourself," Tom challenged her. "You haven't had enough experience yet. You'll meet all kinds of bad road in this weather!"

"I'll drive." Jason interrupted her protest before she could voice it.

"Better yet, why don't you take the Cessna, Mr. Farrell?" Jeff suggested. "It's fueled and ready to go. You won't have any trouble in a moonlit night like this one, and you'll be on the coast in no time. The plane's in tip-top shape."

"Are you sure?"

"Yeah," Jeff answered him. "Dad would want you to. We're going to be in Tahoe a week. We've already decided to drive up. You're welcome to it."

Jason looked at Jan's strained colorless face. "What do you think?"

"I really want to see Sarah.... If you wouldn't mind?"

"No trouble. Get your things together and I'll call in my flight plan now so we can get in the air as soon as we reach the airport."

Jan heard him on the phone as she gathered up the few items she had purchased and stuffed them into the knapsack containing her new ski clothes. Jason took it from her as they left the room. Tom, Nancy and Jeff chorused their goodbyes.

Jan was glad of the soft warmth of the fur as the chill night air hit her. She wrapped it around herself and climbed into the cab. They drove through almost deserted streets, the moon startlingly bright in the dark night.

The plane was waiting for them when they reached the airport, its aristocratic nose pointed toward the dark escarpment of the mountain ridge. Jason threw Jan's knapsack into a rear seat of the four-seater, took off the tan overcoat he was wearing, folded it and put it on the seat with her things. Then he helped her over the wing and into the craft. He hadn't said a word on the trip to the airport. Jan, uncomfortable with the memory of the last time they were alone, held her peace.

Please, Sarah, don't die, she prayed silently while Jason adjusted the headphone, spoke curtly into the thin mouthpiece and flipped switches as he ran through his pretakeoff routine. A few minutes later he taxied down the runway and guided the small plane into the air.

"It's a good night for flying," he commented quietly as the plane climbed. "There's nothing like a full moon on a clear night."

The night was beautiful. Cold but beautiful. Jason called to activate their flight plan and they flew into the star-studded darkness. The interior of the plane was comfortably warm before the lights of Reno vanished. Jan took off her coat and settled back, uneasy in his company, yet at the same time glad that he was there.

"Thank you for coming after me," she said. "I feel it's a real imposition. You must be busy...." Her voice trailed off as he turned to look at her. In the dim lights of the dash she was able to see the tension on his face.

"Since I was responsible for your abrupt departure I felt obliged to find you. It's hard to lose a friend, worse to lose one in these circumstances, I think. You don't owe me any thanks." His words sounded harsh, rough. "I owe you an apology. I didn't really mean to be such a bastard. I got carried away, that's all."

"You did, rather. Let's not talk about it. I just want to forget it."

"Do you?" He gave her a peculiar look. "You may be able to. I find it very difficult."

"Please, Jason," Jan began, "we can't be friends, or even civil to each other unless we just forget it."

"Do you want to be my friend?"

"You're Tom's father. I...." She stopped then, puzzled by the look he turned on her. His eyes were shadowed and she couldn't see them, but the smile he gave her was bitter.

"Yes. I am Tom's father." The statement was abrupt.

Startled, Jan withdrew into silence, feeling hurt and uncertain. This was a day she would never forget. At last the chaotic activity was catching up with her, and she drifted into sleep beside the taciturn man she loved.

Her dreams were uneasy and she awoke frightened and disoriented. The plane was bucking and shuddering. Jason was swearing in a quiet steady way. Jerking herself upright, Jan's eyes flew to the curved glass enclosing the cabin. She couldn't see a thing. The plane twisted with a life of its own, the motor droning steadily in spite of the difficulty it was in.

"Cold front," he snapped at her. "Didn't see it coming. I'll try to take us up out of it."

"O-okay," Jan forced a calmness into the word. "I'm not afraid."

"I sure am. Those wings are icing like mad. If we can't get above this, we've got trouble."

Endless minutes later the plane popped out of the heavy cloud system, pitching in the fierce wind. Jason fought to keep it level, his glance taking in the sections of the wings he could see.

Jan held on desperately. The Cessna rose with the speed of a rocket, propelled by a freezing updraft, then dropped with all the buoyancy of a stone, back toward the earth.

"There's a hole! Hang on, we'll try for it." His shout did little to reassure her.

A hole? Where? What did he mean?

The moonlight turned the top of the cloud cover

into a silver sheet. Then she saw it—a round clear area just ahead of the plane's nose. The clouds weren't filling it. They seemed to be spinning slowly around the edge of a vast hole. Jason took the plane into the hole, fighting to keep it level as it lost altitude and seemed to lose most of its ability to move forward.

"Get that knapsack and those coats." Jan could hear the air rushing by the outside of the Cessna as she reacted to his crisp command. Reaching back she pulled the two coats off the seat behind her and caught the strap of the turquoise and white knapsack.

"We're going down, Jan. There's a mountain lake down there. Jam that knapsack in front of your knees. Keep your head down. Wrap your arms around your legs. Now!" He was barking the instructions at her, his eyes and hands busy as he tried to keep the plane level and out of a stall. Jan obeyed quickly, stuffing the knapsack between her legs and the dash of the plane. She dropped her head and held it on her knees. To her surprise, Jason swiftly threw the fur and his overcoat over her.

The wheels touched the ground and the little plane seemed to tear along at express-train velocity, lurching, shuddering, as it crossed terrain it had not been constructed to handle. The carriage tore away. Jan heard its screaming departure, then Jason's weight came down on her and some object stopped the nightmarish forward rush. The tail rose, quivered a moment at the apex of the arc, then settled back with a crash that shook the trees surrounding the mountain meadow.

Jan blacked out momentarily. She came to as an explosion that sounded like dynamite blasted the area. There in the darkness, held down by an oppressive weight that threatened to crack her vertebrae, she listened to the hissing tearing reverberation of sound with horror. How many times had she heard it in her own mountains?

Avalanche!

Recognizing the deadly sound of the fast-moving wall of snow, she hunched lower beneath the weight bearing her down, expecting the worst any second. The wreck of the plane shook as the monster killer hurled by somewhere in the near vicinity.

Silence fell. Jan was aware of the high squeal of some metal part rubbing against the fuselage, driven by the wind. Jason's inert body sprawled over hers, pinning her down.

"Jason!" she cried. "Jason, let me up."

There was no response and a cold finger of fear touched her heart. "Jason! Can you hear me?" *Please God, let him hear, let him be alive.*

With superhuman effort Jan slipped to her knees. Using her legs to brace herself, she shifted his unresponsive body with extreme care and slid out from under him onto the knapsack that had protected her knees.

Jason lay crumpled sideways over the seats. In the moonlight and the reflected glow of the plane's headlights, his face was ashen. A great gash slashed his forehead. It was bleeding profusely, the skin around it beginning to purple. His arms were still spread out in his attempt to save her from harm.

Still dazed by the force of the crippling impact, Jan stared at him. Pulling herself together, she bent over him and slipped a shaking hand inside the coat of the business suit he was wearing. The strong regular beat of his heart was immensely reassuring. Her relief left her weak.

Maneuvering with extreme care, trying not to shift Jason, Jan was suddenly conscious of the biting cold. Jason must be freezing, but her first concern was to stop the blood flowing from his forehead. Still on her knees, she reached into his back pocket and pulled out the large square linen handkerchief. She folded it into a compress, then undid the silk scarf at her neck and used it to bind the linen compress to his head, tugging the scarf until it was a snug pressure bandage, then tying it. Wriggling out of her half-slip was no easy feat, but she did it, then used the silky fabric to clean most of the blood from Jason's white face.

The nose of the airplane had jammed back into itself on impact, telescoping the little cabin. Jason's body was sprawled across the two seats. Jan managed to climb over him, then dropped back on her knees. She tried to straighten him, moving his feet into the aisle between the rear passenger seats. That done, she half stood and slipped her hands under his body, intending to slide him off the seat into the cramped area of the aisle. Tensing her muscles against his deadweight, she lifted him gently.

Jason moaned and she eased him back, moisture popping out on her forehead. What was wrong? Broken ribs? Or was it his back? His legs and arms seemed to be unharmed.

Kneeling there, Jan stilled her impulse to panic and thought with desperate clarity. No matter what his condition, she had to get him out of the plane, somewhere where he would be sheltered from the cold, safe from hypothermia. And she had to do it quickly. The cold was numbing, eating into her bones, slowing her thought processes.

"Think Jan, think," she commanded out loud. "Jason can't help you. You've got to move."

It was obvious she wouldn't be able to get him out of the hull of the plane by herself. And unless she was able to keep him warm, he was in danger of death by exposure. The cold was eating at her now, striking through the ultrasuede suit, numbing her legs and body.

If only she knew how seriously injured he was! Hunching over him, she ran her hands beneath his suit jacket up the warm length of his body. She could feel nothing broken, but he groaned when she pressed against his ribs. Applying a light pressure, she ran her hand down his spine, her heart in her throat. He gave no sign of distress and she sighed her relief. His reaction seemed to indicate he'd broken or cracked some ribs on impact, but he showed no sign of having punctured a lung.

Fumbling in the reflected glow, she pulled the cushions off the seats. A faint odor of the Cessna's fuel wafted past her nostrils, but she pushed the thought of fire away. Surely if one hadn't started during that horrible landing, it wouldn't now. Mentally crossing her fingers she laid the cushions in a row on the floor between the seats. That would help to keep the bitter cold from creeping up through the bottom, she hoped.

Praying that she wasn't wrong about his injury, she knotted the sleeves of his overcoat, which was wedged beneath him, across the broad expanse of his back, her fingers awkward in the frigid air.

She stood then, bending over his unconscious frame. Crossing her arms under the knotted sleeve, she bent her knees, then straightened them against the pull of his weight. The angle was clumsy, the space cramped, but she raised him with slow and dogged determination, easing his unwieldy body out of the seat and onto the cushions. In spite of the cold, her effort generated heat and warmed her.

She made sure he was on the protective cushions, then, working carefully, she took the overcoat from under him. She picked up the mink and spread it over him, fur side toward his body, then covered him with the overcoat. She was thoroughly chilled by the time she finished. Reaching for the knapsack, she pulled the windproof clothing out of it. Her stiff fingers interfered with her efforts to remove her skirt and jacket, but she finally had the one-piece ski suit zipped up over the after-ski pants Tom had insisted on buying her. She pulled on the thick warm stockings and the knitted woolen cap. She draped the sweater over Jason, under the coats. Lifting his head with extreme care so the gash wouldn't start bleeding again, she put another cushion under his head. She removed his shoes and wrapped his feet in the thermal underwear, rubbing the circulation into them first.

The moon had vanished and only the reflected light from the plane's wildly angled headlight lit the cabin now. Knowing she might need its help before this was over, Jan leaned over and peered at the dashboard until she located the switch. She turned the lights off, and a brief shiver of fear ran through her as the stygian dark engulfed the cabin.

Creeping back to Jason, she pulled on her thick ski gloves and snuggled up to him, her arm flung across him as she tried to share her warmth. Not daring to go to sleep, she lay there listening to his labored breathing, waiting for the dawn. Several times in those endless hours she unwrapped his feet and chafed them with a vigor that produced enough friction to warm them. She worked on his hands too.

Jason didn't regain consciousness, which added to her worry. His breathing became stentorian, frightening her.

During those interminable hours, Jan crept under the coats, not so much to warm herself as to add her own body heat to his. Close against him there in the hostile dark, the wind tearing at the fuselage of the downed plane, she talked to Jason. She told him of her love for him, the frightening depth of her need, her loneliness, the oppressive sense of isolation, her hurt, everything. She told him that she never wanted to leave him again.

CHAPTER SIXTEEN

AT LAST THE DAWN CAME. Huddled beside Jason, Jan watched objects become discernible in the cold gray light.

Would anyone come looking for them? Would they ever be found in this high valley? As she wriggled out of the warm nest she had made, she glimpsed the sky and her heart sank. It was going to snow and snow hard, if she were any judge. They couldn't be rescued until the weather cleared. Jason's chances to live were up to her. He needed shelter that was warm if he were to survive. And survive he must.

The door was warped when she tried it, and it took several minutes of real physical labor to force it open. Finally, it gave way with a screech. Jan swung it back then wished she hadn't opened it.

The snow-fogged landscape that met her eyes was as bleak as a moonscape. Snow swirled, filling the air with powder and obscuring the uneven aspen meadow they were on. Jan considered the desolate scene, then went back into the fuselage.

Taking off her ski gloves, she unwound Jason's feet and rubbed them until they were pink, then pulled off her wool socks and fitted them on him. If she was going to get anything done in the bitter cold, she needed the thermal underwear. The trick would be to get into it before she froze.

Using the ultra-suede skirt as a substitute, she wrapped it and her jacket around her feet, then gritted her teeth and unzipped her ski suit and after-ski pants. She was into the underwear and back into the other two garments in nothing flat, her teeth chattering in spite of her speed. When she took her ski boots from the knapsack, she found a long wool scarf she didn't remember buying tucked under them.

After fastening the thick boots, she took the scarf and raised Jason's head with concern. His face looked so pale in the watery morning light, worsened by the contrasting dark auburn stubble of his beard. Winding the scarf around his bandaged head, she lowered her face for a moment and pressed her soft cheek against his cold one.

"Oh, Jason, my love," she whispered. "Be well, my darling. Be well."

She made sure the pillows supported his head, tucked the coats securely around him and crawled into the smashed tail of the craft, intent on finding anything at all that might aid her in the task of constructing a shelter. She remembered Jeff mentioning his father's fishing trip to a remote area of Mexico and the fact he hadn't unloaded his equipment on his return.

Digging into one of the packs, she felt her spirits rise. Her gloved hand closed over the short handle of a hatchet with a sharp, wicked-looking blade. With it she could build a shelter, one big enough to enclose a bed of soft pine boughs, one that would protect them completely from the wind and the snow she expected to come before too long.

She dumped out the rest of the contents of the duffel bag, hoping to find a shovel. Evidently the fisherman who stuffed the bag hadn't needed one. She did find a battered blackened coffeepot and a frying pan, however, and a long and vicious knife, the sort a fisherman uses for scaling and cleaning his catch. There was also a tin washbasin.

There were matches too, and a camping stove with several tins of fuel. She noticed a pouch on the side of the bag. Unsnapping it, she fished out the contents, a dozen or so plastic packets. With a sudden feeling of elation she read the neat labels printed on each. Food! There was dried-beef stew, chicken soup—even an apple-raisin crumble and some dried-fruit bars. At least they weren't in danger of starving.

Jan opened the second duffel bag and found a rubberized groundsheet and a small pup tent. Jeff's father and his friends were practical men, accustomed to camping out and foraging for themselves. Jan offered a small prayer of thanksgiving as she put everything but the ax aside for future use. Making sure Jason was securely tucked in, she left the wrecked plane, jumping into snow that was at least three feet deep.

She forced a track through the snow to the edge of the avalanche. The snowbank it had created was ten or twelve feet high. It was hard, but it was no competition for the flashing blade of the ax Jan swung with telling precision. Driving a slanting tunnel at a forty-five-degree angle, she burrowed into the ice-packed snow. She smoothed the rounded tunnel roof, making sure it was large enough to allow the passage of Jason's wide shoulders. In forty-five minutes she had an ice cave hollowed out of the side of the avalanche debris. It was large enough for Jason to stand up in the center. After digging a small angled vent through the upper surface of the snow deposit, still two feet thick, she got down to the business of creating a sleeping platform.

It wasn't an easy task.

She attacked one side of the cave she had formed, hacking away at the packed snow and stamping the debris underfoot. When she was finished, she had sliced a shelf out of one rounded wall, three feet high and wider and considerably longer than a man.

The shelf finished to her satisfaction, she deepened the hole in the center to form the essential cold basin. She used some of the snow from the hollowed interior to build a windbreak several feet beyond the entrance to the slanted tunnel.

It had warmed her to work so hard. Knowing the danger of overheating under these conditions, she stopped for a moment or two and breathed deeply. Any perspiration created would freeze, bringing problems she was better off without.

Waiting for her body to cool a bit, she surveyed her handiwork. Thank heavens for the sharp little hatchet. It had speeded the task of forming the shelter immeasurably. The blizzard wasn't far off, she judged. Digging the hollow with nothing but her hands could have been done, but it would have taken hours longer. This cave would do them very well, she decided. It was large enough, and if they were careful they could maintain the conditions under which survival was possible.

The long shelf she had hacked out of the side was long enough to accommodate Jason's injured body and leave room for her to sit. It still had to be insulated with a thick layer of pine boughs.

Jan pulled her knit cap down as far as she could and went back out into the bitter cold. The lining of the ski clothes absorbed the moisture caused by her exertion and trapped the heat she created. Except for her face, she was warm as she struggled through the deep snow to the nearest downed tree. A victim of the avalanche's awesome power as it hurtled down the mountain, the fir lay on its side, branches whipping in the cold wind. Jan cut them with clean brisk strokes, pulling them behind her as she floundered back down the path she'd blazed. After chopping the branches into a manageable size, she pushed them down the tunnel and spread them on the sleeping shelf. Light diffused through the packed snow of her ceiling, making her task easier. Several trips later the fragrant mattress was thick enough to keep the chill from creeping up into Jason's body.

She went back to the wreck then. Jason was still unconscious, his face ashen, his breathing labored. Jan chafed his hands and feet and wrapped them well before she crept back into the wrecked fuselage to retrieve the pup tent.

She tossed it out of the plane, and spread the canvas under the plane's hatchway, keeping the guy ropes untangled. Packing the tent's edges down with snow so the wind wouldn't flip it, she climbed back into the plane.

Her next task proved to be a good deal harder. She spread the groundsheet beside Jason and tucked part of it under him. Then she spent agonizing minutes transferring him onto it. When it was accomplished her muscles and her patience were both strained. Tucking the coats around him, she wrapped him in the rubberized sheet. Turning him on his stomach was a monumental chore. Frightened that she might hurt him, she worked very carefully, breathing a sigh of relieved thankfulness when the job was done.

She inched him through the oval opening in the side of the plane at a snail's pace, sliding out to support him as he finally slipped down to the canvas surface of the pup tent. She looped the guy ropes of the tent over her shoulder and moved toward the ice cave. For the first time the snow on the ground was a blessing as she moved his weight easily to the tunnel's entrance.

When she got him into the cave itself she had trouble again. Her strength was running out, but she couldn't leave him where he was. If he were to live, it was imperative to get him up on the sleeping shelf. Jan solved the problem by tying the guy ropes firmly around his unconscious form, kneeling on the shelf herself and using the loops of the ropes as handles. He moaned as she straightened him out on the springy mattress of fir, the sound piercing Jan's troubled heart.

Had she injured him, pulling him around as she had?

Spreading the tent over the fir mattress, she eased his overcoat under him, tugging it until his whole body was on it. Then she spread the mink over him, fur side down and covered him with the groundsheet.

It took several trips, but she salvaged everything that might be of use from the wreck, including the cushions and a big flashlight she found under a seat. She sorted out the things she had salvaged and put everything in order in the restricted space.

There was no way to heat the ice cave. Even the heat of their own bodies might cause humidity high enough to condense on the inside of the snow structure and freeze. If the snow froze it would lose its insulating ability and the inside of the cave would become as cold as the air they were sheltering from. Since the temperature of the interior was going to hover around thirty degrees Fahrenheit, they weren't going to be warm, but they wouldn't freeze either. And while she couldn't risk lighting the little stove in the cave, if she used it at the entrance to the tunnel, where icing wouldn't matter, she could keep them supplied with water warm enough to drink.

The blasting air was shrieking outside with increased fury, intent on destroying everything in its path. Coming to a sudden decision, Jan ventured out once more, knowing she had little choice. The blizzard was due any moment. Scooping up snow, she packed it into the two duffel bags. She could feel the sheen of moisture on her body. She knew she should avoid overheating, but fear of the impending storm drove her. As it was she finished packing the last bag when she saw the storm howling down on her.

She made for the entrance at a stumbling run, afraid she would be unable to find it once the blowing snow obscured it. Tumbling into the tunnel entrance, she dragged the bags behind her, effectively plugging the opening and shutting out the screeching wind.

Panting with her last effort, she beat the clinging snow from her ski suit before crawling into the ice cave.

The quiet was wonderful, calm and soothing after the high-pitched fury of the wind. It was then she noticed how damp her ski suit was. That was dangerous. It would freeze in the low temperature of the cave. Unless she was able to dry it, she ran the risk of hypothermia.

Moving quickly, Jan kicked off her boots and peeled away the snow-dampened suit. Snapping it briskly, she shook the snow away then laid it aside on the thick insulating mattress of fir extending beyond Jason's feet. She stripped off the rest of her clothes and wriggled into the dry underwear and pantyhose she had purchased in Reno. By then she felt as if she might be freezing, but she was free of the moisture which could be fatal under these conditions.

Her skin glowing pink with the cold, she climbed back into the after-ski pants and cashmere sweater. She was cold but dry.

Putting on the knit cap she moved back to the sleeping platform.

Jason's eyes were open and he was watching her.

Jan blushed in spite of the cold.

"How do you feel?" In spite of the skip of her heart, the question came out crisp and clear.

"Terrible." His voice was a mere shadow of its usual strength. "Where are we?"

"In the Sierras."

"How's the plane?"

"It's a wreck. How's your head?"

"Splitting. Where are we?" He repeated the query, his eyes registering pain.

Jan realized he was asking about the shelter. "We're in an ice cave. We'll be safe here as long as we don't panic. I can't start a fire, so we must keep ourselves from freezing without one. It's a bit difficult, but it can be done indefinitely as long as we keep our heads."

"Tell me what to do."

"You must keep very still. I can't tell whether you have a fractured skull or just a concussion. Either one is going to make your head ache. Badly, I'm afraid. You also have something wrong with your ribs. I'm not sure if I should bind them or not. It's better if I don't, I think. But in that case, you must take shallow breaths so that if one is loose, it will begin to heal before it punctures a lung. The other two things we have to do are get enough water and keep each other warm. I found some dried food on the plane. I just have to figure out how to cook it. We won't starve."

Jason was staring up at her with dark eyes. "How did I get so lucky?"

Jan didn't understand the query. "I'm going to rub your hands and feet and get your circulation going, then I'll melt snow for drinking water. We must be careful not to dehydrate. But first I have to move you enough to put these things under your overcoat so they will dry. Think you can help me?''

"I'll try."

Jason found it impossible to move by himself. Frightened by the possibility of harming him further, Jan moved him with great care. He didn't make a sound but she knew he was in pain. Hastily she smoothed the clothing under the overcoat, then helped him back into place.

His face was paper-white. "I'm sorry, Jason," she whispered. "I'm so sorry. But our lives may depend on my ability to go out once the blizzard stops and there is no other way to dry those things."

"It's—all right...."

"Jan barely heard the breathy whisper.

Her heart beat with a slow painful anxiety as she uncovered one foot at a time and rubbed them briskly.

"Jan—" Jason's voice was stronger now. "Where on earth did you learn to build this cave?"

"Stop talking, Jason. You mustn't until you heal. My father was an engineer. I've told you that. We lived on the mountain almost all my life. Every winter we went out on traplines in all kinds of weather. Dad taught me the dynamics of survival under almost any condition. It's just a matter of knowing a bit about all kinds of things, then using your common sense."

She wrapped his feet again. "I'll go get something for you to drink now."

She set the little stove up, then pushed against the duffel bags blocking the wind. Frigid air whistled in, but it was necessary to ensure no build up of carbon monoxide. Reaching through the opening, she gathered snow into the battered fisherman's bucket, praying it wasn't full of tiny holes.

After lighting the stove, she stirred the snow in the bottom of the bucket, not allowing it to form a frozen crust on top. She added the soup mix, and though it took awhile, she had a couple of pints of lukewarm chicken soup when she doused the stove and pulled the blocking bag into the opening. Scooting back through the tunnel, she took a cup of the broth and hurried to Jason.

"We have to drink this immediately. It may freeze solid if we don't." Raising his head, she put the cup to his lips. "Your head is going to pound, I'm afraid, but you must have fluids."

He wasn't able to finish it all. Jan lowered him carefully, then drank the cooling soup. Jason watched her, his gray eyes inscrutable.

Jan put the cup aside, then sat on the edge of the platform to remove her boots, turning her back to Jason deliberately.

"In order not to die in here, we're going to have to be sensible," she said. "The cave will protect us as long as we keep from icing it up. We do that by not talking much. Our breath will freeze on our snow ceiling and ruin the insulation if we aren't careful. And we don't move unless it's absolutely necessary. Beyond that, we must share our . . . body heat." Her cool voice faltered with her final announcement.

"Meaning?" There was a hint of amusement in the query.

"I'm going to crawl under the mink with you. We can keep each other warm that way."

"That's great." Jason sounded almost cheerful.

"This is no time to be funny," Jan told him, her tone severe. "Our survival depends on our ability to act sensibly."

"Sorry. What do you want me to do?"

"Just be quiet," she said, unable to repress a flare of anger. Moving with care, she lifted the makeshift covers and crept in beside him, blushing as she fitted her slim length against his.

Jason managed not to say a word, but his eyes glinted.

Using extreme care Jan snuggled against his unresisting body. His heat touched her, spread through her and held her.

"D-did I hurt you?" she murmured, pulling the protecting and insulating groundsheet up over them.

"No way, my love."

The words sweet in her ears, Jan pulled the knit cap down over her face, retreating behind the mask it made.

"Good." She forced a businesslike briskness into her approval. "I'll have to rub our hands and feet every half hour or so. And we must drink water every hour. Otherwise, we just lie here, without moving, if possible. Once the blizzard is over, I can go out and scout around."

"I'm so glad you're with me." Jason moved an arm under the warmth of the mink and draped it across her. "Why were you running from me, Jan?"

"I—you—I wasn't running," she lied.

"Weren't you?"

"No...yes I was. Of course I was. I'm sorry. It was childish. But you shocked me, you see. I hadn't thought of—of living with a m-man...for pay, before." She felt the flush heating her. When was she going to acquire enough sophistication to deal with this man on his own terms?

"I thought you knew what I meant, Jan." His voice was soft. "If I apologize will you try to listen to me?"

"You don't need to explain to me." In spite of herself, the words sounded defensive.

"Ah, but you're wrong. I forgot how young you were.... Do you know about Tom's mother?"

Surprised at the question, Jan could only nod. Jason's arm tightened around her waist as he felt her head move against his shoulder.

"It was a hard lesson for a young man, Jan. It cured me of any stray idea about romantic story-book love. At least, I've thought for years it had...."

"Jason, you must be quiet," she interrupted gently. "Even if you were strong enough to talk, we can't risk it here. I'm sorry about your wife, sorry you were treated so badly. But it's none of my business. I have to keep you alive and I won't be able to if this cave ices up." Making a valiant effort, she kept her voice from trembling.

He ignored her little speech. "Men and women need each other. Heaven knows that's true for me. But I gave up the idea of love in those months before my son was born. I've always been careful not to buy the myth of true love since then. The other night when you were so sweet, so willing, I...."

"Just be quiet, Jason." The words were hoarse, torn from her.

"I offended you. I didn't mean...."

"I don't want to hear any more about it." She did her best to sound indifferent. If he said one more thing, she was afraid the tears would flow and never stop.

"You're still misunderstanding me."

"Perhaps." She fought to control a growing sense of panic. "It doesn't matter. Do us both a favor and be quiet, please."

She felt him shrug. To her surprise he fell silent, but he didn't remove his arm. It warmed her even as it created an exquisite intimate ache within her.

JAN DIDN'T SLEEP much the next three days. The blizzard raged, dumping tons of snow in the valley.

She massaged Jason's arms and legs and rubbed color into his face every half hour. Melting snow so they had enough to drink was a constant chore. Jason seemed content in the warmth of the bed she had fixed for him. Jan would crawl back into the bliss of his embracing arm each time her chores were done.

It was an exquisite wonderful agony, lying with him, sharing his warmth and his closeness. If only it could continue!

She knew it couldn't. The realist in her rejected her wish to stay with him, regardless of the consequences. Her dream was over.

That evening in his house when she had been so eager to give, he had played her for the innocent she was. Unable to recognize the love she offered him, he had converted it into a shameful experience she wasn't soon to forget.

Tom had told her his father had been too deeply hurt by the woman he'd married to ever marry again. Jan hadn't believed him, but she did now. Jason would never trust a woman enough to let her get that close to him again. She found it impossible to blame him, and nothing changed the fact that she loved him.

There was no hope for her and she recognized this fact. A man of Jason's intelligence and experience had no place in his life for a naive and inexperienced bumpkin from the backwoods. It wasn't his fault she found him irresistible. Nor could she blame him for misinterpreting her signals to him. How many other women had fallen under the magnetic spell of his powerful masculinity? Jason was an attractive man. Few could resist the call of his commanding sexuality, she was sure. But he was not for her.

And so, sharing a frightening ordeal few could survive, she taught herself to accept the truth even as she shared the poignant intimacy of the close fragrant bed with him. Sometime in those cold danger-fraught hours she said goodbye to him, her common sense finally ruling her impulsive heart. That settled, she was able to care for him without trembling each time she touched him. Almost.

Jason's gray eyes followed her whenever she moved around the ice cave. He didn't talk much, just watched her, his eyes hooded, enigmatic. His searching compelling glance had its effect. Jan couldn't help her response, her heart pounding in her ears, her flesh tingling with the unspoken allure he managed to project. He did nothing to relieve the tension building between them, silently accepting her back into the warmth of the nest their bodies had created each time her chores were done. His arm would slip around her waist, his contented sigh a lovely sound as she settled beside him.

Jan fought his attraction with all the stubbornness of her nature, refusing to become victim to his charm again. By the end of the third day Jason was grim, his attempts to communicate met by a cool aloofness on Jan's part.

"Why is there a hole in the middle of our floor?" he asked.

Darkness had fallen. Jan was using the flashlight, shining it into the cold basement in the center of the floor as she returned with water. It wouldn't do for her to fall into it and break a leg.

"The cold air settles there," she explained, raising his head for his portion of liquid snow. "The heat of our bodies rises and warms the air on this level so that it stays above freezing and keeps us from dying of the cold, as we would if we were outside. We couldn't live out there with only this much heat. Because we are quiet, not moving around in here, we're able to stay alive. As our body heat rises, the colder air is forced down into the hole and we stay warmer than we could without it. It's a natural phenomenon. We're using it, that's all."

Jason, feeling better, showed his interest.

"So you just dug a hole, made a platform for us to lie upon, lined it with fir and kept us alive. A little chilly, but safe." There was incredulity in his voice. "How many women do you think could have done it? Or men, for that matter. Don't be blasé! It doesn't become you."

"It's just a law of physics, Jason. The hole acts as a basement, sort of. It traps the cold. It's no big deal. Anyone can do it."

"No big deal . . . !"

"People who live in cold places like the Himalayas use the principal all the time. It's a matter of knowing about it, that's all."

She finished giving him the water, her hands tender when moving his scarf to a dry spot. She rubbed his hands and feet briskly, ignoring the effect the steady gray eyes had on her. Her own flesh was glowing as she slipped back under the mink, trying to convince herself her warmth was due entirely to her exertion. Jason's arm was around her instantly as he settled her into place.

"How is the storm coming?" he asked.

"I'm not sure." Jan forced herself to concentrate. "It may be lessening. We'll know by morning, I think."

"Great. The rescue team should be here as soon as the storm's over."

"We're buried under several feet of snow," Jan protested, unwilling to have him get his hopes up. "Even if they send planes in, no one can see us. We may be here for weeks."

"They know we're down, Jan. Half an hour after we were supposed to land, they knew something was wrong. They'll be in the air looking for us soon as the snow clears."

"The wreckage is covered by snow. I'll have to get some signal fires going or they won't find us. They won't be able to spot the plane." Cuddled into his side, Jan realized she really didn't care whether rescue came or not. It was one thing to be sensible, to recognize there was no future with him for her. It was another not to want to prolong the wonderful agony of being alone with him, having him dependent upon her like this.

"I filed a flight plan when we left," Jason told her. "They know my course, Jan. And as the plane was instrument-rated, they can track us. We had an ELT built into the tail."

"What's an ELT?"

"It's an Emergency Locator Transmitter. It transmits automatically. It was triggered when the plane crashed. It continues sending the signal for eighty hours."

"I didn't know." Jan breathed a sigh of relief. Now if only Sarah was recovering. She hadn't dared discuss her friend's illness with Jason. He was in no condition to be worried.

The snow cave was brilliant with light the next morning. Jan slipped out of the warm bed, knowing the blizzard had stopped.

Pushing the duffel bags away from the entrance, she was momentarily frustrated by the bank of snow that had drifted across the opening. This called for her ski suit. Still in place under Jason's makeshift mattress, it would be dry by now.

"Storm's over," she exulted, going back into the cave. "I'll have to get my ski things. It's going to be great to get out of here!"

Jason chose to misunderstand the meaning of her words.

"Was the company so bad, Snow Queen?" His eyes gleamed over the edge of the scarf Jan had wrapped around his whiskery cheeks. "I was just beginning to enjoy myself. I'm seriously thinking about staying here forever, just you and I, living in our little snow hut, enjoying each other with no one else around."

"I hope I can shift you without hurting you." Jan made an attempt to ignore his teasing statement as she retrieved her dry clothes.

Her back to him, Jan dressed quickly, the cold bitter against her skin. Jason was staring up at her when she turned to him.

"I'm going out now." Jan didn't know whether he had watched her change, but what did it matter? "I'll get a fire started and see about cooking some breakfast for you."

"Come here, Jan."

"I really must . . . ."

He just looked at her. Jan sighed and sat down on the edge of the platform, unable to refuse.

"I want you to know what these days we've been together have meant to me," he told her. "We'll be rescued soon. I want to have a chance to redeem myself."

"It isn't necessary, Jason. There's nothing to explain. I do understand. Tom told me...."

"About his mother?" he filled in when she hesitated, her color rising.

"Well, yes, a little. He didn't tell me much...."

"He doesn't know much. It's something I rarely discuss. It's the one area of my life that I've closed the book on. I was too young to know what I was doing, but not too young to be left emotionally scarred, I think."

"I can see that, Jason." Afraid she was about to do something foolish, Jan jumped up, tucking the groundsheet around him in a hasty effort to divert him. "You don't owe me an explanation. I must see about food for you now."

Her exit through the tunnel was a panicky flight. How could she stay and listen to him rationalize his reasons for rejecting her love? What did the woman who was Tom's mother, the woman who had taken his first love and destroyed it so thoroughly, have to do with her?

Nothing, nothing, nothing.

The word was a chorus repeating itself as she threw her energy into battering her way out of the ice cave.

When she finally burst through, the snow was a thick blanket over the landscape. It was more than waist deep at the edge of the cave, the wrecked plane an insignificant bump in the smoothness of the snow-filled valley. The meadow stretched away, gorgeous, pristine. In the distance a peak reared up in rosy relief where the soft fingers of dawn's light touched it. Closer to her, tall stands of fir, spruce and pine were captured in pits of snow, their branches laden. The trees climbing the slopes were taller, beautifully spaced, as though planted by the thoughtful hand of a giant gardener. They wove a pattern of loveliness, their snow-draped spears directed at the pale winter sky, the early sun casting long blue shadows toward her.

The air was terrific, invigorating. Taking a deep breath, Jan realized how stuffy the cave had been, even though she'd aired it on a regular basis and kept the vent open.

Jason called, barely audible in the hush of the morning, and Jan turned to go to him. She was on her knees at the entrance when the sound came through the still air, freezing her movement as she listened.

What was it?

When it came again, she knew.

A helicopter!

Leaping to her feet, she searched the morning sky. There were two of them when she finally saw them.

Coming in low over the far end of the valley, they hovered over the flat area where the snow covered the lump of the wrecked Cessna.

Jan popped out of the snow like a cork out of a bottle, jumping up and down, powder flying around her, arms waving madly.

The lead helicopter hovered, clearing snow away in great clouds with the downdraft from its rotating blades. A man lowered himself down a rope ladder and dashed toward her.

"Hi, young lady! Am I glad to see you," he shouted above the noise of the monstrous machine.

Jason was going to live!

Things were hectic for a while, but it wasn't long before the efficient crews had Jason aboard one of the big helicopters and they were airborne.

"Where are you taking us?" Jan asked the question of the man in charge of the air-rescue team. He had introduced himself as Johnny Budge and he seemed in awe of her expertise in keeping a wounded man alive and well in the extreme cold of the blinding blizzard.

"To Sacramento. His son is on his way there now. He was with another team. I'll bet you're glad this is over. I still can't believe you did it. How did you learn the ice-cave technique? Not one in a thousand know about it."

"Is J— Mr. Farrell going to be all right?"

"Thanks to you. How did you know what to do?"

"My father taught me years ago." Her eyes on Jason's wan features, Jan didn't want to be bothered with explanations, but the man's interest was genuine and she couldn't be impolite. "I grew up in the mountains in Maine, you see. He thought survival techniques in winter cold were something I needed. We built ice caves every winter."

"Smart man. Most people think of igloos."

"Those are too hard and take too long unless you are an expert," Jan informed him.

"I know, but not too many realize that fact of life. Jason Farrell was just darn lucky when he picked you for a companion in this adventure. Where were you going, anyway?"

Jan explained about Sarah.

"You'll be able to call your friends as soon as we get in. Once you get rid of the press, that is."

"Oh, no! I can't stand that again!"

He looked sympathetic. "'Fraid there isn't much you can do about it. Farrell's an important man and his disappearance has been all over the news. Sorry."

"It's not your fault." Jason stirred then and looked at Jan. Jan excused herself and went to him. He looked so wan, so still, the darkness of his beard emphasizing the lines of strain in his face. Was he hurt more than she thought? Irrational fear suffused her. It was hard to deal with, but the knowledge she had saved his life was sweet within her. He was alive because she had taken care of him. No matter what the future held, she had that to remember.

"Stay with me," he whispered, his gray eyes fastened on hers. "We need to talk."

"You'll be all right, Jason. I have to find out how Sarah is. If she needs me, I'll have to go to her."

The helicopter was descending now, settling onto its landing pad. The red lights of ambulances flashed around the perimeter, reflecting off the upturned faces of the waiting crowd.

"She'll have to wait. I want you to stay."

"I can't. Surely you can see that?"

"No, I damn well can't!" Jason flushed under his stubble, making no effort to curb his raising temper. "I want you here, not chasing off to San Francisco. I need you!"

At that moment, the helicopter door opened and Lucille rushed by the rescue team, her face paper-white. A dainty hand flew to her slender throat.

"Jason!"

Her scream was piercing. Jan clutched at her, but the distraught woman collapsed onto the ground.

Pandemonium broke loose. Newsmen, ambulance attendants and the rescue team were all trying to crowd into the hutch. Jan took the path of least resistance. Her mind had ceased to function, the significance of Lucille's shock clearly interpreted.

Jason's petite and gorgeous vice-president loved him! A cold little iceberg grew where Jan's heart once beat. So much for those naive longings of hers. Stumbling down the steps that had been pushed up to the doors, she found herself in Tom's strong arms. She clung to him, repressed sobs making her throat ache.

"I thought you two were goners!" His bear hug smothered her as he buried his anguished face in her soft hair. "Oh, Jan! Never do that to me again. No one thought you'd live through that blizzard. How did you do it?" He hugged her again.

Jan clung to him. "Nothing to it," she joked, then added, "I'm so glad to see you."

"You're glad! Think how I feel—and don't you dare cry!"

"I won't." She raised her head from his shirt. It was then she saw the men with the cameras bearing down on the helicopter. "Can we get out of here, Tom?"

Tom followed her stricken gaze.

"Those guys won't see you as long as Lucille is strutting her stuff." His comment was dry. He watched with distaste as the woman in question appeared in the helicopter doorway, wan and lovely in her distress, then he turned to Jan. "There's an ambulance over here. I had them send two. C'mon."

"I don't need an ambulance," she protested, pulling back. "I'm perfectly all right. I have to get to a phone and call Ken. I must find out about Sarah."

"She's not doing well, I'm afraid. I talked to Ken an hour ago. Poor guy's about to lose his mind, he's so worried."

"I know he must be. I'll have to get to San Francisco, Tom."

"Okay. I'll even take you. But first you're going to the hospital for a check-up. Please?"

He looked so worried Jan gave in. "Only if the doctor will see me right away and if you'll phone the airport and get a reservation for me while I'm being examined."

"Okay. Let's go." He pulled the doors of a waiting ambulance open and ushered her in, climbing in behind her. "I want to check on the old man, then I'll go with you to Frisco."

"You don't need to do that, Tom," she protested.

"You'll have to lie down, miss," the attendant told her, scowling at her escort. "You shouldn't really be in here, fellow."

"I'm staying. And I'm going with you." His announcement final, he sat down out of the way while Jan had her blood pressure and pulse taken. "I can't stand being around when Lucille does her act. Did you see that performance she put on for the benefit of those newsmen? The stage lost a good bet when she decided to go into managing other people instead of acting."

"She fainted." Jan knew she'd never forget it. If nothing else, it made her realize how hopeless her love for Jason was.

Fool, fool, fool.

"Ha! I'll bet she did!" Tom remarked, then changed the subject. "Mr. Clark got in touch with me as soon as he heard your plane had gone down. I've been in contact with him constantly. I nearly died of fear, Jan. Both you and dad gone...I don't know what might have happened to me if I'd lost you."

Jan didn't know how to respond. There was so much love, so much distress, in his young face.

The nurse put a thermometer under her tongue, saving her the necessity of a reply. Jan sighed. Why couldn't Jason be as uncomplicated, as unspoiled, as the son he'd reared with such love and care? But then he wouldn't be Jason. Tears burned her eyes.

Tom's searching look was shrewd, his gray eyes reflecting the intelligence he'd inherited from his father. "Lucille really bothered you with that show she put on, didn't she?"

Jan shook her head as the attendant read the digital numerals appearing on the thermometer's tiny screen, then extracted the slender rod from under her tongue.

"Ignore her, Jan," Tom said. "I do. She's been around for years. She still treats me as if I were ten.

She's a pain and she never gives up, but dad isn't going to marry her."

"I know. You once said he'd never remarry." She sounded forlorn.

"Yeah. But I've changed my mind lately." He gave her an enigmatic glance as the ambulance stopped. "Let's get this over with."

"She has to stay on the stretcher," the attendant protested.

"That's not necessary—I'm really fine," Jan said, getting up.

"Turn to your left once you're inside," the disgruntled attendant volunteered. "Dr. Jones is waiting for you."

Ignoring his instructions Jan went straight to the phone and placed the call to the hospital in San Francisco.

"Thank God you're safe, Jan," Ken's relief came clearly over the wires. "Sarah is so upset. When can you get here? She needs to see you."

"I'm on my way. Tell her I'm coming."

"It will mean so much to her. She loves you as much as if you were ours, you know."

"I know. I love her, too. And you. I'll catch the first plane out."

She came out of the phone booth, her mind made up. "I have to go at once, Tom."

"What about the doctor? He's waiting."

"I don't need a doctor. There's nothing wrong with me."

"Sure." Tom recognized the determination behind her statement.

"Good. Thanks. I'll tell Jason I'm going."

"Tell him I'm taking you."

"Tom! You should stay here with him."

"Lucille will take care of him. I'm staying with you."

"Jason won't understand," Jan protested.

"He'll understand. Hurry up. I'll have everything arranged when you get back."

As she went back into the emergency admitting area, Johnny Budge came through the door, her knapsack, handbag and fur coat in his hands. "Thought you might need these, Miss Jordan. In all the confusion you left them."

"Thank you so much." She'd forgotten all about her belongings, the bag that contained the check for thirty thousand dollars and her cash.

"I keep on causing you trouble, don't I?" she said.

"Oh, no. I wish all my rescues were as pleasant as this one. Take care." He gave her a cheerful salute and left.

Jan took her things through to Tom. He was busy on the phone. She left them in his care and went to see the man she loved for the last time. It was foolish, she knew, but her need twisted inside her, a bittersweet longing that would not be denied.

"I'm the person who was rescued with Jason Farrell," she explained to the nurse at the main desk. The woman led her down a passage to the cubicle in the emergency ward where Jason was resting.

Jan went in, a curious emptiness seizing her as she approached his bed. His eyes were closed. She stood looking down at him. He was handsome even with his growth of beard and the unnatural pallor of his lean face.

How I love you, Jason Farrell. If only you could love me. What shall I do when I never see you again? What shall I do?

She knew very well what she was going to do. Walk out and leave him to Lucille or whomever he happened to want for the moment. And she would be left with a broken heart. Well, at least it didn't show on the outside.

Not wanting to wake him, she turned. Perhaps it might be best to leave the news that she was going with a nurse. Unable to suppress a sob, she walked away fighting an impulse to touch him.

"Jan." The sound of her name stopped her. "Where are you going?"

"Sarah needs me. I've just come by to tell you I have to go to San Francisco. I'm leaving immediately."

"You'll come back as soon as things straighten out?"

"No, Jason. I'm not coming back. Not ever. Goodbye." Turning her back to him, she marched toward the door.

"I need you, too, Jan." That resonant baritone reached out, touched her ears, caressing, pleading. "I...."

"Jan, you darling!" Lucille bustled through the door, reaching for her, enclosing her in silken arms and giving her a little hug. "I haven't even thanked you properly for saving Jason. What an ordeal! But, my dear, I can never tell you how grateful I am.

When you saved this precious man for me, you saved my life. I can't live without him.''

"Y-yes. It's all right...." Jan broke away and stumbled into the hallway, blinded by sudden tears.

"Jan!" Jason called after her.

Ignoring him she rushed away, hurrying through the doorway and down the hall.

"It's all set." Tom hung up the phone as Jan came toward him. "We've got twenty-five minutes to reach the airport. There'll be a cab out front." He gave her a curious look but didn't comment on the tears that were streaming down her face. "Did you tell dad I was taking you?"

"I—I forgot."

"I'll call him from the airport if we have time. Or from Frisco. Here's a cab.''

Jan was thankful Tom had decided to go with her. Tired, dirty and very unhappy, she arrived at the hospital in San Francisco. But she was too late. Sarah had just died.

CHAPTER SEVENTEEN

THEY BURIED SARAH on the first of December at Davenport, Iowa.

Jan stayed at the home of Sarah's sister. Ken found solace amid old friends, familiar places. He took Jan around, showed her the high school he had attended with Sarah, the island in the river where he and Sarah picnicked, his eyes misty with the memories of the youth they'd shared together.

"It must be wonderful to have been able to share that kind of love and have it all your life." Jan spoke gently, thinking of her father's lonely existence and the loneliness she had to face because she hadn't had the sense to love wisely.

"I can't complain," Ken said. "I had her a long time. But oh how I miss her! It's something I must face, I know. It's meant a lot to me, the way you've stuck around and held my hand, Jan. You know that, don't you?"

It was because she did understand the depths of his grief and the courageous struggle he was going through that she agreed to go to the ranger station with him. He wanted her to help him sort out Sarah's things. A week after the funeral they went home to Maine.

Jan stayed at the ranger station longer than she had planned. There was so much to do, sorting and boxing Sarah's things. Much of it would be given away when spring came. Some were personal possessions Ken would keep. Others were mementos he thought her sister might like to have.

Ken was mutely grateful for the support and comfort she offered him, and Jan was glad to have something to do to take her mind off the dull aching void left by leaving the man she loved.

Then, two days before Christmas, Sim radioed. He wanted to leave at once. Something had come up. He seemed reluctant to talk about it but he assured her he had to go.

"It is time I was getting home," Jan told Ken when she relayed Sim's request.

"I hate to see you all alone for Christmas, honey," the older man told her. "But of course I'll take you over to the lake. And from the looks of the weather, the sooner the better if you're going to get up that trail of yours before it snows. Is Sim gone for good?"

"I asked him to come back when his business was finished. He said he would if I thought it was okay for him to stay all winter."

"He's a funny old geezer. But he's a good man, one I'd trust under any circumstance."

"I know, Ken. Dad felt the same way about him."

"Well, let's get cracking. I'll go warm up the plane while you pack."

Jan made short shrift of packing a backpack with essentials, leaving the bulk of her things with Ken.

Tom had made sure that she received all of her belongings from his home before she left San Francisco. She had refused to return to the Farrell household herself. She would get her remaining possessions from Ken when the weather cleared and it was easier to transport them from the lake to the cabin. Her mother's picture went into the pack, wrapped carefully, along with the sketch she had made of Jason, as well as the children's story she had started so long ago in California.

She lashed the backpack to its frame, fastened on the snowshoes Ken insisted she take along, and carried her burden out to the plane.

The plane sat on the frozen surface of the lake, its motor revving, skis replacing the pontoons. Ken had it warmed up, ready to go.

"You'll be all right going up that trail?" he asked as they flew across the distance separating the ranger station from her mountain home.

"You know I will, Ken," she told him. "Dad and I used it all winter. It isn't going to snow and there's not enough on the ground to slow me up. You're a dear, but please don't worry about me. I'll be okay."

Her lake came in sight and he banked and glided toward it.

Jan watched out her window as Ken flew in for an expert landing. It seemed like years since she'd left here, innocent, eager, bewildered by awakening feelings. She felt much older now, and certainly wiser.

After they had landed she returned Ken's warm embrace, shouldered her knapsack and tackled the path up the mountain. There was little snow on the ground, though heavy downfalls were due anytime. As a usual event, the cabin was snowed in for Christmas. It gave Jan a sad hollow feeling to realize this was the first time she would celebrate the holiday alone.

Trudging up the mountain, the wind whispering through the spruce and fir, the air clean and crisp in her nostrils, her muscles straining against the drag of the backpack, Jan's spirits began to rejuvenate. By the time she reached the cabin and caught the smell of woodsmoke from the fires Sim had left burning, life was stirring in her, burning out the unhappiness of the last few weeks.

She loved Jason. That was a fact she had to accept. And he was alive because of her. Nothing could ever dim the wonder of that. He would never love her, nor would he ever be able to forget her.

She hugged the thought, warming herself with it. Even if Tom were wrong and Jason did marry Lucille, part of him was hers, the part that remembered the days in the ice cave they had shared.

She caught sight of a movement at the edge of the clearing and smiled.

"Hi, Bandit, you old rascal," she greeted the little furry pest. "Still around begging for your supper, are you?"

The raccoon rose on his hind feet and clasped his paws in front, regarding her solemnly through black masked eyes. Jan laughed, feeling as if it were the first time for months, and continued across the clearing, eager to be home, eager to have familiar things around her. Perhaps some of the heartache would ease now that she was back.

She shrugged out of the backpack and unlashed the snowshoes she hadn't really needed, hooking them on the wall of the cabin. Opening the door, she dragged her backpack across the threshold.

She was straightening to close the door when the blanket came down over her, trapping her in its soft folds.

Jolted into action she fought the smothering cover. Hard hands threw her, struggling, to the floor, and someone sat on her. A rope was passed under the blanket a couple of times, then jerked tight. Feeling the knot being tied, Jan drew up her knees, put her feet on the floor and bucked wildly.

Her accoster's oath was muffled. Grabbing her ankles, his grip painful, he passed the rope around them and tied them. Jan sat up, bringing her head forward with a swift driving motion, hoping to catch him unawares. She felt him dodge as he rolled off her, his feet thudding on the floor.

"So, little cousin, we meet again. This time the surprise is on the other foot, I think."

Peter Goud! Where had he come from?

"Untie me this instant!" Muffled by the blanket's thickness, her demand lost its impact.

"I am not so foolish as that, little cousin. Oh, no. It's far better to keep you trussed like a chicken, I think. Neither of us will suffer damage that way. You lie there and I will ask you questions. If you answer properly, perhaps I will free you. Who knows? After all, we are related. One must always be more lenient with one's kin, is it not so?"

"I'm no kin of yours! I couldn't be! And I can't breathe. Stop this foolishness at once."

He walked away then. Jan heard him cross the floor and leave the room. Struggling, she tested her bonds. She was truly captive.

"Why are you doing this?" she asked as his footsteps advertised his return.

"We will talk. When we come to a satisfactory agreement, I will release you."

He felt for her face then, his fingers fumbling with the thick woven cloth. Finding it, he commanded her to hold still. "I'll make a hole."

"No! Don't!" Jan moved her head from side to side, furious.

"You have a choice. Be still so I can ensure a proper air supply, or lie there in the dark and perhaps be short of oxygen. Which do you choose?"

The thought of ruining one of her good Hudson's Bay blankets angered Jan, but she realized she had to cooperate for the time being. The man was undoubtedly mad, but one did *not* deal with a madman by frustrating him. Time and a chance to reason with him were the most important factors at the moment. It was best to try to mollify him.

"Cut the hole. I must have more air." Closing her eyes, she turned her cheek toward the slicing scissors, hoping he wasn't reckless as well as crazy.

He cut a slash across, intersected it with another, then snipped the four resulting flaps away. That finished, he grinned down at her, his fair skin and blond hair giving him a boyish look the glint in his eyes belied. Squatting, he scooped up her trussed body and carried her over to the long couch.

She lay there while he tended the fire, willing

herself to stay quiet, determined to let him take the lead. If he talked enough, perhaps she might get some clue to his motives. With a little luck she might even be able to talk some sense into his head. But first she had to find out what was going on.

The thought crossed her mind that Sim might have known he was here when she radioed him that morning, then she dismissed the idea as nonsense. After his initial experience with the man who claimed to be her relative, the old trapper wouldn't have been caught off guard. Peter hadn't been here when Sim signed off. Nor would the old man have gone if Peter had put in an appearance before Sim left. That meant he'd probably arrived not too long before she had.

How had he made the trip?

The only way in was by ski plane to the lake or helicopter to the clearing. Bandit hated helicopters and disappeared for days at a time after one set down in what he considered his own territory. Since Bandit was out there on patrol, that left a chartered plane. He'd landed on the lake, then sent the plane away. Funny she hadn't noticed his tracks as she came up the mountain.

The fire roaring away to his satisfaction, Peter picked up the footstool and moved it near the couch. Lowering himself onto it, he took off his jacket and tossed it over the arm of the couch. With his elbows resting on his knees, his square stubborn-looking chin on his laced fingers, he grinned down at her.

"Well, little cousin. Here we are again."

"What is it with you?" Jan demanded. "Why do you keep following me? Can't you see I'm not really interested in the fact that you claim to be my cousin?''

"Ah! But you see, I think your lack of interest is because you have no idea of the situation, so I have decided it is my duty to inform you of certain facts.''

"I can assure you I have very little interest in your so-called facts,'' Jan told him. "I can't understand your persistence in trying to take me to the Netherlands. I don't want to go. My father and mother left there and had no desire to go back. Why should I be interested in doing so? How do you expect to convince me of anything when you treat me like this? It makes me very angry.''

He grinned. "A little anger won't hurt. You keep disappearing on me. Every time I try to explain, you go. I find it a frustrating habit and I feel I must break it for you. So first we talk, then we go to Amsterdam, ja?''

"I doubt whether anything you say will convince me I should go to Amsterdam. Are you still trying to tell me there's supposed to be some kind of fortune waiting for me in Holland? A fortune you hope to share?'' The blanket enveloping her was very warm, but Jan pushed her discomfort aside and concentrated on asking the right questions.

Peter's face lit up. "It's a long way from being a supposition, little cousin.'' He lowered his voice as if someone might be listening over his shoulder. "It's worth millions! Diamonds, antiques, fine houses, gold—many things, but mostly diamonds. The fortune was founded on diamonds, you know.''

"Whose fortune?" Jan asked. "You've lost me completely."

"He looked at her quizzically. "You really don't know, do you?" He reached across for his jacket. "At first I couldn't believe that you knew nothing. Then I thought it over. I realized from your reactions that you might not. So I sent for proof of the things I'm about to tell you." He extracted three legal-sized envelopes from a pocket and threw the jacket back. "First, we have this one."

He pulled a crackling embossed sheet from an envelope and smoothed it out. Jan was able to see an official-looking seal imprinted in the thick paper.

"A birth certificate. Can you read our language, cousin?"

A strange dread creeping over her, Jan nodded.

"So!" he grunted his satisfaction. "I have here a birth certificate. You can see it is authentic. It has the proper seal attesting to that. If you will read it you will see it is the record of the birth of a baby daughter to Juliana and Dirk van Eck. At The Hague. On your birthday, I think."

Jan stared at the certificate.

"Interesting, is it not?" Peter remarked. "Do you know where you were born? On the same day and to the same mother, I believe."

"No, I don't," she whispered, horrified at the implication. "Lewis Jordan was my father. Not someone named van Eck. And I wasn't born in Holland. I was born in the United States."

His smile was cruel. Flipping open another envelope, he produced its contents. "The registry of the marriage of your mother and father. Read it for yourself.'' He held it up for her.

Reluctant but unable to prevent herself, Jan scanned the document with disbelief, her mind registering the translation. It was the marriage certificate of Dirk van Eck and Juliana Goud-Andvers, dated a year to the day before her own birthdate.

"It isn't true. Lewis was my father."

"Lewis was van Eck's cousin. An English cousin, it is true, but his cousin nevertheless. He met and fell in love with your mother while working in Amsterdam for the family. Are you with me so far?"

"Y-yes."

"I was there, you see. I was young, sure. Only ten. But I was old enough. Van Eck was engaged to your mother. He saw the way things were and sent Lewis to South Africa on company business. Juliana cried. I remember that. Van Eck forced Juliana into the marriage within a few days of Lewis's departure, then kept Lewis so busy he didn't get home until you were a month old. Lewis came back, had an interview with van Eck, van Eck's father and an attorney. He was handed his walking papers and the stack of unopened letters they had intercepted, all the letters he had sent Juliana during his absence. Lewis didn't take it without fighting back." He paused to stress the drama of the situation.

Goud would be an easy man to hate, Jan decided. There was little doubt he was enjoying the task of tearing her memory of Lewis to shreds.

"Aren't you going to ask what happened—what this man you knew as your father did?"

"He was my father. The dearest kindest father any child ever had. Nothing you can say will change that."

Again he gave her a smile of pure cruel enjoyment. "I see. Let me tell you how he engineered things so he was able to act as your parent."

He opened the other envelope and pulled out a third document. It, too, was a marriage license, issued to one Lewis Jordan of Winchester, Hampshire, and Juliana Andvers of London. It had been issued when Jan was six weeks old.

"But how could Lewis marry my m—Juliana, if she was already married and had me? It doesn't make sense."

"Simple, my dear. He took your mother and you to one of those obscure villages deep in the English countryside, married her illegally, had you both put on his passport as his dependents and left the country. I must say he covered his tracks well. Van Eck spent thousands trying to trace him. He had been gone three years before my father found the lead and traced him to the States."

"Your father?"

"Van Eck is one of the oldest diamond houses in Amsterdam. My father headed their investigative department. He was brother to your mother. I'm his son. I have told you we are family." Again that derisive cruel smile flashed.

Jan considered him a moment.

"But your father wasn't able to find us." She pointed this out with a small thrill of pride. The lovers had been able to foil their pursuers.

"He found your mother. Or rather, he found her grave. She died in childbirth. Lewis disappeared with you. Since that time, we have had no trace of you until I saw you on the telecast when Lewis rescued Farrell's son and was hospitalized."

"You killed him. You were in that room, weren't you? You went there while I was—was talking to Jason. The shock of seeing you killed him."

"It was most unfortunate. I had no idea his heart was weak or I would have been more cautious. You see, I didn't want him to die."

He paused, daring her to ask the question trembling on her lips. Jan stopped it in time and watched him as he put the papers back in his coat.

"Will you take this blanket off me?" she asked. "I'm very uncomfortable."

"Ah, little cousin! We haven't struck our bargain yet. You don't know why I didn't want Lewis to die. It made me angry, you see. He had unfinished business with me."

"I will not bargain with you. Your business with my father has nothing to do with me. Now let me up."

"I have demonstrated clearly that Lewis is not your father," he protested, a flush creeping across his fair skin. "I prefer you not to say to me that he is. He has given me much difficulty most of my life and I will not have you pretending he was what he was not. Do you understand?"

Jan decided discretion might serve her better than anger with this strange man. It was obvious he was telling the truth as he saw it. Knowing Lewis's stubborn set of mind, his intelligent approach to every problem he ever tackled, she was able to imagine that he could steal the woman he loved and the child of another man. Nor was it out of the realms of possibility that he had covered his tracks so well it had taken his pursuers almost twenty-four years to locate him. Many things she hadn't understood over the years were explained if she accepted the simple fact that the two she knew as her parents had spent their lives hiding from the vengeance of a wronged husband and father.

Father?

It was a jarring note. Lewis had been such a good parent to her. Caring, loving, concerned, he had used every facet of his great intelligence and understanding to bring her up as a well-rounded self-sufficient person. No child had ever been more loved and she knew it. Lewis would always be her father, biological or not. That he wasn't had yet to be proved to her satisfaction. Papers were easy to forge.

She considered the man staring at her. He had such a gloating look.

"I hope you won't take it badly, but I don't believe you. Something doesn't ring true in this tale you're telling me. What do you stand to gain out of this dedicated effort you've made to—" she searched for an appropriate word "—*persuade* me to go to Amsterdam with you."

"The van Eck heirs will be extremely grateful. Dirk died a year ago. He never forgave his cousin for running off with his wife and child. He spent a fortune looking for you and your mother. More than that, he was certain you and Lewis were still alive. He tied up the family assets and they are held in trust and may not be touched, his bequests may not be made until you are found and restored to the family. The carrot and the stick theory. The family doesn't share in the goodies until they find you. It gives more thrust to their determination. At the time of the telecast, when you and Farrell brought Lewis to Boston, I happened to be in the States, tracking a lead. At the moment there are ten members of the family or representatives they've hired here. However, I'm the only one who has located the hideaway Lewis built after Juliana died."

"You expect to be well paid for taking me back with you. Is that it?"

"Well paid, *ja*. There is more." A subtle cunning expression glittered in the light blue eyes. "I want you to turn the rest of Juliana's diamonds over to me. Without notifying the family you've done so, you see."

"Diamonds! What diamonds?"

"Ah, little cousin! So innocent! This time I can't believe your protestation. Juliana took her diamonds with her when she left Holland. They were worth a fortune even then. They were beautiful first-quality stones. Their value has appreciated in the years between. Lewis must have used some of them over the years for this—" Waving his hand at the cabin, he grinned. "He was never one to stint himself, I think. He always appreciated a little of the best. But even his tastes didn't use up too much of Juliana's dowry. Those he never used must be worth at least the original amount given today's prices."

"You're mad! You will never persuade me to believe that my father was a thief." Even as she protested, she remembered Jason's probing questions about Lewis's source of income.

"He most certainly did steal you and your mother, cousin. Why would he balk at cashing in some of Juliana's diamonds? The rest of them are here somewhere. I want them."

"Even if they were—and I assure you they are not—they would belong to the van Eck family."

"Not so, little cousin. The diamonds your mother took belonged to her, not the man she married. Therefore, they belong to my family, not his. Lewis would not have trusted the diamonds out of sight or to anyone else. He has them hidden where he had easy access to them. They are here. You will tell me where."

"I don't believe you in the first place," Jan replied sharply. "Beyond that, I can assure you there are no diamonds hidden here. You are fantasizing."

"We'll see, shall we? If you won't cooperate, I will have to trust my instincts and look for them myself." He stood and stretched, a powerful-looking man. "You understand I will have to take things apart as I do this. I had thought to save you the unhappiness of seeing what a man can do to a nice place if he really searches thoroughly. But first a coffee, I think. Would you like some?"

"Certainly not! Stay out of my kitchen."

"Don't be stubborn, little cousin. If you continue to refuse to cooperate with me, we will be here several days. Maybe longer. Who knows? Perhaps we will be here all winter, undisturbed in this sylvan hideaway. We may even have the time to get better acquainted. A winter together, who can say what may happen, even if we are cousins.''

For the first time, a chilling finger of fear touched her.

''Don't be ridiculous!'' she spat at him. ''I want nothing to do with you. Will you please take this suffocating blanket off me? I can't stand it!''

''I am sorry. I do not trust you. You're too aggressive, not frightened enough of me. Most women would be whimpering by now. You are glaring at me as if you might cheerfully slit my throat. No, little cousin. You haven't played your cards right. You will have to woo me, teach me to believe in your goodwill toward me. Then I might be persuaded to release you.'' He grinned at her and went into the kitchen.

Struggling energetically, Jan went to work on her bonds.

''There are interesting places to hide articles as small as diamonds in the kitchen, aren't there?'' His question drifted back to her as pans began to clang on the floor. ''Is it possible the two of you have hidden them in here?''

Jan heard cupboard doors open, the sound of things being dumped. Then above it came the distinctive sound of an aircraft. Jan held her breath and listened.

A helicopter! Coming to the clearing!

The reason why a helicopter should be flying in wasn't at all important just then. She rolled off the couch, knocking the air out of her lungs with the force of the fall, but it didn't stop her. She rolled to the door, beating Peter by several strides. He ran from the kitchen and grabbed for her, cursing fluently in his native language as he fell over the knapsack she had dragged into the room when she first entered. He kicked it aside and grasped her with hands that hurt even through the blanket folds. Pushing her out of the way, he opened the door a crack. The beating chop of the helicopter blades filled the clearing.

Cursing vividly, he slammed the door and whirled, his darting glance settling on Lewis's deer rifle. It was in a rack over the fireplace.

Peter leaped over the backpack he had kicked away from the door, caught his toe in a strap that was sticking up and fell. He scrambled to his feet, his face livid, picked up the hapless pack, hurled it into the nearest corner and plunged on to pull the rifle from the wall.

The helicopter was almost on the ground as he threw the door open. Reaching the edge of the porch, he dropped to one knee and pumped a shell into the breech.

The helicopter hovered a few inches above the frozen turf. As Jan watched with horrified fascination, two large canvas containers were lowered with extreme care.

A man followed them out, jumping lightly to the ground and giving a thumbs-up to the pilot.

"Get back on that thing and get out of here!" Peter roared as the pilot began his ascent.

Jan stared at the newcomer, stunned.

Jason! How could he be here?

The rifle came up to Peter's shoulder. Jan leaped to action, spurred by Jason's danger. She hurled herself over the threshold and planted her feet squarely in the middle of Peter's back, spoiling his aim and sending the powerful bullet screaming through the helicopter's fuselage. The pilot reacted and the craft shot straight up.

Peter landed at the bottom of the steps, cursing like a madman. Jason didn't wait. Diving for the cover of the woods, he disappeared just as Peter snapped off another shot at him.

Trapped in the awkward blanket, Jan struggled to a sitting position and watched as Peter dashed off in pursuit of the man she loved.

CHAPTER EIGHTEEN

THE BLOOD SEEMED TO DRAIN away from her heart.

Peter was a dangerous man. Wealth was so close at hand by his reckoning. It meant nothing to him if he had to kill to ensure possession of the diamonds he was looking for.

"Jason, be careful!" Her shout was lost in the noise of the helicopter as the pilot brought it back down into the clearing with a bump, shutting off the motor and leaping out, his back bent under blades still turning with lazy ease.

"Is that you, Jan?" He shouted the question at her, starting toward her. "Are you hurt?" It was Mike, from the air-charter service.

"No," Jan shouted back, "I'm fine, Mike! Can you help Jason?"

"I'll see!" He turned and plunged into the forest.

Two more shots rang out in quick succession. Jan groaned and hooked the ropes binding her ankles under the edge of a lower step. Sliding backward, she strained against the knots. The only result was to pull the loops holding her arms to her sides tighter. Evidently he had used the same rope for both restraints. There was no way she could slide the rope off her ankles. The way he'd tied her made it impossible.

Frustrated, angry and frightened all at the same time, Jan became very still as she strained to hear the sounds issuing from the forest. The crashing of men through the underbrush did little to reassure her. Nor did the brief periods fraught with silence.

Three more shots shattered the uneasy quiet. A bullet struck the shingles of the cabin, raining splinters onto the porch. A yell of pure unadultered triumph rang out on the heels of that shot.

Jason! Jan closed her eyes in relief. He wasn't hurt. Not if he could yell like that.

Peter Goud dashed out of the underbrush, Jason and Mike on his heels. His rifle discarded, Peter ran for the helicopter. Jason put on an amazing burst of speed for a man not too long out of the hospital and brought him to the ground just short of his goal. Mike was there in an instant, jerking the blond foreigner to his feet.

The scuffle that followed was brief and predictable. Mike, the collar of Peter's jacket bunched in one capable fist, his other hand administering a punishing hammerlock, marched his prisoner across the clearing, following Jason's flying footsteps.

Jason, his chest heaving, arrived beside the bound bundle on the porch in seconds flat.

"Did he hurt you, Jan?" He dropped to his knees beside her, his grim features white. Before she could answer she was snatched up, her face buried in his leather flight jacket. "If he's harmed you...!"

The harsh threat rumbled in her ear and Jan twisted free. "No," she started to say, the rest of her assurance dying as she met the passionate eyes staring down at her. Startled by the intensity of his gaze, Jan was mesmerized. His head came down swiftly and he kissed her.

The sullen day, the snow-laden clouds, the cold, the sound of Peter Goud's angry words as Mike marched him toward the porch, everything vanished from Jan's circle of consciousness except the wonder of the mouth touching hers.

Wrapped in the blanket, bound by ropes, mummy-like, her response was total as she drowned in the magic of the man she thought never to see again.

"What d'ya want me to do with this bird, Jase?"

Jase! The familiarity of the address registered with Jan as Jason raised his head from hers.

"Take him inside, Mike. Be with you as soon as I attend to an important matter."

There was no mistaking the camaraderie in Jason's words. So she hadn't been mistaken. These two were talking as if they were old friends. When had that happened?

"Sure thing." Mike and his prisoner clumped up the steps.

Jason didn't take his eyes off the face of the woman he was staring at, as if he were memorizing her flushed features. Recovering a bit from his unexpected appearance, his unexpected greeting, Jan met that stare with as much aplomb as she could summon.

"Would you please untie me?" The request was only a little uncertain.

"I don't know." The look in those dark gray eyes gave her an anxious moment. "The way you keep disappearing on me, it's probably just as well to keep you trussed like a Christmas turkey.''

"Jason!" Jan protested. "Please."

He laughed, lowering his lean cheek to nuzzle her flushed one.

"All right, my love." He shifted his hold on her.

"I'm not—"

The look Jason gave her stopped the objection she automatically began.

"Don't say it, Jan." Lifting her up, he strode across the threshold and placed her on the couch in front of the fire. Kneeling on the bearskin rug, he reached for the scissors Peter had used, cutting the ropes and jerking the blanket away from her slender form. Flexing his lithe body, Jason came to his feet. He tossed the severed ropes to Mike, who had Peter leaning face to the wall, his hands against it, head high. The man's feet were spread out in an uncomfortable stance. He was entirely off-balance.

"Okay, buster. Hands behind your back." Mike made short work of binding him securely.

He led him to a chair and pushed him into it.

"Now let's find out what was going on here."

"Want to tell us about it, Jan?" Jason's crisp question had some frost in it. "I hope I'm right in assuming you had no idea your—er—relative would be here when you left Clark's?"

"I didn't, but how did you know I was at Ken's?"

"Would you believe a bird told me?" Jan shook her bright head, staring at him. "Thought not." He wasn't in the least disconcerted. "We'll talk about what I know later, my love. So where did you come from, Goud? And why were you here?''

Peter didn't answer, his look sullen, a stubborn set to his chin.

"He said my mother had some diamonds. He wants them," Jan volunteered. "I think he's crazy. He said dad wasn't my father, as well. I've never heard anything so ridiculous."

"I showed you the papers. They are official. Don't be so damn hardheaded." Peter looked thoroughly disgusted. "There's nothing ridiculous about my claims, little fool!"

"Careful, Goud. Keep a civil tongue in your head," Jason warned. "Where are these papers, Jan?"

"In his jacket pocket."

Jason picked up Peter's coat, taking the stiff envelope from the inside pocket. Peter offered no protest.

Jan found she was holding her breath as Jason examined them.

"This one is a marriage license. For your father and mother." His look questioned Jan. "I can't read the other two."

"One is supposed to be my birth certificate, if Peter is telling the truth. And that one is another marriage license." She hesitated, not yet able to believe the tale Goud had spun.

"It's the official record of Juliana's real marriage." Peter's surly explanation sharpened Jason's glance. "Lewis married her bigamously. To supply her with a passport, we think."

"I don't believe him," Jan whispered. "He's making it all up. Lewis Jordan was my father. I know he was."

"Sh-shh, love," Jason murmured. "Let the man talk." His glance soothed Jan and she fell silent.

Peter wasn't a gracious storyteller, but the tale of Juliana's forced marriage to van Eck, the birth of her little girl and her flight with her true love when he returned and sought her out made fascinating listening even in his reluctant telling.

His words angered Jason.

"You're here to steal, then, are you, Goud?"

"The diamonds were not Lewis's. They belong to Juliana's family—my family."

"If they were her mother's, they belong to Jan."

"She doesn't need them. She inherited millions from van Eck."

Jan stared, incredulous, but was given no time to reply.

"Need doesn't enter into it," Jason told Goud, his tone implacable. "You dared to come here, attack my fiancée, tie her up, hunt Mike and me with a deer rifle...."

Jan stopped listening at the word *fiancée*.

"You shouldn't have interfered," Goud broke in. "It was a family matter."

"When anyone puts a bullet in my chopper, I take it personally." Mike looked as dangerous as Jason. "Just who do you think you are?"

"I don't care who he thinks he is," Jason said grimly, ignoring Jan's stunned look completely. "Want to take him down to civilization and book him, Mike? He needs a lesson in U.S. law."

"Sure thing! Let's go."

Together they hauled the man out of the chair and out of the house. Jan trailed along behind, Goud's jacket in her hand, Jason's bizarre claim ringing in her ears. He hadn't bothered to look at her since he'd made the ridiculous statement. What was he up to now? Why would he want Peter and Mike to think she was engaged to him? Her mind seemed to have shifted out of gear. It was very difficult to follow Jason's thought processes sometimes, she thought grimly as she followed the two men and their prisoner. What was he up to now?

Jason and Mike marched Goud into the cold. They bundled him into the waiting helicopter, Jason climbing aboard to pull him in while Mike shoved from beneath.

Jan felt as if her heart were in her throat as she handed the jacket up to Mike. Jason still hadn't paid her the slightest attention since he'd announced they were engaged. What had he meant, if anything? Was he leaving now to help Mike take Peter to the proper authorities? Why had he come? He hadn't known Peter was here. Questions she didn't have the answer to whirled through her mind in dizzy confusion.

Did she want him to stay?

The answer to that one was a resounding yes.

When Peter was securely tied into one of the back seats, Jason came to sit in the seat beside the pilot. Jan lost hope then. He was going. She didn't care, she told herself, biting her lower lip to stop it from quivering.

Mike started the blades whirling and Jan retreated

from the noisy machine. The day had suddenly turned more bleak. If she trembled she hoped it was from the cold. The two bags Jason had lowered from the helicopter when he first arrived were sitting there, gray lumps in a gray day. Was he leaving them, as well?

The blades picked up speed and Jan caught back a sob.

Then Jason stood, sending her a look that left her breathless as he jumped out of the helicopter. It seemed the most natural thing in the world for him to put his arm around her, shielding her from the aircraft's downdraft with his muscular body. The machine drifted into the gray sky. Mike, grinning, lifted a thumbs-up and the helicopter shot into the lowering cloudmass.

Jan was barely aware of his departure. "What do you mean telling those men I'm your fiancée?" she managed.

He gave her an odd look. "I meant no offense, you know." He made no attempt to remove his arm.

"You had no right...." Jan tried to wriggle away. His arm tightened.

"Oh, no you don't." He tilted her face up. "I want to talk to you about that night, Jan."

"Let me go, Jason." Her panic was rising.

"Impossible, love. I still don't trust you not to vanish the minute I let you go. Will you kiss me, Jan?"

Unable to stop the reaction caused by his husky request, she trembled against him, crushing the impulse to put up a wild struggle. It was too late now to make any attempt to act indifferent to this man.

"You keep trying, don't you, Jason? Can't you believe I'm really not interested in you?"

Smiling, he watched her through those incredible dark lashes of his. "Aren't you going to kiss me, little coward?"

"I think we need to go in. It's cold." Her chin set, she blazed defiance at him.

Her scornful look had no apparent effect on his cool assurance. "Kiss me. I guarantee you won't feel cold long."

"Stop being ridiculous! It really isn't good to stay out here, Jason. We must go in before we freeze." Stubbornly she resisted the pull of his charm, doing her best to be in control even if she knew it was much too late to maintain any semblance of distance from him. He was in her blood whether she wanted him there or not.

"Okay, love. Make me wait. But you won't get away with it forever."

He surprised her again, as he had so often in the past, dropping his arms and releasing her. Jan shivered and ran.

The cold was to blame, she assured herself silently. Jason, his packs in his hands, ran beside her. They crossed the porch together and Jan shut the door behind them.

"Goud do this?" Jason put his burden down and crossed to the kitchen door. "What a mess. Shall we clean it up first?"

Jason worked beside her, calm, efficient and full of teasing good humor. Her guard was down, her sense of danger lulled by the time they finished. Jan put on the coffeepot and busied herself with setting places. Jason stretched his long length, settled into a chair and relaxed, a gleam in his eyes. Jan caught him watching her and blushed in spite of her firm resolution not to be disturbed by him.

"I'll have to go get sugar." Dodging the inevitable, she dashed down the basement steps into the storerooms in the big cellar, intent on replacing the sugar Peter had dumped on the floor as he searched for the nonexistent diamonds.

Jason followed her into the cool depths, marveling at the refrigeration units and systems of storage Lewis had installed.

"I think we should consider Goud's strange tale," he told her casually.

"The man was obviously insane," Jan maintained stoutly. "Do you realize what he was telling me?" She slammed the door of the pantry containing the dry foods with unnecessary force. "He wants me to believe my mother was a—a bigamist, and as good as a thief. And that my father wasn't Lewis, that he ran away with another man's wife and child. Well, I won't!"

"He didn't say that, Jan." Jason took the sack of sugar from her and followed her up the stairs. "The jewels belonged to your mother. He's admitted that. And he was telling you a love story. The love story of two people who cared so much for each other they risked everything—disgrace, disinheritance, isolation—everything, for it. All these years Lewis was true to his love, true to his commitment to your mother. It's a wonderful story. Don't you see that, my love?"

"I wish you'd stop calling me your love. I'm not. You've never loved anyone, Jason. So stop pretending, especially to me."

"Ah, but you are, you see...."

"Stop it!" She turned on him, unable to bear it. "I know I'm unsophisticated, but you don't have to carry on like this!"

He closed the basement door as they came into the cheerful kitchen, his eyes narrowed, his face thoughtful.

"I know I've been a bastard, Jan. I want to make it up to you, to explain myself. If I try very hard to be on my best behavior, will you at least give me a chance?"

"I doubt it. I'm not feeling friendly." Taking the sugar she cut the bag open and poured it into the bin. Jason came up behind her, his hand feathering through the brightness of her hair.

Jan went rigid under his touch. "Don't do that," she whispered, clutching the bag.

Jason smiled. "Okay. If I get my chance."

"Yes. Certainly." Anything so long as he moved far enough away so that the heat of him, the scent of him didn't send her senses spinning. What was there about him that was so potent, so vital to her?

Dropping his hand, Jason moved back to his chair. If he was in any way sure of his ability to arouse her, he hid it well.

After pouring the coffee, Jan put it on the table and sat across from him. Jason sipped the hot brew, his eyes never leaving her face.

"What if Goud really does know, Jan?"

"He doesn't!"

"He seemed very sure of himself to me." His voice was serious. "I don't think he'd go to the trouble he has unless most of his facts were straight."

"But it couldn't be so. My father wouldn't have kept something like that away from me!"

"Are you sure? Seems to me it might be the very sort of tale a man might keep from a girl he'd raised as his own. Especially if he was as in love with the mother as Goud's story indicates Lewis—your dad was with your mother. Providing he couldn't have her any other way, that is. Men do strange things and at times act in ways society finds hard to understand when they are in love. If it was his only chance for happiness, it's understandable."

Understandable! Was this Jason Farrell the cynic speaking?

"No. It can't be true." Even as she said it, Jan remembered Lewis's last words to her the day he'd found Tom and gone down the mountain to the lake to meet the floatplane.

I've committed a serious wrong, he'd said that day. *I must talk to you about it.*

Had this been what he meant? She stared into the milky brew in her cup, rejecting the idea even as her common sense turned it over as a possibility. As much as she hated it, the nagging suspicion Jason was right reared its ugly head. The thought of a family far away in Holland troubled her more than she cared to admit.

Jason watched the shadows chase themselves over

her expressive face, maintaining his silence as he allowed her to work it out for herself.

The wind was whistling outside as they finished their coffee. She picked up the cups and washed them, concentrating on the simple task. Jason left her to her unhappy thoughts and went to tend the fire in the living room. When she finished, he had the last signs of Peter's violent activities cleared away. He was just coming back from carrying the things she'd brought from the ranger station to her room.

"It's going to snow soon. I must see to the animals," she told him in a hasty attempt to put distance between them.

"Right. I'll help."

She found she was unable to resist the pleasure of having him near. She didn't protest. The smile he gave her was full of his awareness of her unease. Jan buttoned her coat, pulling on a green stocking cap and gloves she had knit, along with the matching scarf, which she looped around her neck.

"Here's one for you. Keeps the cold out. Do you want a cap?"

Jason wound the soft brown woolen length around the outside of his own collar, managing to look even more handsome.

"Nope. I'll manage without one, thanks."

"Just don't get chilled."

She didn't see the speculative glance he bestowed on her as he followed her from the house and up the path that climbed to the outbuildings.

Sim had done his usual good job of caring for the animals. Jan allowed Jason to pitch hay down, help her add straw to the thick mat underfoot and see that there was fresh water. While she finished up, he busied himself gathering eggs.

"You had some fair-sized pigs when I was here before," he commented as he rejoined her. "Where are they?"

"Sim dressed them and put them in the freezer locker," Jan told him. "We raise a couple each year for the meat."

"You really do have everything here to live well, don't you?" Jason walked beside her after they had secured the shed doors. Jan heard the speculation in his tone and glanced up at him carrying the basket of eggs.

"Yes, I suppose we do."

The wind played in the thickness of his gleaming russet hair, ruffling the tumbled strands as he stood looking down at her. It seemed so right, so natural, to have him here beside her helping her with the homely tasks of caring for everything!

Realizing where her thoughts were leading, Jan brushed them aside and lengthened her stride.

"Lewis spent a great deal of money to have such a first-class operation so far from civilization, Jan. You must know that."

"I suppose so. We didn't discuss costs." She ran up the steps of the comfortable cabin that had been home all her life. "Dad was an engineer. He knew how to do everything."

"But he still had to have money to accomplish this," Jason insisted, taking off his coat as they walked into the big living room. "After your father died, did you find anything in his papers to give you an idea of his source of income?''

Jan hung her coat in the closet, then took the egg basket from him. "Not a thing. I didn't even find a bankbook, though I know he always went to a bank when he was on a buying trip. I found some cash, that's all." She flushed as she remembered what had happened to it. "I lost it in Boston." Hoping he hadn't had time to observe the flush that climbed into her cheeks, she beat a hasty retreat to the kitchen. Jason was on her heels so she stuck her head into the refrigerator, unsettled and unsure of herself once more. "That's why I had to borrow money from Tom, you see."

"Oh." The syllable was absolutely noncommittal.

"Yes!" His indifference struck sparks and she turned to face him, battle flags flying. "I sent him a money order for all I owed him when Ken and I were in Davenport. From the money I won!"

His smile was so tolerant Jan felt like slapping him. "You didn't think I'd dream of—of sponging off him, did you?" she demanded sharply. "I shouldn't have gone with him. I know that. But he was so insistent and I wanted to get away so badly...."

"Ah, yes. I seem to remember how you kept disappearing."

"You had no right to try to make me go with you," she protested. "And you wouldn't listen. What else could I do?"

"Were you afraid, Jan? I wonder." His glance probed. She wasn't able to meet those keen gray eyes.

"What did you think would happen if I had my way and took you down off your mountain, took care of you as you deserved?"

He took a step toward her. She backed away, her panic obvious. Jason's laugh was gentle.

"Shall I fix something to eat?" she asked. It was a hasty attempt to distract his attention. "Mike won't be back for several hours. We may as well have something."

He considered her. She faced him, proud, defiant, frightened, beautiful in the confusion caused by the emotion she was trying so hard to hide from him. His eyes darkened, an answering flame flickering in their depths.

"I'm hungry," he murmured. "But not for food—"

Jan turned and fled down the cellar steps. He didn't follow. When she finally ventured back with the food in her hands, her head high, he was gone.

Where was he? She peeked into the living room. The fire was roaring away, crackling merrily around the fresh logs he'd laid on it, but Jason was nowhere in sight. The snow was threatening, the sky lowering, gray outside the windows. His pilot's jacket was hanging in the closet when she looked so she knew he hadn't gone outside. Perhaps he was radioing Mike to see when he expected to return. Mike needed to hurry or it would be snowing. But Jason wasn't using the radio, either.

The door to her father's bedroom was ajar, however. Jan heard the shower in Lewis's bath come on, Jason's pleasant baritone rising above the splash of the water in a melody she didn't know. Jason was taking a shower!

Well! He certainly didn't mind making himself at home!

Uncertain whether she found it annoying or not, she went back to the kitchen and fixed a casserole.

The meal in the oven, she hurried into her own room. Sorting through her wardrobe, she regretted leaving all her California finery with Ken. Of course, it hadn't been practical to put the lovely things in her backpack, either. Wanting to look her best for a reason she didn't care to define, she decided to wear a royal blue silk shirtwaister Lewis had bought for her the previous year. It was a dress she'd never had the occasion to wear, charming with its full skirt and patch pockets. Finding an undamaged pair of nylons, she breathed a sigh of relief. Nylons were something she rarely bothered with up here but she was glad she had them tonight. Teamed with black leather pumps, she decided she would look quite presentable.

Showering quickly, she brushed her shining silver-streaked hair until it shone and touched a bit of color to her lips.

As she dressed, she did her best not to think of the evening ahead, not to wonder what Jason was up to.

When was Mike coming back for him? She realized she'd forgotten to ask.

If it started to snow before the helicopter returned, Mike couldn't land. Did Jason know that? He'd have to stay all night in that case. Maybe for several! This time of the year they could easily be snowbound. Was Jason aware of the uncertainty of the weather up here? Knowing she should have mentioned it before, she hurried from the bedroom.

Oh, no! It was too late.

CHAPTER NINETEEN

THE SNOW FELL in a thick white curtain that blanketed the clearing, cutting visibility outside the windows
to zero. Mike would never come back to pick up his
passenger in this kind of weather.

Unable to move, unable to think, she stared
through the window, her heart pounding as she realized the full extent of the situation. Jason was
trapped here with her. Her knowledge of the season
left no room for hope. Winter isolation had arrived
with a vengeance. Short of snowshoes or a long
cross-country ski trek, they were cut off from everyone until Mike could bring his helicopter in again.

There was a sound behind her and Jan whirled, the
blue silk fluttering around her long lovely legs. Jason
leaned against the doorjamb on the other side of the
wide room. His attractive face contained an expression of utter complacency.

About to offer a quick sympathy for the weather
condition, Jan choked, her hand rising to cover the
fluttering pulse in her throat. His gray eyes held hers
captive.

"Where did you get those clothes?" she asked. He
had changed, but the two canvas bags he'd brought
with him were resting undisturbed where he had

stacked them. Jan glanced at them and Jason's smile was cheerful, insouciant.

"I brought them up last week," he said casually. Folding his arms across the white knit turtleneck he was wearing under his fine black wool sweater, he straightened. His black trousers followed the lines of his lean, hard-muscled body as he moved toward her.

"Last week?" Jan backed away.

"Uh-huh. Sim suggested it."

"Sim suggested it?" Feeling idiotic, she parroted the phrase.

"He did. The first time I came. Shall we have more light? It's a bit dark in here." He stopped his advance, one brown hand reaching to touch the button on the tall reading lamp beside the big leather chair.

Jan whisked around the end of the couch and kept the length of it between herself and the amused man who was giving her the definite impression he was stalking her.

"Are you telling me you've been here twice before? Why? And why didn't Sim mention it if it's true? I radioed him several times since Ken and I came back. He would have told me. He didn't say a word. What are you up to now, Jason?"

"Just making a few plans for the future. Mine and yours."

"Yours, perhaps. But it can't concern me. What's going on, anyway?"

"Oh, it concerns you, Jan. More than anyone in the world, it concerns you."

"You're not making sense." Her anger hard to repress, Jan clenched her hands in the folds of her dress and glared at him.

Jason's glance flickered, softening, the expression on his sculpted features enhancing his attractiveness. Sighing, he sat down in the leather chair beside him, stretching his long legs up on the ottoman. He lazed back, lacing his fingers together, bracing his strong chin on them. Jan felt her heart expand, but she steeled herself to resist the pull of his masculinity.

He was so sure of himself, so sure he'd get his own way! Well, this was one time his charm wasn't going to do him a bit of good!

"Sit down, love," Jason said.

She was about to refuse for no other reason than that he'd asked her, then realized she was being childish and sat on the far edge of the couch, keeping what she hoped was enough space between them. Her effort earned her a tolerant smile from her tormentor.

"Why did you come, Jason?" Angry now, she persisted, trying to get him to the point.

He surprised her by saying, "I just missed you at the airport in San Francisco. I had the good fortune, though, to run into Tom."

"The day we left with Sarah? You followed me from Sacramento?" Her question was an accusation.

"Yes." He wasn't in the least bothered by telling her. "I decided not to go after you to Iowa. It didn't seem appropriate, somehow. I caught the next plane east and came here instead."

"You mean—here—to the cabin?"

"Here. To the cabin," he confirmed. "Mike

brought me in. Great pilot. Been a lot of help. So has Sim, bless his heart.''

"But why did you want to come here?" Jan was puzzled. And very, very cautious.

Jason was obviously enjoying her bewilderment. "I needed to tend to a couple of things. You didn't stay around long enough for me to thank you for saving my life for starters. I had to do that. Then I felt I owed you an apology and an explanation. It's so seldom I owe either of these to anyone, I knew I couldn't rest until I'd done it.''

That tidy little speech was so out of character Jan was just barely able to refrain from staring, openmouthed. If asked, she would have said without hesitation that Jason was a direct man, one who didn't waste his time with equivocation. Right or wrong, he acted as he did without the necessity to prevaricate or rationalize. So what was he doing here, acting as if his whole personality might be blighted were he not able to deliver his thanks in person? She examined his dark face very closely, trying to see why he wished to apologize.

His expression was as bland as milk, but the corner of his mouth twisted in a rakish tilt. It took her about two seconds to decide she wasn't about to open *that* Pandora's box.

Suddenly she knew she didn't want to hear what else he had to say, not at all, not for any reason.

"You're quite welcome, Jason. I appreciate the trouble you've gone to. A note or a few minutes on the radio would have done nicely, you know. You needn't have bothered to go to so much trouble.''

"Sorry," he smiled, "sounds much too impersonal. Not my style at all. I had to deliver the message myself."

"It wasn't necessary. Your business takes so much time, according to Tom. Can you afford several days' absence? We'll be snowed in for at least that long the way the weather looks."

"Sim said we would be when he radioed in early this morning. Just what the doctor ordered."

"Sim radioed you?" This time her agitation got the best of her and she jumped to her feet. "What are you talking about, Jason? He'd do no such thing. You've lost your mind!"

"Sorry, my love. I came here when you were still in Davenport. Sim and I had a very serious talk. Wise old codger, that Sim of yours. After I explained how you kept on vanishing every time I thought I had you cornered long enough to really get to talk to you, and after he knew why it was absolutely essential for me to do so, he was a great help."

"I don't understand you." Rooted to the shaggy bearskin rug underfoot, Jan didn't take her eyes off his imperturbable features.

"Well, he calmed me down and pointed out that you would be coming home. He also said the longer you stayed with the ranger, the easier it would make our plans. And he was right."

"Jason!" For some reason she had the feeling he was teasing her, drawing out the tale, pushing her toward the edge of her patience for reasons of his own. "Will you please get on with it? So far you've made very little sense." Her composure eroding, she felt anger stirring.

"You see, it was all a matter of taking advantage of the weather of the area, according to Sim. I went back to arrange my affairs after spending a couple of days up here with him, talking to him. . . ."

"Arrange your affairs?" Jan interrupted again, repeating the phrase as if it fascinated her.

"You're beginning to sound like a parrot, my sweet."

"Jason!" Jan's tolerance was at an end. "What is wrong with you? We're about to be snowbound, maybe for days. You're not going to be able to get out to attend to your affairs—and we're going to be alone here—" There was no way she could find the courage to finish that thought.

In the light of the chair-side lamp his lean features registered utter complacency.

"Wonderful, isn't it? Sim really did know what he was talking about."

"You mean you planned this deliberately?" If he'd suddenly sprouted horns and a forked tail, Jan couldn't have been more shocked.

"Great plan, isn't it?" He looked so self-satisfied Jan felt her fingers itching to throw something hard at his handsome head. "Sim reckoned once it started to snow you'd be unable to get away. Short of building yourself another ice cave, that is. I'm going to use these lovely solitary days. I want you to know me. I want to give us time to learn about one another."

His voice deepened as he stood with the easy grace she loved. He hesitated then. If she hadn't known better, Jan might have thought he suffered from an attack of uncertainty. She stared at him across the distance and felt the tension build. Jason, for reasons only he knew, was determined to have her—and she sensed the inherent danger in that.

"Well, you've made a fine mess of things." Rallying her good sense she took the offensive. What on earth had he done with Lucille? How was she going to cope with him? "It was silly of you to come here. It may snow for days." That bit of news didn't seem to bother him. Ill at ease, she headed for safety. "I'll see to our dinner."

"I'll set the table. I've lived alone so much, I'm great around the house." His voice was teasing as he followed her. "I'm more than a pretty face, you know, lady. Where do you keep the cutlery and dishes?"

As good as his word, he set the table while Jan popped a quick pan of biscuits into the oven with the casserole. He made coffee, too, keeping up a running stream of conversation as he worked.

By the time her meal was ready he had the table set, water poured, and he'd stoked the fire in the living-room fireplace. He made the meal delightful. Setting out to entertain her, he performed with the touch of a master.

Jan tried her best to resist but found herself falling slowly into the magic of his charm. It was dangerous territory, but the prospects were delightful, enchanting her. They took their coffee in by the fireplace after washing up. Jason waited until she sank into the corner of the comfortable couch, then sprawled beside her. The silence deepened, became unbearably intimate.

Jan found her awareness of everything suddenly acute. The soft pop and crackle of the logs burning briskly in the huge fireplace, the faintly acrid odor of woodsmoke, the heat on her face, her body, the easy, contented sigh of Jason as he stretched beside her, the intriguing scent of his cologne or after-shave, the faint murmurs of the house as the snow engulfed it, a total consciousness of a world whose center was the man lounging beside her.

Jason wanted her. He was here because he did. Intuitively she knew he wasn't about to take no for an answer.

Oh, he wouldn't force her into submitting to him. He wasn't that sort. He didn't have to and she was sure he knew it.

What was she going to do about it?

Honest with herself, Jan knew she wanted him. More than life itself, she suspected. She'd probably inherited her mother's fateful turn of mind that would allow for only one love in her life, she thought with some bitterness. If Peter Goud's story were true, then Juliana had given up everything in the world to be with the man she loved. She hadn't counted the cost, had become a fugitive from her own family, an exile in a foreign country, to be with Lewis. However, in Juliana's case, Lewis had loved her with equal fervor.

Would she be able to live with herself afterward if she allowed Jason to become her lover when he made no pretense at all of loving her? What would she do when he became tired of her and moved on to someone else? Was a brief happiness better than nothing at all? How would Lucille feel if Jason decided he wanted to maintain a relationship started here on the mountain? If she started an affair with him, Jan knew she'd go anywhere he asked.

"Penny for your thoughts." Jason took the cup of coffee from her and set it beside the couch with his. He touched the lamp switch, leaving the fire as the only light. Shifting slightly, he moved back, his arm going around her.

Jan stiffened, alarmed, but her body melted.

His face serious in the firelight, he tucked her close. "Talk to me, Jan. What are you thinking about?"

Well, he was asking for it.

"Lucille."

"Lucille? What on earth for?" His amazement was real.

"How does she feel, knowing you're here with me?"

"I haven't asked her. It's none of her business."

"That's not what it sounded like to me." Jan tried to escape but his arm tightened. "She referred to you as her man when she thanked me for bringing you out of those mountains...."

"Lucille's a grandstander." His hand smoothed its way down her arm, causing a reaction that coursed through her entire system. "The cameras were rolling. Our Lucy was center stage. She loved every minute of it. Makes her a great salesman." He bent his burnished head and stared down at her. "You rushed out of that room as if the devil were on your heels. Why didn't you come back when I called?"

"Sarah was sick. I had to go. Besides, I'm sure you're wrong about—''

"Lucille?" He murmured the word, his interest in the gleaming gold strands the firelight picked out in her honey hair. "I've known her since I was five. She's always acted that way. She's harmless."

"You mean she doesn't want to marry you?"

"She wants to manage me. I'm a challenge to her because I've never allowed it. She doesn't love me, Jan." His husky whisper trembled along her nerves. "You do."

Except for the blood singing in her ears and the slow and painful squeeze of her heart, Jan felt as though she had turned to stone. Her breathing stopped and she bounced up, arriving at the door to the bedroom hall without being conscious of the fact she'd moved.

Transfixed, she listened to him. "You do love me, you know. You will all your life and mine. You can't hide it from me, thank goodness. I'm not in a hurry, my love. I'll wait until you know your own mind." His deep voice played its magic with her nerves, causing an irrepressible thrill to shoot through her.

"You're insufferable," she managed. "I don't love you and I've no intention of pretending I do."

"Ah, Jan!"

She fled then, closing the door of her bedroom on the temptation he offered so surely.

What on earth was she going to do?

She felt she might be able to handle an affair with him as long as he had no idea she loved him. But to allow one to develop if he knew how hopelessly involved she was would be a mistake—a one-sided love affair.

He is ruthless, she thought. *It's all very well for him to pretend Lucille doesn't care for him. But I saw her face in the hospital. She does love him and he acts as though it's nothing to him at all. Arrogant cad! I wonder what really happened to Tom's mother?*

Realizing absolute fairness had little to do with her frame of mind, she paced the room restlessly, feeling caged. Never had she been less enticed by the idea of going to bed. Hauling her backpack onto the blanket chest at the foot of the bed, she proceeded to unpack it.

It was half-empty when she reached in and retrieved the packet in which she'd wrapped her mother's picture. As she touched it, she heard the glass grate.

"Oh!" This was too much, coming as it did on the heels of the emotion-charged scene with Jason. "Damn, damn, damn!"

Jason's head appeared around the doorjamb with an alacrity that should have aroused her suspicions. "What's wrong?" Genuine concern touched his words.

"My mother's picture!" She had unwrapped the memento by now. The glass was shattered, shards sticking out of the frame, two or three having pierced the photograph. "Peter broke it when he kicked my backpack out of the way. Oh, Jason, it's the only one I have of her. . . . "

"Don't worry, love. Let me clear that glass away

for you. If it's not too badly cut I'm sure it can be restored. We'll take it to the best restorer in town. I'll
have it fixed for you." He took it from her with
careful hands. Jan followed him as he left the room.
"Put another log or two on the fire while I get rid of
this glass," he smiled over his shoulder on his way
through the kitchen door. "I know it's getting late,
but I would like to talk to you for a few minutes before you hit the sack. Okay?"

"What do you want to discuss?" Successfully side-
tracked, Jan called the query after him.

"A bit of personal history," he answered.

Intrigued, Jan decided to play along. She put the
logs in place as requested, turning on all the lights before sitting down to wait. She sat in the leather
lounge chair this time, not willing to risk the intimacy
of the long couch in front of the fire.

Jason came back into the room and hesitated, an
odd expression on his lean face. The damaged picture
in one hand, the broken frame in the other, he gave
the impression of being uncertain for an instant.

"How bad is it?" Jan asked reaching for the picture, her anxiety showing.

"Oh, it'll be all right with a little work." Jason
handed her the photo, but kept the frame and the
bundle of debris he was holding out of her reach.
"Did your father make this picture frame, Jan?"

"Yes, he did. He loved woodworking." Concentrating on the nicks scratching her mother's picture,
she didn't notice her companion's unusual expression.

"I'll be right back. Don't go away."

He took the broken frame into the bedroom he was using.

"I thought I'd try to mend it in the morning." He answered her questioning look when he came back to relax in the corner of the couch nearest her chair.

"That's kind of you." The prim answer was all she could manage as she held herself stiffly, her skin prickling.

"Your mother died when you were very young, I believe."

Jan nodded mutely, the simple statement adding to her tenseness.

Jason's smile creased his cheeks. "I was five when mine died, Jan. Tilly was the only mother I had for years and she was far too indulgent with me. Tried to make up for mother's absence the only way she knew, I guess. It was wrong of course, and it almost ruined my life."

"Why are you telling me this, Jason?"

"I want you to understand some of the factors that have shaped my attitudes, darling. I can't be entirely objective, I'm afraid, but it's critical that you know why I misread you so disastrously at first."

Darling! So it was about to start! "It doesn't matter...."

"It matters," he interrupted impatiently. "It matters like hell. Just listen for a couple of minutes then I won't bring it up again." His look hardened, his gray eyes angry. "This isn't the easiest thing for me to do, you know. While I probably understand myself as well as most men, I've seldom tried to explain myself to anyone else."

"I see. Why do you want to explain yourself to me, then?"

"Damn it, Jan! Can't you see it's absolutely essential for you to know something about me if this thing is to work?" He moved restlessly, sitting forward, clasping his hands together and staring into the fire.

This thing is to work! What thing? Confusion spun through Jan's head as she stared at his profile. *Surely taking me as a mistress can't be all that complicated?*

"My mother was a beautiful creature, fragile, gentle, sweet. I adored her. Dad was a rover. Even then I knew it. She wasn't able to take the humiliation he dished out. It killed her, I think. I hated him when I was a youngster, you see. I blamed him for mother's death. He was a victim of circumstance, but I was so young. . . and what does a child know? Only what he sees, I'm afraid." He fell silent a moment, lost in his own thoughts.

"I'm so sorry, Jason." Jan resisted the impulse to go to him, to cradle his head in her arms. He looked stern, yet so vulnerable.

"In the end she died. I hated him for years. I defied him every chance I got." His face bleak, Jason ran his fingers through the silken tousle of his thick hair. "When I was sixteen I met Tom's mother. She wasn't the kind a young kid meets every day. Twenty-six, blond to all appearances, she was something else again. I thought I'd discovered heaven and she was careful to see that I didn't have a chance to lose the key. My father had a fit and that made it perfect for me. I'd stopped listening to Tilly, and every time my father opened his mouth I made it a habit to go in the opposite direction. This time I got what was coming to me."

"You don't need to tell me this, Jason." Frightened by the cold disgust on his face, she was sure she didn't want to hear it. "It's nothing to do with me."

"I need to tell you." The firm set of his chin spoke of his determination. "It's the only way you're ever going to be able to make a correct assessment of me. I want you to know me, Jan, to really know me. I want you to understand my motivation, understand my weaknesses and my strengths. Otherwise, how will you be able to put up with them, to tolerate me?"

"Put up with them? Tolerate you?"

"Don't be obtuse, darling. It doesn't become you."

That accusation stunned her into silence. What on earth was he talking about?

"Do you know what it means to a kid of sixteen to be seduced by a woman like her?" His voice hardened, took on a bitter tinge. "I was a sitting duck, of course. I was always in trouble at home, always trying to get dad's attention any way I could. I had everything I wanted but his time and his love. Then I found what I thought was love somewhere else and I went for it, full tilt. I thought she was beautiful and I was sure she loved me."

"Oh, Jason."

"I was stupid and hardheaded. When I ran away with her I took all the money I could get my hands on. It was mine. My mother left it to me. I had to leave the largest hunk behind. It was in trust. She stuck around hoping I could get my hands on the principal. In those months I discovered the difference between love and lust. The money I'd taken with me was almost gone when I discovered she was pregnant. I stayed until Tom was born, then I took him and came home. God! I was seventeen and had a child to raise. I was frightened out of my skull."

"So you stayed for your baby's sake." Jan's heart felt as if it might be melting. What a hard lesson he'd had to learn. She controlled her impulse to reach out and touch him.

"Yes."

"Didn't she object when you left? Didn't she want to keep her child?"

"Keep her child? I threatened to cut her out of any kind of settlement at all in order to keep her from having an abortion, Jan. I bought Tom from her. It cost me every penny remaining in my inheritance and drove a permanent rift between dad and me, but I had my son. I've never regretted that for a moment. I took him back to Tilly, determined he wouldn't suffer from the lack of love that ran in the family."

"I don't understand."

The smile he gave her wrenched at her heart.

"My father had been neglected all his life. It took me years to find out. Granddad was a reprobate and a rogue. My grandmother died when dad was born. The old man chased his mistresses and left dad to his own devices. My father was only following the example set for him. I was luckier. After Tom was born I woke up to the reality of it all. I made sure my son had nothing of that sort to blight his life.''

"What are you telling me, Jason?'' Alert to the undertone in his words, Jan examined the troubled countenance he turned toward her.

"I found out early that love, romantic love, didn't exist, you see. I had my mind made up about that. Once I'd learned not to chase the will-o'-the-wisp, I was able to handle the drives a man has without involving myself beyond a primitive level.'' He stood then, going to lean against the fireplace. Folding his arms across his broad chest he stared down at her, his gray eyes melancholic. "Do you know what I'm talking about, my innocent one?''

Jan felt her color rise.

"I think so. You've had your affairs, but you haven't invested much in them.''

"Of myself, no. They've cost me, but they've been easy to terminate. And I've never neglected Tom for a woman.''

Remembering the recollections Tom had shared with her of the places he and his father had visited together, the sports they shared, the affection Tom had for him, Jan knew Jason was telling the truth. His child had come first in his life.

"Why are you telling me this?'' she asked again, restless under his unyielding scrutiny.

"I had my life all worked out, Jan. I knew that the kind of relationship I longed for when I was too young to know better just didn't exist. No woman is the only woman in the world for a man. There's always someone to fill in the space when an affair ends.

Nobody in his right mind loses his appetite and the ability to sleep because of a female. If you slip up and get a little involved, it's easy to change course. Go on vacation. Find another woman with enough charm to move you out of danger. The plan worked and I was looking forward to becoming the world's prototype of the happy and successful bachelor.''

He grinned then, looking very much like a small boy caught up by his own mischief. "Little did I know.''

The rueful tag caught her attention. "What happened?''

Jason moved away from the rough stone facing, intent written in the lines of his face. Jan was out of her chair in an instant, her instinct warning her of danger she wasn't sure she could face.

"It's late, Jason. I'm tired. I'm going to bed.''

The hasty statement stopped him in his tracks. He flashed her an indulgent smile. "All right. Run if you must. Get your beauty sleep. I'll tend the fires.''

"Thank you,'' she mumbled, marching past him with a swish of silken skirts.

Go ahead! You won't get far, the challenge in his eyes told her. He looked both irritated and amused by her quick retreat.

"Good night. Sleep well.'' The amount of intimacy he invested in his send-off shocked her. Unwilling to trust herself with him a second longer, Jan hurried to her room, shutting temptation out.

The next morning she awoke to a snow-covered world. Dressed in jeans and a hand-knit pullover, wool leggings cuffed around the high tops of her boots, she walked into the living room. Jason was rattling pans around in the kitchen. The enticing odors of perking coffee and frying bacon filled the house. She barely had time for a swift check of the snowy landscape before he called.

"Sit down, m'lady. Your breakfast awaits," he said cheerfully.

Jan looked him over with care as she did his bidding.

"It isn't snowing." She flipped her napkin open, searching for a safe topic of conversation. "The storm may be over."

"Radio says not. More snow on the way. We'll need a snowplow to get to the barns as it is." He set a warmed plate bearing a fluffy omelet in front of her. "Compliments of the chef." With a flourish of his hand, he bowed before her, and Jan couldn't help laughing.

He kept her amused as they finished breakfast then washed up.

Jan found a pair of Lewis's boots for him and they were a perfect fit. When it was time to do the chores Jason led the way through the new fallen snow, breaking a path through drifts that were waist deep. A cardinal flashed across the clearing, a streak of scarlet against stark white. Jason saw it, his laugh of pure enjoyment ringing out.

Jan regarded him carefully a moment. What had she been afraid of last night? Why had she dodged the issue she was fated to face? Was it really so unreasonable to surrender to the man she loved? She was a woman now....

A sweet kind of joy touched her as she realized she had come to a decision.

"Well, shall we?" Jason looked up from the barn-door latch he'd opened. His perceptive glance roved over her flushed face.

"Sorry." She realized she hadn't heard him say a word.

He grew still as he examined the telltale expression she couldn't conceal. A slow happiness lit his eyes.

Jan blushed, her long lashes fluttering downward.

"I asked if we might go find a Christmas tree." He sounded odd, a husky thread of happiness in the suggestion. "As soon as we finish the chores? We'll bring it back and get it ready for old Kris Kringle to do his stuff. What do you say, my sweet?"

"Christmas!" Laughter bubbled up as she realized she'd forgotten today was Christmas Eve. "Kris is going to have to outdo himself," she told him. "I haven't a thing to give you."

"Ah, Jan. How can you think that?"

Jan met those warm eyes and blushed scarlet. Suddenly unable to say a word, she dived into the cosy shelter and busied herself with the milking. Her body pulsed with sweet awareness of the man working with her.

Jason, content with what he'd seen in that revealing, flushed face, went about throwing down hay and feeding the animals while Jan talked to the goat as she milked. He'd gathered the eggs and was waiting by the time she finished.

Jason proved to be surprisingly adept when it came to handling himself on snowshoes. The morning was hushed, full of cold beauty, the snowfall damp. It clung to the branches of trees and filled the clearing with interesting sounds. The sky was overcast but they didn't miss the sun as they trekked away to search for the perfect tree.

"Snowshoes remind me of duck feet," he remarked as they returned to the cabin, dragging with them the little blue spruce they'd finally agreed was flawless. "Great clumsy duck feet."

"Don't tell a duck that." Jan felt as light as a snowflake herself, full of quivering expectancy.

In a spirited mood, she scooped up a swift snowball and aimed it at Jason, hitting him on the back of the head. Snow spilled down his collar. Jason's howl of anguished protest echoed through the forest. Dropping the tree, he bent to take revenge. In seconds the air was filled with flying missiles.

Out of breath and outclassed, Jan turned and ran. He caught her, of course, tumbling with her into the snow. His kiss was long, slow and wonderful. It lifted Jan up, filled her with yearning expectancy. When he drew away she couldn't move. She was immobilized by the incredible promise of his lingering caress.

Her lashes tangled with snowflakes as she slowly raised them. Jason smiled down into her dazed green eyes. He brushed her cold cheek with the back of his hand before jumping to his feet, leaving her in the dazzling snowbank. Jan, unable to move, watched his broad back until he disappeared on his way back to the abandoned Christmas tree.

Then she was on her feet, fleeing like a rabbit, intent on escaping to the security of the cabin. By the time Jason arrived with the tree, she was busy in the kitchen, a turkey from the freezer on the countertop, her hands flying among onions and fragrant herbs as she readied the bird for dinner the following day.

"I have to make a couple of pies and get ready for Christmas dinner," she told him when he came into the room, bringing the fresh scent of the outdoors with him.

"I see." Those gray eyes told her he did indeed see. Too much. Shy, she masked the flicker of her own awareness. He chuckled. "I'll go ahead and set the tree up for you. We can trim it when you finish. Where shall I put it?"

"Just anywhere." Too breathless to argue, she tackled the turkey.

"Okay." He left without further comment. As she prepared the big bird, she could hear him working away, singing snatches of carols in that soothing baritone of his.

She delayed the inevitable as long as possible. The pies were in the oven, a batch of bread, properly punched and patted, rested in the huge bowl under a spotless towel, smelling yeasty, tempting. The turkey was thawing in the pantry, the dressing mixed and ready beside it.

Jason had been in the kitchen the last forty-five minutes. Sitting at the polished oak table, he had been repairing the picture frame Peter Goud had kicked apart.

He didn't talk much but every time Jan glanced at him she met those gray eyes. Warm, intense, a flicker that she couldn't afford to interpret in them, his smoky gray eyes were a weapon of attack. Jan felt her defenses melting like snow in summer.

Without a word he wooed her, heightening each sense to an exquisite peak of awareness. She became a living, pulsating being of light walking on air. Her heartbeat and her nerve endings fused, throbbing together, pulsing to the rhythm fluttering in the base of her throat, drumming deep in her body. Her breath caught, flickered, became unreliable as the drumbeat thickened, threatening to shake her slender figure. Every scent in the cabin seemed to assault the dainty little nostrils quivering above the sweet curve of her mouth. The touch of her clothing enmeshed her in sensation from which she had no wish to escape. Her response to the unspoken demand of the man sitting there so quietly was total, instinctive and wonderful.

Jan became aware of herself, blissfully, completely, fully aware of what it meant to be a woman for the first time in her life.

Jason watched her, his expression teasing. He bided his time as it became obvious she had no idea how to handle the situation, then he smiled, and rose to his feet. Jan's heart thudded wildly as she looked at him, startled.

"Come on, Jan. We've got a job to do."

He decorated the tree, refusing to allow her to help but demanding her criticism as he trimmed the boughs with lights and colored ornaments.

Jan spent the next few hours in a torment of indecision, trying to find enough courage to let him know she had made up her mind to become his lover. She knew she couldn't fight his powerful allure much longer, knew she must go to him soon, tell him she would be his lover, be anything, do anything he wished her to. Yet her proud and stubborn nature wasn't quite ready for unconditional surrender. What if he didn't want her? After all, what did she really know about men? What if she was misreading, misinterpreting his reason for being here? It hardly seemed likely, but what did she know about sophisticated men like Jason?

Come to that, what would any sophisticated man want with her, a gauche, untutored young woman from the backwoods?

That did it.

Tomorrow, she decided, jumping to her feet. Tomorrow she would tell him of her decision. If she could find a way.

"Good night, Jason," she murmured hurriedly. Her swift movement took him by surprise. She was through the hallway and into her bedroom before he could protest, but his gentle laughter followed her as she fled.

CHAPTER TWENTY

IT WAS AFTER MIDNIGHT when Jason finally retired.

Jan, her senses tuned to every soft rustling move he made, stayed in her lonely bed and felt her longing melt her bones and her will.

She was going straight out of her mind, she thought, making one more restless toss as she tried to find comfort in the sheets. Unwilling to bear it another instant, she leaped out of the nest of covers, pulled on her robe and slippers and headed for the kitchen.

Giving in to impulse, she detoured to the tree, deciding it might help if she turned on the lights and looked at it awhile. She plugged in the lights then stood stock-still.

The skirt of the tree was deep in gaily wrapped, beautiful parcels of various sizes and shapes. Where on earth had they come from? Jan dropped to her knees, knowing the answer to that silly question. She touched a gift tag with tentative fingers.

"To Jan, the love of my life," it read. The next one said, "For the only woman I've ever loved." Fascinated, awed, she read each one, rustling through the pile to find each little card. They were all signed with that distinctive, slashing J. By the time she finished, tears were running down her cheeks and she was sobbing with soft happiness. She sat back on her heels, pressed her hands to her face and let the tears come.

When Jason's arms went around her, she turned to him and buried her face in the strong column of his neck, wrapping her arms around his broad chest, too occupied with burrowing into his strength to notice it was bare.

Jason held her and rocked her, whispering words that added fuel to the flame already consuming her. Wild with the ache the repression of her emotions had caused, she covered his neck with kisses and heard him moan softly. The sound thrilled her, filled her with quivering excitement. Lifting her head she looked up and met blazing gray eyes. He kissed her then, that fine mouth flaming against the hunger of hers.

Jan lost all sense of self, all sense of time as she gave herself to him. She stood, the robe slipping from her of its own volition. For an instant he was immobilized by the sight of her naked beauty, then he gathered her into the strength of his masculinity, her curves a perfect fit against his hard, muscular frame.

He smoothed his hand down her hips and held her, arousing such pulsating waves of delight that Jan clung to him, trembling, shaking with the force of it. He laughed again and tilted her yearning mouth up to his, drinking deeply of the beauty she was offering. His tongue touched hers and Jan cried out in wonder, trembling with the need to get closer to him. He swung her sensitized body into his arms and carried her to the fireplace, placing her gently on the fluffy bearskin rug. The soft fur was exciting, sensual. Jan wriggled with pleasure, opening her eyes as she reached for him.

Jason laughed and backed off. Once again she had the breathtaking pleasure of seeing him naked, the firelight dancing on his superb body. She lifted her arms and he watched her a moment, his eyes hooded, a tender smile creasing his face. Then he came to her and her world exploded in his kiss. When he raised his head, Jan almost gasped in protest.

He touched her breasts with his lips and tongue and her pleasure became a delirium she could not control. Moaning, she writhed under the searing sweetness. Without thought or direction, she arched against him. The response of his masculinity was awesome.

She lost herself then, becoming one with him, his heartbeat, his need, his movement.

Jason watched her, guiding her, holding himself in check as he taught her how to give herself, how to please him as he pleased her. Completing their union, his first thrusts were unbearably gentle as he eased her from girlhood into womanhood. Jan barely felt the transition. Her body responded naturally, rhythmically until at last they spiraled into perfect fulfilment.

Jan lay in the shelter of his arms, the rug a soft dream beneath her, the fire warm on her back, reveling in the afterglow of their lovemaking. She felt Jason's fingers trail lingeringly across her flushed cheek.

"So, my love," he whispered, "will you marry me?"

"Marry you?" Jan's eyes popped open. She stared at him, dazed. "You want me to marry you?"

"Sweetheart!" There was contrition in the darkening gray of his fine eyes. "I did apologize for asking to let me set you up, you know! I don't want to do that. I thought you knew. I didn't want to even then, you see?"

"You didn't?"

His look severe, he kissed her eyes shut. "Don't look at me like that. No, I didn't."

"Then why did you ask?" Jan quivered at the touch of his lips, like velvet on her skin.

"I had to have you, my lovely." His smile was tender. "I planned to take you with me, lock you away and let you grow up while I taught you how impossible it was to live without me."

"But I was grown-up," she protested. "What did you think you were going to teach me, Mr. Farrell?"

"I've noticed the grown-up part." He spent several minutes demonstrating just how adult he knew her to be. Jan snuggled into his embrace. "You enchant me, little witch," he murmured huskily. "You have since the first moment I saw you. Do you remember that?"

Jan blushed. "You dragged me out of bed. You were horrid to me."

"Ah, yes. So I was. But first I stood and looked at you. I was entranced. You looked like my dream of love, a dream I had long forgotten. And there you were, your arms around my son. I am not a jealous man, but I was jealous then, sweetheart. And of my own son. I didn't believe in love, didn't believe what happened to me that night. I did fight it, you know. I hated it, but it just...grew." His kiss was deep, passionate.

After a time Jan caught his head in her hands and held him away from her.

"What did you want to teach me, Jason?" she asked.

"Why, to love me, of course. You had to love me! I was going out of my mind. Do you know what you put me through, Jan Jordan?"

Jan watched the firelight play over his bronzed skin, his dark head, the strength of her feeling for him taking her breath away.

"It wouldn't have done much good, you know. I was already mad about you."

"Oh, Jan," he groaned, drawing her closer. "If you only knew the torture I went through. I couldn't eat, couldn't sleep. Every time I tried to concentrate on anything, I'd wind up thinking about you. I was depressed—I was a mess. And I didn't know where you were for weeks. I haunted Sim, you know."

"Y-you did?"

"And made Mike a rich man. I was on this mountain every spare minute I had, waiting for you to come back."

"And you got Sim to trust you?" The wonder of that little miracle in itself showed her how powerful this man's charm was. Sim trusted no one, as a rule.

"I had to, or go completely crazy. You've a lot to answer for, you know."

"Why didn't you tell me?"

He sat up, shifting her in his arms so the firelight danced on the sweet planes of her body. His embrace tightened, the passion in his eyes deepening as he watched the effect of the flickering light moving over her soft bare curves.

"I knew you were attracted to me, my love. But I had to make sure you loved me, as well. I thought you did, but I couldn't have tolerated anything less from you. I wanted you to come to me, give yourself to me. And you did. Oh, Jan—" his husky, choked whisper would echo in her ears the rest of her life "—I can't tell you what it meant to me! Nothing in my life will ever be as fantastic as this wonderful night!"

He buried his face in the burnished honey-brown of her hair, a shudder running through him. Jan was filled with wonder. Still as a startled doe, she absorbed the glory of the love offered by the strong man holding her, the throb of her heartbeat an answer to his call.

Jason raised his proud head, his eyes fierce in the firelight. He kissed the bridge of her nose, then moved down to experience the sweetness of her mouth.

"You will marry me, Jan?" The question carried a definite note of command.

Jan couldn't resist the impulse to tease him a little. Her eyes closed, she touched the corner of his mouth with the tip of her tongue, ran it around the firm shape of his lips and felt him shudder against her. "Maybe. Is that the best you have to offer?"

"Why, you little witch!" He rose onto his knees,

pressing her into the bearskin with a firm hand. "You're asking for it, my love."

Using his mouth, his hands, his tongue, he attacked with the knowledge of an expert. Caressing her, teasing her, he drove her to a heightened state. Jan matched his demand, and when she was sure she could bear no more, the sensations peaked and their union was complete.

IT WAS LIGHT when she awoke. Jason lay with his head on her shoulder, one arm tucked around her, holding her firmly in place. Jan touched him with gentle fingers, loving him with a strength that left her breathless.

Here, in the arms of this man, was the meaning of life. She was finally content.

The house was warm but the fire in the fireplace was a smoldering heap of ash. Fearing he might catch cold, Jan eased herself out of his arms without waking him and went to fetch an afghan to cover him.

Then, humming to herself, she took a shower, touching her body with wonder and reverence.

What a beautiful, beautiful thing love was!

When she finished dressing, she noticed Jason's picture propped up on her nightstand. Picking it up, she examined it with care.

At last she understood what her fingers had known that night. The picture she had created was the real Jason. How could she not have guessed? Wondering at her own obtuseness, she kissed the image she had created.

"May I see it?"

Jan whirled around, color climbing into her cheeks as she hid the picture behind her. "Oh! Jason! You startled me."

"Who were you expecting? Santa Claus?" Wrapped in the afghan, he looked spectacular as he moved through the morning light to her side. Shrugging off the knitted cover he reached for her, kissing her with a thorough hunger she enjoyed.

"Now let me see." He sounded breathless as he raised his head.

Jan surrendered the drawing, her own breath taken by his beauty as he stood naked before her.

When he had examined it, he gave her a long look, a banked fire in those gray eyes.

"When did you draw this, my love?"

"I don't know exactly. A long time ago. When I was in California."

"You mean you didn't do it this week?"

"No, I—I told you. . . ."

He reached her in a stride, tossing the picture on the bed and folding her against the broad expanse of his chest. "Thank you from the bottom of my heart, my darling. I guess we have the basis for a good marriage in spite of the way you've acted sometimes."

"I don't know what you mean."

"Yes, you do." He kissed her with an intensity that stirred her newfound instincts. "If you drew that some time ago you were already seeing me as I am, not as you thought I might be. Why didn't you tell me?"

"I don't know." She fingered the tangle of his hair, smoothing it, distracted. "I just drew it and loved it. But it was hard for me to believe in it. Until now.''

His kiss was infinitely tender, and Jan thrilled as she felt his body stir against hers. He laughed.

"I'm going to shower or we'll spend Christmas in bed." Dropping his arms he left the room with that lithe grace of his. Jan, feeling strangely bereft, went to get breakfast.

Jason came to the door of the kitchen as she finished, startlingly handsome in fitted black trousers and a fine-knit V-necked sweater, the sleeves pushed up to his elbows.

"Time to eat," she told him with a shy smile. He sat down, patting her affectionately as she came to spoon scrambled eggs on his warmed plate.

"Look what I found, woods sprite." Producing a flat key and a thin silk-wrapped packet, he put it beside her plate.

"What is it?"

"I don't know. It was in the back of your mother's picture, taped to a cardboard retainer. I found it when I took the frame apart yesterday."

"Yesterday? Why didn't you give it to me then?"

"I didn't want to. Things were going too well. I didn't want to interrupt your concentration on me and I thought there might be something in it that might take your mind off on another track. I wasn't about to let that happen."

"You're insufferable, Jason. Do you know that?" She sat down, staring at the packet and the key.

"Yeah, I know. But I'm lovable as well, and I have the picture to prove it. Oh, Jan, how I love you."

Her heart tripped, the blood rushing into her cheeks. She picked up the parcel to distract his attention. Enclosed was a letter from her father. In block letters the heading read simply, IN CASE OF EMERGENCY.

It contained the name of a bank with an address in Boston, the name and address of an attorney and the address of van Eck et Fils, Diamond Merchants, Amsterdam.

Wordless, she handed the paper to Jason. He looked at it and whistled.

"Looks as if Goud may have been telling the truth. I know the bank, and the attorney is a member of one of the area's most respected firms. What's in the envelope?"

Janet opened it and unfolded the single sheet of paper within.

My dearest Jan, I am writing this to tell you how much I love you and to assure you Lewis is your real father if not your biological one. It is my wish for you that you find a love as wonderful as my own. Tricked into marriage to another, I was unable to stay. I could wish Lewis were your father, but he is not. You have been raised with his love and mine. Love is the most powerful force in the world and must be protected beyond all else when it is found. It never dies, no matter what the circumstance. I followed my heart, never regretting an instant, my darling. Now, in my last moments, I leave my love to care for you. Forgive me if I have been selfish. I love you. Take care of each other, be happy, and know I love you both more than life itself.

Your loving mother,
Juliana

Her tears falling softly, Jan looked up at Jason. He came to her side with a muttered curse and lifted her out of her chair, carrying her into the living room and cradling her against him, his hand soothing her as he stroked her back.

Handing him the letter, she buried her face in his neck, weeping quietly.

THEY SPENT A WEEK on the mountain, waiting for Sim to return. As Jason was quick to point out, they couldn't possibly leave the animals untended.

He made good use of his time. He taught her what it meant to be loved by a caring sensitive man, what it meant to be a woman in the true sense of the word. Jan glowed with her love, learning to express it, to glory in it.

Every day he spent time at the console of the short-wave set.

"Lucille is getting into gear," he told her one evening. They were sitting before the fireplace and he pulled her into his arms. "You look gorgeous, woods sprite."

"Lucille!" Clad in her old flannel robe, lamb's-wool slippers on her feet, Jan couldn't imagine looking gorgeous. Dodging his seeking lips, she tried to break away. Lucille was the last person she wanted to think about at that moment.

"What do you mean? What have you asked Lucille to do?"

"I've been in touch." Jason didn't let her go, kissing her anyway. "She's arranging the details of the wedding for me—for us," he amended mildly when he raised his head.

"Who said I was going to marry you?" Jan demanded. "And how will Lucille feel, knowing you're not going to marry her?"

He concentrated on the rim of the ear nearest him, his teeth and the tip of his tongue making short work of her effort to resist him.

"Hmmm. Did I forget to ask? Will you marry me, Jan Jordan? The moment we get down off this mountain? You might as well agree. I'll just keep you here forever if you don't."

"I'll think about it."

Jason's response was a long and searing kiss that left her breathless. When he finally released her, Jan went back to her original question.

"Lucille is in seventh heaven," he told her. "She always wants to manage me. This time I'm letting her, if you don't mind too much. She's very efficient. I want her to get all the details thrashed out without bothering me. I have other things on my mind." He gazed seductively at Jan and she couldn't help but laugh.

"It just seems strange, that's all."

"Nothing strange about it. When we do get out of here, I'm going to have my hands full before I can spirit you away to a place where I can have my way with you—" he leered at her teasingly "—until you beg for mercy. Lucille can manage anything. She assures me she wants to do it.''

"But I thought she...." Jan's voice trailed off. Jason tilted her face up and kissed the tip of her lovely nose.

"You thought she was in love with me. She never has been, my darling."

"But there in Sacramento, she called you her man...."

"I told you she gets carried away when she's the center of attention. It was a dramatic thing to say at the moment, so she said it. It didn't mean anything, sweetheart.''

"Oh.''

"Is that all right, then?" A sweet and lingering kiss destroyed any of her residual resistance. Jan clung to him, her hungry body responding to the potency of his allure.

"I've asked her to have Nancy Stone come to my place in New York. She and Lucille will stay with you while you shop and get ready for our honeymoon. And two of your uncles are coming from Holland. I got in touch with them today, via transatlantic telephone. They'll come to the wedding then go on up to Boston and take Peter Goud out of the hands of our authorities. Tom will fly in from California. He's to be best man." His voice thickened as he stared at her soft mouth. "Are you going to marry me, Jan Jordan?''

"Have I a choice, Jason Farrell?''

"Absolutely not. Come here and I'll show you why not.''

Jason spent the remaining days until Sim put in his appearance doing an excellent job of showing her exactly why life was impossible without him.

CHAPTER TWENTY-ONE

"THESE EARRINGS are exquisite!" Nancy exclaimed, touching the dazzling crystal drop. "And to think you found so many of them, Jan! The whole story's like a dream. I've never seen such beautiful diamonds. Have you, Lucille?"

Busy with a comb as she arranged the nervous bride's shining hair under the perfection of the veil, Lucille smiled. Her lovely eyes approved Jan's stunning appearance.

"Never," she agreed. "Isn't it wonderful you were able to locate your father's vault and retrieve them, Jan? Jason tells me you found several pieces of lovely jewelry and some perfectly gorgeous unmounted stones."

Jan found she felt no jealousy toward Lucille when Jason left her in the other woman's care. No lover had ever been more convincing in his demonstration of the strength of his feelings. Jan had come down from the mountain knowing the depths of his feelings, glorying in the miracle of his love.

No other woman could ever be a threat to her happiness! Even if she had hardly seen him all week, she was sure of his love.

Lucille placed Jan's bouquet in her hand, then

stepped back to view her handiwork. "You look wonderful. Doesn't she, Nancy?"

"Jason doesn't have a chance," Nancy twinkled saucily.

Jan blushed. She had lived here in his penthouse for a week and not laid eyes on him. Busy getting things in order so he would be able to leave on a protracted honeymoon as soon as the ceremony was over, he had deliberately stayed away, much to his fiancée's dismay.

Lucille and Nancy had been in charge, taking Jan on a shopping spree she wouldn't have believed possible. The two had spent the week with her to astonishing advantage. Nothing she'd said, no protest she'd made interfered with their instructions from Jason to outfit her in a manner becoming to his intended mate. Nor had they paid the slightest attention to the strenuous objections she'd raised about the incredible amounts of money they'd spent.

Nothing had persuaded Jason to come near her all week. She hungered for the sight of him, losing her temper finally when he continued to phone but stayed away. Friday evening when he called, she slammed the phone down in a fit of temper.

Denying herself the luxury of his teasing nightly call since then, she was in a sorry state on her wedding day.

"I'm not sure I want to see him at all," she muttered, squirming as she thought of his intransigent behavior.

"What! Call it off and disappoint those magnificent men out there? Your uncles wouldn't understand,'' Nancy teased. ''From what I saw, they certainly approve of Jason.'' She had met the two men at the airport, delivered them into Jason's hands and stayed to lunch with them.

Afterward, the three had left Jason to last-minute details and met Tom after his flight from the coast.

Jan had loved her uncles on sight. Nancy and Lucille had finally managed to break up the nonstop effort to cram almost twenty-four years of information into a two-hour rapid-fire attempt to catch up.

Since the plans were for them to leave shortly after the ceremony, Jan promised that she and Jason would visit Holland in the spring. Her uncles were to go on to Boston after the wedding and pick up Peter Goud and take him back to Amsterdam and the family wrath. Peter, they informed her in no uncertain terms, was not one of the shining examples of her family.

Jan was much too happy to condemn him. Jason and Mike had dropped the charges, and her cousin was free to leave the country on Monday.

Jason had called Holland every day after the initial contact. Her relatives had been delighted to learn of her existence. Messages had flown back and forth while they were snowed in on the mountain. By the time Mike was able to come in after them, Jan felt she knew a lot about her mother's family—or rather families, as her father's van Eck contingent refused to be left out of the love story.

The two sides of the family had sent representatives, an uncle each, to be at her wedding. Jan was content.

"Jason has your relatives eating out of his hand," Nancy commented mischievously as she stood before the radiant bride.

"Your uncles are absolutely gorgeous!" Lucille remarked. "Umm, let me see...." She fluffed the bride's hair a bit more beneath the charming juliet cap. "What do you think, Nancy?"

"Fantastic! Jason's not going to be able to move when he sees her. He'll think he's died and gone to heaven!"

"She is rather beautiful, isn't she? She's a credit to that entrancing man she calls uncle." Lucille's laugh sounded slightly embarrassed.

"Hah!" Nancy picked up the clue. "Which uncle, Lucille?"

"Hans van Eck, of course. He's promised to come to Boston for another visit soon."

"Sounds like Lucille has contracted something, doesn't it, Jan?" Nancy twitched the ivory satin of the wedding gown and stepped back, her bright head to one side. "I think Brainard Goud is the best looking. Imagine! Two widowers as handsome as they are! And as rich, apparently. Talk about waking up in heaven...wow! If I were a little older...!"

Absorbed in Jason and the preparations for their wedding, Jan hadn't bothered with the details of her inheritance yet. Not that the idea of being independently wealthy had made much of an impression on her at this point. Engrossed as she was with Jason, her love pushed everything else to the back of her mind.

Lucille glanced at her watch. "It's almost time."

A knock rattled against the door. Nancy, looking beautiful in her bridesmaid's gown, opened it. Tom came in, his appreciative whistle splitting the air.

"I'm going to have the world's most beautiful stepmother!" he exclaimed, grinning happily. "When dad does something, he doesn't fool around!"

Jan blushed. "Tom!"

"Being snowed in on a mountain sure agreed with you, mom. What the heck did you and dad do up there?"

Flushed scarlet, Jan did her best to look stern. " 'Mom' indeed! And don't be so nosy."

"Yeah, I know." Handsome in his tuxedo, Tom exuded charm. "Kids should be seen, not heard. Life has a fair chance of becoming intolerable. Let's go, ladies. Jase is useless already. He's going to pass out if we don't get this over with, I'm afraid."

"Oh, Tom." Jan's knees quaked suddenly.

Her soon-to-be stepson grinned at her and offered his arm. Jan clutched it as though it were her last support, trembling, her vision swimming. Lucille and Nancy fussed, arranging her skirts into picture-perfect folds as Tom led her into the huge living room of Jason's penthouse.

Music sounded.

Jan clutched the drift of her bouquet as her gaze sought her lover. Jason smiled at her across the distance of the room, a smile that caused her heart to brim with happiness. Tom heard her sigh of contentment and grinned as he led her to her destiny.

ABOUT THE AUTHOR

The Awakening Touch is Jessica Logan's fourth Superromance. Jessica is still amazed that she ever found time to practice her writing while she was growing up. The eldest of twelve children, she traveled extensively with her family because her father was an engineer, sent by his company to various locations throughout North America.

A teacher with a master's degree, Jessica has co-authored several children's books and a teaching manual with her husband, a retired psychologist who is still an active professional musician. Her husband acts as editor and researcher for her Superromances.

Writing is ideal for Jessica. It's something she truly enjoys, and seeking out the perfect background for her novels allows her to travel, indulging the itchy foot she inherited from her parents.

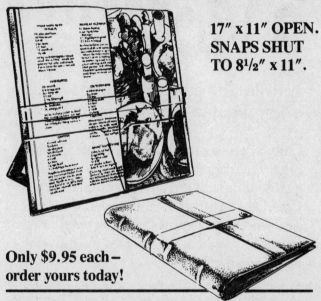